Other titles by this author
Bequia Mystery Series
Dead Reckoning
Deadeye
Deadlight

Science Fiction
Geborah's Seed

Map of the Eastern Caribbean and The Grenadines

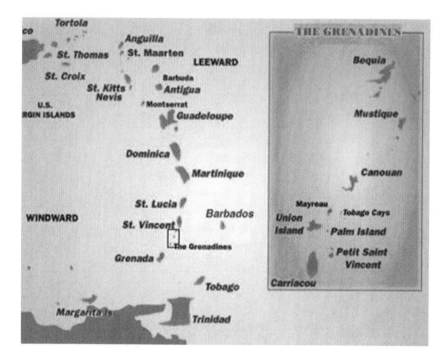

Bequia Map

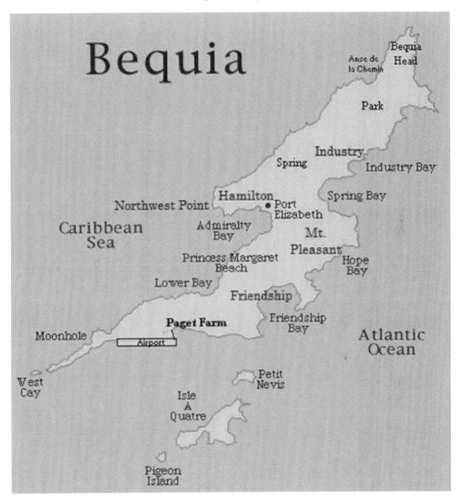

Dead Reckoning

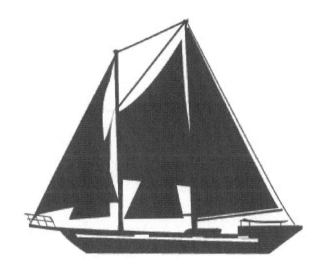

A Bequia Mystery

Michael W Smart

Copyright © 2011 by Michael W. Smart
First published 2014
Available in print ISBN: 978-0-9914008-0-5
Availabe in ebook ISBN: 978-0-9914008-1-2

Cover Illustration Copyright © 2013 by Michael Smart
Cover design by: Denise Kim Wy
http://www.coveratelier.com)
Editing by: Heather D Sowalla, Windy Hills Editing
Author photograph by: Camilla Sjodin
(www.sjodinphotography.com).

Published by Michael W Smart at CreateSpace

To Julia and Jason, two extraordinary people

Dead Reckoning:
To navigate without precision by estimating a current or
future position from a known position in the past

.

CHAPTER 1

I settled into plump cockpit cushions; a tumbler of straight up Mount Gay rum in my hand; anticipating a leisured ending to another day. Like the day before, and the one before that.

I ignored the ringing cell phone. The second time its insistent tone had beckoned. Instead I gazed into the distance at a blood red sky. Mesmerized by its fiery glow; its subtle shifting streaks of amber and gold. And the sun, the color of a ripe peach, melting into the horizon, leaving a scarlet sliver at the merging of sea and sky.

Dusk turned to evening. Details ashore dimmed and blurred. Lights flickered on. In the darkening bay anchored sailboats swayed in silhouette against the lighter western sky. High above, pinpoints of light appeared in the gathering darkness.

I rose from the cockpit. Cringed at the familiar ache in my lower back. Climbed through the hatch and down the companionway into the salon. The phone lay on the navigation table, behind the salon, port side.

Two missed calls displayed on the small screen, and the voice message icon. Jolene's number. Something unmistakably wrong. Apparent the moment I heard her voice, hesitant. Uncertain. A tremulous quality in place of her characteristic confident tone. Not what I'd expected.

The message obliterated the leisured evening I'd imagined.

"Gage. Mike's been shot," the words halting, stuck in the back of her throat. Forced out in spastic gasps. "I'm at the Port Elizabeth hospital now. Call me as soon as you get this."

I'd make it to the hospital in less time than it'd take to return her call, listen to halting explanations; questions and answers back and forth.

A disconcerting dread occupied my thoughts as the dinghy skimmed across the harbor. A haunting, constant companion dormant in the back of my mind. A nagging itch I struggled to ignore. Never going away.

Ashore, I ran to the hospital located inland from the harbor, at the foothill of rising terrain marking the boundary between Port Elizabeth and Union Vale. The new, rudimentary three-story brick building had replaced an older structure barely adequate as a clinic.

I entered the emergency area. 'Trauma' as it's locally called. Unusually crowded given the clinic had closed hours before. People stood inside the entrance and hallway. Idle. Silent. Somber. Blank stares reflected a shared bewilderment. Witnesses to a dissolving illusion, a tranquil island paradise where such violence isn't supposed to occur. A mere mirage, swept away like dust in the wind.

The bystanders mostly duty staff and curious passersby from the street. On Bequia everyone's business is soon common knowledge; the topic of island gossip. News of the shooting had already taken wing.

I noticed a treatment area against the far wall. Bloody swabs littered the floor. An attendant in a brown tee shirt and worn jeans swished a mop through pools of blood, spreading it more than removing it. A uniformed nurse packed away equipment in a desultory manner. Another gathered and wrapped bloody instruments.

I approached a van driver I knew. "What happened?"

"Somebody shoot de commisshunah. Dey tek him to surgery."

The small hospital, no more than fifty beds, hadn't the equipment or staff to handle much beyond routine medical cases. Most patients were shipped over to St. Vincent or to Barbados for advanced care. Those able to afford it travelled to the States.

I took the inner stairs up through the building to the surgical ward and operating rooms located on the top floor. Exiting the stairwell I observed a knot of police presence at the far end of the hallway. The smell of hospital laced the air. A mixture of disease, antiseptic and disinfectant.

Jolene stood in hushed conversation amid the small group. Three uniformed constables, the Port Elizabeth Station Sergeant, and a plain clothed CID detective. I kept my distance at the other end of the hallway; idly gazing down at the rough wood benches and lavender cherry blossom trees outside the clinic's waiting area. My ever present dread at the forefront of my thoughts.

A past I expected to someday catch up to me. Perhaps affecting the lives of people I now called friends. I didn't have friends. Hadn't for a long time. The emotional place where friendship might dwell and be nourished long since scraped raw and scabbed over. I'd lost too many. In senseless ways. In senseless places. Until only a scarred void remained. Dead and infertile. Or so I'd believed. Until it'd been miraculously revived, in great measure by the person lying unconscious on an operating table fighting for his life.

I sensed Jolene's approach and turned to meet her. Her eyes puffy, the whites slightly pink, but not teary. At least not at the moment. Her face as if set in stone. The normally supple contours chiseled into sharp, severe lines. Her dark curly hair tied in a tight chignon accentuated the severe effect.

She'd sent the men off on their assigned tasks. Two of the uniformed constables remained on guard at the entrance to the operating room. Free of her colleagues' presence the iron grip she'd clamped on her emotions relaxed. But not completely. She hadn't yet allowed them free rein. She maintained control.

Gazing at her strained face, normally as radiant as freshly varnished teak, I expected the worse. She wrapped her arms around me. Rested her head against my right shoulder. I held her close. We stood frozen in the moment. When she raised her head an errant tear streaked her cheek. She wiped it with the back of her hand. A sniffle to clear her nostrils.

"They took him into surgery a few minutes ago." She said. Her speech hesitant. Large, moist hazel eyes, amber-grey under the fluorescent light, gazed woefully into mine.

"The doctor said touch and go. Thank God most of the teaching staff was still here," referring to the hospital's attending staff. Competent and experienced expatriates and visiting volunteers who provided medical training to the local nursing staff, community health aides, and the local medical school.

"But they won't be able to handle his injuries here. He has a collapsed lung. Maybe other internal damage. They won't know until they open him up. And he's lost a lot of blood. All they can do here is try to stop the bleeding, replace the blood loss if they have enough of his type available, and stabilize him for transport."

She broke off, choking down emotions threatening to overwhelm her. She squeezed my upper arms in a tightening grip. Tighter and tighter. Until she regained control.

"What happened?" I said.

"Don't know," she said. "Trying to piece it together now. We found him over in Hamilton, just off the road, by the market. He managed to call on his cell before passing out. God knows how. His sidearm was holstered. When I got there...." her voice broke again, and this time, recalling the scene, still fresh in her mind, her friend and mentor on the ground in a pool of his own blood, she almost lost all control. She sniffled again. Wiped a hand across her face. Gathered strength.

"We're processing the scene now. Mon Dieu. Stuff like this isn't supposed to happen on Bequia," anger rising in her voice.

She abruptly changed the subject. "A Coast Guard vessel's on the way with Deputy Commissioner Coffe. Bumboclaat trou de cul sacrament." The curse hissed through clenched teeth, in a muted undertone. The combination of Bequia Patois and Québécois French her usual habit when agitated or provoked.

I led her to a bank of connected plastic chairs. She flopped down on one. I settled into another next to her. Her hand clasped in mine.

"We don't know why he was there, or what he was doing. He'd stopped into the station for a few minutes after arriving from Kingstown. Said he had to make a stop before heading home."

"Has anyone called Jen and his kids?" I said. Mike had two grown children. A daughter, a surgeon in Virginia, and a son, an engineer somewhere in California. His ex-wife lived in New York.

"Oh God." Jo buried her face in her hands. "Gage, I forgot. I need to call her. She should hear it from me, not some official notification. Definitely not from batty mouth Coffe." The pejorative nickname derived from the resemblance between the Deputy commissioner's mouth and the sphinctered orifice at the other end of the digestive system.

Speak of the devil. A figure entered from the stairwell. Dressed in crisp pressed grey uniform slacks, starched and ironed white shirt, black tie, grey uniform tunic. His shoulder epaulets and collar bars bore the rank insignia of Deputy Commissioner of Police, Royal St. Vincent and the Grenadines Police Force. His stride possessed a military bearing as he approached us, followed by a phalanx of uniformed and plain clothed officers.

Deputy Commissioner Coffe, pronounced like the drink, had a complexion also like the drink, without milk or cream. Black, like coal. Tightly curled well-groomed hair bordered a bald pate extending from his forehead to the back of his head. He wore thick spectacles in large black frames. A thin black moustache on an otherwise clean shaved face. And he carried a sliver-topped swagger stick tucked under his left arm. Under his right he carried his uniform cap. Its black peak beneath decorative white braids shined to a mirror like glaze.

He frowned when he saw me. A stern gaze settled on Jolene. She rose at his approach. Stood before him in a posture approximating attention and saluted. He returned the salute and they hurried to the other end of the hallway.

Deputy Commissioner Coffe and Jolene appeared to be in a heated conversation. Difficult to tell - he always appeared heated. A perpetual frown had etched deep parentheses from his flared nostrils to the corners of his small atypical mouth. Thick tightly pursed lips contributed to his derogatory nickname. That and the crap usually issuing from it. He glanced in my direction as he spoke. He didn't like me. I liked him even less.

A short, heavyset woman wearing bloodstained green surgical scrubs, mask hanging around her neck, exited the double doors of the operating suite. All heads turned towards her. I tried to discern the news by reading the faces, the lips, the body language of the small assemblage.

The surgeon's back towards me. Unable to see her face. I paid particular attention to Jolene. Observed no gasping inhalations, no abruptly bowed heads, no grief-stricken expressions. Coffe's stern frown remained unchanged.

Jolene returned to where she'd left me sitting.

"They've stopped the bleeding," she said. A measure of relief in her voice. "Now they're trying to reinflate the lung and stabilize him. That's all they can do for him here. He needs to be airlifted stateside for more surgery and advanced pulmonary care. Gage, I don't know what's keeping him alive." Almost a sob.

"The surgeon said he took three hits, one in the upper arm, one in the shoulder, and one entered under his left armpit, hit his collarbone, and ricocheted into a lung. It's still touch and go. Problem is, they don't know when they can get a flight to airlift him out." Fear and concern rose in her voice.

"He's tough Jo. He's a fighter." I said. The words meant to reassure. Normally there'd be truth in them. But Mike wasn't a young man anymore. At fifty seven, three years older than me, I knew all too well at our age we didn't heal as quickly. Or as well.

She rose from the chair. "I've got to call Jen. Where you gonna be?"

"Dunno. Reach me on the cell. Any change, any news, okay."

"Yeah. Talk to you in a bit."

As she walked away Deputy Commissioner Coffe took her place, as if he'd been waiting for the opportunity. He stared at me. His expression presumably meant to instill respect. I saw only an officious, narrow-minded little man, obsessed with his own self-importance. A bureaucrat who enjoyed the perks, if not the actual work required of his position. I'd caught small indications Mike felt similarly about him. The Deputy Commissioner a thorn in Mike's ass we seldom discussed.

"Sorry about the Commissioner," he offered. The words unexpected. And surprising coming from Coffe. Maybe the shock of an occurrence so unthinkable, so unexpected, happening to one of their own. Even someone he didn't like. Or maybe he considered the words proper form, without much meaning beyond the fact they were expected. A formality he'd been obliged to perform. The next words out of his mouth indicated the latter.

"I know you and the Commissioner are friends, but this is a police matter," the words rolled and pushed out of the small round mouth as though he were spitting marbles. "I won't tolerate interfering friends, or overemotional girlfriends either," shifting his gaze to Jolene down the hall, still in conversation with the surgeon. "Do I make myself clear, Mr. Gage?"

Jo's earlier Patois/French invective sprang to mind. The pejorative nickname appropriate. Definitely an asshole. Finally in charge, and prepared to take full advantage of Mike's misfortune and absence.

I departed the hospital. Emotions roiled within me. Amid the rampant random thoughts colliding in my brain I remembered I hate hospitals. Hate the way they sound and smell and feel. Like being trapped and captured. I'd spent my share of time in hospitals. Always believed the sooner I escaped the better-off I'd be. A great place for patching injuries and wounds; sometimes snatching life back from death's greedy grasp. But the worst place for mending and getting well.

I walked toward the harbor. Paid scant attention to the small brick homes on either side of the dimly lit, deserted, rut filled road. Or the muted lights visible behind curtained windows.

Raw emotions bubbled to the surface. Bewilderment, dread, guilt, anger. Like ocean swells they flowed into one another, merging, building, feeding upon each other; gathering strength. Rolling inexorably onward. Evolving into a towering wave packing the power to overwhelm and destroy. I'd faced that wave before. Knew diving beneath it before it broke, allowed its destructive force to harmlessly wash over me. At other times I'd stood before it like a rock at the base of a cliff, absorbing its smashing onslaught. In either case erosion an inevitable consequence. Bit by little bit. Until all feeling, all emotion was washed away.

Unable to shake the feeling I'd somehow been responsible. The guilt ridden thought more than plausible. A definite possibility. Perhaps even an inevitability. My perpetual punishment for past sins. A nemesis from my past perhaps, bent on retribution. Or an attempt to bury secrets no one wanted unearthed.

I'd been careful. I'd left no traces, no signature, no loose ends. It'd been my mantra. But I'd made enemies. Still out there. People with long reaches and longer memories. I needed to consider the possibility. Or definitively rule it out. And if I were the intended objective, the guilt accompanying that scenario hung over me like the inhospitable dark side of the moon.

I arrived at the Frangipani bar without conscious memory of walking there. Long suppressed emotions percolated to the surface. Uncharacteristic of me. And strange, like the taste of sour milk.

I had a decision to make. If the shooting was connected to me I faced two options. The most basic of reactions, fight or flight.

I'd slip my mooring and sail away tonight. Abandon the relationships I'd formed here. The life I'd settled into here. Resettle someplace else. Start over again. I'd done it many times before. But the break needed to be complete. No half measures. No goodbyes. It used to be an easy decision. A no brainer. One I'd never had to wrestle with before. But the prospect of leaving and starting over held less attraction than it once did. Maybe because I'd grown older. Maybe a new unwillingness to so easily let go.

And of course Jolene, An unexpected and wonderful complication I'd been learning to navigate my way through. From the outset it'd seemed an impossible relationship. Our age difference for one thing - my being twenty years older. For another, I'd never been open to such emotional attachments. An axiom I'd lived by for so many years it'd become second nature.

In my former life such attachments never ended well. I'd needed to maintain an emotional detachment. Prepared to leave everything and everyone behind without hesitation or explanation. But Bequia held an irresistible attraction, like a moth to a flame. The island and its people conjured a sense of home. A home I'd never had, or knew I wanted. When Jolene had entered my life the ground beneath me shifted, imperceptibly at first, but reconfiguring my terrain as assuredly as an earthquake.

She possessed an uncommon sensibility. A measure of maturity beyond her years I found difficult to resist. A grounded stability I appreciated and enjoyed. She managed to reconnect me to the world. Funny, strong willed, and comfortable in her own skin. She'd somehow managed to breach my defensive walls. She made me feel again. Made me feel different, better. Had thawed a part of me long since frozen, and resurrected emotions I'd considered buried and lost forever.

A part of my mind rationalized they'd both be safer if I disappeared. If someone were after me, they'd follow the trail I'd lay down, leading them away from this place. Or they, whoever they were, might use the people I cared about to lure me back.

Fight or flight.

They'd have me in the open if I stayed. On the other hand I'd be able to see them coming. A kaleidoscope of thoughts and exhumed emotions raced around my brain. Mike and Jolene; my unexpected, maybe undeserved, new lease on life; strategies, tactical situation, logistics, all colliding, fracturing, recombining, fleeting and inconclusive. But bottom line, someone had tried to kill my friend. Perhaps to get to me.

Anger got the upper hand.

Later in Wherever's cockpit I poured another glass of rum. I pulled the cell phone from my pocket, plopped down on the plush cushions I'd abandoned earlier, my bare feet up on the binnacle. I activated the phone's encrypted mode and placed a satellite call to the States.

CHAPTER 2

I awoke in the same spot in the cockpit the next morning. Didn't remember dozing off. Didn't remember if I'd dreamt. The phone hadn't rung. I checked it for any missed calls or voice messages. Dreading I'd see Jolene's number.

The sun rose above Bequia's highest point, spreading the light of a brand-new day across the sloping hillsides. Bright sunlight reflected off the bay. The rippling blue surface sparkled like millions of tiny diamonds.

I stripped, stepped to the aft rail, plunged headlong into the sea. Its bracing chill completed the wake up process. Instantly refreshing. I dove deeper, until sandy bottom rose before me. I kicked along the bottom, stirring up a mist of fine powdery sand.

Looking upward at the silvery surface, I rose slowly. Small bubbles trickled upward as I gradually expelled air from my lungs. Just off to my right, and a little behind me, Wherever's dark deep keeled hull hung in the clear water. The tide ebbing I observed, pulling me farther away in its undertow.

I surfaced. Inhaled a deep breath of fresh, morning sea air. Salt taste in my mouth. Normally I'd swim a couple of miles toward the mouth of the bay and back. But I heard the chiming ring tone of my cell phone. I stroked for Wherever's stern ladder.

The phone ceased chiming before I reached it. I stood naked and dripping in the cockpit, contemplating the screen. A missed call from Jolene. My dread returned.

She answered on the second ring. "Gage?"

"What's up?" I expected the worst.

"He's out of surgery, and stabilized. He's critical. But they're worried Gage. They've done everything they can here. An airlift won't be available for at least twenty four hours. They don't think he'll last that long."

I'd expected as much. Assuming Mike made it through the night. "Tell the docs to prep for the flight. Wheels up around noon."

"What?" Her voice strained. Tired.

"Did you get any sleep?"

"Ah.... No. I've been here all night. And coordinating the investigation. I may have dozed off for a while. Don't know for sure. I got hold of Jen. She'll call the kids. I told her he'd be transferred and I'd let her know when and where." Her voice trailed off.

The phone silent. Then, "What's this about a flight?"

"A buddy of mine will be landing in a couple of hours. Quick turnaround to get Mike, equipment and personnel on board. Have him ready."

She didn't waste time questioning. "He'll be ready."

Her tone told me he would be, and God help anyone who got in her way. Where Mike was concerned Jolene was as loyal and protective as a Lioness towards her cubs. Beneath her genteel surface lay a fierce, fiery strength, like a dormant volcano.

"You're the guy, Nick."

I'd never figured out what she meant by that. She used the expression often. Usually when I'd done something that pleased her, or surprised her. And she'd used my first name, which she seldom did, only in our private, tender moments alone.

Anyway, I had to get a move on.

I bundled up my clothes from the cockpit, climbed down into the salon. First things first, coffee. Had to get the body's cylinders lubricated. From the galley I tossed the clothes onto the queen sized berth in the aft cabin. I stuffed a new strainer into the coffeemaker, spooned in ground hazelnut, filled the water container for four cups, and hit the start button. I figured I wouldn't get to eat for a while. I fished out the fixings for scrambled eggs and sausage on toast.

The coffee finished brewing. Ready at the same time as the eggs and sausage. I ate while standing naked in the narrow galley, cleaning and stowing the skillet at the same time. The plate empty, I rinsed it in the sink, dried it, stowed it the locker alongside its mates.

I entered the aft cabin. Roomy for a sailboat. Technically Wherever was a yacht. The bed unmade, as I'd left it two nights before. Three short steps from the foot of the berth to the aft head and shower. I stepped into the full-size tub, drew the curtain. Washed the previous night and sea salt away.

I rode a dollar van to J.F Mitchell airport. The airport dangerously small. Built on landfill in the sea off Paget Farm on the south side of the island. Landfill the only method of acquiring an area on Bequia long enough, flat enough, and straight enough to construct a runway. Why Bequia needed an airport remained a topic of disagreement among Bequians. Its sole purpose to convey more people to the island. A good thing, or not so good thing, depending on who you asked.

Monk still an hour out when I arrived. I headed for a café shack next to the main terminal building. Old man Sam waited behind the varnished counter. He had the wizened face and leathery skin of a man who'd seen hard times, and good times. Like most Bequia men he'd been at sea for a few years. Had lived stateside for a few years. He wore full upper dentures which he sometimes forgot to put in, giving his sun wrinkled face a skull-like appearance. Tall and still muscled, even at his age, which I guessed to be around seventy.

Old man Sam was an Ollivierre. A descendant of one of the oldest families on Bequia, dating back to the eighteen seventies. They'd been shipbuilders, seamen, and whalers. Sam's Brother the last living hand Harpooner on Bequia. The last of his kind.

"Hey boss," he greeted as I slid onto a stool. Old Sam called everyone boss.

"Too bad bout de Chief," he said, pouring me a mug of coffee. My mug, even though I didn't own it. Whenever I came in he'd always give me the same chipped blue and white ceramic mug. 'I'd rather be flying' lettered on it.

"I teking him Miami jus now," I told him, speaking in Patois as I activated my cell phone.

"Dah's great boss." He turned away to the kitchen behind the counter.

When Jolene answered I said, "How's it going?"

"We're all set. Leaving now." I wondered what kind of strings she'd pulled and how many regulations she'd trampled to make it happen.

"See you in a bit," I said.

As I ended the call I heard the unmistakable high-pitched drone of Pratt & Whitney Turboprops lining up for landing. With only three thousand six hundred feet of runway, Monk needed to execute his best short field technique. He'd accomplished it in worst places.

I stepped onto the blazing-hot black tarmac as he completed his rollout. The sun almost mid sky, a blinding white orb in a cloudless expanse of pale blue. The engines grew louder as an Air Force grey, hightailed De Havilland Dash 8 wheeled onto the ramp and rolled to a stop. The forward door of the aircraft containing a built in boarding ramp opened. I approached the boarding steps as Monk appeared at the doorway.

Gin colored eyes scrutinized me, set in a rugged, sun bronzed face, beneath a head of contrasting white hair. Not sure whether to hug me or slug me. He ducked through the doorway, his large six foot four frame skipping down the four short steps. He wore drab green flight overalls tucked into flight boots.

"Monk," I called.

Monk's real name was John Taggart. For some reason lost to both our memories, I'd called him Monk from the first time we'd met. For his part he called me Raul. He knew it wasn't my name and I wasn't Hispanic.

Monk hailed originally from Dearborn Michigan. Had spent most of his adult life in the Air Force, never rising above the rank of warrant officer, flying and repairing every type of aircraft in existence. A rare breed possessing the ability to get his hands on impossible to find and get items. Whether a thanksgiving turkey deep in the Bolivian jungle, bottles of single malt in Mogadishu, specialized equipment when none were available, or front row seats to a sold out event; Monk could get it. I'd never learned the secret behind his feats of 'procurement'. And learned early on to stop asking.

No longer in the military, he continued to wear military issue flight jumpsuits. The jumpsuits efficiently utilitarian. Something the military excelled at. Monk considered every flight a 'mission' and the jumpsuit's array of zipped pockets and Velcro attachments came in handy.

Not a fist. Instead he embraced me in a crushing bear hug, lifting me off my feet, squeezing the breath from me.

"Raul," he yelled. "God, it's good to see you. But you have some nerve buddy."

"Yeah, yeah, I know. We went through all this last night. So maybe we're even, or you still own me, or maybe I owe you. I forget."

He laughed, a boisterous happy sound like china smashing on a tile floor, accompanied by a hefty slap between my shoulder blades.

In addition to his 'procurement' skills Monk was equally adept at bartering, his primary form of currency. He used cash rarely, preferring personal IOUs. He'd render a service, you'd owe him. Out of the blue one day you might get a call. Time to pay up. Failure to do so entailed unpleasant consequences. Given his reputation this seldom occurred. And when he owed you? Like gold in the bank.

"Good to see you too," I said.

"How's our patient? He good to go?"

The ambulance, a white Land Rover led by a Toyota Police jeep, had already entered the access road. It turned onto the ramp as Monk finished the question.

"He's hanging in," I said.

We gave the ambulance room to pull up to the boarding ramp. The air shimmered around the aircraft. The breeze negligible. The tarmac blisteringly hot.

Jolene exited from the Land Rover's passenger side. The driver walked to the back of the vehicle and opened the rear doors. A doctor and nurse hopped from the back, helped the driver slide the gurney out. They carried it bearing the unconscious and intubated Commissioner of Police toward the aircraft.

Monk stopped the doctor on the way in. "I rigged clamps onto the seat rails for the gurney." The Doc nodded and continued into the empty cabin.

Jolene stood next to me, observing the transfer. Monk's eyes undressed her.

"Monk, this is Jolene Johanssen, I said, introducing them. "That's Superintendent of Police Johanssen to you."

"Good to meet you." He shook her hand, his rakish smile washing over her. That much hadn't changed in the years since I'd last seen him.

"Any change?" I asked her.

"No. They've put him in an induced coma. I'm just glad we don't have to wait." She put an arm around my waist and patted my shoulder. An arched eyebrow from Monk. Followed by a quick glance at me, and a sly smile.

The medics returned to the Land Rover, unloading equipment and supplies.

"Go help them settle in," I said to Jolene, disentangling her. "Monk and I need to go over the flight plan."

He'd been flying close to six hours. And had probably been up most of the night reconfiguring and prepping the aircraft. I planned to fly the return leg. Give him a chance to catch up on sleep. The flight plan details didn't worry me. Monk had taken care of that. No pilot I trusted more. He'd flown me in and out of more hellish places than I cared to remember. And more than a few nasty situations. He preferred helicopters, while I never fully trusted them. Though I appreciated their tactical utility.

I hadn't flown a Dash 8 in some years. But a plane is a plane. All obeyed the same laws of physics. The same principles of flight. All equipped with similar flight controls and switches. Some more advanced than others. You just had to know what the switches and levers did and where they were located in the different types. The Dash 8's operating specs and performance data also didn't concern me. Much of it stashed somewhere in my memory, ready for recall. And anyway Monk represented a walking operator's handbook for almost any aircraft type.

"How's the fuel situation?" I asked him.

"I topped off in Antigua. We have long-range tanks and auxiliaries. Plus extra tanks I installed on board. No need for a fuel stop."

I nodded. "Weather?"

"Nothing to speak of. Smooth and clear all the way down. Some high cumulus over the Florida peninsular, but nothing significant in the forecast."

"Terrific," I said.

We talked as we walked around the aircraft, inspecting the fuselage, the control surfaces, props and landing gear. Following the walk around we entered the aircraft. Monk made for the cockpit while I inspected the cabin. The gutted interior possessed a forlorn appearance without the customary passenger seats. In their place Monk had installed four rectangular aluminum fuel tanks, two either side, complete with feed lines and shut off valves. A faint odor of kerosene permeated the cabin.

The medics had secured the gurney to the seat rails on the port side. Life support and monitoring equipment with self-contained power packs had been strapped in place along the cabin fuselage. Intravenous bottles hung from hooks in the ceiling.

Mike lay in peaceful oblivion on the gurney. A stocked med bag lay between two facing seats on the starboard side, occupied by the doc and nurse attendant. I checked they were properly strapped in. Checked on Jolene, strapped into another seat against the port bulkhead facing the head of the gurney.

Monk had the engines spooling when I turned to the door. I hauled it closed. Secured it. Squeezed my way into the cockpit, taking the right seat. I unplugged the bulky headset, hated those things, and plugged in the twin jacks for the earpiece and boom mike I'd brought along.

The Pratt and Whitneys spun to a high-pitched, screaming whine. The noise lessening as increased RPMs turned the props into blurred disks. Monk completed the checklists, reset the communication and navigation avionics, and the GPS suite in the center of the panel. The electronics had the flight plan. Monk received our clearance from the tower and taxied out to the single runway.

We'd be taking off from East to West. I glanced up, scanned the overhead panel. All switches in their proper positions. The annunciator panel showed clear. All indicators showed green. I read out the takeoff checklist as we taxied out. The checklist complete, we were ready.

A sudden loss of power during takeoff is a pilot's greatest worry. There are procedures for safely aborting a takeoff. Provided you have sufficient runway, or an overrun area ahead. Or sufficient power to climb to an altitude safe enough to turn and return for a landing.

Bequia's thirty six hundred foot runway provided barely enough length to get the Dash 8 airborne. Carrying a full fuel load in the wing tanks, and extra fuel in the waist, we were close to maximum takeoff weight. But Monk had chosen his equipment well. The Dash 8, though usually a short-haul machine, had been designed for short field landings and takeoffs.

The blue Caribbean Sea stared back at us from the opposite end of the runway. Even if we made it into the water in one piece; even if we survived the wreckage, Mike would be doomed. Monk's take off briefing accordingly and appropriately succinct.

"Engine out on takeoff, Shit Outta Luck."

Monk checked, double-checked, and triple-checked the gauges and switch positions. He advanced the throttles while standing on the foot brakes. He'd deployed flaps fifteen degrees. While he concentrated on the takeoff, I scanned the gauges and annunciator panel a final time. All green. Panel clear. Monk released the brakes. We were rolling.

I'd never liked the cockpit view of the Dash 8. The top edge of the panel sat high in the cockpit, the seats low. I preferred to sit high, eyes above the panel, looking out and over the nose. I cranked the seat as high as it went. Still couldn't see the nose of the aircraft.

We accelerated down the runway. Paget Farm's dusty green and brown landscape flashed by on the right. The deep blue of the Caribbean on the left. The airspeed indicator came alive. Runway pavement disappeared with astonishing swiftness in front of us.

Monk didn't wait for rotation speed. Immediately upon attaining sufficient airspeed to fly if one engine quit, he hauled back on the column mounted yoke. The heavy machine leapt off the ground, flying in ground effect scant feet above the runway. No obstacles at the end of the runway. Just water.

The runway beneath us vanished.

White speckled blue water flashed by less than fifty feet below. Monk allowed airspeed to build before commencing the climb. The nose lifted. Blue sky beckoned. Not a cloud in sight. Soon we were headed up and away at two thousand feet per minute. Mike would've thoroughly enjoyed sitting up here.

We cleaned up the airplane, flaps, landing gear, and adjusted the power and cabin pressure settings for the climb to twenty four thousand feet. Passing through ten thousand feet I activated the flight management system. The Dash 8 took over piloting itself.

The flight promised to be long and tedious. Nothing much to do but monitor the instruments and systems, and make position reports to oceanic air traffic controllers.

Monk slept on and off, waking to some internal computer when we needed to switch fuel tanks. We burned off the onboard tanks first, careful to maintain the aircraft's center of gravity within operational limits.

The Pratt and Whitneys droned on. Never missing a beat. Never a false note. Returning to the cockpit after a trip to switch tanks Monk turned to me.

"So what's the story with your guy back there?"

"He's the Commissioner of Police, Royal St. Vincent and the Grenadines Police Force," I said. "And my friend."

A raised eyebrow from Monk. "When did you start having friends?"

I didn't answer.

"I don't hear from you in like seven years, and all of a sudden out of the blue I get a call and find you sunning on a tropical island needing a quick ride. So what you been up to man?"

When I didn't respond to that either, he left the question hanging in the silence.

"Suit yourself," he said finally. "I know you're as tight-lipped as a Washington DC madam. But it's a long flight and we got nothing better to do."

"I met him here on Bequia," I said. "A couple years before I retired."

"I'd heard you went off the reservation. Didn't believe it though. Thought you were probably dead in some godforsaken hellhole."

"It's funny," I continued, smiling at the memory. "I'd just sailed into Port Elizabeth, a stopover on my way south to Panama, and maybe the South Pacific. It'd been raining, hard, with rainwater flowing over the roof gutters. I hadn't had a freshwater shower in two weeks. So I took off my shirt, stood under one of the roof spouts, fresh rain water pouring over me when this dude, with this silly grin, walks over and hands me a bar of soap. That was the first time I laid eyes on Mike Daniels."

"Still seems weird you and him being pals. Him being a cop and all."

"Go figure. But since the day we met, even when I'd disappear for months and reappear, he'd never asked me what I did or where I'd been. He always had this look in his eyes though. Like he knew."

"So how'd he end up on a stretcher in the back of my airplane?"

"Dunno. Something I'm gonna have to look into. Could be a rival. Someone he pissed off maybe. But why now? That part doesn't track. He's made enemies. And there's been active resistance within the police force to the changes the Prime Minister brought him in to make. Not to mention the old boy's club resenting him for being an outsider.

"Outsider?"

"He's American. Used to be Sheriff of Monroe County in the Florida Keys before retiring to Bequia.

"Maybe it's someone from his past," Monk mused.

"Again, why now? Unless it's someone who just got out of prison. He also served in the National Guard, part of a unit training local police forces after the Grenada thing back in eighty three. Fell in love with the place and bought a little house off the beach when he retired. That's how he met the Prime Minister. They got to be friends and the Prime Minister asked him to run the police force. Wanted Mike to modernize the force, upgrade training, equipment, improve their capability, especially with a growing crime rate being fueled by drug trafficking and guns. Guess he figured Mike a good choice because of his experience in the Keys.

"How so?"

"Similar geography. Both chains of small islands. And both gateways for drugs into the States."

"What about the girl?" a lascivious smile aimed at me. "You and she doing the deed."

Another silence. I'd already said more than was characteristic of me. And Jolene another topic altogether. One I wasn't sure I could, or wanted to explain.

"So it's like that." The smile disappeared, replaced by a piercing stare. "What you getting into here buddy? This ain't nothing like you."

"I've got a different life here Monk."

"Uh uh. Not that I blame you. She's a stone fox." He glanced behind through the cockpit door, ensuring he hadn't been overhead.

"Smart too," I added. "Educated in the States. Master's Degree in Psychology. Could've had any number of lucrative careers in the States, or Canada where she grew up. Instead she came back here."

"Why for Christ sakes?"

"She was born here. Mother's Vincentian, father's French Canadian. The Dad was down here for a few years working on some agricultural training project for the government."

"And how in hell did you manage to hook-up with her?"

"Mike introduced us. She worked for him. One of a handful of female constables on the force when Mike took it over. None with any real prospects of working in the field, or advancing into the commissioned ranks. Mike changed all that. Another reason the brass resents him. She's good. Has good cop instincts and her educational background was a plus. Mike recognized that. Put her and other women to work in the field. And he recruited more women onto the force."

As though she'd known we were discussing her, Jolene popped her head into the cockpit.

"How you guys doing?" handing us thermos cups of hot coffee and a couple of BLT sandwiches.

Where'd she find time to manage those? I wondered.

"So this is what a Dash Eight cockpit looks like," she said, taking a long appreciative glance around. "Beats the hell out of the little Seneca."

"You're a pilot?" said Monk, a new respect in his lascivious eyes.

"I'd offer you a seat up here for a while, but I don't trust this goat alone with you," I said.

"Oh he wouldn't be too much to handle," she smiled.

"Well you can have this one for a while," Monk said, rising from the seat, his tall frame bent over in the cramped cockpit. "I have to check our fuel situation."

He squeezed past Jolene and she took his place in the pilot's seat.

"How's Mike doing?" I asked.

"No change. It's a miracle he's alive. And another miracle we're able to get him stateside so fast. Maybe one day you'll explain to me how you arranged all this. But for right now, I love you."

"How're you doing?" Accompanying Mike to Miami didn't surprise me. I wondered what it might end up costing her. "How much grief you gonna get for this?"

"Coffe will have a shitfit. But I don't care. If it weren't for Mike I'd never have had the opportunity to do meaningful work. Change the self-serving culture of that place."

The vehement note in her voice set me wondering again why she'd joined the St. Vincent Police force. When asked she'd alternately claim it'd been a whim; seemed like the right thing at the time. I'd always suspected there'd been more to it than that. The question itself seemed to scrape a raw nerve.

"Most of all," she said smiling at me, "I'd never have met you. Where are we?" She asked, quickly changing the subject, scanning the panel in front of her.

I tapped the navigational display in the center of the panel, "You tell me."

She studied the display, scanned a few other instruments. "Seven hundred fifty miles out, level at twenty four thousand feet, heading two eight seven degrees. ETA two point six hours."

She gazed out at the pale azurine sky, scattered clouds far below, and the cerulean Caribbean Sea almost four miles beneath us. Monk must've gone to sleep in the cabin, allowing us time together. Enough time for her to make the next two position reports.

Seventy miles out I placed the aircraft in an easy fifteen hundred foot per minute descent. Halfway through the descent, the Florida coastline growing ahead, Monk reentered the cockpit.

"Time to go strap in back there," he said to Jolene. "Mind checking the others for me? Make sure they're belted in and ready for landing."

"Certainly, Captain," she said, a teasing flight attendant lilt in her voice.

After she'd departed Monk said, "Much as it weirds me out saying this, especially to you, I think you've got a keeper there pal." He folded himself into the seat. Once settled, he turned to face me, concern in his eyes.

"I've been thinking. Any chance this business might be something coming back to bite you in the ass?"

I didn't answer him.

"Yeah, well," he said in the silence, turning his attention to the panel and the approaching shoreline. "People get a mite slower with time, you know. And skills get rusty from disuse."

"You saying I'm getting old Monk?"

"Hell Raul, when you're seventy you'll still be the most dangerous son of a bitch I know. I'm just saying. Keep checking your six real careful old buddy."

"Always," I said.

I contacted Miami center. Received guidance into Miami airspace. As a Medivac designated flight, we received priority handling.

I'd decided to fly the landing. I punched up and studied the approach for Miami International on the GPS display. The electronics still commanded the aircraft. I'd go hands on to fly the approach segments. I had the approach and landing checklists ready to go. Monk would handle the checklists and callouts. The US coastline grew steadily in the windshield.

"When was the last time you landed one of these things?" Monk asked.

"You should know. You were there."

"That's what I thought." He frowned. "Sure you want to do this now?" his chin gesturing toward the cabin.

"I've got it Monk. She's like an old girlfriend. I remember every touch and feel."

A smile spread across his face. "Okay."

The flight into Miami airspace proceeded uneventfully. Miami Approach vectored us inbound without delay, handing us off to Miami tower. We were on an instrument approach, but the sky over Miami remained clear. Only a few scattered cumulus. Monk and I completed the approach and landing checklists. We dirtied up the Dash 8, deploying flaps and landing gear. Crossed the outer marker at one hundred forty knots.

Dusk had set in, still enough twilight for a visual approach and landing. The tower controlled high intensity runway lighting a muted glow. The precision approach path lights flashed in tandem toward the runway centerline. The forward view over the panel not to my liking. Fortunately the Dash 8 like most De Havilland models has a steep approach angle. An almost straight down view at the runway. The downside, the flair and touchdown required exquisite timing.

My position in the cockpit; my sightlines forward and to the sides; my perception of main gear in relation to the aircraft's height; outside references; target point on the runway; all raced through my brain as I bled off power and airspeed. My feet rode the rudder pedals, applying slight pressure to hold the nose aligned with the runway centerline.

The approach to that point, airspeed and sink rate, right on the numbers. Steady on the localizer and glide slope. A good landing is all about the approach. Good approach, good landing. Bad approach....well you get the idea.

The Dash 8's electronic callout activated. "Five hundred," the mechanical voice announced.

"One hundred."

"Fifty."

The runway threshold, broad while lines streaked by black rubber, rushed to meet us, filling the windshield.

"Forty" reported the mechanical voice.

"Thirty."

I timed the flare, pulling back gradually on the throttles, easing the column mounted yolk back toward my stomach. Steadily. Evenly. Held it there. The Dash 8's nose leveled, settled slightly nose up. Airspeed wound down.

"Twenty," said the mechanical voice.

"Ten,"

A slight thump as the main gear met the asphalt. No jolt. No bounce. The tires stuck to the pavement like a fly on sticky paper. The aircraft raced down the long wide runway. I held the nose up. Ground spoilers deployed. The aircraft decelerated. I lowered the nose wheel onto the runway. Propellers to reverse pitch. Gentle pressure on the foot brakes. The big De Havilland slowed. Slowed more. Until it rolled forward slightly faster than taxi speed.

I cleaned up the aircraft. Turned off the active runway onto the taxiway. Received taxi instructions to the general aviation ramp where an ambulance waited for Mike.

CHAPTER 3

Jolene and I planned to meet for lunch at De Reef. Like most other beach bar/restaurants in the Grenadines, De Reef featured an open-air design, the multipurpose room separated from the beach by a low stone wall.

We'd returned from Miami to an island transformed. In our absence Bequia had been invaded. Overrun by news reporters. Not to cover the attempted murder of the Commissioner of Police. Rather to cover the story of a white female tourist from New York who'd disappeared from the island without a trace.

Since Natalie Holloway such disappearances acted like chum to stateside cable news networks. Coverage of the disappearance dominated cable news. Bequia received stateside programs via satellite, allowing its inhabitants to follow the coverage.

The foreign news media besieged St. Vincent's police force. Deputy Commissioner Coffe proving less than useless. Neither investigation had provided any tangible results. The only silver lining, the mountains of cash poured into the local economy by the newshounds. An off-season tourist bonanza.

I sat at a wood table. Bare feet crossed at the ankles atop the low wall. I gazed out between two short coconut trees at the surf frolicking on and off the beach. Out in the bay Wherever rocked gently on her mooring.

Jolene arrived. A vision of her former self, rested, confident, alluring. The trip to Miami, despite the circumstances, had rejuvenated her. She wore her uniform, grey slacks and tunic, rank insignia attached to shoulder epaulets, black low-heeled closed toe shoes. A regulation handbag hung by a long leather strap from her shoulder.

Not off-the-shelf fare from the local uniform supplier. The slacks tailored and formfitting. The tunic cut to her chest size, tapered at the waist, and flared over tantalizing hips.

Naturally curly brown hair, pinned back from her face, fell around her neck and onto her shoulders. She wore no makeup. She seldom did. Maybe a touch of eye shadow and light lip gloss occasionally when off duty.

Even without the uniform she commanded attention. Tall and slender, she had an erect posture and squared shoulders reflective of some paramilitary training. Her elegant face, a light mocha complexion burnished by the tropical sun, featured delightful cheekbones, neither too high nor too wide; straight nose with a small flare to the nostrils; delicious mouth; full sensuous lips; dimpled cheeks when she smiled; a strong jaw line and dimpled chin.

And astonishing hazel eyes, their color shifting with changes in light. In totality an exquisite combination of her ethnically mixed parentage.

She sat next to me. Pulled a large manila envelope from her bag. Placed it on the table. I knew she carried a service weapon in the bag too. She picked at the platter of conch, coleslaw and French fries in front of me. Took a gulp of my Heineken. She ate like a bird, preferring to pick from my plate rather than ordering a whole meal for herself. I'd gotten used to it. Considered it endearing.

I opened the envelope. Withdrew a stapled sheaf of papers. Also a dozen eight by ten photographs. She continued picking at my plate.

"Anything new on Mike?" I asked. I scanned the photocopies accompanying the CID case file.

"Nothing new since yesterday." She bit into a conch morsel. "He's out of the woods but the docs say it'll be a long recovery."

Mike's condition had improved in the five days since he'd been in a Miami hospital. The tracheal tube had been removed. He'd resumed breathing on his own. His vitals stronger. He'd even woken up for a few lucid moments. But still critical, and any number of complications might prove fatal.

"How about you?"

"Dealing. The station is a madhouse. Whole Island is. And nobody knows how to deal with it. Especially batty mouth. We're a ship in a storm without a rudder. Maudet stupide fils de puted. He's so full of himself he can't see he's over his head with the US press. Not like our local reporters he can finagle and browbeat. They'll eat him alive."

"How're you handling it?"

"Keeping my head down. Let Batty mouth stand in the spotlight and take the heat. And it keeps him out of my way so I can concentrate on Mike's case. And now this missing tourist. Not making much progress on either."

I'd been perusing the file and studying the photos. "You guys collected a lot from the scene. You've got the slugs taken from Mike, the caliber, the place, a timeline. All you have to do is find the weapon, or shooter. Match it. Find one and it'll lead you to the other."

"Oh is that all?" Her quick wit and sarcasm making an appearance. "And maybe you can tell me exactly where to find either of those."

"You're looking for a real shooter. Maybe even a professional. Anyway someone who knows how to shoot. Three rounds, three hits. Tightly spaced. But Mike was moving. May've seen it coming. Definitely not some local too stupid on rum. And you didn't find any casings. Either a revolver of the shooter policed his brass. You should also look for a connection to the missing woman."

Jolene stopped chewing. Her eyes narrowed in a familiar questioning stare. The irises amber toward the center, grey-green around the edges. The colors subtly changing in the shifting sunlight. She studied my face, a slight pout to her lips. I wanted to kiss them.

"What about the woman?"

"I don't believe in coincidences. Mike gets shot. She disappears around the same time. I'd search for a connection."

Her eyes remained locked on mine.

"How do you propose we do that?"

"You're the detective. Anyone hear the shots?"

"No, the boatyard and slipway were deserted at the time. We interviewed people who'd been in the vicinity close to the time of the shooting. None can remember seeing or hearing anything useful."

"Unusual. Unless the weapon was silenced. Also points to a professional. You need to ask what would bring a professional shooter to Bequia. And how does it involve Mike and this woman?"

I gathered everything and stuffed them back in the envelope. "Let me study these some more. Maybe do a little digging."

"Keep it. They're copies."

I rose, leaned over, lightly kissed her luscious lips.

"Gage," she said, halting me as I turned to leave. Concern lined her brow. "The PM's getting pressure to call in the FBI."

The prospect didn't thrill me. As she'd been aware. I nodded, Thanked her for the heads up. Kissed her again. I Left her with the remnants of my plate.

The thing about digging, it attracts attention. As discreet as you attempt to be, word inevitably gets around. Especially on a teeny island like Bequia. People talk. And no way did I want to tango with Coffe or his cronies. More importantly, I had no idea yet what the shooting, or the woman's disappearance, meant. Or what might be waiting on the ground.

The two incidents may be connected. Maybe not. I'd proceed on the assumption they were. So what were we dealing with here? Had Mike been the intended target and somehow the missing woman got involved? Or had she been the target and Mike happened to be in the wrong place at the wrong time? Whichever, it represented unknown territory. And a connection between the shooting and my past still couldn't be ruled out.

An amateur wanted by the police, especially for shooting a cop, the top cop no less, wants to get as far away as possible, as fast as possible. The impulse is to hide. Ironically, it's where they make the most mistakes. A sudden disappearance or break from routine draws attention. A fleeing person leaves a trail.

But If this had been something else, as I believed, having organization and resources behind it, the next step involved remaining put, blending in, watching, and sweeping the trail. I'd need to find those signs. Locate the watcher. The thought raised a concern I should've considered before. I dialed an encrypted number. Waited for the other end to answer.

My search required information. More than available in the police file. Or available on the news. The cable news coverage all garbage. Speculation posing as news. Subsumed in a herd mentality, the various channels repeating the same concocted narrative; the same inane questions. Not one original take or question anywhere.

Desk anchors interviewed a parade of self-proclaimed, self-promoting experts. Retired detectives, retired FBI profilers. One idiot whose claim to expertise involved a television reality show in which he purported to be a bounty hunter. The preposterous and ultimately useless format a mainstay of cable news coverage.

Worst of all, a biased predilection for criticism and controversy. Targeted on a small, unsophisticated police force desperately treading water. Bequia's obscure vital statistics flashed across television screens around the world. Not the type of coverage the tourist board would've preferred.

Deputy Commissioner Coffe basked in the limelight. Holding news conferences and popping up in interviews on every network. His fifteen minutes of fame. Unaware he'd become the latest meal of a ravenous beast.

At any rate I needed more information on the missing woman, Sarah Holmes. And the rampant uninformative useless speculation posing as news wouldn't provide it. A needless waste of time.

Her disappearance, frankly, concerned me only as it related to the attempt on my friend's life. The news media on the other hand regarded the shooting as a mere sidebar. A drop in. And in doing so missed the irony of the story - Mike had been transforming the very constabulary they portrayed hourly as ineffective and third world.

Sarah Holmes had purportedly grown up in Madison Wisconsin. After graduating High School she'd moved east to attend Columbia University in New York City. She'd also attended Grad school there, receiving a Master's Degree in Business. She'd landed an upper level management job with a prominent Wall Street Bank. Considered a rising star.

I'd need to confirm her history. In my experience birth certificates, passports, social security certificates and other identifying documents were easily faked. I had no reason to believe it might be the case with Sarah Holmes. But I'd learned the hard way never to take anything for granted or at face value.

Thirty four years old, same as Jolene. Single. At the time of her disappearance a senior manager with Global Investments LLC, an investment-banking firm in Manhattan. She'd been on a vacation cruise on the Caribbean Star. It'd sailed from Miami where she'd boarded. She'd apparently done the typical cruise and touristy things until she'd mysteriously vanished without a trace. The extent of my knowledge regarding Sarah Holmes.

From the outset the investigation of her disappearance had focused on Bequia. The last place any of the passengers or crew remembered seeing her. I found references online regarding the ship captain's statement. Apparently he'd been unaware of a missing passenger until after the ship had sailed. He'd notified his corporate headquarters and then the authorities, who'd established Bequia as the last place Sarah Holmes had been seen.

The local police investigation had turned up no leads and no suspects. According to Jolene the CID had interviewed anyone who'd seen her, spoken to her, poured drinks for her, served her anything to eat, or came in contact with her in any way, shape or form. All amounted to nothing.

Speculation filled the void, running the gamut from suicide by jumping overboard, foul play on board ship, foul play on the island; to her running away for some undetermined reason. None of the theories supported by evidence.

Throughout the investigation Deputy Commissioner Coffe remained ineffectual. While the cruise line pushed the land theories to deflect any responsibility from their ship, its crew, or corporate management.

I needed a source. Figured the best place to find one might be Hamilton, a collection of small homes and shops on the north side of the harbor. The hamlet also sported a supermarket, at least Bequia's version of a supermarket, and a boatyard and slipway for hauling out. A few reporters had taken up residence at the marina's small hotel. Those with larger budgets had rented whole houses.

A reporter provided the ideal cutout and cover I required. Their job entailed asking questions. In places I couldn't. The downside? The risk of exposure. Becoming part of the story. Even as an anonymous local source. A scenario I'd need to prevent. And of course avoiding cameras at all costs.

I needed a print reporter. Someone I'd be able to manipulate without arousing suspicion. Someone I'd steer in the direction I wanted. To persons I deemed of interest. The questions I wanted answered.

I sat at the far end of the bar spanning one end of the open aired room. The room overlooked the harbor on one side, Hamilton Beach on the other. A cool evening breeze sailed through from the gorgeous tropical night beyond. The kind of night depicted on postcards, or in movies.

The opposite end of the room had a raised stage for live bands. In front of the bandstand, an empty area reserved for dancing. The remainder of the room occupied by dining tables covered by blue linen tablecloths. Each table surrounded by four wicker armchairs. Lamps hung from overhead beams provided muted lighting, supplemented by colorful shaded Chinese lanterns placed in the middle of each table.

I sipped a rum punch. Pink in color. I nixed the little straw umbrella normally accompanying it. The drink contained a mixture of rums, fruit juices, and a sprinkling of nutmeg. The hotel's signature drink. The kind that went down smooth and tasty, with no immediate discernible effect. Until three or four glasses in. Followed by an incomprehensible heavy tongue and change in speech pattern. 'Incomprehensible' all but unpronounceable. 'Unpronounceable' a challenge too. Along with walking. Wondering what had hit you. You'd only had three.

Happy hour had passed. Dinner being served. On either side of the bar swinging doors to/from the kitchen in constant motion as wait staff passed bearing platters of conch, crab legs, lobsters; a full menu of entrees. A full menu of delectable odors setting my stomach growling. I hadn't eaten yet.

Drinks flowed. The table banter low-key boisterous. Bob Marley's 'No woman no cry' thumped from speakers around the room. Locals I recognized occupied the bar. We exchanged greetings.

The tables by contrast, occupied by joyous strangers. Mostly white. The women mostly blond. There hadn't been anything new to report for days. But day after day the on camera talent stood in the same places, repeating the same old items, discussing the same baseless speculations. Back in the stateside studios anchors asked the same worn scripted questions, displaying a studied ignorance about the island, its people, and its culture.

"Hey Donny," I greeted the tall, lanky bartender. Donny also captained a charter ketch moored in the harbor. And sang vocals in a local band. He had light grey eyes and the light complexion of his Scottish-Carib forebears. "Look like yuh fullup."

"Yeh," he said, smiling. "CNN, NBC, ABC, de hole alphabet," pointing to tables and groups as he spoke. He put another rum punch on the bar in front of me even though I hadn't asked for one. "Newspapahs too."

I scanned the room. My gaze rested on the lone occupant of a table on the far side, close to the bandstand. One of Donny's 'I dont nohs.' Absorbed in a blackberry. Oblivious to anything but the tiny electronic screen in her hands. Thumbs urgently typing. If she'd ordered, the food hadn't arrived yet. The table empty, except for a tall glass of a dark liquid on ice, and a bulging cloth handbag with large wood hoop handles.

Petit. Difficult to tell with her sitting. I had a side on view. Maybe five four or five standing. Slim figure. Nice breasts. Straight, silky brown hair parted on one side fell to her shoulders. Her face shrouded in the dim light. Good-looking though. Attractive. I wondered why she sat alone.

I surveyed the crowd while nursing my drink. My gaze kept returning to her table. I didn't allow my eyes to linger. Some people can sense when they're being watched. Attractive women especially. Though the blackberry seemed to effectively override any guydar she might possess.

I spent the next day following her around Port Elizabeth. In the evening I sat in the same spot at the bar as the night before. Switched from Rum Punch to my usual Rum and Coke. She sat at a different table. Still alone. But I knew more than I did the night before.

Like her name, Nora Austin. On assignment for AP. I'd googled her. Had even read some of her work. I liked it. Surprising. Clean, concise, crisp reporting. Informative. She possessed a talent for weaving a compelling story using the known facts. No speculative embellishments. No preconceived point of view. She'd filed two stories from Bequia. One on the shooting of the Police Commissioner. The only comprehensive coverage of the subject I'd seen by anyone.

I'd been unable to determine from following her what particular angle of the story she might be working on. Maybe she'd just been gathering background material. At least she'd been out talking to people, getting to know them. Getting to know the island. A few of the cable news folks did the same.

But none of what they did or learned made it on air. Segment producers and editors figured it didn't procure eyeballs.

Something else I'd learned about Nora Austin provided the hook I needed. I picked up my Rum and Coke and headed to her table. She didn't notice my approach or my presence. The ever-present blackberry commanded her complete attention, blocking out the sultry country music filling the room; the gaggle of conversations around her; the appetizing aromas of beef, chicken and fish emanating from surrounding tables. Her world began and ended with the blackberry.

From my vantage point above her I glimpsed the smooth, creamy tops of her breasts beneath a low cut blouse. She looked up. Eyes the color of caramel. Natural Long lashes, high cheekbones, pert nose, thin lightly glossed lips. An altogether attractive package.

"I hear you're looking to charter a boat?" I said.

She responded as if a switch had been turned on. Instantly animated. Snatched back to the present from the tiny screen. Her thumbs halted their syncopated dance. Empty ring finger I noticed. Finally, a tentative smile curled the corners of her mouth.

"Yeah...ah...yes. How'd you know that?"

"Small Island." I said, beaming my most disarming smile.

"Well, thanks anyway," her initial excitement waning. Replaced by a worldly wariness. "It's true I'm looking to charter, but you guys charge more than I can afford."

I pulled out the chair opposite her, sat down. She pulled back, visibly more wary. Arms crossed around her bosom. A sure sign I'd invaded her space. Her brown eyes surveyed me. Her brow furrowed in consternation. The lines added strength and character to her face. Her years worn with an alluring grace and poise. Mid forties I guessed.

"Where're you looking to go?" My manner nonchalant. My smile turned up a notch.

"Look. I don't want to waste your time. The big bucks are over there," a quick arm gesture towards the rest of the room. Then crossed again. Her smile quick and easy. Her mouth provoked a titillating effect when she spoke.

"Well it's up to you. But until I know where you want to go, I won't know what it's going to cost." I had to put her at ease. I sensed her personal alarms going off. I dialed down the smile quotient. Sipped of my drink. Didn't know if it worked. She maintained her closed posture. Arms still folded like a personal shield.

The room's ambient noise filled the silence between us. Willie Nelson replaced Shania Twain. I twirled my glass on the table. Crossed my legs. Got comfortable in the chair. My body language projected a nonthreatening posture. No hurry to leave either.

Finally she leaned forward, both arms on the table, glanced around the room. Locked her eyes on mine.

"I need to go down to Union Island. Spend a few hours, maybe a day, and return," her manner coy, playing me along, waiting for an answer which would put an end to my intrusion. But this was my game.

"Why don't you just fly down on the island hopper?" I said. "Or take the ferry? It's not that expensive. And it's quick."

"I may need to visit some other islands too. I won't know until I get to Union Island."

"Shouldn't be a problem. How much you looking to pay?" My question threw her off balance. Not the bargaining ploy she'd expected. She didn't know what to make of it. If the offer were real, how much was too much? How much too little?

"Tell you what. Come up with a number you can afford. I'll tell you if it works for me." In truth, I didn't need the money. I'd have taken her to Union for nothing. But that'd be like showing a mouse the cheese and the trap you planned to set it with.

Her head tilted to one side. Gaze askance. Her eyes searched mine. Brow lined in contemplation. She even screwed up the corners of her mouth a couple of times. The entire effect enchanting.

Finally she said, "How's five hundred US. There, wait, and back?"

"Deal," I said, sticking my hand halfway across the table to her.

She stared at my open hand. Shifted the stare to me. Perceptive brown eyes, lively, and aware. Appreciative of my male attention. Yet wary. Probing. Questioning.

"How do I know you truly have a boat? Or that it's not some broken down tub not worth even that much? And you don't sound like you're from around here." The corners of her mouth curled in a coy smile. Playful. Convinced my presence was nothing more than an attempted pickup.

"You're a reporter. Check it out for yourself." My arm hung heavy in open space. She took it. A quick up and down shake. Soft, pleasant touch. Firm grip.

"Half when we leave, half when we get back," she said, still clasping my hand and staring into my eyes.

"Done," I said. She let go of my hand.

"So what now?" she asked.

I turned the smile back on, "You eaten yet?"

CHAPTER 4

"What's shaking?"

"Not a whole lot." Jolene said. "Nothing new on Mike's shooting or the Sarah Holmes disappearance. And our person of interest is a dead end." Delivered with a bucketful of sarcasm, referring to a characteristically inane remark Coffe had made in an interview.

"The only solid thing we have is a timeline. Looks like whatever happened did happen here. She was last seen walking along the harbor. But Gage, I can't find any connection between Mike and this woman. From what we've put together they'd never even met."

"The connection isn't necessarily between them. But with the two incidents. Keep looking. How's Mike?"

"Heavily medicated. He's in and out. But doing better than expected. The doctors think he's out of the woods. Jen and the kids are still with him."

"Great news Jo. Listen, do they have any security on his room there?"

"Yeah. Sure. The Diplomatic legation requested security. There're also a lot of cops in Miami who still remember Mike. And he's the only witness to an attempted murder."

"Good." I didn't say more. She didn't need to know about the extra pair of eyes I'd arranged.

I sighted the dinghy heading out from the beach. Rodney, my longtime deckhand, expertly navigated the inshore surf before accelerating up on plane.

"I'm gonna be gone for a couple of days. A charter to Union Island." I said.

"Really? Since when do you take charters?"

"More like research. You can reach me on the cell or sideband."

"Okay. See you when you get back."

Rodney brought the dinghy gently against Wherever's starboard side, by the boarding ladder. Held it there while Nora climbed aboard. As she reached the deck I extended a hand to help her over the gunwale.

She pushed big Hollywood style sunglasses up onto her head. The glasses held her hair back from her face like a hair band.

"This is a joke right?"

"Excuse me?"

"This is your boat?"

Her gaze swept the fifty eight foot length of Wherever's sturdy white pine deck. Past the sunken cockpit, the spoked wheel, the custom designed binnacle and instrument cluster. To the white mahogany trimmed coach roofs, one over the salon, a much smaller one over the forecastle hatch. With her bowsprit Wherever measured another eight feet. Her waterline measured only fifty four feet due to a sharply sloped transom.

The angled rake of her stout wood masts gave her a sexy elegance. And also had a practical effect, allowing her to point higher in the wind than most schooners normally could.

"Technically she's a yacht," I said. "A staysail schooner. But yes, she'll all mine."

Nora turned to face me, right hand on her hip. Belligerence in her eyes.

"Okay, so what's the deal here?" Belligerence in her voice too.

"The deal is, you give me two hundred and fifty bucks and I take you to Union Island."

I kept my eyes riveted on hers. She searched mine. Convinced I'd been playing her. The usual game. Local guy on the prowl for tourist pussy. And if she caught me checking her out; the trim figure; toned creamy legs flowing out of khaki shorts; the curve of her butt; supple breasts beneath a tangerine short-sleeved shirt; it'd only confirm her suspicions. Anyway I'd already surveyed those enticing features. I maintained eye contact. Rodney headed below with the small bag she'd brought along for the trip.

"So, we're going or not?" I said, turning up the smile.

Her evenly spaced almond shaped eyes softened. The corners of her mouth crept upward. She shifted her stance.

"Rodney," I called.

We cleared Port Elizabeth on a light breeze from the north, a bit of east in it. Wherever reached on a starboard tack, headed for West Cay. The northern headland sheltering Admiralty Bay blocked the breeze's full potential. Too light to provide much headway. Too light to kick up much of a swell. The sea lapped gently at Wherever's hull as she glided towards the point. No heave or roll to her. After rounding West Cay we'd be on a run. I contemplated setting a spinnaker. Decided it entailed too much work.

"How long will the trip take?" Nora asked, settling into the cockpit cushions.

"With this breeze about seven or eight hours."

"That long. It won't give me much time on Union Island. Can't we go any faster?"

"Only as fast as the wind will carry us."

"Don't you have an engine on this thing?"

I shrugged off creeping annoyance. "You ever sailed before?" I asked instead.

"No. Not really. I've been on boats before, powerboats. My uncle had a boat. He and my dad went fishing all the time. Growing up I'd go out with them sometimes."

A mouthful. More than she'd probably intended to say. A nervous reaction perhaps. Her self-revelation also produced a bit of self-consciousness. She busied herself gazing at every area of the deck. She gazed out at the sea. At the land sliding by. Everywhere except at me. She remained silent.

Clear of West Cay I turned the wheel a few spokes to port. Wherever's bow came around, her eight foot bowsprit leading the way. She settled on a southerly heading. Rodney hauled down the foresail. I gave her a few more spokes, jibing the huge mainsail and heavy boom. They swung to the starboard side in a loud thump and clatter of blocks and ropes. Meanwhile I loosened the jib sheets. Rodney swung the jib over and I took up the slack on the port sheet. Wherever ran wing on wing, her snow-white Dacron sails spread on either side, rolling gently, the wind and sea from behind.

Nora watched in silence. Her legs wrapped beneath her. Her face lifted to catch the sea air. Stray strands of brown hair ruffled in the breeze.

"So why are you going to Union Island?" I asked, breaking the silence. "I assume you're working on the Sarah Holmes story. What does Union have to do with her?"

Hesitation. Instinctively protective of her information. "Can't say for sure. Maybe nothing."

"What's your theory of what happened?"

About to say something, she choked it off. It happened so quickly she probably thought it'd gone unnoticed. Noticing those small signs second nature to me.

"I don't have a theory," she said. "I just work the story. I go where it leads me."

"What's leading you to Union Island?"

"The cruise ship spent the day there before her disappearance."

"Do you think she disappeared from Bequia, or from the cruise ship?"

"Hard to say. Right now everything points to her never making it back to the ship."

"Makes it even stranger that the local cops haven't been able to come up with a single lead. Maybe she did disappear on her own. Running away from something. Or someone. Skeletons in her closet maybe. Or something at work."

Her gaze rose to meet mine. Brown eyes curious, contemplative. But she didn't take the bait.

I Pondered other openings to probe when Rodney emerged through the hatch carrying a large bowl of cut fruit, mangos, strawberries, watermelon, pineapple, bananas. He placed the bowl on the cockpit table. A nod and smile toward

Nora. He handed me a cold opened bottle of Red Stripe beer. He went aft, busied himself rigging the trolling line. Maybe we'd catch dinner.

Rodney crewed for me regularly. A reliable first mate, deckhand, chief cook and bottle washer. And an excellent cook. His expertise with local dishes surprised and delighted the occasional guest or charter I might have on board. There weren't many. I wasn't in the charter business. But occasionally I'd have a guest aboard, like Nora.

Rodney had crewed for me since I'd first arrived in Port Elizabeth. A boy when we'd first met. Maybe thirteen or fourteen. A stray, sort of. No permanent home, bouncing from place to place for meals and a place to sleep. He never spoke much about his family. I never pressed him. I knew his mother lived somewhere on Bequia. Sometimes in conversation he'd mention her.

Just turned eighteen, he had the strong, muscular physique typical of outdoor living and manual labor. Medium height. His skin the color of coal. He had short, tightly knitted black hair. And an open and friendly manner. Always a ready smile. And a spontaneous laughter, erupting at the oddest times, at the most ordinary of things. Most times I had no idea what had amused him, setting off his laughter. Something peculiarly foreign I'd done, or said.

"So Mister Gage," Nora said after sampling the fruit. "What's your story?"

"No story? And please, it's just Gage."

"Okay 'just Gage'. Don't give me that no story baloney. You give the impression you're a local, but you're from the states. And this boat. I mean yacht. Everyone has a story. What's yours?"

"Sorry to disappoint. Just a retired civil servant spending the rest of my days on the sea."

"Retired from what?"

The lie on the tip of my tongue, a disturbance on the water a mile to port offered a timely distraction. I turned to call Rodney. He'd seen it too, already making his way toward the foredeck. Nora noticed our concentrated attention. Her question, my story, temporarily forgotten.

"Something wrong?"

"On the contrary." I smiled at her. "Wind's shifting and stronger now we're out of Bequia's shadow. We may shave some time off the trip after all."

The new air brushed my skin before we reached it. Rodney already had the staysail untied from the boom. We'd sailed many sea miles together. He knew Wherever as well as I did. We required little communication. A look. A nod. Both in tune with Wherever and each other.

I loosened the jib sheet. Rodney tugged the light billowing sail to the starboard side. I retrimmed the jib until it acquired a smooth cambered curve. Rodney moved to the staysail halyard. The triangular sail rose on its stay. The foresail followed.

Wherever caught the new breeze. She picked up her pace like a stallion given its head. She heeled. Her bow wanted to head to wind. I held her down, simultaneously adjusting the mainsheet. Rodney trimmed the foresail and staysail. Made a minor adjustment to the jib.

Wherever came alive. She heeled onto her side, her lee rail closer to the water. She settled on a beam reach. Blue and white water swished along her sides.

Nora struggled to stay balanced in the cockpit seat on the high side. I helped her over to the low, lee side. She plopped down onto the cushions, an anxious expression on her face, her eyes darting nervously between the canted deck, the low rail, and blue water rushing by.

Reassured as Wherever settled on her course, Nora turned toward the fresh breeze and her face relaxed, taking on a serene countenance. Her brown hair streamed away on either side.

"More like it?" I smiled at her from where I stood at the wheel.

"This is great."

"That's the difference between sailing and motoring," I said.

I allowed her time to savor the sensation of wind and rushing sea. I watched for signs of queasiness. Not much of a sea running. No real swells. Just short lumpy chop. Wherever brushed them aside in her headlong glide.

"I notice there isn't not much coverage about Commissioner Daniels, you know, the shooting." I said, attempting a new approach.

"Did you know him?" she asked.

"Small Island. Yeah, he's my friend."

"I'm sorry. How's he doing?"

"Better. Looks like he'll pull through, barring any complications. Still a long ways to go though."

"One of the first stories I filed covered the shooting, " she said. I didn't mention I'd read it. "I guess everyone's more interested in the Sarah Holmes story. That's my assignment anyway. This is the third disappearance in the Caribbean in as many years, not to mention the number of disappearances from cruise ships in the past few years."

"Really?" I said, exaggerating my interest, attempting to draw more from her. Again she refused the bait. Instead she looked off to port.

"What's that over there?" pointing to an island low on the horizon. A long dark mound sandwiched between azure and cerulean blues.

"Mustique. Mostly private villas. Hideaways for rock stars and assorted royals."

"Just off the bow there," I said pointing, "Is Savan Island. And beyond it, Canouan."

"What's that big one ahead, on the horizon? Is that Union Island?" She pointed at a low-lying landmass about nine miles off the starboard bow.

"That's actually two islands. From here it looks like one, but there's a wide channel between them. The point you see jutting out, with the little rise at the end, is Union Island, about four miles farther on."

"We seem to be moving pretty good. How much time now?"

"We're doing about seven knots, I'd say four to five hours with this breeze. What's your plan on Union Island? I know the island, most of the folks. I can introduce you around, be your local guide."

The curious gaze returned. Her eyes wary, questioning. The occupational reluctance to reveal information perhaps wavering, yet still firmly in place.

"Not sure about that either," she said. "Need to just start talking to people. See where it leads. Maybe then I'll have a better idea."

"Anything in particular?"

"I'm getting an odd feeling you have more of an interest in this than you're letting on Mister just Gage," the questioning stare rooted on me.

Perceptive. And too close for comfort. Saved by a shout from Rodney.

"Hey skip, I tink we have dinnah." Rodney stood at the aft rail. A purposeful grin covered his face. The trolling line stretched taut in Wherever's sudsy wake. He painstakingly worked the line in. Something big on the other end.

"Maybe a Bonita or yella dolphin from de feel," he yelled.

Rodney soon had the fish under the transom. A final heave and he hoisted it over the rail. A huge Bonita thudded onto the deck. Black and glistening. The large silver hook visible in its open mouth. Rodney raised a wooden mallet among the fishing gear. Swung it. A flawlessly accurate blow to the head of the violently thrashing fish. It lay still. Rodney went to work using the rest of his kit.

In minutes he had the large Bonita gutted and cleaned. The head and tail severed to be saved for soup. He neatly sliced the body into steaks. Before heading below he washed down the blood streaked deck using scooped buckets of seawater.

"Looks like tuna steak on the menu this evening," I said.

Nora had watched the entire operation in rapt fascination. And gradually wind and sea worked their inexorable magic. She relaxed, enjoying the sail. Her impatient get-there-itis vanished. The direction of our conversation if not forgotten, at least tabled for the moment. A delightful smile fixed on her upturned face.

And in that instant my plan went to shit. Observing her, serene and contented, slim legs tucked beneath her, face radiant in the sun, hair streaming in the wind; the first stirring of doubt hit me like a punch to the gut.

In the aftermath of Mike's shooting I'd been acting instinctively. My actions dictated by old habits. My conscious mind suppressing any rising doubts, any contemplation of the demons still lurking inside. Denying the nagging fear of resurrecting them, their potential to consume me, as they had before.

Developing an asset to gain an objective had been as straightforward as using a key to open a lock. There'd never been qualms. And the euphemisms, assets, marks, targets, had assured the required separation. Forestalled any attachments. Kept the eye focused on the prize, the mission. Pawns to be manipulated, used, forgotten.

Not anymore. I forced the incongruous thoughts to the back of my mind, postponing contemplation of the unexpected dilemma. Retreated instead into piloting Wherever. Being exactly where I wanted to be. On the sea; a heeling deck under my bare feet. The sun on my back and the wind in my face. My slice of peace on earth. A peace offered by an endless sea and sky.

The hours wore on. The sun's silvery disk climbed higher in a sky so blue and bright it required a perpetual squint. The sun arced through its zenith into afternoon. Mayreau Island slid by to port.

We entered the South passage between Mayreau and Union Island. I brought Wherever's head up ten degrees, countering the strong current running through the channel. We beat through the choppy sea, Wherever shouldering the chop and rising swell, throwing rainbow hued spray across her foredeck. Her rail lay closer to the water now. Her deck at a twenty-degree angle.

Nora wore an apprehensive expression again. Her clutch on the cockpit coaming tightened.

"Feel like taking the wheel?" I smiled down at her. My offer meant to reassure, indicating everything was alright. The slanted deck normal.

"Are you nuts? I don't know how to drive this thing."

"Come on," I insisted, reaching over for her hand. "It'll give you something to do instead of sitting there feeling queasy and thinking about throwing up."

She hesitated, but eventually took my hand. I pulled her up to the wheel. She immediately grabbed it and gripped hard.

I stood next to her. Slightly above due to the heeled deck. Her hair streamed back from her face and shoulders. Her closeness electrifying, titillating.

"Don't grip it like that." I said, easing her grip on the wheel. "Hold it lightly. Let it vibrate against your fingers and palms. You have to feel her".

She held the wheel as though driving a car. Hands on the spokes in the ten and two o'clock positions. I rested my right hand gently on top of hers. Eased the wheel back and forth beneath hers.

"Fantastic," she said after getting the hang of it. She turned to face me. Her upturned face lit by a self-satisfied smile.

"You're doing great." I said in encouragement. In truth Wherever practically steered herself once her sails were properly trimmed. With her fine entry at the bow, and long deep keel, she tracked through the water as straight as an arrow shot from a bow.

"If you weren't paying for the trip I'd ask you to take the watch for a while".

"Oh I don't mind. But you're not going anywhere right? I mean you're not going to leave me here alone, right?" A glance in my direction for reassurance.

I smiled. Stepped away from the helm. Sat on the high side of the cockpit.

"Just keep it up?" I said. The words evoked a distant memory, eliciting a smile across my face. A private joke. A memory from another time. Another place. Another woman.

We crossed the South Channel. Union Island on our lee. Little Palm Island and Petit St. Vincent to windward, stealing our wind, diverting it southerly. Wherever had been beating close-hauled through the passage. With the wind backing, I put gentle pressure on Nora's hand beneath mine on the wheel. Wherever's bow eased off.

"Just hold her there. Steer for that point ahead," I said.

I left her at the helm. Moved to the lee sheets. Eased them out. Wherever's sails bellied out. The slant in her deck decreased. She picked up a new heading straight for the harbor's entrance.

"What's that you guys keep doing with those ropes?" Nora asked, curiosity replacing her earlier apprehension. She gazed up at Wherever's rigging.

"They're called sheets," I said. "They control how far in or out you need the sails to be, depending on the direction you're sailing and where the wind's coming from." A gross oversimplification but providing her the gist. "We adjust the sails whenever the vessel or the wind changes direction. It's called trimming."

"What about those ropes there, against the poles?"

"The masts." I laughed. "Against the masts. Those are halyards. Any rope used to raise and lower sails on the mast is called a halyard. The sheets and halyards and some of this other gear we call the running rigging. Most of what you see attached to the masts are called the standing rigging. They support the masts from the front, back and sides."

An hour later we crossed in front of Clifton Harbor. Curling whitecaps marked the top of a horseshoe shaped reef surrounding the anchorage. The entrance marked in typical Grenadine fashion. Meaning no markings at all. No buoys. No bells. No lights. Local knowledge required to recognize the landmarks ashore, range them in line, and steer for the white water-free passage.

I navigated the opening from long experience while Rodney shortened sail. I explained the sail handling and maneuvers to Nora, standing beside me.

Uncrowded during the off-season, Clifton harbor contained only a handful of moored yachts. I recognized them as regulars based in the Grenadines. A forty eight foot catamaran moored close to the concrete breakwater. Owned by a retired couple, Trinidadian husband, American wife. In the middle of the harbor the 'Pearl', a staysail ketch in the charter trade, owned by an absentee American, captained by a Bequian. And the 'Dugong', a steel hulled gaff-rigged schooner, built and captained by an eccentric American hippie forever living in the sixties.

Scattered around the harbor a few locally built Grenadine schooners, snug on their moorings. Working vessels, rust stained paintwork; old tires hanging over the sides as fenders.

We cruised past them into the harbor, heading downwind of our mooring. Wherever's sails, except for the mainsail, on deck. I turned her into the wind. Mainsheet off the winch and free to run. Wherever slid forward under momentum alone. Closed on the mooring buoy. Rodney wielded a boat hook, snagged the leader and pulled the end of the mooring line through the starboard hawser. He dropped the loop over Wherever's Sampson post.

Nora had returned to her seat in the cockpit throughout the maneuvers. She watched us clean up the deck. Running lines coiled down. Halyards secured. Sails furled and lashed to their booms. Cockpit awning rigged.

A little after three in the afternoon when I tethered the dinghy to the jetty in Clifton, close to the town square. At the end of the jetty a stone walkway led to 'Lambi's Bar, Restaurant, and Guest House. The bar and dining area, constructed on stilts over the water, provided a panoramic view of Clifton Harbor.

Across Clifton's Main Square a high chain-link fence enclosed the single runway airport. Ahead the town of Clifton rose above the harbor. The rising terrain dotted by brightly colored rooftops scattered amid the greenery.

I grabbed Nora in time to prevent a fall when we stepped onto the dock.

"Easy", I said, steadying her. "Now you have your sea legs you have to get used to being on solid ground again".

"Whoa. That's weird. Thanks." No indication of her earlier self-consciousness. Or embarrassment. The sail down had put her at ease. Her touch as she leaned against me, natural, comfortable.

"Where you headed?" I asked, recalling her reaction the last time I asked, and attempting to sound not too pushy or overly interested.

"I need to talk to some cabdrivers," she said, her earlier reticence absent.

"Van drivers you mean. No real cabs on the island. Best place to start is over there," I said pointing to the main square surrounded by pastel painted shops, restaurants and bars.

"I'll be over there if you need me," indicating Lambi's open-air bar. She headed off toward the square. I continued up the stone path to Lambi's.

June, owner of the catamaran, sat at a table nursing a cold, dark drink. Probably her usual Rum and Coke. Something in common we shared. The sole occupant of the room, she sat engrossed in a novel. Another shared passion. A voracious reader, she devoured any mystery, suspense thriller or political history novel within reach. We constituted a two-person book club and swap library. I wondered where her husband Nigel might be. Probably off with Dee, their Rodney, on a tennis court somewhere, or busy with maintenance chores on the catamaran.

"What you got there?" I said.

June looked up through thick reading glasses.

"Hey sailor," her smile wide and welcoming. "What brings you to these parts?" Her voice deep and raspy. Years of heavy smoking and drinking I figured. The odor of stale cigarette smoke hung around her. A butt filled ashtray on the table in front of her. I leaned over to plant a kiss on her sun-wrinkled cheek.

"Nothing much. Short charter. A reporter needed a ride down."

The lines on her face, around her mouth, above her dark brown eyes, rearranged themselves into a sneer, before transforming into curious amusement.

"Must be some special kind of reporter for you to be doing a charter number one. And hanging around reporters number two." Hairy eyebrows arched behind the square amber frames. "I expected to see you anchored down here yourself. Away from the circus on Bequia. Same as we did."

I'd turned to get a clearer view of the open square. I spotted Nora. In conversation with a group of drivers lounging on a bench. The shops around the square idle. Not much activity or business during the off-season. Their owners already taking in sidewalk stalls and wares. Preparing to close for the day and head home. The bars and cafes by contrast preparing for the evening. Around the square islanders engaged in spirited discussions of the topic dejour. Usually politics, women, or cricket.

Three Nissan Minivans, decorated in bright primary colors, were parked around the square. Probably belonging to the drivers in conversation with Nora. June's table provided an unobstructed view of Nora and the men. But I hadn't intended to disturb June's reading. Or her solitude, yet another thing we shared in common. I'd intended only a quick hello. But before I had a chance to disengage myself she asked about Mike.

"How's he doing?" She'd already dog-eared her page and laid the book on the table. A Dick Francis mystery. She extracted a Dunhill from a pack on the table and lit it.

"Better." I pulled a chair out from the table. I sat, maintaining my view of the square. "The worst is past, I guess. The docs say barring complications he'll make a full recovery. But it'll take time."

"Doesn't make any kind of sense," shaking her head. She blew a column of smoke through her mouth and nostrils. Her voice like a nail on a cheese grater. "Whoever heard of such a thing on Bequia?"

"Changing times," I said.

"To hell in a hand basket," she snorted, releasing another cloud of smoke.

"Where is he?" she asked after a pause.

"Jackson Memorial, Miami"

"He's in good hands there Gage. That's where Nigel had his bypass surgery. They were fantastic. Saved his life."

I noticed Nora heading back. From her expression, without finding who, or what she'd been searching for. She still hadn't given me much, but in the short time I'd known her I figured she wouldn't be on Union unless she'd caught a scent, or running down missing pieces of the story. She stood apart from the cable news herd. Following leads uniquely her own.

Nora disappeared from view, heading in the direction of Lambi's entrance from the Square. She spotted me when she entered. Headed over to the table.

"Doesn't look like it went too well," I said.

"I learned the name of the driver I need to talk to. But he wasn't there. Won't be around until tomorrow. Some family thing."

I noticed June appraising Nora. She stubbed out the cigarette.

"Nora, this is June, a friend of mine. June, Nora Austin. One of those pesky reporters you came down here to get away from."

They shook hands. Nora, a bit uncomfortable given my remark. June, amused and mischievous.

"Don't mind him dear. That's just his usual cynicism rearing its head."

"I didn't get that impression of him." Nora said, glancing at me, and increasing June's playfulness.

"Well before you two start talking about me like I wasn't here. What do you want to do next?" turning to Nora.

"Nothing to do until tomorrow."

"In that case, pull up a chair and join us." June said. Before anyone had a chance to protest she motioned to Denise behind the circular bar.

Nora and I returned to Wherever after a pleasant, carefree, chatty two hours spent in June's company. Mostly the two of them getting acquainted. June recited stories of her career at the United Nations. Nora recited stories she'd worked on. Places she'd been. Famous and not so famous people she'd interviewed. June ate it up in avid appreciation, putting Nora at ease.

The women talked and laughed like old friends. I contributed occasionally. Nothing beyond my time in the islands. I spent most of the time fending off June's frequent sly innuendos.

Wherever smelled like a five-star restaurant when we climbed aboard. Rodney had set the cockpit table. The three of us sat around the table conversing, eating, savoring a meal of fish soup, salad, and steamed tuna garnished with dill, and smothered in sautéed onions, butter and a wine sauce. Desert consisted of sliced mango with a vanilla ice cream topping.

"Who knew you could eat so well on a sailboat," Nora enthused. She wiped her mouth on a napkin and fell back into the cushions. "Rodney, that was fantastic. You could have a career as a chef."

"Tanks mom," A Cheshire cat grin lit his entire face. He proceeded to clear the table.

"Did he just call me mom?" Nora asked as he disappeared down the hatch.

"Ma'am," I translated. "Just sounds like mom when he says it." I passed the remaining empty dishes to Rodney through the hatch.

"That was the best meal I've had in a long time. And your friend earlier, June? I liked her."

"I noticed. Great people here in the islands. Treat you like family once they get to know you. You'll see that once you get outside the press bubble."

"Ah. The cynic makes an appearance," she said. "Maybe you can show me around. Introduce me. Does your offer of tour guide still stand?"

"It does," I smiled. "Might have to charge you extra though."

She smiled in turn. Her face, framed by hair pulled back behind her ears, glowed in the pale lamplight beneath the awning. I felt her heat next to me. Inhaled her faint feminine scent carried like pheromones on the night breeze. Another time, another place, maybe.

I fell asleep accompanied by delicious thoughts of Jolene.

The next morning Rodney dropped us ashore. I left him with instructions for Wherever after Nora departed. I'd solved my problem. Not that it changed the situation much. She was a reporter, and she'd do what she came here to do. I had no control over her. She'd pursue her story. With or without my manipulation. I'd watch her trail as originally planned. But no longer as a pawn. Rather a knight to be protected.

The main square already busy. The day well underway. Union Islanders out and about pursuing their normal daily routines. The atmosphere lackadaisical and unhurried. Shops on both sides of the square open for business. Their pastel pinks, greens and yellows cheerfully reflected in the bright daylight. Their merchandise festively displayed to attract the tourist eye. Only a smattering of those around this time of year.

Small trucks and minivans, Nissans, Toyotas, Mitsubishis, navigated the narrow streets. Their bleating horns a constant background refrain, amid the strains of reggae and soca music blaring from their speakers and from storefront boom boxes.

Nora must have found the driver she'd been waiting for. She climbed into the front cab of a small green Mitsubishi truck, the rear compartment covered by a green canvas awning with red and yellow tassels hanging down the sides. The van headed off in the direction of Ashton.

I lingered in the square after the van's departure. Observing the activity on both sides of the square. Nothing out of the ordinary caught my attention. Or set off any mental alarms.

I ambled into the square. Approached a driver I knew.

"Hey Leon."

"Gage. Wat yuh doin dis side man?"

"Ave a charter just leave in dat van." I said, slipping effortlessly into local Patois. "Whose van dat be?"

"Bainsey van," he said, referring to Noah Baines, a driver I also knew. A Barbados transplant. A Bajan in the local vernacular. Noah had married a Union Island woman and made Union his adopted home.

"Yuh need go sumweh Gage?"

"Yea man. But I need de van. Dohn know how long. I pay yuh fe de hole day."

I pushed a wad of US bills into his hand. An illegal arrangement, strictly speaking. Leon had no license to hire out vehicles. And Union Island possessed no car rental agencies. If anyone asked, especially the police, he'd loaned me the van. The bills I'd given him amounted to more than he'd make in a day of driving. He smiled, and waved me toward a red canvas covered Nissan parked in front of a pink batik shop. I had a hunch where he'd spend the remainder of his day.

I climbed into the driver's seat. Right hand drive. Started up the van. Threw it in gear, and headed in the direction Noah's van had taken. Past the Barclays Bank. The pharmacy. The shops on either side of the narrow street heading out of Clifton.

For the remainder of the morning, into the afternoon, I trailed the green van on its tour of the three square mile

Island. From Mount Taboi overlooking Ashton in the south, to Bloody Bay Head in the north. And Point Lookout in the east. The van stopped frequently. Nora disembarked at these spots. She gazed out at the scenery. At the blue-green Bays. At the surrounding islands. Not merely sightseeing. And no one paid her any undue attention. Didn't diminish my uneasiness. If someone had been watching her, it meant they were good.

By late afternoon Noah deposited Nora back in Clifton. I parked Leon's van on the opposite side of the square. I watched Nora walk off toward the beach before I approached Noah.

"Hey Bainsey. Dat me chartah. Weh she been man?"

"I tek she all ovah. Sightseeing."

"Sightseeing? She tol me she a newspapah repotah."

"Well she ax me to tek she all de places weh dat missin woman been. I was she drivah yuh noh." Even though he spoke like a Vincentian, Noah's accent retained the singsong lilt peculiar to Barbadians.

"Yuh drive dat missin woman?"

"Yeh man," he answered, a proud lift in his voice. As though the attention surrounding her disappearance boosted his celebrity by association. "Tek she all ovah jus like yuh chartah. She tek piccha everyweh."

"She was tekin picchas?"

"Yeh man. Everyweh she go she tekin picchas."

"Wait fe me." I said. "I have fe get me chartah. Wherever over in Chatham."

I walked over to the stone jetty where Nora stood waiting.

"Hey Gage," she greeted. "Would it be possible to make a couple more stops on the return trip to Bequia?"

"Don't see why not. Where?"

"Tell you later. I need to get back to the boat and write up my notes. You sure it's okay? You don't have to get stuff, how do you call it, provisions, or anything if we don't head straight back?"

"We're fine. In fact, Rodney already took care of the provisioning. Anyway, we need to take a ride."

"A ride? Where?"

"Over to Chatham Bay. Rodney moved Wherever over there earlier."

She didn't question why. But I didn't miss the curious expression etched on her face.

"Just a few maintenance items I needed done over there," I explained, forestalling any questions and concealing the real reason, a precaution born of occupational paranoia.

We returned to Noah in the Square. Boarded the van and drove out of Clifton. The town's cheerfully painted shops and narrow streets gave way to green open spaces, hillside woodlands, tropical fruit trees, and grazing goats as we wound into Union's interior, our route climbing above Ashton township. The landscape green and dusty brown. The scent of rich soil in the air. Modest island homes briefly visible amongst thick trees bordering either side of the narrow winding road.

We dipped into a valley. Open green pastures on either side. The road climbed again, topping out on a forested ridge overlooking the blue, green, white capped water of Chatham Bay. A single yacht, Wherever, rode at anchor in the picturesque bay. Noah deposited us at the Beach Sands Hotel. I paid him generously.

"See yuh latah Bainsey.

"Shuh man. Latah."

I hailed Wherever from the Beach. Rodney had been keeping a watch for us. He vaulted over the rail. Landed expertly in the dinghy. Fired up the outboard. Headed for the beach.

"I didn't understand a word you two were saying the whole ride over," Nora remarked while we waited on the beach. "Weird how you just slip back and forth in the language like that. Anyone who didn't know better would take you for a local."

"Comes naturally when you've lived here a while. I use it to play a little game on self-indulgent tourists sometimes."

"Yeah. I bet you do."

I laughed. "Meaning what?"

"There's more to you than meets the eye, is all. And there's more to your story than you're willing to let on Captain just Gage." She smiled at me. Her manner easy. Playful. Nonthreatening. But also a smart, perceptive reporter, I had to keep reminding myself.

"Speaking of which. You'd do me a huge favor if the rest of your colleagues thought of me as just another local charter captain."

"And why's that?"

"Can you do me that favor or not?"

She searched my eyes. Her curiosity further aroused.

"My lips are sealed," she said finally. I took her word for it. Hoped she wouldn't pursue the subject on her own. I'd given her no reason to.

We'd been aboard Wherever only moments when my cell phone rang. I checked the incoming ID, a secure sat line. I ambled off to the bow, out of earshot, to answer the call. A call I'd been expecting.

I needed to get stateside. Fast.

CHAPTER 5

I needed to enter the States unnoticed. No immigration and customs station. No airport surveillance cameras. The last time I'd flown in, Mike comatose on a gurney, we'd had diplomatic credentials and clearances arranged by the government of St. Vincent and the Grenadines. The formalities had been quick and perfunctory.

I flew from Union Island to Martinique. From there to Port-au-Prince, Haiti. At Port-au-Prince I boarded a C-130 operated by my preferred airline. The second time in as many weeks I'd called on Monk for transportation.

Monk operated charter flights throughout the Caribbean, and Central and South America. Mostly cargo. He operated in remote areas not served by commercial carriers. Or anyone else. Oftentimes involving unsavory characters and clandestine cargo. He sometimes flew off book missions for the U.S government. It provided him a measure of official protection.

He had a perfect setup for trafficking, drugs, weapons, people, whatever. A sure bet he'd been approached any number of times. He made regular aid flights into Haiti and the Dominican Republic. Key staging points for narcotics headed to the U.S. But drug trafficking wasn't Monk's thing.

He limited his smuggling to food, medicines, crop seeds, and people having legitimate, as defined solely by Monk, reasons to get in and out of places unnoticed. The jobs Monk accepted had to pass his personal moral sniff test. And his extralegal activities reflected a well-disguised altruism, the basis for our bond of respect, and even trust.

I departed Port-au-Prince sitting in the back of Monk's C-130 surrounded by a half load of empty and partially filled cargo pallets. A long, noisy, bumpy, monotonous flight. Nothing I wasn't used to. The back of a C-130 as familiar to me as business class to a traveling salesman. I slept.

I arrived in Miami eight hours after departing Union Island. I'd left Rodney instructions to take Nora wherever she needed to go. I'd told Nora my attorney had called from the states concerning an urgent matter requiring my personal attention. The lie had come easily. As practiced as a three round grouping into center mass. Before leaving I'd grabbed a cover ID and a stack of cash from a concealed compartment in Wherever's aft bilge.

The aircraft taxied to the General Aviation area on the periphery of Miami International Airport. Two Immigration and Customs agents greeted it in Monk's hanger. The aircraft's paperwork and manifest in order. The port of entry formalities routine. Monk's aircraft, crew, and operations familiar to the inspectors.

I presented a legitimate U.S passport. The name a cover known to no one else. The passport carried the appropriate Haitian port of entry stamps, provided by Monk. Who'd also provided documentation identifying me as a UN relief worker returning to the States briefly for a conference on relief aid to Haiti. The documents passed inspection without question. I also carried a Florida Driver's license and credit cards in the same name.

I found the blue BMW 735 parked where Monk had said it would be. He'd handed me the keys in the hanger. I activated the aftermarket GPS. Entered the North Miami address in case my memory failed me. Dialed a number from my cell phone as I exited the airport.

"Just arrived in Miami," I said when the other end answered. "Status?"

"We had to intercept. Couldn't take a chance waiting. We'll brief you when you get here."

"Should be there in about thirty minutes."

Early evening by the time I arrived at the house in North Miami. I'd left the airport clean. No undue attention. No tail. I pulled to the curb in front of the address I remembered. I'd purchased the property some twelve years before. Had personally used it only twice in all that time.

I stepped out of the car. Straightening up proved a challenge. I'd been sitting for long stretches. Travelling in the back of a C-130 hadn't helped. And despite sleeping for most of the flight my body possessed a weary lassitude. The stiffness in my lower back announced itself painfully. Not just my back. Every joint screamed its own complaint. I ached all over.

I studied the block. One end of the street to the other. A quiet residential street. No traffic. No one moving about. One of the reasons I'd chosen this area. That, and its proximity to two major highways. Its character hadn't changed much over the years. Lights shone from the curtained windows of small single family homes along both sides of the street. A hint of fried chicken scented the evening air.

I approached the house, painted pale pink. It had a red tile roof, and green aluminum sunshades above heavily curtained windows. The modest two bedroom stood back from the street, fronted by a small, well-kept lawn and a sickly looking palm tree. A chest high chain-link fence surrounded the small yard. A dark SUV sat in a covered carport on the right side of the house. I opened a gate in the fence, followed a narrow concrete path leading to a raised stuccoed landing by the front door.

The door opened in response to my knock. A smiling giant filled the doorway. Max Garibaldi. Big, six foot four, two hundred plus pounds of beef, bone and muscle. I hadn't seen him in years. Had forgotten how imposing he appeared in person.

"Gage," in a song like elongation of the syllable, "Long time man." His voice soft, melodious. A surprise in someone his size, Conveying the impression he might be a singer. And disguising a trait familiar only to those who knew him well. The softer more mellifluous his voice grew, the more danger he represented. He wrapped me in a bear hug as he dragged me through the door.

As I entered I spotted Mendez sitting in the small kitchen. The remnants of a fast-food meal and a beer on the table before him. He rose when I entered the room, opened the refrigerator and fished out another beer. He twisted the top off and handed me the cold beer me as I approached.

"Cheers boss."

I'd known Mad Max and Mendez, aka mole, from back in the day. A study in contrasts. Max tall, chiseled features, strong jaw line and a prominent cleft chin. Contemplative grey eyes. The more cerebral of the two.

Mendez on the other hand, short, stocky, a scrapper. Quick-tempered. Piercing brown eyes. And an encyclopedic knowledge of chemistry. Particularly chemical explosives. Capable of speaking the Queen's English when called for, but he preferred the vernacular of the streets, perfected during stints of undercover work with the DEA.

Like me, both were clean-shaven. Uncharacteristic for the three of us. Usually we'd accumulate a three or four day growth, sometimes a full beard, shaving in the field a low priority. Unless our cover called for it.

Max and Mendez, along with two others, represented the only team I'd worked with in an otherwise solo career.

"Sure was a surprise getting your call," Max said. "Haven't heard from you in years. How'd you know where to contact us?"

"Sorry about that," I said. I took a long thirsty chug of beer. Didn't answer his question. They didn't need to know I'd been keeping tabs on them over the years, or how.

"Sort of an emergency," I said. "Thanks for the help with this. Hope I didn't pull you guys away from anything important."

"Nothing won't keep," Mendez said. He didn't elaborate. "Heard you were out for good."

"Where'd you hear that?"

"Here and there. Kinda figured when you dropped off the radar like you did. Heard some people aren't too happy about that. Nervous you might suddenly appear somewhere they don't want you to, know what I mean?"

"They've got nothing to worry about as long as they leave me alone."

"Well here's to you G," Mendez said, raising his beer bottle in salute. "You deserve it."

I hadn't heard the one letter nickname in a long time. Didn't particularly care for it. What it represented. And I'd spent a great deal of time putting it behind me. But as we sat around the table chatting, catching up, and seeing them together, hearing their voices, it was like stepping back in time.

I put thoughts of the past behind by turning to our current business. The irony not escaping me. The current business dredging up the past.

"What've we got?" I asked.

Mendez pushed a manila envelope across the table. "Name's Victor Ricardo, 'Ricky' on the street, like in Lucy."

I pulled a sheaf of five by seven color photographs from the envelope. Images of a slightly built man in tailored shirts and slacks. Sometimes wearing a sport jacket. Five nine or ten. A buck fifty pounds maybe. Thin face, prominent cheekbones and a moustache. Slicked black hair.

The photographs had been taken at various locations around downtown Miami. A few in Miami Beach. More ominously, at different locations around Jackson Memorial Hospital. On the back of each photo a notation of date, time and location. I listened while studying the face and locations in the photographs.

"Been on the DEA's radar going back a few years," Mendez continued. "Most of what we know about him I got from contacts over there. They've tied him to maybe a dozen bodies all over south Florida. But never been able to pin anything on him. He's chief enforcer, fixer and executioner for

Philippe Calderon." He paused. I continued studying the photographs.

"And?" I prompted in the silence.

"You don't recognize the name?"

"Should I? Never heard of him."

Max and Mendez exchanged glances.

"He's the biggest drug importer in South Florida Boss," Mendez said. "Feds been trying to take him down for years. Nothing sticks. He's well-connected, ruthless, and smart. Models his organization after the old mob families, but he doesn't seem to be connected in that way. Most of the old Miami mob's been dismantled by the feds anyway. Besides drugs, he controls the port, loan sharking and prostitution. They think he's also into human trafficking. Establishing his own supply of girls. He owns some legit clubs, restaurants and other businesses. Washes cash through them. Not much happens in South Florida he doesn't get a piece off."

"Independent or connected?" I asked

"No one knows for sure. He's local, homegrown, tagged as a heavyweight about ten years ago. As the major player for the past five. He's definitely in bed with the Columbians, but no one's sure if he was recruited, or formed a business alliance."

"And we know for sure he pointed the gun?" I stared at the last photo in the pile.

"No doubt."

"How long before he starts wondering where his guy disappeared to?" I stared at the image. Victor Ricardo's corpse. Two gunshot wounds in his chest.

"Not for a day or two. And only if he doesn't hear anything about your pal on the news. That's from the horse's mouth."

"We had to take him down quick and hard G," Max interrupted. "The clock was ticking. We didn't want any nasty business in the hospital, or even close to it. Anyway we were able to get a little from him before he shuffled off his mortal coil."

"Was he the shooter on Bequia?" I asked.

"Said he knew nothing about it. Had never been there. Never even heard of the place," Mendez said.

"And you believed him?"

"Yeah. He would've told us Boss." I didn't need to question that assessment.

"So what's the connection?" I thought out load. "Why would this Miami drug guy want to target Mike if he had nothing to do with the original shooting?"

"Don't know. Maybe a contract. But outside contracts aren't usually in this guy's portfolio."

"Okay." I said, stacking the photos neatly like a deck of cards. "Thanks guys. Good work."

"So what's the next move Boss?" Mendez asked.

"Tomorrow I'll visit my friend in the hospital. Then I need a chat with Mr. Calderon."

"How're you gonna arrange that?"

"One-on-one under my control." I said

They exchanged glances again. "Figured you'd say that. We already did the recon. Best scenario is a snatch and grab on the street."

I smiled. An unconscious reaction. Despite the intervening years, still in sync. Smiles emerged on their faces too.

"Lay it out," I said.

All business again. Max led off. "Calderon's estate and all his offices have tight security. Both uniformed rent-a-cops and plain clothes guards and patrols. And they carry heavy-duty firepower. There's also electronic surveillance and countermeasures at the estate and offices. We'd need a larger team for an extraction. And it'd probably get loud and messy."

Mendez picked up the briefing. They'd divvied up the surveillance. Max the physical spaces. Mendez the man himself.

"There's one, maybe two bodyguards when Calderon's on the move," Mendez said. "Especially when he's at dinner at one of his clubs, or meeting privately. His ride is an armored limo. It's never left unattended away from the estate, but there's ways to jack it. Best scenario is a snatch with the limo. Once we get him inside he's ours. Like Chinandega back in ninety two."

"Timetable?"

"The sooner the better. He's gonna start wondering about Ricky soon. May send in a backup. Or he may go into lockdown. We know his movements and his routine. We know where he'll be tomorrow night. All we need is to pick up some gear. Make some arrangements."

"What about the bodyguards?"

Mendez continued. "Muscle mostly. Professional shooters. But not too smart about personal security."

"How'd you manage to put all this together so fast? Sounds like at least a month's worth of recon."

"Try years. DEA's been watching him for that long. I've got some hooks over there," Mendez said.

"And they gave you access. Just like that?"

"You have to know how to ask." Delivered with a conspiratorial smile. "They don't know I have it."

I knew better than to ask. The mole had struck again.

"Okay. The intel looks good. Something still doesn't feel right though. I can't see a guy like Calderon being this vulnerable."

"Thing with this guy Boss," Mendez said, "he's looking in all the wrong directions. He expects surveillance, expects penetration. He's compartmentalized his operations, eliminated the competition, and bought a whole lot of official protection. He's sitting on top of the heap with no opposition. Other than the Feds, someone stepping outta line or trying to muscle in on his territory, he thinks his bases are covered. That's his weakness. He's not looking for outsiders like us."

"Okay. Set it up, we'll op spec it later. I'll pick up cash for you before visiting Mike. Get what you need. And put together everything you have on Calderon for me."

We spent the remainder of the evening in more reminiscing. People we'd known. The other members of the team. Those still among the living. Those not. Surprised by my reaction to seeing them again. Being in their company again. Hearing their voices, their familiar banter and laughter. Like coming home after a long absence. A home I no longer recognized or felt a part of, or wanted to be a part of.

The next morning I handed Max cash I picked up from a secure lockbox I kept in Miami. I bought extra clothes, changing in the store's fitting room.

When I entered Mike's room a nurse had just completed her morning ministrations. Mike lay comfortably on fresh linens. A swath of bandages covered his upper torso. A nasal cannula strapped to his face. No longer hooked up to life support as when I'd last seen him.

He managed a weak smile when he saw me. Tried to raise an arm. I hurried to his side. Took his hand and arm in both of mine. Gently laid his arm back at his side.

"Take it easy partner. No need to stand on ceremony with me."

He smiled again. His voice barely above a whisper. "Good to see you Gage. Don't tell me you came all the way stateside just to say hello."

"Some business to take care of. Thought I'd look in as long as I was in the neighborhood."

Even in his current state, the familiar, curious cop-like suspicion crept into his brown eyes. He held my gaze, probing, questioning. He let it go.

"So how's life on Bequia without me?"

"Jo hasn't been bending your ear?"

He smiled again. "I guess. But I only get bits and pieces. And I tire quickly. Most of the time I'm in a drug induced fog."

"Well, you'll be up and about soon, unless you're as stubborn and ornery as I get in hospitals".

"Make it a regular habit do you?"

I laughed. Spontaneous but subdued. I patted his shoulder. "You never give up do you?"

"Not normally in my nature."

"Good. It'll go a long way to getting you out of here and back home."

I paused. Silence hung between us. I needed to get onto the other reason for my visit. The timing had to be right.

"What do you remember about the shooting Mike?" I waited for it. For his eyes to lock on mine; for the unsettling, interrogative stare. Intense and piercing, even though dulled by drugs under half closed, puffy eyelids; peering into my soul. I smiled inwardly. Our gaze remained locked on each other. I didn't doubt he'd discerned the reason behind my question. And wondered what, if anything, to do about it.

Finally he said, "Not much. Happened fast. I remember seeing a guy. Something wrong about him. Nothing I can explain. He was just wrong, you know?" I nodded.

"But I wasn't expecting a weapon. I walked right into it. Stupid, stupid."

"Don't beat yourself up Mike. Could've happened to anyone. You're not the first. Won't be the last."

Wrinkles around the corners of his eyes conveyed a somber smile. His eyes teared. I didn't know whether from emotion or medication. He looked away.

"Didn't feel a thing then. Sure do feel it now," he said. "Can't believe all those years as a cop in the Keys; the crazies I've tangled with over the years. And I get capped on peaceful little Bequia."

"Can you id the shooter?"

His penetrating gaze returned. Our eyes locked again. His moist, plaintive. Questioning. What are you up to? Why are you doing this? Why get involved?

"I'm not sure," he said. "Everything's still fuzzy." He blinked away tears. They spilled from the corner of his eyes, trickled across his temples. I found a gauze pad on the bedside table, gently dabbed the sides of his face.

I fished a photograph of Ricardo from my shirt pocket. Not the one of his corpse. Or any of him around the hospital.

"This him maybe?"

He studied the photograph. "No. That much I can tell. The shooter was dark. But I don't think Hispanic. Maybe darkly tanned white. But it might've just been the light. Anyway he had thinner hair."

It confirmed Ricardo's story. "Who is he?"

"Just someone of interest, as you guys would say?"

"What about her?" I showed him a photograph of Sarah Holmes.

"The missing woman?"

"Yeah."

I noticed no television in the room. They'd probably kept newspapers from him too. Although on the mend he still required intensive care. I knew he'd been visited by various police agencies, including the FBI. They'd undoubtedly questioned him about the missing woman, their main interest.

"Don't remember seeing her. Sorry Gage."

"Don't sweat it. Probably nothing."

He smiled. "Hey Gage. I hear I have you to thank for my taxi ride."

"No problem."

"Someday you'll have to tell me how you pulled that one off."

"Someday. Right now your only concern is getting better and getting home."

"Thanks anyway," genuine gratitude in the dark brown eyes. Maybe referring to more than just the medevac ride.

"Anytime," I said, returning his gaze. He turned away again. Appeared to drift off. Time to leave.

"I'll let you rest. I'll be in to see you before I leave town."

"Gage," he called as I turned from the bed. "Be careful."

"I'll see you later." I said.

I had a date with a Miami drug lord.

CHAPTER 6

Night again. Raining. Not a hard storm driven rain. Rather a constant steady downpour. The rain gave the night a clean, fresh smell. Like the city's dirt and grime had been rinsed away. The rain also a good omen, if you believed in omens, providing cover for the planned op.

I focused on the club on the west side of Collins Avenue in South Miami Beach. Mendez and I waited in a black cargo van parked on the opposite side of the Avenue. From outside, the nondescript one story building didn't have the appearance of a nightclub. Not like the trendy neon lit nightspots farther along the strip. Storefronts attached on both sides. A boutique on one side. A hair and nail salon on the other. High-rise apartment buildings towered over it in the blocks behind.

Rainfall streaked the windshield, magnifying and distorting the scene outside. The colored lights like bright blossoming flowers. The buildings and trees along the wide avenue reflected in rippling patterns on the wet pavement.

Max stood concealed near the limo, parked down the block from the club. Dressed in a Metro Dade Police Officer's uniform. I sat in the van's shotgun seat, my role to provide covering fire if needed. A suppressor equipped Heckler & Koch MP5 lay at my feet.

The police disguise provided a number of contingency options. Including an abort option. It allowed Max to approach the limo without arousing the driver's suspicions. If the limo had been parked in front of the club entrance, in the red fire zone, Max would have instructed the driver move it. Not too far as to raise suspicion. Just out of the red zone and the club's entrance.

A neon sign lit the entrance. A single security camera, positioned on the inside, recorded anyone moving through the swinging double glass doors. The doors being glass, the camera also picked up activity on the sidewalk. Earlier recon had spotted the camera. The only one in the area. The lampposts at both corners of the block, and the traffic lights hanging across the intersections were clear.

No pedestrian traffic on the sidewalk. Another benefit of the rain. The riskiest part of the operation about to unfold. We didn't have eyes on the target inside. According to our intel Calderon would have dinner, then depart around ten pm to visit another of his clubs. The after dinner clubs interchangeable. The only unpredictable part of his routine. We expected him to be inside for at least another hour. But he might walk out at any time. Might be on his way out at that moment for all we knew.

Max waited for the right moment to make his move. The go, no-go call for the op his alone. Leaving concealment and taking control of the limo had to be accomplished in one fluid movement. Max adept at waiting. As I was. Silent. Immobile. A predator hidden in tall grass. Capable of waiting days for a target, in jungle rain, in desert heat, in freezing cold. Waiting for the right moment to pounce.

The sidewalk clear, no one approaching from either direction, Max made his move. He approached the driver's side of the limo. Tapped on the window. He'd be unable to see inside the limo's heavily tinted glass. But the driver could see out. He'd see the police uniform.

The position of the parked limo blocked Max's actions from my view. I visualized the scene in my mind. The driver's window descending by its silent electric motor. Max's hand coming up. The hiss of compressed gas. The dart embedding in exposed flesh. Max reaching in, opening the driver's side door. Pushing the driver from behind the wheel and sliding in beside him. If everything went as rehearsed.

Max disappeared into the limo. A second later. Confirmation.

"I'm in," said his voice through the tiny earpiece pushed into my right ear.

Mendez started the van. We weren't out of the danger zone yet. Calderon might exit the club during the transfer. We had another plan for such a contingency. Mendez pulled away from our parking spot. I moved to the side door in the back of the van. Mendez maneuvered the van alongside the limo.

"Now", came the signal in my ear. I slid the side door open. Stepped onto the wet pavement. Opened the front passenger door of the limo. The limo driver in position as expected. I reached under his armpits, grasped his torso and heaved backward. The doorsill of the van connected with the back of my knees. I fell backwards. Continued to fall flat on my back on the floor of the van. The driver on top on me. I rolled him off me into the van. Swung my legs up and in. Closed the sliding door. The van kept on rolling. Less than five seconds.

I returned to the passenger seat as we approached the intersection. Mendez made a right turn. We doubled back around the block. Mendez parked in the spot we'd vacated less than five minutes before.

More waiting.

Sitting in the van, the MP5 nestled against my leg, the bulk of a forty five caliber HK Mark23 pressed against the small of my back, my thoughts questioned my presence here; the course of action I'd set in motion. Flashbacks to other places. Other faces. Before the darkness.

It'd been different then. I'd been different. I'd relished the adrenaline rush. The primal exhilaration of life on the edge. The irrational faith in my own invincibility. And a self-righteous belief in my purpose. All obliterated by time, experience, and age. The novelty worn bare. One too many narrow escapes. One too many bodies. One too many corrosive lies and betrayals. Faith, belief, identity, purpose destroyed. Replaced by a despondency so deep, a despair so pervasive, the sun turned dark; a black hole in the sky. And the world disappeared.

I'd somehow survived. Had managed to find my way back. Had buried my demons. And the person who'd possessed such unquestioning righteousness in his heart and flag on his shoulder I hadn't seen in many years.

Now hunting again. Stalking again. Ready to kill again. Heading down that dark road again. A road ending in a familiar, even darker place.

But I'd changed. The torturous road back not without its uncertain ambiguity; its share of blood in a redemptive effort to set things right.

I refocused my attention on the club. Pushed aside the nascent doubts swirling in my mind. Familiar now with that dark road, and the invisible demons lurking along the way.

Earlier we'd observed Calderon enter the club accompanied by two men. One a bodyguard. The other unknown. The unknown man exhibited neither the posture nor carriage of an armed bodyguard. Perhaps a business meeting. No predicting how many people might exit with Calderon. According to Mendez's intel Calderon usually traveled alone after dinner. After the last club of the night there might be a female companion.

Twenty minutes later the earpiece delivered a message. "Heads up. Eyes on target."

Two men existed the club. Calderon behind the bodyguard. The bodyguard held an open umbrella over Calderon and scanned the street. Calderon cast a gaze at the rain filled sky. He buttoned his overcoat. At the same time the limo pulled up to the entrance. As they expected. Neither man waited for the driver to get out and open the passenger compartment door. Maybe not their usual routine, the driver always remaining in the vehicle. Or maybe they wished to escape the rain as quickly as possible.

The rain continued working to our advantage. And the bodyguard's disadvantage. Both his hands occupied. One holding the umbrella over his boss. The other opening the limo door. Leaving him distracted. And preoccupied. Unaware of any danger.

Mendez's assessment correct. All muscle. No brain. No clue regarding personal protection. His boss inside the limo the bodyguard hurried around the vehicle to the front passenger side. He opened the door. Turned away to close the umbrella. Another mistake. He slipped into the seat, ass first, his back to the driver. His final mistake.

"Target secure," came the message through the earpiece a moment later.

The clock now running.

The limo pulled from the curb and headed away. Mendez followed a few car lengths behind. Both vehicles headed north on Collins. Turned west onto Fourth Street. Crossed Washington Avenue, encountering only light traffic. We turned onto Michigan. After one block we made a left onto Fifth, heading for the MacArthur Causeway.

On the East-West Expressway we traversed the rain-drenched city at a steady pace. Miami's lights a colorful kaleidoscope through the rain streaked glass. At the Palmetto we headed north. The limo turned left into an industrial area west of Miami International Airport. The limo's lights went out. Mendez did the same in the van.

The limo rolled to a stop in front of a warehouse. Max exited the vehicle. He spent a few moments at one corner of the building. A large door slid open.

Max drove the limo into the dark, cavernous interior. Mendez and I waited in the van. Max retrieved the unconscious limo driver from the van, abandoning the limo, unconscious bodyguard, and driver in it. He closed the warehouse door and relocked it before joining us in van. We headed for the second exchange.

Mendez drove into a long-term parking area at the airport. We exchanged the van for a black Range Rover. Calderon unconscious in the backseat, we headed for our destination.

"Time?" I asked.

"Maybe two hours before his people start getting nervous. They'll be worried they can't contact the driver or bodyguard. Probably won't make a move until morning though. I took care of the cell phones. They'd already disabled the factory GPS and on-star tracker on the limo. May have installed a tracker of their own though. In that case they'll probably find the Limo by morning. The driver and bodyguard should be up and around by then anyway. The trail ends at the warehouse. Owned by a Calderon company. And if by some long shot they connect the van and locate it, it'll trace back to another one of his companies where we lifted it. We should have more than enough time with Mr. Kingpin here." Max's dulcet delivery sounded like a song.

We traveled west on the Tamiami Trail. Headed into the Everglades. I turned to Mendez. "What's the downside if this guy disappears?" I asked him, an uncharacteristic ambivalence still gnawing at me. I already had an idea of the answer. Already certain how this scenario must end. But wanted to hear his take anyway.

A questioning sideways glance at me. His gaze quickly returned to the slick black ribbon outside illuminated by twin high beams.

"When he disappears," Mendez said, emphasizing 'when' in place of my 'if', "It'll be doing the world a favor. You've read the file. Dude's vicious through and through. Got a lot of shit to answer for. There'd be chaos in his organization for sure. A power struggle for succession. Dead bad guys turning up around South Florida. Distribution will take a hit, for a while, but his suppliers will shift to other routes. Not much downside. And with everything shaking loose the Feds might finally have an opening to bring the whole house down."

He glanced at me again. I merely nodded.

After another hour Mendez turned off onto an unmarked road. It soon turned into a dirt road. Eventually just tire tracks in high bush heading into a black void. Mendez stopped the vehicle. Max hopped out. He'd changed into night combat gear. He'd take position on the outer perimeter. Farther on Mendez stopped again. He switched the SUV off.

Black night surrounded the vehicle. The sky and stars obscured by an unseen overcast. And loud. With the engine off the full nocturnal chorus bombarded my ears. Mendez lathered himself with insect repellant. He tossed me the tube. He'd said there'd be a safe house here. I saw only blackness.

Mendez exited the vehicle. A powerful spotlight appeared as if by magic in his hand. I joined him. Immediately the black night enclosed me like a coffin. The air thick, dank, and humid. The odor stale, and fetid, like rotten eggs. Mendez handed me the spotlight. He reached into the back for Calderon. Hefted the big man unto his shoulder in a fireman carry. He pointed off to the right.

I aimed the light in the direction Mendez had indicated. The beam illuminated a thicket of trees. Mendez nodded. Took back the light. Motioned me to follow him.

"Stay exactly in my footsteps," he instructed before setting off. Calderon's weight didn't appear to bother him.

We moved into the trees, wending our way around them. I followed Mendez's instructions, treading in his tracks. The light illuminated our path. Anything beyond its beam invisible. Until a small shack, in the middle of a clearing, materialized out of the dark.

More than a shack I observed as we approached it. A sturdy, one room log cabin. Raised about three feet off the ground on pilings cut from surrounding trees. Split Logs formed steps leading to a planked porch along the front. Mendez mounted the steps. He carried Calderon without discernible effort. He reached out, opened the door to the cabin, stepped inside.

Mendez had chosen the location. Ideal for our purposes, he'd claimed. I'd never been to the place before. Had no idea how Mendez knew of it. But I immediately discerned its purpose. Mendez deposited Calderon in a chair and exited the cabin. Shortly afterward I heard a faint rumble, barely audible. A bare light bulb hanging in a corner flickered on, revealing the contents of the single room. Three folding cots against one wall, an unfinished wood table, and the chair Mendez had dumped Calderon in.

No ordinary chair. Bolted to the floor, constructed of unfinished wood like the table, and shaped like the electric chairs used in executions, leather restraints provided for the torso, arms, legs and feet.

Mendez returned. He too had changed into night combat gear to take up position on the inner perimeter.

"Hidden generator, muffled," he said. From a corner of the cabin he fetched a halogen lamp. He positioned it in front of the wood chair, before prepping and strapping Calderon in.

Mendez hung an intravenous bag from a pole attached to the back of the chair. He connected the IV tube to a needle inserted in Calderon's right arm. Before exiting the cabin he laid a filled 12cc syringe on the table.

Calderon sat, stripped naked, his hands, arms and legs secured to the chair. I switched on the halogen at low setting. Doused the hanging light bulb. I contemplated the man bathed in the halogen glow before me. I studied the slim build, the hairless chest, probably waxed, the Hispanic features. He used heavy mousse in his straight black hair. Pencil thin moustache, neatly groomed, midway between his upper lip and nostrils. A perpetual menacing scowl had etched creases across his forehead, between his eyes, and around his mouth. The lines crisscrossing his face relaxed in his drugged state. His expression almost peaceful.

The intel I'd read provided little of use for an interrogation. It didn't get me inside his head. He had no immediate family. His mother had been a junkie prostitute. Killed when Calderon was nine years old. By his father, a pimp and local heroin dealer who'd been sent to prison for the murder. Calderon had bounced around in the system until his early teens.

No wife or kids. According to the file he liked to sample his own girls. The ones fresh off the boat. Not gentle about it either. He'd come up the hard way, killing his way to the top. I'd encountered his type before.

Stripping him naked removed the outward accoutrements of his identity. The identity he projected to the outside world. His power. Rendering him exposed and vulnerable. Diminishing his capacity to bluff and bluster.

In theory anyway. The tactic succeeded or failed depending on the strength of his mind. His sense of identity without the trappings. His inner core. His sense of self. How grounded his personality. What he believed in. What he feared the most. Growing up and surviving on the streets had hardened him. But had it strengthened his core as well? I'd find out soon enough.

The intravenous drug took effect, counteracting the sedative cocktail we'd fed him after the initial dart. I watched as his conscious mind surfaced through the darkness, like a drowning man bursting to the surface gasping for air. He awoke disoriented and belligerent. Every cell of his being revved up for survival. For fight or flight.

I waited, timing the moment when he'd be susceptible to questioning. The drugs in his system already being metabolized. Using more drugs to facilitate the interrogation too risky. I needed him aware, if not completely lucid.

I observed him closely. Patiently. Watched him pass through the stages. The sudden conscious awareness. The accompanying panic. The frantic efforts to move his limbs. The realization of being alive. But something not right. Not fully comprehending where, or how, or why. Dawning memory. Dream or reality? Taking stock. Strange sensations. Dryness in the mouth. Breathing air again. But where?

I pushed the middle switch on the lamp. The harsh light hit him in the face like a slap. He recoiled. Tried to raise his arm to shield his eyes. The arm wouldn't move.

"Welcome back," I said in a neutral voice. "Glad you can join me."

He recoiled again, as if from a second blow. My voice his first inkling of another person in the room. He swiveled his head from left to right, attempting to see me through squinted, unfocussed eyes. I remained out of sight behind the lamp.

"What's this about? Where the fuck am I?" The words slurred around a leaden tongue. Renewed agitation. Aggression in his manner and tone. Not the meds this time. He struggled in the chair against his restraints. A mistake. His agitation not allowing his disoriented brain sufficient time to reorient itself, regain its equilibrium; determine his status and his environment. His continued struggle against his restraints instead working to my advantage.

"You have any idea who you're fucking with?"

My voice calm and neutral as before. "Where you are doesn't matter. Who you are doesn't matter. What matters is the mistake you made. You tried to kill a friend of mine. I want to know why."

His expression changed. His manner calmer. A hint of a smile despite the agitated fear still evident in his bloodshot eyes. But he thought he recognized the game now. Knew how to play it. He'd been here before. This would all boil down to making a deal. His way out. After which he'd use all the resources at his disposal to hunt me down. And kill me. No one did this to him and walked away. Or so he thought.

First he'd need to know who to deal with. "I don't know what you're talking about. You obviously made a mistake. Got the wrong guy. But we can work this out. Just tell me who are you. Not FBI. This isn't their scene. DEA maybe? What it is you want."

"You're what I want." I stepped to the side of the lamp, still out of his vision. I stuck my hand in front of his face, holding the photograph of Victor Ricardo's lifeless body. Bright red stains in the middle of his chest.

He stared at it for a moment. "Never seen him before."

"Okay Philippe. That's the way you want to do this. Let's get down to it." I circled around him. Outside the circle of light; moving at a slow pace; stepping deliberately; embedding the sound of each footfall in his consciousness.

I paused behind him. "You're a businessman, Philippe. Ready to get down to some business?"

I didn't wait for an answer. I bent close to his right ear, from behind. "Here's the deal. You tell me what I want to know and you walk away from this alive. You keep fucking with me and I still get the answers I want using that needle in your arm. But it'll kill you in the process."

He glanced down at his arm. Saw the intravenous needle taped there. Probably aware of it for the first time. And the rest of his lower body. Suddenly aware of his nakedness.

"You're a fucking dead man, you hear me?" his fear and agitation returned in full force. His voice a malevolent hiss muted by the drugs. His tongue still too thick to form words properly. His dry lips exhibited signs of cracking. He ran his tongue over them. To no avail.

An innate meanness evident in his bourbon colored eyes, the whites splotchy red. Their pupils dilated, almost fixed. And in them the first small hint of desperation.

"We all die Philippe. From the day we're born we start dying. But here's a question. Who's better off? The person who doesn't know when their life will end? Or the one who knows exactly when, where, and how? Like you Philippe."

I halted at his side. Extended my hand into the light again. This time it held the MK23. Its attached suppressor ominously ugly and menacing. I pressed it gently against his right knee. The frantic struggle resumed. He attempted to move his leg away. Grunted with the effort. Unable to move.

"Philippe," I said, my tone soothing, encouraging, like a therapist drawing out a patient. "Why did you send Victor Ricardo to kill my friend?"

"What're you doing? What the fuck're you doing?" Desperation the dominant force now. In his voice, in his face, in his renewed struggles, in his addled brain. Another mistake, preventing him from thinking clearly. And indicating I had him. One more small push.

Still using my soothing therapist voice I told him, "I'm going to shoot out your kneecap Philippe. It's called kneecapping. I'm sure you've familiar with it. Then I'm going to shoot out the other one. You'll never walk again, but you'll live. Though I'm not sure how long someone in your line of work will last confined to a wheelchair. Lots of ambitious people around you right. It'll be like shark chum in the water. And after I've blown out your knees, if you still haven't told me what I need to know, I'll use the drugs. And then you'll tell me Philippe. Everything I want to know. But I guarantee you it'll burn up your insides and then it'll kill you."

Although inflicting pain might produce useful information in an interrogation, it also produced too much uncertainty. I had no intelligence to corroborate anything he might tell me. And depending on the subject, the psychological anticipation sometimes proved as effective as the actual infliction of physical pain.

I had him. The calculated bluff pushed him over the edge. I noted the change in his blood streaked eyes, desolate, resigned, furtive. Not the game he'd originally thought. The rules set by the person holding him captive. The one holding the gun; holding the drugs. He'd give up what he knew. Figure out what to do about it later.

"Why'd you put a hit on my friend?" I asked in my therapist voice.

"It was just business," he sneered, the rationale understandable in his mind. "I don't even know the guy. It was part of a deal, a favor, I got a call."

"Who called you Philippe? Who asked you to do this?"

He hesitated. Eyeballs swiveled in his head. His glance darted back and forth, searching for a way out. Perhaps concocting a plausible explanation. The suppressor pressed hard against his bare knee changed his mind.

"No. No. Don't shoot."

"Then give me the name Philippe." I thumbed the hammer back on the HK for emphasis. My finger curled on the trigger.

His wide-eyed stare focused on the round suppressor pressed against his bare knee. A soft sob escaped his lips as an amber puddle spread on the rough hewn wood between his thighs.

He spoke a name, almost whispering it, as if saying the name out loud would strike him dead. A name I recognized. And which made no sense. Hearing it I thought Calderon had thrown it out merely to end his ordeal.

The name he'd whispered appeared on the target list of every U.S federal agency. A few European and South American ones too. It didn't make sense. I didn't see a connection to Mike. Why would the head of a Columbian drug cartel want Mike dead?

"Why did he ask you to do this Philippe?"

"I don't know. He didn't tell me and I didn't ask. He wanted it as part of a transaction we had going. Just part of the deal," the words flowed freely, unhindered by any attempt at deception.

"Okay Philippe. We're done now."

I stepped away from his side. Dimmed the lamp. His head limp, chin resting against his chest. He paid no attention to me as I closed the IV clamp. I picked up the syringe from the table. Aware of its contents. Aware of what it represented.

Inserted the syringe into the IV tube's injection site. Squeezed the lethal dose of potassium chloride into the line.

His heart already ceased beating by the time I closed the cabin door behind me.

Light when I stepped outside. A dim, diffused light. Barely penetrating the lingering overcast. The light surprised me. I'd lost track of time. The harsh halogen lamp and blackout curtains had made the night seem perpetual.

Dense tree growth surrounded the small clearing, concealing the cabin from view. Cypresses I think, rising from pools of green and black swamp water. The water blended into mounds of dryer, firmer ground. The trail leading to the cabin obscured by thick moss, and algae covered roots running between the swamps. A natural defense against anyone unfamiliar with the trail. One small step away from becoming alligator food. Mendez had navigated it with surefooted familiarity.

The Cypresses rose straight and tall. Their trunks covered in green moss. Their drooping branches and intertwined vines created a sparse canopy overhead. The guys nowhere in sight. I walked to the end of the narrow porch. Drew a deep breath of stagnant air smelling of decay. Craved a cigarette. A habit I'd given up. But there were times when I missed the comfort of a deep soothing drag.

I peered out around the corner of the cabin. Noticed for the first time a landing between the trees, an airboat under camouflage netting, at the end of a winding ribbon of swamp water,

Mendez materialized like an apparition from the swampy mist. The MP5 slung across his chest, ready for use. A M25 light sniper rifle, Leupold sniper scope and suppressor attached, slung across his back. I stepped off the porch to greet him.

"Get what you needed?" he asked.

"Yeah. Got a name. Not sure what it means though."

He nodded. "What about him?" jerking his head toward the cabin.

Calderon's fate had been sealed the moment I'd decided to snatch him. Mendez knew it. Max knew it. I knew it, despite the equivocating in my brain. Calderon hadn't seen our faces. Had no idea who we were. But putting him back into circulation would be like cleaning up trash only to dump it back on the floor. A loose end we couldn't afford returning to bite us. Particularly Mike. And someone the world would be better-off without.

My ambivalence generated not by the act itself, but familiarity of what lay down that road. A familiar sensation clutched at my chest, emanating from a place I never wanted to return to; leaving a sour aftertaste, and a foreboding sense of impending doom.

"Boss?" Mendez said. I remembered I hadn't answered his question.

"We need to clean this place," I said.

He nodded. "Figured we'd need to. Got everything I need." He squeezed the push to talk button on his radio, spoke through the boom mike at his cheek.

"Bring it in Bro." He turned to me. "I'll walk you out to the car. Max will meet you on the way out. I'll finish up here. Max will come get me later."

"That doesn't make sense. This is on me. I need to clean it up. Then we can all get out of here together."

"I got this boss," his tone emphatic. The set expression on his face invited neither argument nor debate. Something regarding this place Mendez didn't want me to know. Things I didn't need to know.

"Dude's gonna be famous Boss," he said chuckling, removing a bit of the sting from his dismissal. "They'll mention his name in the same breath with Hoffa."

Back at the dirt track Max popped out of the underbrush like a foraging animal. Daylight revealed the vehicle track, bordered on either side by swamp. How Mendez had navigated it the night before remained a marvel.

Max and I drove back to the house in North Miami. Mostly in silence. I immediately crashed on the nearest available soft surface. Later he returned to the Everglades to retrieve Mendez.

That evening we debriefed at the house over Thai takeout. I gave Mendez the name whispered by Calderon. Asked if they were free for the next two or three weeks. They were. No hesitation.

I returned to the hospital the next morning. The same uniformed cop as the day before stood, or rather sat, guard by the door. Mike awake and visibly better.

"How you doing? I greeted him. "Looking better today."

"Feeling better too. I think they're turning down my meds. Still tired all the time. Docs say my lung function's still impaired. Getting better though. They're optimistic."

Speaking took a toll. He paled. A short bout of coughing. I handed him a cup of water from the side table. He sipped through a straw. Lay back on the pillow.

"How'd your business go?" his discerning stare capturing me.

"Finished," I said, returning the stare.

I hesitated on how much to tell him. My natural instinct for secrecy maybe. Or his lifetime commitment to the law. Not wanting to compromise his values. Or maybe not wanting to burden him with more worries until he recovered.

"You're safe here now," I said.

The probing brown eyes searched mine. Mine answered his. Understanding conveyed in our nonverbal communication. He turned away.

"You good?" Now my eyes did the asking when he turned to face me.

"Yeah Gage." Pausing. "Yeah I guess so." A subtle shift in his expression. A conflict resolved perhaps? A hint of worry maybe?

"Gage," still holding me with his stare, "Thanks. Although this makes me think there's more going on than just a cop getting shot for being in the wrong place at the wrong time."

"We're working on it. But you're okay now," I repeated. "Heading back today. Any message for Jo?"

"Give her a kiss for me. Not one of yours, one of mine. What the hell, give her one of yours for me too."

I laughed. "See you soon buddy." I patted his shoulder affectionately. Exiting the room I sensed his piercing eyes on my back as I walked along the hallway.

Both aware this, whatever this was, was a long ways from being over.

CHAPTER 7

Home aboard Wherever. Rodney had left her in prim pristine shape on her mooring in Lower Bay. She'd been my home since I'd completed refitting her thirteen years earlier. More than simply a home, also a companion. She'd saved my life. If a ship could be said to have a soul, she did.

Inanimate when asleep, spread her Dacron wings and she'd awaken. Come alive. Her hull, deck, spars and rigging a living, breathing organism. She spoke to me in the sounds of her rigging; through my fingers on her wheel; in her vibrating deck beneath my bare feet.

I'd first seen her lying abandoned in Port Antonio, on Jamaica's north coast. A dark period of my own. I'd lost my sense of purpose. My will to live. Had reached a point, staring into the abyss, when I didn't care if it swallowed me whole.

I'd been lying low. Wasting away. Waiting for it all to end. Contemplated hastening its arrival. I'd lost my soul. Sold it to the devil. Who'd arrived to collect. Why not just hand what remained of it over already? I'd completed a particularly dirty operation. Had defied my handlers and my orders. Again. Strengthening their belief in my unreliability. And my belief in my own deserved demise.

I hadn't known it at the time, but the derelict yacht, sitting alone in the blue bay, would change the course of my life. And in so doing save my life.

She'd possessed a curious, touching beauty. An irresistible attraction. She captured the eye, from the sharp bow and fetching curves of her cutwater, to the sensuously sloped sheer of her transom. She grabbed my attention whenever I'd pass by the port. The more I'd tried to ignore her, the more she summoned me.

She'd been my hideaway during the two years it took to affect my escape. The latest in a string of failed attempts. There'd been days when I believed there'd be no way out. No way to exorcise the demons. Kick the adrenaline high. While a corrosive disillusionment distorted my reality; my will to survive. And dark demons slowly devoured me from within.

The forlorn schooner had provided the means. Not only of my escape. But my salvation. Enabling a peace only found a thousand miles from the nearest land. A quiet and timeless world possessing the promise of new hope. Where I'd pondered the big questions, discovered my answers, and recovered my soul.

I'd almost renamed her 'hideaway'. But in shedding my former life, like molted skin, I'd answer "wherever" when people asked "where're you off to now?" The name suited us both. A journey with no defined destinations; no precise positions. Only an ever distant horizon and the promise of new expectations and new hope.

She'd been designed by Lewis Francis Herreshoff, known for his graceful lines and fast hulls. The son of another well-known yacht designer, Nathanael Herreshoff, affectionately known as the wizard of Bristol. She'd been built by the Herreshoff manufacturing company in Bristol, Rhode Island in 1928, and she'd lived a storied history through a succession of owners. During World War II she'd served in the U-boat watch patrol off the New England coast.

Her last owner had been a Hollywood mogul who'd died suddenly. She'd lain forgotten while his heirs squabbled over his estate. Abandoned, she fell into disrepair.

That's when we'd met.

I'd shipped her to Rhode Island after purchasing her through a dummy corporation. I restored her. In the process she restored me.

She'd retained the sturdiness of her original construction. Her white oak keel and frames, her double planked heart pine hull, still sound. A previous owner had removed the canvas originally covering her deck. But her oak deck beams and white pine planking required only minor repairs and recaulking.

I redesigned her interior, using the same cypress, walnut and mahogany trim she'd originally possessed. I replaced her Douglas fir spars with Sitka Spruce. I converted her gaff rig to Marconi, making her easier to single hand. I replaced her standing and running rigging. Installed new bronze hardware and stainless steel winches for her sheets. A new Ford Lehman diesel replaced her dead engine. I gave her a new shaft and bronze propeller. I redesigned and rewired her electrical system, her plumbing, and her cockpit, adding modern electronics. In everything, I endeavored to retain her traditional ambiance, melding the new into her original classic design.

Seaworthy once again we'd sailed to Guyana. The three-week passage our maiden voyage. The voyage sealed our relationship. I got to know her. Her likes and dislikes. Her best points of sail. The combinations she preferred in different weather and sea conditions. What made her sluggish. What made her skittish. I learned her language, and how to listen to her. She got to know me.

One particular night, a night as dark as pitch, heaving and rolling amid twenty foot swells, she'd handed me an epiphany. The night of my rebirth.

I gazed in reminiscent affection across her deck and over her rigging as I emerged from below, changed and heading to Jolene's place ashore. My time evenly divided between Wherever and Jolene's two-bedroom house nestled into the green wooded hillside overlooking Lower Bay. It'd been in her mother's family. Handed down through three generations to Jolene. Her front verandah provided a view, through the trees in her front yard, of Admiralty Bay's wide expanse. Including Lower Bay's small cove, where Wherever rode serenely on her mooring.

The house, her furniture, her pictures on the walls, her books, her potted plants and flowers, reflected Jolene's personality, open and cheery; spontaneous and deliberative; funny and cerebral; affectionate and ferocious. My only contribution a two-person hammock hanging between two trees in the sloping front yard.

She preferred natural scents, in her home and on her person. The rooms scented by strategically placed potpourri and oils she'd made from the leaves and petals of local plants. A varying redolence of rose, chamomile, lavender, lilac, gardenia and jasmine.

Earlier on my way through the harbor I'd picked up fresh fish. Delightfully lost in preparing dinner when Jolene walked through the stained double doors. The tired, morose expression on her face transformed when she saw me. Her eyes widened and brightened. Her mouth opened in silent surprise. She sprang across the room, enveloped me in strong arms, pinning mine against my sides, still holding the long tined fork and spatula.

She kissed my mouth. Hard at first. Then softening, lips parting, tongue probing, mingling, tasting. We savored the long, welcome home kiss. My hands, clasping the utensils, pressed into the small of her back, pulling her into me, pushing her through me. Her uniform belt dug into my waist. I inhaled her lavender scent, conscious of a throbbing between my legs.

"Hmmm," disengaging her lips, head held back, eyes closed. "You don't know how good it is you're back."

"That kiss is from Mike by the way." I said.

Her eyes sprang open. An amused chuckle escaped her lips.

"Well thanks for delivering it. And well delivered too. So when do I get yours?"

"As soon as you give me my arms back."

"Maybe I like you pinned and helpless Mr. Nicholas Gage."

"In that case." I leaned forward to bring my lips gently against hers. Her mouth opened. The eager dance of tongues repeated. She raised her arms. Laid them around my shoulders. Using one hand behind my neck she pulled my head harder against hers.

Our lips finally parted. We opened our eyes, both staring into the others; both smiling.

"I need to get out of this god-awful uniform and forget about this dreadful day."

She breezed out of the kitchen. A whiff of lavender in her wake. I heard her start a bath. A luxury given Bequia's water shortage this time of year. I popped a Kenny G CD in the player and went back to my fish. Slightly overdone due to recent inattention.

We ate by candlelight on the verandah. On the hillside, a constant breeze kept mosquitoes and other flying pests at bay. For the most part. A full moon rose. Bright and round and white as bone, casting a silvery light across the bay, and shadows across the front yard. The surf crashed in rhythmic cadence against the shore below, providing a soporific background soundtrack, as soothing as a lullaby.

"How's he doing, Gage? I mean really. He sounds so weak on the phone. Makes me feel so helpless."

"He's doing well," I assured her. "Getting better every day." Her eyes, light grey in the subdued light, searched mine, seeking truth in them. Not sure she really wanted to know.

"His lung is healing, not functioning at full capacity yet. Makes him tire quickly, especially after talking. But he's getting better Jo."

Relief in her eyes, as if she'd been holding her breath. I refilled our wineglasses from the bottle of Pinot Noir on the table.

"And just what mysterious business got you tearing off to Miami in such a hurry?" Her tone teasing, but containing a serious edge too. Like always when she'd ask about my past. Things she wanted to know about me. Things I didn't know whether, or how, to tell her yet.

I'd been dreading the question since departing Miami. And I'd resolved to tell her the truth. At least part of it. Mike not only her boss, but a mentor and dear friend. A surrogate father at times. And she the lead investigator on his case. She had a need to know. But with one important caveat.

"I'll tell you, but there's a condition."

"Serious?" Eyebrows shooting upward. Not the response she'd expected, accustomed to my chronic evasiveness.

"Serious."

"What condition?"

"You can't repeat what I'm about to tell you to anyone. It's for your ears only. If that compromises you as a police officer, then I can't tell you."

Surprised again. And shaken. "Now I'm not so sure I want to hear this." She picked up her glass. Swallowed a mouthful of wine. Turned away, gazing into the moonlit yard. Reached a decision. She turned back to face me, her eyes finding mine.

"Being on the force is just my job, Gage. And until Mike came along a seemingly meaningless, impulsive mistake. My first loyalty is to Mike. I'd never allow the job or anything else to stand in the way of protecting him. Or you." She paused, appearing to want to say more, lapsing into silence instead.

A reticence I'd grown accustomed to. A reluctance to divulge her reasons for joining the force in the first place. An anomaly, given her background and education. A whim, she'd say when asked. Seemed like the right thing at the time. I didn't buy it. More to it, I believed. She could be whimsical, even impulsive and spontaneous on occasion. A childlike playfulness I admired and enjoyed. But not concerning a life changing decision. She made such decisions only after careful consideration, and usually with purpose.

Some significant event had occurred I speculated. Perhaps not to her. Maybe someone close to her. She too had a past, and secrets. She'd speak of it when ready, in her own time. Like me.

"You know what worried me the most, for a long time? About us?" She said. Rhetorical. She didn't wait for an answer. "That learning about you, your secrets, would change the way I see you, feel about you. And maybe, I don't know, maybe you're afraid of the same thing too. It scared me. Being in love with someone knowing there's a part of you I'd never know. Never be able to reach. I don't feel that way anymore. I've been close enough to you to know with all my heart you're a good person Gage. No matter your past, whatever it was you had to do. I couldn't love you otherwise. She reached over, took my face in her hands. Kissed me softly on the lips.

Her eyes stared into mine. "There's nothing inside you that scares me, Gage. Nothing you can say will make me run away."

Wow. My turn to be surprised. Not the revelation I'd expected. Or the way her words touched me, evoking emotions inconceivable only a few years ago.

"Remember when I asked you if Mike had security on his room?" I said.

"Yeah. I told you Miami Dade was providing security."

"Well just in case, I asked a couple of people I know to keep a watch on Mike."

Her eyes widened in surprise. "When I was on Union I got a call. They'd spotted a guy nosing around. Casing the hospital, the ICU, Mike's floor. They intercepted this guy, who turned out to be a triggerman working for Miami's biggest drug dealer."

I paused. Waited for her reaction. She sat in stunned silence. Her mouth agape. The expression in her eyes a mixture of astonishment, curiosity, confusion and concern.

"I went to Miami to make sure Mike was alright. And I had a chat with Mr. Drug lord."

Her initial shock wearing off, She found her voice again. "And what did you find out?"

I hesitated.

"Gage?"

"He won't be a danger to Mike anymore," I said.

Her eyes stared hard into mine. Asked the silent question. Found the unspoken answer.

"You didn't answer the question," she said, a pained, gentle sympathy behind the amber irises.

"He had no connection to Mike. Seems it was a favor for his Columbian supplier. Part of a deal."

An abrupt transformation in her demeanor.

"Crisse sacrament. What the Bumboclaat is going on Gage?"

"Don't know."

"Does Mike know any of this?"

"Not in so many words. He's safe for now. But I still have to find the connection to the Columbian."

"Well maybe I can help. What's his name? And who was the Miami drug Lord?"

Her use of the past tense in referring to Phillip Calderon didn't escape me.

"Jo," I said, a sharp edge in my voice. "No." The single word emphatic. "You're the only one who can know about this.

At least for now. Until we figure out what the hell is going on. Right now you don't need to know the Miami guy's name, or the Columbian's. Not yet. You can't put any of this information out there. We don't know who may be listening or watching. It might put everyone in further danger, Mike, you, me, and the guys baby-sitting Mike in Miami. Understand?"

She nodded. Deflated. But accepting. I folded her into my arms. Stroked her soft lavender scented curls. Kissed her forehead. She gazed at me, concern in her eyes. At what, I wasn't sure. The danger? Or what I'd done in Miami? I hadn't said it in so many words, but she, like Mike, astute enough to read between the lines.

"Anyway, I've already got someone putting together information on both these guys. Maybe we'll find the connection to Mike. Figure out what we're dealing with. What's happening here. Until then it's safer if you're not completely read in."

"Crisse. Bumboclaat."

I laughed out loud.

"Probably better anyway because right now everything's out of control," she said. "The FBI's sticking their noses into our investigation because they're getting no cooperation from shit for brains Coffe who is totally mismanaging the situation and alienating everyone involved. Officially the ministry's still fending off the FBI. But they may not be able to for much longer, and they're looking for a way to get back on the Fed's good side. The investigation's become a political and diplomatic cluster fuck. All the effort going into damage control. Every time Coffe opens his mouth there's more shit needing cleaning up. But his latest fiasco about the body may be the last straw. Word is the PM is out of patience and considering giving him the boot. At least off the case."

"What body?"

"Oh. Right. Happened right after you left for Miami. Someone reported finding a body over in Hope Bay. Story spread like wildfire. The news people swarmed all over it. Everyone claiming it might be Sarah Holmes. Coffe called one of his beloved press conferences, before waiting for any information or confirmation. Which of course gave credence to the story. So when it turned out there was no body we were left with shit on our face again. No one knows how the rumor got started. But Coffe really stepped in it. And made the force look even worse than the media vultures already think we are. Surprised you didn't hear about it. Been all over the cable news."

"Didn't have much time for TV in Miami. I was kinda busy."

"What really vexes me though," she continued, allowing what I'd said about Miami to pass unremarked. "Both cases are at a complete dead end. We've got no leads in either one. Maybe we're really out of our depth. Truthfully, I don't know if we going to get to the bottom of any of this without outside help."

"You've been watching too much cable news," I said.

"Don't have time either. But maybe they're right."

"One thing you can do if you haven't already, is get hold of the list of Sarah Holmes's personal effects. Better yet, the effects themselves. Particularly the photographs she'd been taking around the Grenadines."

"They sealed her cabin until the ship docked in Miami. The FBI probably has all that, and I'm not sure we're going to get anything out of them. Why her photographs in particular."

"Dunno. But it seemed a particular interest of hers on Union Island."

"That's a particular interest of most tourists."

"Yeah. Still might be worth looking into."

"I'll see what I can do."

"Be careful who you talk to, and what you say. Especially with the Feds."

"Did you talk to Mike about Sarah Holmes?"

"A little. His memory's still fuzzy. He thinks he remembers seeing her around the harbor, but no details on when or where."

"Anything about who shot him?"

"No. A photo might jog his memory though, if we had one to show him. When I showed him a picture of the Miami guy he was certain it wasn't him."

"So what're you gonna do next?"

"I've got to go back to Union. Follow up some things there."

"Ah yeeeess. The reporter," her lilting emphasis teasing and mischievous. "She's been looking for you, by the way." I swirled the wine in my glass, took a sip. Gazed out into the bay. Didn't take the bait.

"She's kinda attractive, don't you think?" A tripwire. As in 'do these pants make me look fat'?

I maintained my silence, avoiding the trap.

"I mean you must have noticed." Not giving up easy.

"You working this weekend?" I said instead.

"On call. Like always. Hazards of rank my love. Why?"

"I was thinking of flying Mike's Seneca down to Union. Quick hop down and back. But let's take Wherever instead. Make a weekend of it."

"That, my sweets, is the best idea I've heard all week."

CHAPTER 8

I'd sailed the passage to Union Island many times. Every time a new experience. Wind, sea, weather, perpetually changing. No day the same as any other. Every passage as unique as though it were the first.

Early Friday evening. Three weeks and three days since Mike's shooting. Four days since I'd returned from Miami. Jolene arrived aboard Wherever from the office. She changed into jeans and a tee shirt found among the assortment of clothes she kept on board.

We cleared Admiralty Bay, the sun a silver ball descending in the sky ahead. The horizon pink and amber. A light shore breeze bore Wherever down to Wes Cay. The sun sank lower, turning the pink sky a deep claret, and the bases of drifting clouds a blackish grey.

Clear of Bequia and in open water the wind and swell increased. Jolene took the wheel while I handled the sails. The main and foresail already set from the run out of the harbor. I trimmed them for the new course. Unfurled and hoisted the jib. Followed by the staysail. Her sails set and trimmed Wherever surged ahead like a runner out of the starting blocks. The sea a moving series of small hills and valleys.

Wherever rose on each swell, slid sideways into the valleys, shoving aside mounds of blue and foamy white water.

The sun slid below the horizon. Its departure punctuated by a thin crimson line stretched across the sea. Darkness enveloped the schooner like a soft blanket on a cool night. I switched on Wherever's running lights. Settled into the cockpit behind the wheel. My bare feet on the spokes. My gaze lost among the emerging stars.

I loved night sailing best of all. Embraced in a solitude magnified by the dark. The entire world reduced to a slim lighted cocoon gliding through the night. Self-contained. Cradled by the dark sea and sky. The silence, and the slow rhythmic heave and roll, engendered a soul nourishing peacefulness.

Jolene nestled against me, staring up at the starry night sky. Lost in her own private reverie. I picked a star high and bright above the mainmast, used it to keep our course for Mayreau Island. Wherever scampered along, chasing the black horizon, alive in her element.

The hours slipped by. And the sparsely lit islands to port. A half-moon rose, its pale silver light dancing across the water. Jolene and I shared the night in companionable silence. The sounds of wind, sea, and Wherever's passage through the night a harmonious accompaniment to our silent thoughts.

Our shared appreciation for solitude, for quiet, among the gazillion tiny things I loved about Jolene. A shared ability to find comfort in our silent thoughts. It'd been a reliable, consistent companion during hours and days of monotonous waiting; of silent stalking..

Like me, she welcomed solitude as a dear old friend. Her ego required neither the sound of her own voice nor the chatter of others; the need of external artifacts to give meaning to her existence. She possessed an abiding sense of self. An enduring strength in her person. I loved her for it.

I seldom used instruments sailing among the islands. I knew the passages well. Even at night. But as the dark mass of Mayreau approached, silhouetted in the moonlight off the port bow, I activated the GPS and depth sounder mounted on Wherever's custom designed binnacle. I planned our approach.

Saline Bay, on the southwestern end of the stingray shaped island, loomed in the dark. I planned to anchor off the crescent shaped stretch of beach. No other yachts in the bay. Jo had the wheel again. I went forward, shortening sail.

Wherever slowed, skipping through the light chop under jib and main. We tacked twice across the Bay, closing on the beach, the water shoaling as we approached. Jolene called out depths. At the target depth I let the jib fall. Jolene let the mainsail sheet run free.

Wherever slid closer to shore under momentum alone. The mainsail flogged in the light breeze. She eased to a stop. I kicked the brake from the anchor windlass. Chain links rattled over the sprockets and through the pulpit rollers, shattering the silence. A loud splash as the Danforth anchor hit the water.

The noise ended as abruptly as it began. Rope replaced chain, running out in a long line as Wherever fell back on the breeze. I gave the line sufficient scope, tying it off to the Samson post. I stood at the bow, an arm wrapped around the inner forestay, gazing out at the moonlit beach a short distance away. The smell of salt air in my nostrils. I inhaled a deep breath. Observed the anchor line stretch and straighten as Wherever put tension on it, setting the anchor into the sandy bottom.

Almost midnight. I folded and tied the sails. Coiled and hung Wherever's running lines. Hadn't given a thought to food. But wondered about Jolene. Neither of us had eaten. I set an anchor watch on the GPS. Headed back to the bow for one last check of the anchor line.

Jolene slid in behind me. Her arms encircled my waist. A diaphanous sarong wrapped around her, wearing nothing else. Food clearly not on her mind.

I awoke to the sun's warmth on my face. Still wrapped in the folds of the jib on the foredeck where we'd fallen asleep, sated and spent. A contented murmur from Jolene as I untwined myself from her arms and legs.

I made my way aft, went below to set coffee brewing. Returned topside, still naked, and plunged into the warm, translucent sea. I surfaced, strong even strokes propelled me toward the beach. When my feet touched sandy bottom I turned. I breast stroked leisurely back toward Wherever. Ahead of her bow I dove, savoring the caress of seawater against my skin. I swam along the bottom until I came upon her anchor, set deep in the sand. I followed the chain and line up to the surface.

Jolene greeted me as my head broke the surface.

"Morning sailor."

She dove from the fore shrouds. Her lithe toffee colored body sliced the water, creating scarcely a ripple. Surfacing next to me she rose straight up head first like a graceful dolphin. Seawater glistened in sparkling droplets from her hair and shoulders as she threw her arms around my neck. I pulled her close, her naked flesh against mine, and tasted the salt water on her lips.

Our bodies merged, melded. Her thighs wrapped my waist. Her arms folded behind my neck, clasping me tight against her. She encased my erection deep within a warm velvet enclosure. My hands cupped her soft supple bottom, pulling her hard against my groin. I locked my mouth over hers, sealing it as I sucked the air from her lungs, dispelling it with mine through my nostrils. We sank amid a rising stream of bubbles, like a submarine blowing its air. We drifted downward. Locked in a tight languorous coital embrace. Her pelvic muscles clutched and squeezed, producing a throbbing ache in my groin. Until subtle signs signaled her need for air.

Clutching her tight against my pelvis I kicked my legs beneath her. The motion accentuated the pleasant fulsome friction inside her.

We burst above the surface. The deep, gasping intake of air pushed us over the threshold. She held me squashed against her as soft guttural moans escaped on each exhalation. A still rational section of my brain recalled our calculation of her cycle the night before. In the safe zone, I surrendered to the sensations, peaked with her; erupting inside her in a rapturous rhythmic throbbing.

She leaned back on the sea's smooth surface, arms spread to her sides. She unwrapped and opened her legs, releasing her grip on my waist. A satisfied sigh as she gently floated away on the tide.

We breakfasted on eggs, sausage, toast and coffee.

"You going ashore?" she asked.

"Yeah. Not for long. I want to see where Nora went. She stopped here with Rodney on the way back to Bequia. When we get back we'll shoot over to Union."

"What'd you think she was doing here, and on Union?"

"Not sure. I think she was retracing Sarah Holmes's movements. I know your guys talked to anyone who might have had contact with Sarah. But I think Nora wanted to see the locations herself, and trace a timeline of Sarah's movements in the Grenadines."

"I wanted to do that too. Even started working on it. But Batty Mouth ordered everyone to focus on Bequia. I haven't had time to finish it."

"Well Nora did the legwork for you. See if it squares with what you have. Might not be a bad idea to compare notes with her. If she's still around."

"She is." Jolene said. A statement of fact.

Mayreau's small population occupied a single hilltop village in the center of the one and a half square mile island. The village provided a magnificent view of the island's lush green landscape and turquoise bays. To the north, secluded amongst the trees, the small, cozy Salt Whistle Bay Resort. Empty now during the off-season. To the east, the spectacular Tobago Cays. And south, Palm Island, Petit St. Vincent, and Union Island. We stood in the same spots as Nora had, according to Rodney. Gazed out at the same panoramic views she had.

By midday, the sun beating down in a brilliant blue sky, Wherever once again lay on her mooring in Clifton Harbor. Jolene and I went ashore. Crossed the square to the police station, where Jolene borrowed an early model Mini Cooper, its top cut off. Her CID colleague and friend, a woman, had the duty shift at the station. She eyed me between teasing glances at Jolene.

Jolene and I toured Union Island in the Mini Cooper. Jolene drove. We retraced Nora's, and Sarah's steps. The tour didn't take long on the small island.

We lunched on conch rotis and potato fries from a local eatery. We met and chatted up acquaintances along the way. I revisited the locations Nora had stopped at during her visit. I gazed at what she had gazed at, searching for something, anything, to jump out at me. A eureka moment which never came.

No eureka, but a familiar prickling of the hairs on my skin. Its cause unknown. We'd topped Mount Olympus, overlooking the green, white crested waters of Chatham and Bloody Bays.

I turned to Jolene. She'd been gazing into the distance at the indigo expanse of Caribbean Sea, and the islands dotting it like a strand of emeralds. Absorbed in the silent reverie of her thoughts.

"Hey Jo,"

Her sun browned face turned toward me. Eyes shielded behind aviator sunglasses. Her simple, unselfconscious beauty striking.

"I need you to do me a favor," I said, pausing, thinking. How to approach this? Just come out with it. "I want you to start wearing a vest."

"What!" eyebrows converging, wrinkling the top of her nose. "You can't be serious? I hate those bloody things. Besides, we don't have the type you can wear under clothes. I can't walk around wearing the type we have. They're only meant for tactical situations."

"I have something might suit you."

"Gage, even the inner wear ones make me look skoochy."

"What the hell is skoochy?"

"Never mind," she snapped.

"I'm serious Jo. This whole business is giving me a strange feeling. I'm still alive because I learned to pay attention to that feeling. I'd rather see you looking skoochy, whatever the hell that is, than see you as a corpse."

"What're you saying?" She removed the sunglasses. Eyes the color of witch hazel searched mine through squinted lids. The eyelids flickered. The imagery of a corpse, her corpse, unsettling. And something else in those startling eyes. I'd mentioned my past. Both still unaccustomed to such forthcoming. On the verge of speaking, she decided against it. Silence instead.

"Look," I said, a serious edge in my voice, but also a reassuring calm. "I thought I might get a scent of something. Maybe someone watching Nora's trail. But if someone is watching her so far they've been invisible. Then this cartel involvement. Something's going on here we can't see yet. And whatever it is started before Sarah Holmes even got to the Grenadines. We're in an unmarked minefield Jo. I have to assume you are, or will be, in the line of fire too. You're too close to this not to be. So do me a favor and wear the vest."

Concern, not fear, in the alert hazel eyes. And a fierce determination; protective instincts kicked in.

"So what's this thing you have for me," the sunglasses back in place. An anticipatory smile on her face.

"It's a surprise," I said, smiling back at her. "One more thing."

"What's that?"

"We need to see Sarah Holmes's pictures, now more than ever. The ones she took the day she disappeared probably disappeared with her. But we need to see everything she took before that."

"You keep coming back to that. You think there's something important there?"

"Dunno. But everywhere she went she took lots of pictures. Maybe there's something, or someone, in them might give us a lead."

CHAPTER 9

We returned from Union Island early Sunday evening. Jolene lay in bed, blissfully asleep. She had to be up early for work the next morning.

I headed to the beach. I planned to spend the night at home, aboard Wherever. My cell phone chimed. I pulled it from my trouser pocket and checked the caller ID. Not a number I immediately recognized, but vaguely familiar. Memory snapped into place. Wherever's alarm.

In the dim moonlight I spotted Wherever bobbing on her mooring. I lifted my gaze to the top of her mainmast. A small red strobe, in the same housing as her anchor light, blinked a silent signal.

I tapped the 'accept call' icon on the phone. The alarm automatically switched from silent mode to normal mode if I didn't answer by the fifth ring. Normal mode activated rotating strobes mounted toward the top of the foremast. And a piercing siren. The electronic gadgetry comprised a state of the art system possessing some remarkable bells and whistles.

For one thing, remote operation, responding to inputs from the phone. Answering the call activated a prerecorded message. I didn't listen to the entire recording. I knew what it said. I'd recorded it. Instead I tapped the pound key on the phone's touch screen, accessing the system's main menu. I listened to the prompts. The alarm had activated so infrequently since I'd installed the system, I'd forgotten the catalog of menu and submenu items.

I thumbed the number one on the simulated keypad, accessing the room monitor menu. Obeying the prompt, I touched   the number one key again, activating tiny microphones spread throughout Wherever's interior. I heard faint sounds. Lockers   opening and closing. Sounds of movement inside the cabin. More lockers opening and closing. Someone searching inside. An intruder would find nothing of importance. Like the weapons cache. Or the cash and cover IDs. They were too well concealed. But the break in worried me for other reasons. And pissed me off.

I tapped the back arrow key. The screen returned me to the previous menu. The number two key next, video surveillance mode. Tiny cameras concealed around Wherever's interior, like the microphones, transmitted wirelessly to the alarm's compact main console mounted beneath the nav table. The console connected to a similarly compact DVR containing a built in video server.

The phone connected to the URL address of the video server. The small screen in my palm remained blank. Or black. Difficult to tell which. Though deprived of real time video, the system had been recording since the alarm's activation. I'd be able to enhance the video on playback later. My immediate concern involved figuring my next move.

I pondered this new development. Was the intruder's purpose mainly to search? Plant surveillance? Maybe something more deadly? An ambush? How many involved? Did he have eyes on the beach to alert him when the dinghy shoved off? I decided to leave the dinghy where it sat. I turned away from the beach.

I hiked up Lower Bay's steep road. At the top of the climb the road connected to the main road leading to Port Elizabeth. I savored the cool night air. And the view of Admiralty Bay's broad expanse. The rippling water shimmered in moonlight.

From the higher vantage point I noticed a double-ended rowboat, a 'Bequia dinghy', tied to Wherever's port side. The side hidden from the beach. The Bequia dinghy's thin silhouette low in the water, hidden in Wherever's shadow.

I continued along the main road until I reached a spot overlooking Tony Gibbons Bay. I followed a well-worn foot path down through a thick growth of mango, breadfruit, and coconut trees to Princess Margaret Beach. I found a comfortable spot on the beach. My back against the foot of a coconut tree. My view of Wherever unobstructed.

I settled in for the night. In years past sitting in a hide night after night hadn't been a big deal. But a necessary requirement. Accomplished in stride. Now my thoughts fixated on the spreading ache in my lower back, and my comfortable bed. The surf's soporific splash and sigh along the beach didn't help.

An ambush for sure. It didn't require all night to search the schooner. The intruder was waiting for me.

Dawn's first faint light brushed the eastern sky when a figure crawled from the cabin into the cockpit. The person kept low. He swung over the rail. Climbed down into the rowboat. The boat tipped with his weight, almost capsizing and dumping him into the water. Bequia built double-enders notoriously tipsy, like canoes or kayaks. The intruder steadied himself following a series of frantic gyrations. Hilarious at any other time. His awkwardness ruled out a local. The distance, and dim light, obscured his features.

He pushed away from Wherever's side. Rowed clumsily toward Princess Margaret Beach. Another clue indicating a nonlocal.

I made myself invisible.

He reached the beach. Leapt from the dinghy into the surf, pulling it next to two others beached high above the surf line. He'd probably taken it the night before, assuming it wouldn't be missed until morning. He crossed the remaining stretch of beach, heading into the dense line of coconut trees.

An easy take down. If I wanted. In my element. Invisible. Homing in on a prey unaware of my presence. Until my arm encircled his neck. Or my blade sliced his throat. Instead I needed to see where he went, who he met. Who he was.

I followed him from the beach. The strenuous climb to the road left him panting. Good to know. A van rounded the corner, catching him in its headlights. His face turned away from me. But the light provided a clear impression of his physical build, carriage, and his clothing. The van driver beeped the horn at him. Another van not far behind. And scattered pedestrians, heading into Port Elizabeth to catch the morning ferry.

The intruder turned off the road at the entrance to the Gingerbread Hotel. I followed him down the steep driveway, using mango tress bordering the driveway for cover and concealment. Invisible in the shadows. He had no idea he'd picked up a tail. In the Gingerbread parking lot he unlocked a yellow Kawasaki all terrain dirt bike. Started it up.

The bike's stuttering four-stroke motor revved high as it climbed the steep hill back to the main road. I left my concealed position. Sprinted through the Gingerbread Hotel grounds to the beach. Sprinted along the beach past the Whale Boner and Frangipani Hotel.

The rider and I reached the harbor at the same time. The bike rounded the last corner into Port Elizabeth, raced past the Anglican Church, turned onto the crowded wharf.

Sitting astride the saddle he walked the motorbike through the chaos on the wharf. Passengers, vehicles, handcarts, goods and cargo piled high, all jostling for maneuvering room on the crowded wharf.

Two ferries in the process of loading. The Bequia built wood schooner 'Friendship Rose', and a yellow steel hulled light freighter 'Admiral I', a vehicle ramp lowered from its stern. They lay on opposite sides of the dock. The man rode-walked the bike onto the vehicle ferry, where he disappeared from view.

I waited until both ferries departed. The 'Friendship Rose', slower of the two, departed first. These its last passages as a ferry. An anachronism of another time, the gaff rigged 'Rose' had been replaced by larger, faster, modern motor vessels, possessing creature comforts like air-conditioning and a galley serving hot meals. But lacking an ineffable ambiance soon to be lost by the 'Rose's passing. Rumor was she'd be going into the daytrip charter business.

I flagged down a dollar van leaving the harbor for the south side. The van empty for the return trip from the harbor. I hopped aboard.

It dropped me at the turnoff to Lower Bay. I paid the dollar EC fare. I paused at a promontory where the steep rutted road bends left before descending to the bay. A spot I seldom passed without pausing to absorb the view.

Twilight gave way to sunrise. The sky turned from slate to periwinkle blue. Wooly cumulus materialized in the brightening sky, their eastward facing edges tinged saffron by the ascending sun.

Admiralty Bay emerged in the spreading light. The 'Friendship Rose' disappeared around Northwest Point at the bay's northern extent. In the distance, West Cay marked the southern boundary. Inshore, turquoise water frolicked across the white crescent shaped beaches of three inner bays. A handful of sailboats, sloops, ketches, a yawl, a couple of schooners, a catamaran, lay at anchor in the Bay.

Back in Lower Bay, I retrieved the dinghy. Pushed it into the surf. I didn't start the outboard. Instead I detached the oars from their Velcro straps, fed them through the oarlocks and rowed. I approached Wherever silently. From astern. The cabin monitor indicated no one aboard. I preferred to be safe than sorry.

I swung onto the aft deck in a crouched position. Paused, listening. Moved to the cockpit. I opened a watertight compartment housing the VHF and intercom handsets. I punched in the disarm code on the intercom's keypad. Moved to the main hatch.

The main hatch had a keypad combination lock. The hatch hadn't been forced. I noticed scratch marks on the keypad. It'd been pried open. The internal circuitry shorted or somehow circumvented. A weak spot I'd have to rectify. I unlocked the hatch. Flipped the lid up and pushed the hatch cover back a crack. Enough to get my arm through. I reached under the sliding hatch cover, gingerly feeling around the coaming.

I didn't expect to find anything. The intruder hadn't impressed me as knowing much about boats. If he'd left anything behind that went boom, it'd be somewhere inside. The hatch clear, I pushed it fully open. Daylight illuminated the opening and companionway ladder. I checked for trip wires or triggers. Clear. I opened the hatch doors. Climbed down the companionway into the main salon.

I painstakingly inspected the bulkhead openings at head, chest, knee, and ankle height. I worked my way forward. No tripwires or anything else out of the ordinary. The forward area cleared I went aft. Performed the same inspection in the nav area, galley and aft cabin. I checked all the exposed surfaces, and inside shelves, drawers and lockers. I checked under surfaces too. The dinette, under the salon cushions, the bunks. I lifted the bilge covers, checked all the bilges. Area by area I methodical cleared Wherever's interior.

Next I swept the interior for transmitting devices. Audio or otherwise. Found no RF signals. The intrusion clearly not aimed at surveillance, strengthening my suspicion of an ambush.

Last, I checked the concealed compartments in the aft stateroom, and under the false aft bilge. Weapons, cash, IDs; everything intact. Undisturbed. The compartments ingeniously concealed, impossible to find without tearing the yacht apart. Before closing the last compartment I removed a tactical SIG 226, its custom suppressor, two magazines of fifteen nine millimeter jacketed hollow points each, a Boker HK12 knife, and custom tactical eyewear.

I cleared and reset the alarm system, disarming it a second time. I brewed coffee. I sat at the nav station sipping the steaming mug of mountain roast while I viewed the digital recording on my laptop.

Later that morning, back in the harbor, I awaited the first ferry from St. Vincent. Port Elizabeth fully awake and alive. A bustling hive of activity. Boutiques, souvenir shops, the fresh produce market, all open and lively. Colorful handmade sundresses, blouses, hats, shawls, sarongs, batiks, hung in windows and on sidewalk racks and stalls. Souvenir shops displayed their wares on every conceivable surface. Dollar vans decorated in splashy colors and ornaments, music blasting from oversized speakers, deposited passengers, picked up others. Pedestrian traffic ebbed and flowed in every direction.

I headed toward a huge almond tree in the center of Port Elizabeth. Better known as 'parliament', a gathering place to 'lime', gossip, and idle the time away discussing the topic dejour, usually politics. I sat on a wooden bench constructed around the tree's massive trunk. I observed the varied activities around the harbor. I exchanged greetings with passersby.

"Mawnin Mr. Gage"

"How it go bredda?"

"Irie"

"Wha gowan Gage"

Van drivers double tapped their horns. A vehicular way of expressing "Good Morning."

A blazing hot sun made the day a scorcher. Custom sunglasses shielded my eyes from the dazzling glare. More than mere sunglasses. Tactical protective eyewear. Designed to protect against sun, wind, dust, and fragment impacts. Also designed for surveillance, a powerful miniature camera built into the nose bridge. When activated it transmitted to my cell phone. The phone cached the video images, transmitting them to the DVR on Wherever when the cache reached capacity. Interchangeable lenses provided ultraviolet and infrared vision.

A red and white ferry rounded Rocky Point. A few minutes later it tied up alongside the wharf. A sparse sprinkle of passengers disembarked. Mostly off-season tourists. Either visiting Bequia for the day, or the final leg of their travel after overnighting in Kingstown to catch the first ferry to Bequia.

Bequians who'd crossed on the morning ferry still busy performing their mainland chores. Not expected to return until the first midafternoon ferry. I scrutinized the crowd, my eyes hidden behind dark polarized lenses. The lenses sharpened the contrast between the indigo blue of the deep-water channel and the lighter turquoise closer to shore.

My intruder not on Board. I waited for the wharf to empty. Decided to wait at the Frangipani for the next ferry. Headed there an unsettling sensation prickled my skin, like a sudden chill. The goose bump raising kind. An inexplicable sixth sense. Undefinable. Eminently familiar. A pair of eyes watching me.

Change of plans. I hiked out of the harbor in the opposite direction, along the main road toward Hamilton. Past the gas station, the model boat shop, the electric generator plant and the spot where Mike had been found bleeding to death. I continued past the slipway, and small residential homes tucked into the foothills of steep rising terrain. I headed to the beach. Doubled back along the sand to the Hamilton Hotel Marina. At the Marina's gas dock I hopped aboard a water taxi and motored over to the Frangipani. I hadn't been followed. The watching eyes no longer present.

I arranged to meet Jolene for lunch. Spent the interval indoors at the Frangipani reading month old Time and Newsweek magazines. The Comfortable armchair in the Frangipani lounge faced open doors looking out into the harbor, providing a view of anyone passing outside.

I leafed through the stale magazines without much interest. Stateside politics and news held no interest for me. A data mining program on my laptop sifted select online news sites for anything correlating to my past activities, or anything potentially hazardous to my current lifestyle. Plus other early warning systems I'd left in place after going inactive and retiring to Bequia.

Shortly after midday I returned to the harbor. A marked contrast from earlier. The harbor quiet. Empty. Not completely, but nearly so. The shops and other businesses closed and idled for lunch. Sparse vehicular and pedestrian traffic. Lunchtime on Bequia customarily extended well into the afternoon as everyone sought refuge from the scorching midday heat. Strolling through the harbor I experienced the chill of unseen eyes again. Like a blast of cool air. I'd ruled out a tail. For now the hidden eyes merely watched. And only in Port Elizabeth.

Jolene and I had agreed to meet for lunch at a family restaurant on Back Street. The dining room, on the building's second floor, overlooked the rooftops of one story shops lining the harbor road. The view included the road and harbor. The ground floor had rooms rented out to tourists in season. Some taken by the cable news people. I'd chosen the restaurant slash hotel for its clear view of the wharf, and the exits out of Port Elizabeth. And its location around the corner from the Port Elizabeth Police Station. Convenient for Jolene.

"Tante Lou" I called, entering by the kitchen. Stevie Wonder's 'She's so lovely' floated across the room. Louise Williams, Tante Lou, large, buxom, dark chocolate skin, wearing a blue floral tent dress, looked up from a large pot on the stove.

"Gagey. Ow yuh doin bwoy? Any news bout de chief?" She continued stirring the gurgling pot as she spoke.

"Doin good. Getting better. Be home soon. What yuh have hot today Tante Lou?"

"Curry goat. Fish. Jerk chickin."

"I'll take a goat plate."

"Ge me a few minits."

Three men sat on stools at one end of the bar, nursing beers. The only occupants of the large open-air dining room. Two drove dollar vans. Probably waiting for the ferry. The other Donny, the Hamilton Hotel bartender and charter captain.

Noel, one of the van drivers, greeted me. "Wha gwan Gage?" Another Ollivierre, related to Old Sam who ran the airport café. Donny also an Ollivierre. Lots of Ollivierres on Bequia.

"Yuh tahk wid de Commisshunah Gage? How he be? Cyan get nuttin from de news." Noel said.

"Him doin good. Bettah." I said, joining them at the end of the bar.

"Cyan believe such a ting breddah," said Lionel, the other driver. Sumbady can jus gun down de poliss commisshunah like so? And dem cyan find who do it."

"Is dat touris woman," Donny said. "Everybady lookin fe she. Nobady worrying bout de commisshunah."

"Well cyan be no Bekweh man," Lionel said.

"Why nat? Sum stupid crazy man pon Bekweh yuh noh. Speshally dem labah pahty people," Noel said, referring to the political opposition party, The Unity Labour Party. "Dem nevah like de commisshunah," Noel concluded.

I listened to the back and forth, not contributing. Their voices conspicuously expressed the outrage of most Bequians. And despite the windfall cash infusion from the free spending press, a subtle change had occurred in local sentiment, pleasant welcome morphing to silent resentment.

Jolene entered from the wraparound verandah. She wore a black skirt and white tunic. By regulation while on duty the skirt reached just below her knees. Tailored to fit comfortably, it hardly concealed the shapely figure beneath. The male eyes at the bar followed her approach. Her warm smile greeted the guys. A quick peck on the cheek for me. We headed over to an empty table providing a clear view of the wharf.

She removed the regulation handbag hanging from her shoulder, placed it on the table. I checked her chest, just above the last button of her white tunic. Gratified to see the collar of the vest I'd given her on our return from Union Island. A female model with elastic expandable breast cups. The classified high tech material fit her like a regular undershirt, or chemise. The design made it impossible to tell she wore a tactical ballistic vest.

"God you look tired!" she said

"Didn't get much sleep last night." I hadn't told her about the intruder. I would eventually. At the moment I had no idea what it meant.

"You should've stayed over, slept in."

"Then neither of us would've got much sleep."

She laughed. "What had you up all night?"

An initial, quick impulse to lie. "Tell you later," I said instead.

Casey, one of Tante Lou's several nieces approached our table carrying a tray. The aroma arrived first, eliciting a salivating, stomach growling response. Jolene ordered a bitter lemon, her gaze glued to the fragrant plate of curried goat, rice and peas, green vegetables, and plantains. I ordered limeade and asked for another fork.

On Bequia lunch takes a while. It's a full meal. A ritual harking back to the eighteenth century when the noon meal, the first full meal of the day, had been called dinner. Not to be confused with supper, the last meal of the day, traditionally lighter fare.

No Bequian expects to move much after such a lunch, especially in the midday heat. It's a time for leisurely digestion. For relaxing in the shade. Maybe a nap. Bequia's version of siesta. Port Elizabeth wouldn't reopen for business until midafternoon.

Jolene consumed more than her usual bird sized portion. She ate in concentrated silence. Also atypical of her. I wondered if she'd been having another frustrating day at work. Wondered whether to ask.

I didn't get the chance. The ferry rounded the point. Its imminent arrival signaled by a blast of its horn. I followed its approach to the wharf. Watched it tie up stern-to. The vehicle ramp lowered to the accompaniment of a grease starved metallic grind.

More passengers this trip. More Bequians. Fewer tourists. A handful of reporters returning from the capital. The wharf, empty and quiet moments before, transformed into purposeful chaos. Passengers disembarked in a horde. Vehicles, handcarts, animals, scrambled their way on and off the wharf.

The yellow Kawasaki dirt bike among the last disembarking vehicles. Its loud stuttering four-stroke audible even at this distance. I observed the rider wending his way off the wharf. Same person as before. He turned left onto the main road, made a right onto the road rising toward Pleasant Hill.

I followed the sound of the bike as it disappeared from view. It reappeared through the open shutters on the opposite side of the room. Tall breadfruit and mango trees obscured the view partway up the hill. The top of the hill, where the road forked, visible in the distance above their leafy branches. The bike took the left fork, the road to Spring and Industry.

Jolene had been speaking to me.

"What?" I said.

"Where were you?"

"Not following."

"You had that faraway look you get sometimes. Like your mind is on some other planet."

"What're you talking about?"

"Don't give me that 'what're you talking about'", exasperation rising in her voice. Concern in her eyes. On edge about something. "Forget it," she said in a calmer voice. "I just wonder sometimes."

"Wonder about what?"

"What takes you away like that. Where you go in your head. What you're thinking."

"Didn't realize I was doing that."

"It's okay," she said. Though I had the impression she'd reached a silent compromise. A measure of her abundant assuaging patience. Another of her many attributes I'd been attracted to.

"Anyway, go take a nap. Get some sleep. You gonna be by later?"

"Maybe. Don't know yet. Have some things I have to do first. I'll let you know."

We finished lunch. She'd eaten most of it. I paid and thanked Tante Lou. Walked Jolene to the station. After she'd disappeared inside, I headed in the direction of Pleasant Hill. Took the winding footpath through the graveyard, crossed the grade school playing field, reached the Pleasant Hill road. At the top of the hill I took the fork for Spring and Industry.

I loved hiking around Bequia. As much as I loved swimming its beaches and bays. Both provided a measure of exercise, replacing the arduous training and workouts I no longer regularly performed. The SIG, concealed in a specially designed pocket holster of my cargo shorts, brushed against my right thigh. The suppressor and extra magazines in the left cargo pocket. The Boker knife, in a hidden horizontal sheath on my belt.

I hiked at a leisurely pace, absorbing the lush scenery around me, listening for approaching vehicles. Particularly the characteristic stutter of a four-stroke engine. The steep hillsides heavily wooded, and vibrantly green despite the dry season. Fruit trees and wild flowers lined both sides of the narrow concrete track serving as a road. I had my choice of luncheon desserts. I passed up a variety of mangos as too messy for my immediate purposes. Until I spotted a type which didn't require hand and mouth washing after eating. Soft and elongated, I bit a hole in its fleshy tip, large enough to suck the juicy innards out while squeezing from the other end. Like sucking toothpaste from a tube. A handful of ripe guavas supplemented the menu.

Sugar cane grew alongside the road. I passed those by. I rounded a corner into a sparsely populated area called Spring. An old sugar plantation stretched out before me. Long since abandoned. Occupied now by rental villas. Mostly foreign owned. More springing up each year as foreign money poured into the island. A positive or negative development depending on where you stood regarding unbridled tourism.

Partial stone walls overgrown by vegetation marked the places where plantation buildings once stood. Amid the weeds and tall grass, the ruins of an old mill. Groves of orange, grapefruit, and tangerine trees covered the landscape. Their bright yellow and orange fruit a conspicuous colorful contrast amid the greenery.

Acres of coconut trees lined the opposite slopes stretching to the bay, and as far as the eye could see. Their palm branches permanently bent by the strong winds on Bequia's windward side. I stuffed two oranges and a grapefruit in my pockets for later. I anticipated a period of waiting in my immediate future.

I surveyed the homes as I passed. Vacant for the off-season. No sign of a motorbike.

I arrived in Industry. A wide crescent shaped bay on my right. I walked past the Crescent Beach Bar, careful to avoid being seen. Still no one in sight. I hadn't passed a soul during my trek from the Harbor. I strolled along the water's edge toward a hotel where the concrete road ended.

If memory served the hotel's three, maybe four bungalows were set back from the beach, nestled among towering coconut trees. Next to the closest bungalow I spotted the yellow motorbike, parked on its jack stand. I found a spot on the seaweed-strewn beach concealed by a dense growth of manchineel trees, native to tropical beaches in Florida, the Bahamas, the Caribbean and Central and South America. Commonplace on Bequia beaches. It's innocent apple tree like leaves and small green fruit disguised its potently poisonous nature. I gazed out through its branches to the empty white capped bay, careful to avoid its leaves or sap touching my skin. I also kept watch on the bungalow. And I waited. Again. Stalking is all about the waiting. I peeled the first of my oranges.

I'd been waiting and observing the bungalow all afternoon. No one entered or departed. The sun progressed steadily across the sky, disappearing behind Bequia's elevated spine. The ridge blocked the view of the sunset. On the Industry side dusk settled in, accompanied by deepening shadows and a darkening sky.

I wondered if anything might happen tonight. I figured if the intruder meant to make another run at me, it'd be at night, like the night before. I figured he'd want to recon first. Wait for Wherever to be unoccupied. Maybe he'd adjusted his plan. Changed his tactics. Prepared an ambush in a new location. He hadn't budged from the bungalow. Maybe he'd been sleeping. If so it gave him an edge. I hadn't slept in thirty hours.

I contemplated calling it a day when the door to the bungalow opened. The guy emerged. Mounted the bike. It sputtered to life and roared away from the bungalow. Its feeble headlight beam stabbed the darkness, bouncing as the bike crossed the uneven ground, until it reached the concrete pavement. It accelerated past the Crescent Beach Bar. Its tiny red taillight vanished around a curve.

Land crabs made their appearance, emerging from holes in the sandy ground, crawling sideways in the detritus at the foot of coconut trees, scavenging for food. As tasty as sea crabs, nightfall or early morning before daybreak the best time for bagging them.

Time to return the favor. I rose to my feet, cramped and stiff. An awful ache in my lower back. Unable to stand fully erect until I worked out the knots and kinks. God I felt old. Didn't think of myself as such. But my body told a different story. Though the aches and stiffness not due to age alone. I'd worn this body hard. It'd been damaged and repaired. Too often to count. It'd withstood blistering heat, subfreezing cold, devastating deprivations. It survived explosive shock waves and the spine jarring shock of parachutes opening after a two-mile free fall. A lifetime of strenuous overuse had taken a toll on joints, cartilage, sinews and muscle.

I approached the bungalow. A dim light burned inside. I withdrew the SIG, attached the suppressor, screwing it in place. I held the elongated barrel against my thigh.

I shed the thick-soled flip-flop sandals beneath a bush next to the bungalow. Brushed my bare feet before stepping onto the concrete entrance patio. Checked my trail. Made sure

I'd left no sign of my approach. At the front door I checked for telltales. I didn't think the guy that sophisticated. Or had any inkling I'd made him. But discipline dictated I not underestimate him either. The door had a simple doorknob lock. Easily picked. I slipped inside.

I double-checked my trail. Made sure I hadn't tracked sand or anything else as I made my way across the tile floor, through a short, narrow hallway. It led to a living room. Contemporary furniture. Comfortable. Devoid of personality. Like a hotel room. A sofa by the front picture window; a wicker glass topped coffee table; a couple of armchairs, shaded lamps on side tables. One of the lamps left on.

On the opposite side, a small kitchen alcove and dining area. Behind me, at the end of the hall, a bedroom, the double bed unmade. Sliding French doors flanked by thick green drapes led onto a stone patio, providing a view of the bay.

I searched the bungalow thoroughly, methodically. Careful to disturb nothing. Careful to not touch any surfaces and leaving everything in place as I'd found it. The bungalow sterile. The only sign of habitation the unmade bed, two dirty glasses in the sink, a small duffle on the bedroom floor containing tee shirts, slacks, socks and underwear.

Nothing to identify him. Or indicate his interest in me. Nothing to indicate who his contacts might be, or anyone else he might be working with.

The Bungalow held nothing else of interest. Ready to leave, I reached for the doorknob. Halted. Sound of the dirt bike returning. I moved into a dark corner at the far end of the room, my back pressed against the wall. The SIG held in both hands down in front of my body. I waited.

Heard the key in the lock. The front door opened and closed. Heavy footsteps approached. He threw the key on the coffee table on his way to the kitchen alcove. He opened the refrigerator. Removed a cold beer. Pried the cap off. Threw the cap into the sink. Halted at the counter while he drank from the bottle.

Before he turned I said, "I'd prefer if you didn't turn around."

My voice froze him in place. Beer bottle poised midair. He recovered quickly. His hand flashed to the waistband beneath his shirt.

"I wouldn't do that either," I said evenly, deliberately, remaining in shadow. "Hands to your side, slow and empty."

He hesitated. I imagined his mind churning. I read his thoughts, figuring the angles, his next move. As I would in his place.

"You could try for it," I prompted. "You'd never make it." I cocked the SIG's hammer to emphasize the point. The weapon now on hair-trigger single action.

He responded to the sound by lowering his arm, holding it slightly away from his body. He kept hold of the beer bottle in his other hand. The only weapon immediately available. He started to turn, thought better of it. When I said nothing he continued, turning to face the direction of my voice.

"Who're you?" he stammered. An American south western accent.

"Bottle on the counter," I said. A deadly calm in my voice.

He regained control of his. "What do you want? I don't have any cash or jewelry."

Nice try. No doubt he already knew this wasn't a burglary. He still held the bottle.

"Bottle on the counter now," I said, a sharper edge in my voice. "Or this ends right now."

He placed the beer bottle on the kitchen counter.

"I think you already know the answer to those questions," I said, never leaving the shadowed corner of the wall. "We need to have a little talk. Have a seat. That armchair facing the window. The one with the back to me. And both hands visible on the armrests please."

He hesitated. His eyes swiveled frantically from side to side, searching for a way out. He squinted in my direction. Calculated my position, still unable to see me. I hadn't asked him to remove his weapon. Had not approached him to take it. He may have figured he still had a chance. Didn't matter to me. Before he could grab and draw it, raise it on target and fire, he'd be down. Wounded or dead. Maybe he'd reached the same conclusion. He moved toward the chair.

He sank into the armchair. Hands on the armrests as instructed.

I heard the sharp tinkle of breaking glass nanoseconds before he jerked back in the chair. Another. And another, accompanied by the shattering of window glass. At the first shot I'd dropped to one knee. The silenced SIG up and pointed in a two-handed grip, searching for a target. Ready to fire. The gunshots had been muted. Either suppressed, or a long range weapon.

Not breaking cover when he'd first entered the room, or after I'd announced my presence, had been unconscious. Instinctual. An inbred habit. And it'd saved my ass. Again.

I remained locked in firing position on one knee. My weapon moved wherever my eyes moved, ears straining for any errant sound. Senses on heightened alert. Nothing moved outside. Nothing moved inside. The shooter may or may not be aware of my presence. If he was, he'd wait for me to move. Or wait for me outside. If he wasn't, maybe he'd enter the bungalow to check his kill.

An eternity passed. Probably only ten minutes. I shifted position, but remained in shadow against the wall. I gave it an extra few minutes. Just to be on the safe side. But reasonably sure the shooter had departed.

The shooter either knew this guy, knew where he'd been staying, or had followed him. I opted for the former. I didn't believe it a coincidence my intruder had been taken out after missing his chance at me. And whoever had silenced him somehow knew I'd made him. Or that I would eventually. The hidden watcher in the harbor maybe.

I moved to the front of the armchair. Stared down at the body animated in life just minutes before. Nothing I hadn't seen countless times. But it affected me differently the older I got. Maybe a reminder of my own mortality. Fewer years ahead now than behind. Truth is I hadn't imagined I'd survive this long.

A familiar odor rose from the body. The coppery scent of blood and the pungent stench of fluids and gasses released at the moment of death.

Gazing at the lifeless body my thoughts recalled recent events in Miami Beach. And the Everglades. What the hell was I doing here? yelled a part of my rational mind. My involvement in this, whatever this might be, a bad idea. It'd be difficult if not impossible to limit my exposure. Fly below the radar. Maybe already too late.

I stared at the tight spaced brown blotches staining the center of his tee shirt. The wider spread of red below. His mouth hung open. His sightless eyes stared into an empty infinity. The same face dimly captured by Wherever's cameras.

I searched his clothing. Reminded myself my involvement stemmed from the attempt to kill my friend. Maybe the dead guy had been Mike's shooter. Killed by another unknown shooter. So it wasn't over. Far from it. More players popping up like weeds. Their connection to Mike nebulous. The circumstances more convoluted. And Jolene might be in danger too.

I found some local currency and about sixty US dollars in his pockets. He carried no wallet. No identification. Not even a passport. I hadn't found one in my earlier search of the bungalow either. The weapon tucked in his belt under his shirt a Taurus nine millimeter, threaded barrel. Same caliber used in Mike's shooting. Ballistic testing would determine if it matched the slugs taken from Mike.

Questioned again my involvement. Bodies dropping around me. Drawing me ever closer to the dark place, and the period in my life when living or dying had ceased to have relevance, or meaning. Would I be able to evade those consequences if I continued down this road?

I found a suppressor for the Taurus in a pocket of his pants. A cell phone in another. I left the weapon and silencer where they were. Pocketed the cell phone. Satisfied he had nothing else concealed on his person, I stepped back, made a quick, final survey of the room. The doorknob the only surface

I'd touched. I wiped it inside and out before exiting the bungalow. I made sure the door locked behind me.

I went to the bike and searched it too. At least as well as possible in the dark, and by touch. A glove box on the bike contained only the bike's paperwork. No saddlebags, no other compartments. I turned and walked away.

I didn't dwell on the conflicted psychological shenanigans bouncing around in my subconscious. They'd sort themselves out eventually. My sole motivation at the moment to protect Mike and Jolene. Which meant getting to the bottom of whatever this was.

I returned to the harbor. Used a pay phone outside the closed and deserted tourist information booth to call the Port Elizabeth police station. In a high-pitched excitable voice I reported maybe seeing a body. "I tink he ded," I exclaimed in Patois, using an appropriate amount of hysteria.

Aboard Wherever I fought off encroaching drowsiness and a pounding headache. But sleep had to wait for the moment. I waited for Jolene's call. Certain it would come. It did an hour later.

"We're got another shooting," she said without preamble, the strain evident in her voice. At lunch I'd perceived her day hadn't been going well. Now this. Shootings, missing persons, murders; not commonplace occurrences on Bequia.

"I know," I said. I waited.

"You know what?" she asked after a moment's hesitation.

"I know about the shooting."

"Gage, I know Bequia is small, but we just got here and nobody else knows about this yet."

"I know," I said, my manner cagey.

I needed to tell her everything. From the moment I'd spotted the intruder the night before. And my presence at the bungalow. But not while she remained at the scene, surrounded by her subordinates. Certainly not over the phone. Which reminded me of something else I needed to do. I hadn't considered it critical until this latest incident.

"What're you saying Gage?"

"I'm saying we need to talk, not now. Not tonight. I'll meet you for breakfast at De Reef if you're free."

Silence on the other end. After a pause, "Okay. See you in the morning. Get some sleep." A concerned, worried edge in her voice.

CHAPTER 10

A slate grey sky. Low-lying, moisture-laden clouds. Farther west the clouds stood in tall squall lines, marching in evenly spaced rows above the white-capped sea like parading soldiers. No rain, yet, but I smelt it in the air. A westerly wind churned up rollers in the normally tranquil bay. I headed for the beach and my breakfast date with Jolene.

She'd arrived before me. Dressed in formal uniform. The full regalia of brass and braid on the crisp grey tunic. Her black cap, belt and shoe leather polished to a lustrous shine. Shoulder epaulettes bore the police coat of arms and rank insignia. I checked her chest as I had the day before. She wore the vest. She appeared rested, morning fresh, for someone who'd probably been up most of the night.

She didn't waste any time. "Tell me."

Hunger pangs took precedence. I called to Thelma, busy opening up De Reef. I ordered breakfast. Whatever the kitchen might have ready. Nothing for Jolene. Or so she said.

Jolene leaned over, kissed me on the cheek. "Morning, by the way. Did you get any sleep?" Not waiting for a response she pressed on. "Tell me," she repeated.

De Reef empty. Jolene, me, Thelma, and a couple of other girls opening the kitchen its sole occupants.

"I was there," I said.

"What?" A pause. Consideration. "Gage, you didn't....?" in a low, tentative voice. Another pause, as though incapable of asking the question.

I peered deep into her eyes. Allowed her to search mine.

"No. Was in the bungalow when it happened though. The shots came from outside."

I pulled a folded computer printout from my shirt pocket and handed it to her. She unfolded it. Examined it through squinted eyes. The low contrast image difficult to decipher. He eyes widened when she recognized the dim photographed face.

"That was taken by the security cameras on Wherever two nights ago."

Her attention shifted from the printed image back to me. Amber-green eyes met mine. Her mouth open.

"He waited all night for me to come aboard. But he didn't know about the alarm. I waited him out and tracked him back to the bungalow in Industry. Someone shut him up before we had a chance to talk."

"Mon ostie de saint-sacrament de câlice de crisse. Wha de bumbo fuck going on?" her quiet agitation reflected in the mix of Canadian French, English, and Patois. "This puts a whole new angle on the investigation. You're saying the dead guy is somehow connected to Mike."

"Very possible. His weapon is the same caliber as the one used to shoot Mike. You're testing it I presume."

Breakfast arrived. Fried sprat and hash brown potatoes, fresh rolls, pawpaw, and coffee. I put a hold on the conversation while Thelma set the table. I asked her to bring an extra fork. Miss 'I'm okay, I don't need anything' eyed my fish and pawpaw like a hungry lioness stalking prey.

I waited for Thelma to deliver the extra fork and depart before continuing.

"There's more," I said around a mouthful of juicy pawpaw. From my pocket I pulled the cell phone I'd taken from the dead guy. Pressed a few buttons. Passed the phone across to her. "I took this cell phone off him."

The fork with a speared piece of fish halted halfway to her mouth.

"Holy mother of Jesus, Matthew, Luke and John," she said.

"Exactly what I said," chuckling at her.

"Gage," she sighed, a stunned expression on her face, unable to shift her eyes from the image of Sarah Holmes on the dead man's cell phone. "I'm out of my depth here. I'm not sure what any of this means or what to do about it."

I sympathized. I'd just handed her another twist in an already frustrating investigation. "I'm not sure what it means either. But now we know for sure Mike, this guy, and Sarah Homes are all connected. Just not sure how yet. See if you can get a dump of the phone records. But don't give the phone to anyone, or let anyone else know about the connection to Sarah Holmes. And whatever you do, keep me out of it," I said, emphasizing that last part.

"Goes without saying my love."

She chewed a mouthful of fish and potatoes. Her burdened expression lifted, at least a little, replaced by a convergence of delicate curved eyebrows. Her thoughts focused on redirecting the investigation.

"I've been making some progress with the FBI," she said. "On the down low. Coffe still doesn't want anything to do with them. But I've been in contact with the liaison agent in the embassy on Barbados. We've established a tentative working relationship. A sort of quid pro quo. If they can't get in on the ground, at least they're in the loop. He's faxing me the list of Sarah's personal effects. And sending me her photographs. I'll give him this cell number and ask him to run it for me. It won't be part of the local investigation. At least for now."

"We need to find out how all three are connected," I said. "And how they're connected to a Columbian drug cartel."

"There'll be more on the dead guy back at the office by now too," she said. "We sent off his prints last night. And we got the name Frank Tesca off the bike's rental documents. My guys are checking the bungalow rental this morning. Why'd he search Wherever?"

"No idea. Didn't get a chance to talk about that. Or anything else. I don't know how or where he first picked me up. But remember I told you on Union I had a strange feeling. Maybe he'd been dogging me for a while." I doubted it, and I didn't mention the unseen watcher in the harbor.

"Have your guys checked the transient yachts in the harbor?"

"Not yet. Thank goodness it's off-season. Not too many to check out. We planned to get to that today too."

"What about airport surveillance. You have cameras at Immigration right?"

"Picking those up today too. We'll go through them, pull the dead guy's immigration arrival card. What're you thinking?"

"Can you get me copies?"

"Sure, I can burn a copy for you. Why?"

"Not sure. See if anything pops out at me."

"Okay," she said, finishing a last bite. "Gotta go."

"How come dress uniform today?"

"Got a meeting at the ministry later this morning. By the way, I haven't had a chance to thank you for my present. I can't believe the way this thing fits and feels. Sure beats the hell out of the ones we have."

"Or anything else the public knows about," I reminded her.

"Still classified. I haven't forgotten. Capable of stopping even a fifty caliber round. Absorbs greater impact energy, so no bruised ribs or internal hemorrhaging. The question is my sweets," a sly tone in her voice, a mischievous twinkle in her eyes, an amused curve around her luscious lips, "How you just happened to have one handy on board, in my size?"

"Special order," I said, smiling back at her.

Hazel eyes held mine in an affectionate stare. "You're the guy." She leaned close. Pressed her lips to mine. A last lingering look, before she breezed out of the room.

I had nothing pressing to do all day. On such days I'd tinker around Wherever, catching up on maintenance chores. Or I'd spend languorous hours in a hammock in the company of a good book. The weather outlook didn't appear conducive to either. And I felt out of sorts, restless. As frustrated as Jolene. Not to mention fleeting flashes of foreboding and doubt.

I still needed more data points. Had not followed up with Nora. After this latest shooting not sure I should. Probably safer for her if I kept my distance.

I whiled the day away ashore, aimlessly, ducking into shelter when the rain finally arrived. A short-lived transitory shower. Jolene called around midday. Informed me in an excitable voice about incredible events unfolding. No hint of what they might be. The investigation I assumed. Said she'd be staying overnight in Kingstown, further whetting my curiosity. Said I had to watch the news. Exasperatingly coy. I tried prying more from her, discern what had her so excited. Her turn to be cagey and tight-lipped.

Four o'clock, ensconced at the Frangipani bar. The only patron there, sheltering from another passing shower. The bartender, Desmond, had little to do behind the bar, except to periodically hand me another cold bottle of Hairoun beer. We passed the time playing backgammon. Something from the cable news channel in the background caught my ear.

"Des, turn up de TV."

The anchor announced breaking news in the Sarah Holmes missing person case. The image switched to a live satellite feed of their reporter in front of the ministry building in Kingstown. Reporting from Kingstown, she explained, the capital of St. Vincent and the Grenadines, located on the main island, not the smaller island to the south where Sarah Holmes had disappeared. The geography lesson characteristically redundant, I thought. Repeated ad nauseam since the story first aired.

The reporter said a press conference had been called by the police, scheduled to begin 'any moment now'. Clearly not accounting for 'Vincy time', I snickered to myself.

In the interim the anchor recapped the story of the missing woman. Pretty sure their cable audience were already aware of the highlights, I thought. But if you happened to have been visiting another planet over the past few weeks, here's what happened. At least they didn't possess any dramatic video, like a fire or explosion, repeated on an endless loop. They cut away to commercials instead. Their bread-and-butter.

Our backgammon game suspended, Desmond and I stared at the plasma screen above the bar when the press conference commenced. Prime Minister Julian Defretas, tall, light brown complexion, waves of long black hair, groomed mustache, salt and pepper beard, entered a large conference room, followed by a phalanx of officials. Jolene among them. He stopped at a podium, the flag of St. Vincent and the Grenadines, and the Royal St. Vincent and the Grenadines Police Force banner, limp in the background. Jolene stood slightly behind him.

A statement from the Prime Minister opened the press conference. "The people of St. Vincent and the Grenadines continued to hold the missing woman and her family in their hearts and continued to hope and pray for her safe return," he said. He announced that Deputy Commissioner Coffe had been reassigned. He'd no longer be heading up the investigation. Stunned silence in the audience, followed by a flurry of shouted questions from the assembled reporters. Stony expressions on the faces lined up behind the podium.

The Prime Minister ignored the pelted questions. Instead he spoke of the island's own tragedy, the shooting of Commissioner of Police Michael Daniels. That investigation also continuing, he told the gathered reporters and cameras. The lack of questions following the announcement paralleled the reporters' lack of interest.

It gave him great pleasure, he said, to announce good news regarding Commissioner Daniels' continuing recovery. He'd been removed from intensive care, expected to make a full recovery. Doing so well in fact, he'd be coordinating the investigations from hospital until his return home soon. In the meantime, Superintendent of Police Jolene Johansson would be heading the investigations locally. He introduced Jolene amid tepid applause from the officials lined up beside her.

Jolene stepped to the podium, replacing the Prime Minister. She addressed the room in a calm businesslike manner, but I imagined her heart pounding in her chest. Strikingly telegenic on camera. Glamorous without the faux trappings of glamour. Resplendent in her crisp, tailored uniform.

"Yea miss Jolene," Desmond erupted in spontaneous admiration, wearing a huge grin.

Jolene made a brief statement before taking questions. Yes, the investigations were progressing, leads being followed. No, so far no suspects. The FBI? Yes she planned consulting with the FBI, but the Vincentian Police remained in charge of the investigations. No comment regarding Commissioner Daniels. She referred the questioner to the Prime Minister's earlier statement. No comment regarding specifics of an ongoing investigation.

A female reporter, wearing a khaki shirt, rolled sleeves and lots of pockets resembling the clichéd bush jacket of a foreign correspondent, asked about reports of another gunshot victim on Bequia. No comment Jolene responded. Has tourism been effected by the recent crime wave, the same reporter shouted in follow-up. Crime wave? I thought in disgust. Another no comment response from Jolene. How was the local police coping with this new crime wave, she persisted. Again with the crime wave. The camera captured the subtle change in Jolene's glare. But she made no comment.

"No further questions at this time," Jolene said, concluding the press conference. She stepped away from the podium. Her performance an exhibition of poise and grace. Unlike Coffe, she'd controlled the process from beginning to end.

The blond, freshly tanned reporter filled the screen once more. She recapped the new developments, describing the investigation thus far as confused and fraught with misinformation and missteps. Misinformation and confusion largely promulgated by the press themselves; by their uninformed reporting and on-air hyperbole. A truth lost on an introspectively challenged tone deaf news media, where on-air personalities, gimmicky sets, clever sound bites, and paid punditry trumped real news and informative reporting.

The anchor asked the reporter what was known about Commissioner of Police Michael Daniels and this Superintendent Johansson. About time, I thought. The reporter hadn't done her homework. She had no specific information to offer except that Commissioner Daniels had been in law enforcement in Florida before taking the job on St. Vincent. She responded in general terms. Repeating the conventional narrative regarding the local police. The anchor apparently not caring she hadn't answered the question or provided any useful information.

The news droned on, turning to other topics. Focused on U.S politics. I'd already tuned out. In the midst of settling my bar tab my cell phone chimed. Jolene.

"Incredible huh?" she said the moment I answered. She sounded short of breath, like she'd been running.

"You look good on TV," I said.

"Got a question for you," all business again.

"Shoot." An inappropriate word choice given recent events, I reflected, too late to stifle it.

"The reporter you took to Union. What do you think about her?"

I hesitated. Not sure it wasn't a trick question. She jumped into the silence.

"I mean, what sort of reporter is she? Can she be trusted?"

"Hell, I don't know. Be trusted with what?"

"I need to do an interview. Damage control. Set the record straight. Clean up Coffe's mess, put some questions to rest. Not a cable network. Print. No cameras. Someone I can do a one-on-one interview with."

"You think that's a good idea?"

"Gotta be done. The first step. After that I won't be the public face of the force. We're setting up a new Public Information Department. I'm searching around now for a camera friendly face. Someone smart enough to deal with the press, and able to stick to a script.

"When did you get so PR savvy?"

"Still learning. But I've got a good teacher. Been on the phone most of the morning with Mike."

"I wondered about that. You sure he's up for this so soon?"

"He's doing great Gage, thank God. The Docs even think he'll be ready to come home in another week or so. The PM saw him a couple of days ago. Knew Coffe had to go, but wasn't sure how to engineer it and still keep the investigations going. He wanted Mike's take on it, and he hadn't seen Mike since the surgery. Anyway Mike convinced the PM he was up to it. They made the decision about Coffe and came up with this plan."

"Okay. Not much I can tell you about Nora. I've read her stuff, including the stories she filed from here. She's thorough, does her homework. Doesn't have an axe to grind. Clear on her facts. Whether that means you can trust her or not, I don't know. Want me to sound her out for you?"

"That'd be great. Let me know. Have you seen her by the way?" her tone switching from businesslike to playful.

"No." Defensive. "Not since Union Island."

"Well behave yourself and let me know what you think. Gotta go. I'll be back tomorrow. Love you." She hung up.

I hadn't seen Nora since I'd left her on Union Island. I hadn't been exactly avoiding her. But I'd decided a little distance might be safer for her. I'd abandoned the idea of using her as a cutout. And given the latest events, I'm glad I did. I'd no intention of placing her directly, or even indirectly, in harm's way.

Keeping my distance served another purpose. No question I liked her. Felt the attraction. A carnal stirring in her presence. But trust? Still a long, long ways away. Only a handful of people, Mike and Jolene included, had ever breached that defense.

The sky hadn't changed much as the day drew closer to evening. It'd cleared a bit here and there, but the gray overcast predominated. If Nora had been at the press conference she might be on the next ferry. Maybe not. At any rate as good a place as any to find her. I'd wait for the ferry. If she wasn't aboard I'd continue over to the Hamilton Hotel. I replanted my butt on the Frangipani bar stool. Desmond and I resumed our Backgammon match. I reopened my tab.

A horn blast drew our attention to Northwest Point. I bid Desmond and our unfinished Backgammon game "so long" and headed for the wharf. Passing under 'parliament's' almond tree, the familiar chill brushed the base of my neck. My watcher. Still around.

Passengers streamed in a crowded rush from the ferry onto the wharf. Many loaded with goods and supplies from Kingstown. I nonchalantly scanned my surroundings as the crowd dispersed in all directions. Some headed out of the harbor on foot. Others boarded waiting minivans departing to other parts of the island. Nothing, and no one, triggered any mental alarms. But the unseen eyes pinned me like a laser dot on a target.

I spotted Nora. Hard to miss her. Despite her petit size, and surrounded by milling stragglers, she stood out in a flower-patterned sundress like a solitary rose in a vase of ferns. I set off in her direction. The watcher's eyes followed me toward the wharf.

"Hey," she greeted me as she strolled off the wharf. "Here to welcome me?"

"Kind of. I was on my way to look for you."

"Great." a wide smile crossed her face. "I tried finding you a couple of times. Always seemed to just miss you."

"I've been a little crazy," returning her smile. "Had to drop a bunch of things in a hurry. Which is why, if you're not busy, I want to take you to dinner. Make up for running out on you before."

"And here I was thinking you were one of those one-night-stand type of guys who never calls afterward."

Uncertain what to make of the 'one night stand' metaphor. Decided probably just her manner of speaking. Not sure though. Writers tended to use words precisely.

"Never in life, my dear," I said, imitating the eighteenth century colloquialism of a favorite fictional sea captain and offering her an ingratiating smile.

We walked comfortably side by side in the direction of Hamilton. Her closeness ignited a pleasant, tightening sensation in the pit of my stomach. Passed the spot where Mike had laid bleeding at the side of the road. The watching eyes no longer present. No one following.

"You haven't given me an answer about dinner," I said, almost at the marina.

"Sure. Let me grab a shower, change, and I'm all yours." Again, teasing choice of words. Maybe my imagination, reading too much into her words.

"Okay. I'll meet you back here, at the bar. Say a couple of hours?"

"Works for me. I'll see you then."

My senses at peak alertness as I walked back through the harbor. Evidently I didn't need to be followed. Surveillance unnecessary. The watcher able to find me whenever he/she wanted. Not difficult on a seven-square mile island.

Who was my watcher? And why now? If not for recent events my candidate list might include any number of black shops. One I'd done a job for. More likely one I'd pissed off. But the timing suggested a connection to Mike, the missing woman, and the dead intruder. Either scenario presented a problem. And possibly substantiated a fear I'd had from the outset.

Best-case scenario, the watcher was connected to Mike's case, the missing woman, and the Columbian connection. Or maybe I'd tripped a red flag somewhere. Had exposed myself and popped up on someone's radar.

Worst case, everything so far, commencing with Mike's shooting, had been designed to draw me out.

CHAPTER 11

Two hours later I waited at the Hamilton Hotel bar nursing a Heineken. Dressed in island casuals, faded blue jeans, striped short sleeved shirt, the shirttail hanging out, and flip-flops.

Nora entered. A tangerine sleeveless sundress draped the curves of her alluring figure. A wide black belt around her middle accentuated her bosom and waist. Lustrous dark hair framed a freshly scrubbed face. Large hoop earrings hung daintily from her lobes. The scent of soap, shampoo, and just a hint of perfume hovered around her.

My mouth formed a silent "Wow".

An appreciative smile. "Didn't think you were that easy to impress."

"You trying to impress me?"

Her smile widened, exposing straight ivory white teeth.

"Well I am." I said. "Hungry?"

"Starved."

"Let's get out of here then."

I led her to the gas dock where I'd tied the dinghy. Exhibiting a practiced ease she hadn't possessed a week before, she stepped in, sat on the center athwart seat. Her hair streamed around her face in the breeze created by our passage across the bay, conjuring memories of our sail south to Union Island.

I ran the dinghy onto the beach in front of the Green Boley. Pulled it far enough out of the water allowing Nora to step out onto sand. She climbed the stone steps from the beach to the front yard of the Green Boley, her sandals dangling from her hand.

The Green Boley stood back from, and slightly above the beach. A favored haunt, the owner-proprietor Winston, his wife Rona, their numerous children and grandchildren, like extended family to me and Jolene. Bob Marley's reggae vocals and rhythms pulsated from the small green and yellow bamboo structure. Bamboo shutters on the sides opened upward, exposing the small dining room and bar to the open air, the night breeze, and the sound of rollicking surf.

Before stepping onto the painted concrete floor we rinsed sand from our feet in a plastic basin of water placed for that purpose at the entrance. Linen covered tables and plastic chairs furnished the room. Against the far wall, a varnished wood bar separated the dining area from the kitchen. Liquor bottles lined wall mounted shelves behind the bar. I'd spent many evenings there helping Winston tend bar.

An array of appetizing aromas, fish, conch, chicken, escaped the kitchen and saturated the air. Winston, medium height, ample beer paunch, stood behind the bar.

"Evening Winston," I greeted him, leading Nora to a table close to the beach.

"Gage," Winston acknowledged, a broad grin on his honey hued face. He cast a curious glance at Nora.

The surf scampered to and fro along the beach, making a gentle splashing sound, accompanied by a nocturnal chorus of crickets and land frogs. Inside, reggae and calypso melodies filled the room from speakers hung in the corners.

An elaborately decorated bowl containing a burning candle sat at the center of each table. The bowl, made from the hard shell of the Boley fruit, inspired the bar's name. Boley trees of varying sizes populated Winston's yard, including a large tree in front of the family's residence. The Boley trees shared the yard with other large, shady fruit trees, tambrin, cashew, breadfruit and guinep.

A connecting section between the bar and residence housed a small boutique operated by Winston's wife. It offered a variety of handmade clothes, batiks, postcards, and other souvenirs.

The Boley fruit grew in different shapes and sizes. Scoop out the pulp, clean and dry the inner shell, and what remains is a ceramic-hard container Bequians utilize in a variety of ways. Large ones cut in half served as soup or salad bowls. Some as planters. Small slimmer ones as drinking mugs. The outside of the bowls often painted and decorated in elaborate patterns, like the candleholders on the tables.

Winston approached our table. I introduced Nora.

"Winston, Nora," I said, "Nora's a repotah."

His curious gaze fixed on her, he extended his hand. When she took it he bent and raised the back of her hand to his lips, his smile designed to charm and enchant.

"Pleashah to meet you," he said in accented English.

Amused by Winston's chivalrous display, Nora smiled back at him. "Same here," she said.

"What can I get yuh from de bar?"

"De usual for me," I answered. "You?" Indicating Nora.

"A glass of white wine please." Winston turned and headed for the bar.

"That was weird," she said, still amused.

"Don't mind him. He's just having some fun with you. Or maybe me."

"I've been taking your advice you know," she said after Winston delivered our drinks.

"What advice?"

"About getting out. Now I understand what you meant by Bequia growing on you. The homey feeling. And the weirdest thing," her eyes expressing a curious, questioning gleam as they stared into mine. "Whenever I mention I know you, I get a surprising reaction, like suddenly I belong."

"You're going around telling people you know me?" Perhaps a bit more defensive than I'd intended. The subtle shift in her eyes indicated it hadn't gone unnoticed. She ignored it.

"I'm not. It just comes up in conversation sometimes. Though I have to admit, I'm curious to see people's reactions when it does happen."

"So what've you learned?"

"That you're well liked. Respected. They consider you one of their own. I've experienced incredible generosity and hospitality. Offering me food wherever I go. Inviting me in to eat, or for tea. Speaking of which does this place have a menu?"

"Mainly for tourists. We'll have whatever the family's having."

"Like family," she said. "Noticed that too whenever your name was mentioned." Perceiving she'd touched a raw nerve earlier she abruptly changed the subject.

"You're not a fan of tourists are you?"

"What makes you think that?"

"Just an impression from listening to you and your friend June. And I keep hearing a slight tone in your voice when you say the word tourists."

"I try to stay out of their way," I said.

"What do you have against tourists?"

"Nothing."

"Not buying it."

Another subject I didn't wish to get embroiled in. But I answered her. "I get it," I said. "People want a better life for themselves and their kids. They need tourism to do that. But it's a double-edged sword. The benefits come with a cost."

"Like what?"

"Destruction of the environment. Negative impacts on tradition and culture. Over commercialization and overdevelopment. "

Ann, one of Winston's teenage daughters, approached the table carrying a loaded tray. Saved by the food. Nora had correctly perceived my attitude. But it wasn't the time or place to get into it. To express the depth of my feelings regarding the false Gods of progress and development, or the distinction I made between visitors and tourists. The former welcome, while the latter invariably exhibited an obnoxious ignorance of the people and culture around them, displaying an arrogant, almost colonial attitude of entitlement. In any event secondary to my need to remain invisible, particularly around strangers on the island.

Ann deposited two steaming bowls of soup on the table. Nora eyed hers. Unsure. Her eyes interrogated mine. "Smells delicious. Looks like spinach but it isn't. What is it?"

"Callalou. Made from a leafy vegetable, like spinach. Mixed with coconut milk, chili peppers, boiled green bananas, flour dumplings, seasoned with local herbs and spices," I explained, dumping a hefty helping of fiery hot sauce on mine.

I lifted a spoonful to my mouth. Nora smiled at my reaction, a long, drawn out appreciative "ummm", my head thrown back and my eyes closed.

Nora sampled hers. "Omigod. This is terrific. What's the little meat chunks?"

"Conch. A house specialty."

Comforted, she attacked the callalou soup.

"How's your story coming?" I asked her.

"Which story?" she asked between delicate slurps. "There's more than just the Sarah Holmes story going on here."

"Like what?" I said.

"Like who shot your police commissioner. And the other recent shooting the police won't officially confirm."

"What are your colleagues saying about it?"

"Not much interest. But the fact the Ministry and Police won't comment makes me think it's more than just coincidence."

She waited, possibly hoping for a reaction, or a comment.

When I did neither she continued. "Frankly, until something new happens in the case, I've been focusing on local atmospherics. The people, and the effect all this is having on them. I'm working on an article about that now."

She paused. Didn't elaborate. Pretended to focus on the soup. Occupational caution. I empathized.

"And?" I said, hoping to draw her out.

She placed her spoon in the empty soup bowl. "I'm sensing a change in local attitudes. A growing resentment against the news people. Their presence here, and the things they're saying and reporting."

"No shit," I said.

"Some people won't even talk to me until..." she paused. Sudden discomfort in her body language.

"What?" I said.

"The way people react when I mention your name. I sort of take advantage of it sometimes."

"Shameless," I said smiling, my earlier defensiveness absent. Damage, if any, already done.

My reaction put her at ease. "You don't mind?"

"Anyone but you and I might," I said, my smile reassuring.

"It's just that before you seemed defensive when I mentioned it."

"Perceptive," I said.

Ann returned bearing platters of steamed fish, rice and peas, greens, roasted breadfruit and sweet plantains. She placed them on the table. Removed our empty soup bowls.

Her earlier uncertainty regarding ingredients banished, Nora dug in. A healthy appetite I observed. Unselfconscious as she sorted, picked, chewed, savored each mouthful, occasionally pausing to continue our conversation.

"Anything new on the Sarah Holmes disappearance?" I asked, feigning an appropriate degree of disinterest and casual curiosity.

"You tell me," she said, a sly playful smile around her mouth.

"What's that mean?"

"Nothing," The playful smile still in place but a businesslike edge in her voice. "The trail's gone cold. No new leads. Three years ago I worked a story about human trafficking. A global slave trade, mostly women and children, especially young East European girls."

"I know," I said. I'd read her story. More than that, I'd had personal experience regarding the subject.

"You know?" her perceptive, curious stare fixed on me again.

"Yeah." A memory percolated to the surface. The face of evil personified. A face no longer among the living. The faces never haunted me. But they remained grafted onto my memory. Even the ones seen only at long distance. A small image centered in the mil dot reticle of a scope. A face one moment, a cloud of pink mist the next. I sensed Nora's eyes staring hard at me.

"What was that?" she asked, a mixture of concern and curiosity in her voice.

"What?" I said.

"You kinda zoned out there for a second," she said. "Like you were thinking about something far away."

"Sorry," I said.

She continued to stare. Undecided what to make of it.

"Anyway, I looked into that angle with Sarah Holmes. One of the reasons I wanted to backtrack her. But that kind of trafficking isn't prevalent in this region. And none of the usual signs are there. And she doesn't fit the profile. Too old for one thing. But I had to rule it out. Stranger things have happened on the trail of a story."

Our plates empty, I sat back from the table. Full. Contented. Nora the same from all appearances. She pushed her plate away. A mouthful of wine washed down the last morsels. The subject of Sarah Holmes tabled for the moment.

"Fantastic," Nora said, using the cloth napkin to delicately dab her mouth and lips. "I'm full. Think I need to work some of this off."

"Any suggestions?" I said.

No misinterpreting the gleam in her eyes. No questioning my imagination this time. The room dimmed, and blurred, leaving only her in focus, and the unmistakable invitation in her eyes, in her posture.

I leaned across the table. "Why Miz. Austin. I do believe you have naughty thoughts on your mind."

She blushed. The pink flush in her cheeks noticeable even in the dim lighting. But the time had arrived to put an end to the playful flirting. Before it transported us to a place I didn't want to be.

"Sorry," I said. "Didn't mean to discombobulate you."

She laughed, a spontaneous outburst, vocal, but not too loud. Pleasant, like the twittering of birds. An unrestrained mirth shook her. I joined her infectious laugher. It broke the tension.

"Oh, you're funny" she said, barely containing another wave of laughter.

"Nice to see you laugh," I said.

"Funny man."

The awkward moment passed, but the subject, and the tension, still alive between us.

"Sorry," I repeated. "Maybe I've been sending the wrong signals. I don't want to give you the wrong impression."

"You haven't," a serious note in her voice, a bemused expression in her bourbon hued eyes. "I'm surprised it took

you so long. You don't strike me as the shy, clueless type." She
said.

"What type do you think I am?"

"At first, another local guy on the prowl." She paused,
searching for a reaction. When she got none, "Now..." elbows
resting on the table she leaned toward me, eyes squinting as
she peered hard at mine, "I think you're controlled, cautious,
way smarter than you want people to think, perceptive, and oh
so mysterious. An extraordinary man trying to appear
ordinary. Do you have any idea what a potent mixture that is?"

"So I've been told," I said.

She raised her arms off the table. Rested her chin on
the back of entwined fingers. Her head slightly tilted. Her eyes
scrutinized mine.

"And then there's your interest in Sarah Holmes."

The remark caught me by surprise. Probably as she'd
intended. Her crafty interview technique growing familiar.

"Just curious," I said. "But I never take what I read or
hear in the news seriously. Figured you might have a different
perspective."

"Huh huh," her smile, her eyes, indicating my
explanation hadn't swayed her in the least.

"Figured you might know something about her that's
not in the news," my smile one of amused disinterest.

Her smile mischievous. "I don't," an amused glint in
the intelligent brown eyes peering into mine. "The research
my editor provided is pretty much the same as what's being
reported."

"No personal impressions?" I said.

Her smile widened, turning into a Cheshire Cat grin.
Her eyes continued to hold mine in an attentive stare,

removing any doubt in my mind she'd read me correctly. And was having fun playing some little game of her own.

"Won't know until I get back and can interview the people around her myself. Form those impressions you're curious about," obviously enjoying herself.

"But?" I said, sensing a hint of something left unsaid. Careful to moderate my tone, keep it conversational. Not pressing.

I observed her hesitation. A tensing of shoulders, and around her throat. Micro-expressions flitted unconsciously across her face. An almost imperceptible shift in her eyes. A blink. The stare momentarily unfocussed. Turned inward. Sighting the mental boundary she'd established regarding how much to reveal. The smile still present though not as playful. The eyes questioning, contemplative. She sipped her wine, providing a momentary delay. Reached a decision.

"She mostly kept to herself aboard ship. Didn't really mingle with the other passengers. Didn't join in any of the shipboard or shore activities. Went off on her own. Did her own thing. One of the reasons it took awhile for anyone to realize she was missing. And the other reason I wanted to retrace her steps." Her thoughts focused inward as she spoke, analyzing her own words, searching for meaning in the impressions she'd verbalized, probably for the first time.

"Not sure how much of a help that will be," she said, her gaze refocused on me.

"What do you mean?"

She leaned toward me, her chin again resting on entwined fingers, the naturalness of the pose enhancing her subtle allure. The gleam back in her eyes. The Cheshire Cat grin back in place.

"Something else I learned talking to folks on the island," she said, the playfulness back in her voice. "Kept bumping into it wherever I went."

"And what, pray tell, is this great revelation?"

"Superintendent Jolene Johansson." She paused for effect. Observed my reaction.

"Small Island," I said. "And you're very good at what you do?"

"Yes, I know."

"Modest too." I said, smiling at her.

Her soft twittering laughter reached me across the table.

"So there you have the whole story," I said.

"In my experience the whole story usually isn't even half the story. She's a bit younger isn't she?" The remark not intended to offend. I'd grown aware of her casual forthrightness, designed to elicit unguarded reactions, attentively observed. A potent trait for a reporter. I appreciated it.

"It works for us," I said. "For now."

"For now?"

"I don't have a crystal ball. And life has a habit of throwing wonderful and terrible things at you. Sometimes all at once."

"You've seen a lot of that haven't you?" her eyes searching mine again.

"I'd bet you have too," I said.

Something about my remark amused her. She smiled. "So you can pass on what I've told you. Like I said, I hope it helps."

Now I understood the mischievous smile, the amusement in her eyes; the coy playfulness. She'd known all along the person leading the investigation and I made pillow talk. The knowledge didn't deter her from exploring the possibility we'd delicately set aside earlier, but not completely settled.

"This isn't something I'd normally do, or even consider, but somehow I feel differently with you. Two ships passing in the night, about to go our separate ways, our one chance to share a moment that will never happen again."

"We're sharing a moment now," I said.

She laughed again. "Cute. You know what I mean."

"A few years ago, without hesitation. But here, now, not possible."

Her eyes searched mine. A long silent scrutiny. Contemplative; registering faint disappointment and an envious approval.

"Lucky woman," her voice soft, almost a whisper.

"She wants to meet you," I said.

"What." her chin sprang up off her hands.

"You were at the news conference today?"

"Yeah?" renewed curiosity creeping into her voice.

"She wants to give an interview. One-on-one. I gave you an excellent recommendation."

Skepticism in the perceptive brown eyes, but also an opportunistic, calculating gleam. "An exclusive?" She asked.

"An exclusive," I confirmed.

"How can I turn that down, for a lot of reasons. First, because you asked," a forefinger crocked in my direction emphasizing the 'you'. "Second, she's a get no one else will have. And third, I can't wait to meet the woman who commands your loyalty. When?"

"She'll be back tomorrow. I'll set it up and let you know."

We spent the remainder of the evening chatting. Amiable and comfortable. The flirting game and its attendant sexual tension put to rest. We ordered more drinks. We absorbed the music, and enjoyed the company of locals and itinerant yachties who filled the Green Boley as the night wore on. Those who knew me curious about Nora. I introduced her, deliberately omitting her occupation. By morning all kinds of rumors will have taken flight on gossipy wings.

We lost track of time. Until close to two in the morning, only Winston, Rona, and a yachtie expatriate with whom I occasionally closed the bar remained. Nora and I had moved to the bar earlier to join them. Our conversation provided her a candid local perspective. I helped Winston close up. Nora didn't mind waiting. She'd thoroughly enjoyed every bit of the evening.

I shuttled her back to Hamilton. Walked her to her room. At the door she turned to face me. Reached up, brought her lips against mine. I returned the kiss. Didn't prolong it.

"Sure?" she whispered.

"Positive." I answered. "See you tomorrow."

I headed home to Wherever.

CHAPTER 12

"Well?" Jolene asked when I called her.

"She'd love to. Can't wait. You're a 'get' as she puts it. When and how do you want to do this?"

"This evening. Dinner at my place. I have a few details to tie up here, but I'll take the ferry over this afternoon."

"You sure this wouldn't be better at your office?"

"I want it informal. I don't want it to appear like I'm dissing the other news outlets, which of course I am. But this way it's not so in their faces. Mike's idea."

"Okay. I'll let her know. When?"

"Around seven. I'll arrange dinner for the three of us."

"Why do I have to be involved in this?"

"Because you are. And besides I need you there to give me a signal if you think there's something I shouldn't answer or talk about."

"Jo..." I hesitated, uncertainty in my voice. "That makes sense, but I'm not sure about this. Shouldn't this just be between you and Nora?"

"Mike said it'd be okay. He gave me a set of ground rules she must agree to before we go ahead. Most of them involving you. He said you'd know how to play it. Said you and

I should set some signals before meeting her, and I should follow your lead."

Mike had put this scheme together. He knew the risks. We'd never spoken openly about my past. But I always had the impression he knew, at least guessed, more than he'd let on. It meant he wanted me close to Jolene, protecting her. I had no doubts regarding Jolene handling herself in an interview. But the information we had needed to be guarded. We still had no idea what we were dealing with.

He'd also be setting up Nora. The same ploy I'd devised to obtain information from her. One I'd decided not to play. I needed to protect her too.

"Gage, he wanted me to ask if you're sure of this person before we go any further."

"Can't ever be sure of anything Jo. The most I can say is she's a good bet."

"Well, Mike said it's your call."

"Okay. I'll set it up."

"So what'd you two do last night?" I imagined her smiling at the phone as she asked the question. Imagined the mischievous twinkle in her eyes.

"Dinner at Winston's. Talked. Drank. Nothing much."

"I'll have to reward you for your good behavior."

"Can't wait," I said. "See you later."

The next order of business, contact Nora. I left a message for her. Next, I dialed a Miami number.

"What's up boss?" said Mendez's voice on the other end.

"You tell me. What's shaking up your way?"

"Word on the street is there's some sorta drug war going on. Seems this big drug guy disappeared and everyone's trying to get a piece of his organization."

"How about our guy?"

"All quiet. Lots of visitors recently, but all official, and family. Boss, it's going to get harder to cover him with all the increased traffic since he got out of intensive care."

"It's okay. Time to break cover anyway. He's going to be running the investigations from his hospital bed so the traffic may not lighten up. Make contact and read him in. Full briefing, everything you've got, including the Columbian. But dress up the part about Calderon. And no need to get into your biographies. Set up security on him and stay close. And give him a hand with the workload," I said in an afterthought. "He'll fight you on it but be insistent. Don't need him having a relapse under the stress."

"Will do boss. Anything else?"

"Anything more on the Columbian?"

"Yeah. We've put together a jacket on him. An even nastier piece of work than Calderon."

"Give it to our man. Use the email address I gave you to send me a copy. It's secure. And what about that other photo I sent you?"

"Still working on that. But no obvious connection to our Columbian."

"Okay. Need you to get a few items for me. I'll text you the details for contact and pickup. And from here forward only secure coms."

"Will do."

"Talk to you soon then," I said before hanging up.

The remainder of the day passed in what had been typical fashion before people shooting people, people disappearing, and people spying on me, displaced my blissful daily routine. Swimming, walking, attending my fish traps, eating, drinking beer, shopping, yacht maintenance, napping, reading, more beer, more eating, switching to rum, sunsets, more eating, more rum, Jolene. Finally crashing in a cool, comfortable bed or hammock.

I arrived at De Reef early. I'd taken a circuitous route. Impossible to tail without being spotted. My eyes swept the large open room. All clear. A sprinkling of patrons at the bar, locals who lived in Lower Bay. Four men at a corner table engaged in a domino match. a game of 8 ball in progress at the pool table. Soca music from the speakers, succulent odors from the kitchen.

No reporters. They didn't venture much beyond Hamilton and Port Elizabeth except to visit the beaches. I ordered a cold Heineken from the bar. Wandered through the kitchen to the back of the building, hidden from Lower Bay road behind coconut and manchineel trees. I sipped my beer and waited.

Before long Noel's van carrying Nora passed along the road. I waited and watched. No other vehicles or foot traffic on the road since Nora's arrival. I headed back to the bar through the kitchen. Spotted Nora by the concrete walkway leading onto the beach. Her gaze fixed on the silvery moonlit bay, lost in the view. She wore dark denim jeans, flat sandals and a short sleeve shirt flared at her waist. Not wishing to startle her I called her name before approaching her from behind.

"Hey", she said, turning, smiling as I approached.

"Gorgeous night," I said, indicating the bay.

"I can see why someone wouldn't want to leave this place."

"Bequia captures another wandering soul," I said. I took her arm. "Let's go this way," pulling her onto the sand.

We walked toward the water, veering off to our left before reaching the lapping surf. We passed under a group of trees, fishing dinghies pulled up beneath them. Fish nets hung from their lower branches. A footpath led from the beach onto a narrow paved road.

I led her along the road in the direction of Moon Hole. The road steepened as we walked. Clear behind us. A bit farther I guided her off the road onto a gravel and stone path, and a series of stone steps, dimly lit by moonlight. The path lined on both sides by cherry trees, plum trees, lime trees and wild flowers. Jasmine and Lilac perfumed the air. A chorus of nocturnal creatures serenaded the night.

The path wound around a rosebush, ending in a grass lawn sloping away in the direction we'd come. Stone steps shaped in a half circle led to a wide verandah surrounding the house on three sides. Hanging lanterns lit the front verandah, and muted light spilled from inside through open windows and a wide front entrance.

I ushered Nora into Jolene's house. Her gaze swept across the comfortable, homey furniture and book lined shelves; framed art photographs on the walls, including a pair of Ansel Adams prints.

I called out to Jolene. Earlier, after arranging our signals, I'd left her in shorts and a sweatshirt busily making everything ready and setting the table.

She entered the room wearing an ankle length, turquoise and seashell pattern halter-top sundress. Her gold streaked curls pinned on one side, falling onto her shoulder on the other. Long earrings, a dainty blue butterfly wing motif, hung from her earlobes. They drew the eye to the elegant curve of her neck.

A touch of eye shadow her only makeup. Her face as fresh as a flower blooming in spring. Her smile warm and welcoming as she walked over to Nora, extending her hand in greeting.

"It's so nice to finally meet you," she said, shaking Nora's hand.

Nora momentarily stunned by the vision before her. Jolene had that effect.

She recovered quickly. "A pleasure to finally meet you too," Nora answered. "I've heard so much about you."

"Oh? What has he been telling you?" turning to me and planting a big welcoming kiss on my mouth. Marking her territory perhaps? Jolene had never exhibited a jealous side. Knew she didn't have to compete. But she did have a playful side. And she liked to play.

Nora observed this interaction, the same bemused expression on her face as the night before.

"Not so much from Mister. tightlipped here." She answered, tossing me a glance. She retuned her attention to Jolene, their eyes communicating something they both understood. Both turned their gaze on me, both now wearing similar amused expressions. "But the local folks I've interviewed have all said only good things about you," Nora said.

"Thank you. Nice to hear," Jolene said. "Why don't we get some drinks and sit outside? What will you have. It's Nora, right? I'm a wine fan myself."

"Wine will be fine."

"Terrific." She ushered Nora out to the verandah, leaving me to fix the drinks.

I decided the occasion called for something special. I selected a pricey Chateau Lafite Rothschild Pauillac from Jolene's collection, eavesdropping on the conversation continuing outside as I uncorked and poured it.

"So tell me, what've you been hearing about me?" Jolene asked.

"Small island. I've done my homework. Especially on members of the police involved in the investigations."

She hadn't answered Jolene's question. And Jolene not one to give up easily.

"Come on. Spill. Tell me what've you heard?" The playful Jolene in attendance.

"Maybe I'll save it for the interview," Nora said.

"If there is an interview."

"What do you mean?" Nora said. "I thought we....."

Jolene cut her off. "I do want to do this interview," she reassured Nora. "But I need to set some ground rules before we begin. Nothing I think you won't agree to. And anyway, Gage vouches for you. How did he put it? 'You're a good bet'."

I reached the verandah as Nora's laughter trailed off. I handed out the wineglasses.

"He makes me laugh," Nora finished.

"One of his many talents," Jolene agreed, touching her glass to Nora's and staring into her eyes.

"So before we get to dinner," Jolene said, "Why don't I tell you my ground rules, and if you still want to do the interview, fine. If not, we can still enjoy the evening and dinner together."

Nora set her wineglass down. "Okay. Let's hear it."

Jolene cupped her wineglass in her hands. Faced Nora. Made direct eye contact. "First," she said, A down to business edge in her voice "You can take notes, but no recorder. And no photographs."

"Not a problem," Nora said.

"Second. My personal, private life is off limits. And specifically, anything regarding Gage and our relationship. In fact, as far as anything you write is concerned, he doesn't exist."

"That doesn't surprise me," Nora said, glancing at me. "We've sorta had this conversation before. But your personal story might be important background for the article."

"My official profile, official record, anything about my life on the police force, is open for discussion. But my private personal life and Gage is nonnegotiable."

Nora considered a moment. "Okay," she said. "What else?"

"One last thing. How do I know you won't disregard our agreement once you've got your interview?"

Their eyes locked, taking each other's measure. I studied Nora's face. Read her eyes, mahogany in the subdued lighting.

"I swear I think mine is the only profession with a worse reputation than lawyers," she said. "I don't work like that. If I had a reputation for burning my sources just to slant a story, no one would ever talk to me."

Jolene glanced in my direction. Confirmation in my eyes. Nora hadn't lied.

"I've done my homework too," Jolene said. "You rep is pretty good. You're particular about who you write for and about editorial control. Tenacious when you catch a scent. Usually an angle no one else is covering. Not deadline-centric until you have the full story. Couple of prestigious awards. And I like your writing. Liked your article on Commissioner Daniels. Especially how you captured the atmosphere around the story."

"Thanks," Nora said, genuinely pleased, and astonished by Jolene's knowledge of her and her work.

Jolene didn't disclose one of her sources had been her brother. A foreign correspondent for a leading Canadian periodical. He and Nora had even crossed paths on one or two stories.

"The type of stories I do, the angles I'm interested in, aren't what the tabloids or cable networks want," Nora said. "Their only interest is capturing eyeballs. My interest is the story behind the story. By the way, how's Commissioner Daniels doing?"

"Are we already on the record here?" Jolene asked, sipping her wine. Her eyebrows arched as she tasted it, recognizing its expensive scent and flavor.

"Personal interest. I know he's close to both of you. But yeah, for the record too."

"Thanks for asking." Jolene said, the ice broken. Warming up to Nora. To this point they'd been circling each other like prizefighters in a ring.

"He's doing well," Jolene said. "We expect he'll be home soon."

In truth Mike's recuperation continued to surprise everyone. Better than expected. And Jolene and I were already planning his return. Sooner than most people realized. That bit of information we weren't ready to disclose publicly. Not yet.

"I suspect there's no truth to it," Nora said with uncharacteristic delicacy. "But how do you respond to the rumors about you and the Commissioner? That you only got to your current position by sleeping with him? You seem to have a preference for older men," she said, again glancing in my direction. The last remark a quick jab to elicit a reaction. I'd warned Jolene about Nora's tactic. She didn't take the bait.

"Just one," she said, smiling in my direction. "But to answer your question. Those rumors were probably started by elements in the Police Force opposed to Commissioner Daniels' appointment, and the changes he was brought in to make. And that he recruited more women and promoted them into traditionally male areas, like the CID. This is still a patriarchal culture, and that change, among others, didn't sit well with the old boys club. As to how I deal with it. I learned a long time ago not to allow such nonsense to distract me. And the old boys on the force have learned by now not to say it to my face."

"Anyone on the force in particular?"

"No comment. Doesn't matter anyway. The Commissioner had the backing of Government, and the changes occurred anyway, slowly, not easily, but eventually. Commissioner Daniels is a friend and mentor."

"Why did you join the police force?" Nora asked, changing tack. "Given your background, your education, and your looks by the way, you could've had a lucrative career in the States, or Canada. Probably as a model or actress."

"It seemed the right thing at the time," Jolene said, smiling. "A whim." Her customary response. "I figured it might be a way of contributing, here at home. Make a difference. God knows the salary when I joined couldn't support a goat. The work was meaningless and demeaning, and I was seriously thinking about leaving when Commissioner Daniels was appointed."

Nora eyed her skeptically. Her heightened perceptiveness sensing something odd in Jolene's response. Not buying the 'did it on a whim story' any more than Mike or I did.

Nora didn't pursue it. Instead, "What about your parents? What do they think about this career choice?"

A quick glance in my direction. Answered by a quick blink of my eyes. No more than a nanosecond. Nora caught the silent exchange anyway.

"I'm sorry," she said. "Off-limits?"

Jolene smiled. "Let's just say both my mother and father have always been supportive of me."

Nora nodded. They continued conversing through another round of wine. Jolene related her history on the Royal St. Vincent and the Grenadines Police Force; Commissioner Daniels; the battles they'd fought together to transform the Force; the reasoning behind many of those changes; the qualitative results vindicating those efforts.

I remained silent throughout their exchange; watching, admiring.

Eventually Jolene said, "Dinner's waiting. Let's continue this inside."

Jolene set out bowls of split pea soup before taking her seat at the table. A bowl of cornbread, another of sweet rolls, hot sauce, salt and pepper, sat on the table before us. The scents wafting from the table accelerated our appetites.

"This is just my curiosity," Nora said after a few spoonfuls. "Off the record. But how did you two meet?"

Jolene glanced in my direction. My response noncommittal.

"Through Mike, Commissioner Daniels. He introduced us. This pirate had been hanging around Bequia for a while, they were friends, and one day Mike invited me to go sailing with them. At the time I was consumed with work. Not in the least interested in a relationship. Not to say he wasn't attractive, but like you say, older. But after that day sailing I couldn't get him out of my mind. I was fascinated and intrigued."

"Intrigued. That's the perfect word," Nora said around another spoonful of soup. "He has no idea the effect he has on women, does he?" eyeing Jolene, a conspiratorial twinkle in her eyes.

"Sometimes I think he does," Jolene, playful co-conspirator, said. "He only lets on like he doesn't."

"I know what you mean," Nora said, glancing at me, returning her gaze to Jolene.

"I happen to be right here and can hear you, you know," I said, smiling. Taking no offense. Instead enjoying their interplay. Aware they'd both been trying to get a rise from me.

"Anyway," Jolene continued. "With Commissioner Daniels a common friend, we couldn't avoid running into each other. And one thing led to another. You know?"

"I can imagine," Nora said.

"It's been challenging," Jolene added. "But never dull. Always full of surprises."

"Not hard to imagine either," Nora said, still smiling, both women gazing at me.

Jolene removed the soup bowls. Returned carrying a large loaded serving bowl, and another containing a garden salad. She set them on the table.

"You're going to love this," She said to Nora. "It's a Vincentian specialty. Simple, but delicious."

"What is it?"

"It's called Pelau. Rice, black eye peas, chicken, and a bunch of other things all cooked together in coconut milk. And hot peppers usually, but this made mild for you. You can add pepper sauce if you want."

"It smells wonderful," Nora said, visibly inhaling the aroma. "I've got to tell you," after Jolene served her a large helping, "I've enjoyed local cooking since that first night on the boat....yacht," she said, correcting herself. "Before that I'd only order things on the hotel menu I recognized. But after the trip to Union Island I took Gage's advice and started sampling more of the traditional cuisine. I've had some fantastic meals."

For some reason both were staring at me again. But soon the Pelau had our complete attention. The rice and peas just the right soft, succulent consistency. The chopped chicken lifted effortlessly off the bone, melting in the mouth. Complemented by the sweet taste of plantains.

Nora ate as she had at Winston's. Her pleasure obvious. Jolene's helping smaller than mine or Nora's. She ate small bite sized forkfuls in between conversation.

At one point Nora asked. "How do you respond to the criticism leveled at the police force regarding whether you're up to handling the investigations? How's it affecting the force? Their morale?"

"The CID is investigating about a dozen cases right now," Jolene said. They don't get the visiting media's attention. They're of no interest to the outside world. But there're just as important to us. We may not have all the resources, or the expertise, but we've come a long way since Commissioner Daniels took over. And we have some smart, professional investigators. They resent the way they've been portrayed."

"So how would you characterize the current status of the three major cases, the shooting of the Commissioner, the Sarah Holmes case, and this latest shooting? Which you guys still haven't officially confirmed. By the way, have you identified the victim?"

Another Nora tactic. A quick succession of questions. Like a boxer's punch combination. Designed to throw the interviewee off balance. Give them little time to think. Time only to react. But I'd prepared Jolene for it. She ducked.

"At this point we're not making any public statements about the specifics of those investigations. What I can say concerning the Commissioner's shooting is we have a lot of physical evidence from the scene, and we're pursuing some promising leads."

"In my experience that response usually means you don't actually have anything."

Jolene smiled. "Be that as it may, it's all I'm prepared to say."

"And the Sarah Holmes case? Do you believe you'll be able to solve that case?"

"To be honest, the trail's gone cold. We still don't know what may have happened to her. We don't have a body or a crime scene to investigate. But we have a ton of information to keep us busy. And we're sharing information with the FBI and other police forces in the region. The FBI is working the case from the stateside end. We're working the local end. We're following any leads developed from any of that information. We've had reports of sightings on Martinique, in Miami, Guyana, even Canada. The FBI has been running down those reports."

"How has the cooperation with the FBI been?" Nora asked. "The news has been reporting a great deal of friction and lack of cooperation. And you guys appear reluctant to ask for their help."

"We did enlist their help from early in the investigation," Jolene said. "The public squabbling has been unfortunate and provided fodder for cable news chatter. But privately, the relationship has been cordial, cooperative and beneficial."

"Do you think she's still alive?"

"We're still investigating this as a missing person. As I said we have no body. No crime scene. No indication of what may have happened to her. Or any evidence to suggest foul play or otherwise."

"What do you believe, personally?"

"Can't answer that Nora," Jolene said. "I don't have the luxury of speculating. And whatever I say, officially or unofficially, is going to send one kind of signal or the other to everyone involved, the media, the family, the public, the FBI, the perpetrator or perpetrators, if they exist."

"Off the record," Nora persisted.

Jolene picked up her wineglass, took a sip, glanced at me. Her attention back on Nora. Contemplative. Her brow furrowed in thought. Avocado hued eyes locked on bourbon brown.

"I honestly don't know," Jolene said finally, without elaborating. She took a big swallow of wine.

Nora wore an expression of uncertainty. Probably perceiving her interviewee had held something back. Something she sensed as being important.

The conversation slash interview wound through dinner, dessert, coffee back on the verandah. Well into the cool tropical night. A light breeze rustled the branches overhead, and spread the subtle fragrance of wild flowers. The moon arced across a star speckled sky, creating light and shadow across the lawn.

I observed their back and forth, like a spectator at a tennis match. Their earlier sparring a thing of the past. Despite the obvious boundaries I sensed they liked each other. Shared a kindred spirit. When not discussing the case they conversed like lifelong girlfriends.

Nora had been thorough, probing, building her understanding of the three cases, fleshing out the personalities and details involved; the obstacles frustrating a solution. Her questions followed a logical line of reasoning. She linked the three cases, impressive, a premise Jolene neither confirmed nor denied. For her part Jolene had been straightforward and candid, but revealing only as much as she intended.

In the wee hours, not long until dawn, while I cleared the kitchen and took care of the dishes, Jolene offered Nora her guestroom.

"Thanks, but I need to get back. I'll be up working anyway. I want to start writing up my notes while everything's still fresh."

"When do you think your article will be published?" Jolene asked.

"Considering everything we covered, I'm thinking it'll be a series of articles. From different perspectives. At least three. Maybe four."

"Well, I have to tell you I enjoyed the evening," Jolene said, standing next to Nora on the verandah before parting. "It was such a pleasure meeting you." She wrapped her arms around Nora, squeezing her in a friendly good-bye hug.

The gesture caught Nora by surprise. But she reciprocated. "Same here," she said.

"And while you're on Bequia, don't be a stranger," Jolene said. "Anything you need let me know.

"Thanks. I may have some follow-ups once I begin writing."

Jolene kissed me on the mouth before asking, "Coming back or staying aboard?"

"You have to be up in a couple of hours," I said. "I'll sleep aboard. I'll see you later."

"Love you," she said, planting another kiss before heading inside.

Shore transportation unavailable at that hour, I ferried Nora across the bay by dinghy. I helped her out onto the jetty at the Hamilton Marina. Walked her to her room.

"You're a good man, just Gage. And she's a lucky woman," she said, soft lips touching my cheek. She turned and entered the room. Closed the door behind her.

CHAPTER 13

The first of Nora's articles appeared a week later in the International Herald and USA Today under the AP tag. The day I departed for St. Lucia. The article detailed the current state of the investigations, providing background on Commissioner of Police Michael Daniels, Superintendent of Police Jolene Johanssen, and the Royal St. Vincent and the Grenadines Police Force's Criminal Investigation Division. Nora covered the shooting and the disappearance of Sarah Holmes in detail, including the current status of both investigations.

Interspersed throughout the article she illuminated the impact both cases, and the attendant media coverage, were having on the local community and police force. The details of those aspects to be featured in later articles in the series. She accurately summarized mistakes made in the investigation, without being judgmental. And illuminated the difficulties faced by the investigators, including the scarcity of resources, and the lack of a body or crime scene in the Sarah Holmes's disappearance.

She detailed inaccuracies in the cable news coverage, characterizing their reporting as misinformed and misleading.

She enumerated specific examples where reported details were inaccurate, and clarified them.

Overall, an example of informative journalism, accomplishing much of what Mike had intended. An accurate account of what had been done and not done; the possible and not possible; the known and unknown. And cleaning up Coffe's mess.

Other news outlets, including the cable networks which had already packed up and departed Bequia, commented on the article. Used it to fill truncated segments on the Sarah Holmes story. The disappearance by then old news. The anchors interviewed their usual 'experts' to provide analysis aimed at 'helping viewers understand' the latest information. As if anyone reading the article weren't capable of understanding it for themselves. Characteristically followed by a new round of uninformed punditry and speculation.

The day bright beneath a scorching sun. The clouds like swaths of white paint smeared across the sky. An intense glare reflected from every surface, causing eyes to squint; making the green landscape greener; the bright rooftops brighter; the Bay more sparkling, its colors blended seamlessly from light green along the beach, to aquamarine in the channel, cobalt where it merged into the Caribbean Sea.

Rodney released Wherever's mooring line. A Northeast wind in the offing, blowing lighter across Bequia's protected inshore bays.

I had a charter. A young German couple, mid-twenties, unmarried. Peter tall, lanky, blond, blue eyes and melanin challenged fair skin which had turned a fierce red in the tropical sun. Kristin in contrast, long brown hair erotically tangled by wind and salt. Long, shapely legs, the firm sexy figure of youth. Provocative in a bikini. Skin that bronzed rather than reddened in the sun. No Arian purity there, I mused. Perhaps a bit of Mediterranean Europe in her gene pool.

They'd been on holiday in the Grenadines, hiking, camping, exploring the islands, making their way around inexpensively. They, or at least Kristin, the type to end up remaining on Bequia. It required only the means to support oneself, and a return ticket out of the country. Peter might fit comfortably into the small German expatriate community on Bequia. Kristin not so much I figured. Too much of a free spirit. I'd offered them passage to St. Lucia, the last leg of their tropical vacation, from where they'd fly home.

Wherever fell off the wind. Her bow swung around, the light wafting breeze on her starboard side, catching and filling her hoisted mainsail. I hauled on the mainsheet until the huge sail bellied out and drew. Wherever skipped forward.

Rodney hoisted the foresail as Wherever glided out of Lower Bay into Admiralty Bay proper. Her staysail and jib followed. Her sheets taut and sails filled, Wherever broad reached out of the harbor until we rounded Devil's Table and Northwest Point.

My guests sat in the cockpit. They weren't technically a charter, since they weren't paying. More like hitchhiking. I needed a credible cover for sailing to St. Lucia. And I wanted a couple of days at sea to think. Time to piece the puzzle together. I had no idea if I had the key pieces. Or what the pieces even looked like, much less any idea of the whole picture.

We lay over in Wallilabou Bay on St. Vincent's sheltered leeward coast, the western side of the island. Once a quiet deserted anchorage, the bay had been transformed by the Pirates of the Caribbean movies which had used it as the primary shooting location. Movie sets depicting early nineteenth century buildings erected in a corner of the Bay drew tourists to the once secluded anchorage. Now Wallilabou Bay provided docking and mooring facilities, yacht services, a small hotel, restaurant and bar, and the attendant 'boat boys' hawking fruit, souvenirs, anything they could get their hands on. Stolen dinghies and yacht break ins had also increased.

Once a favored layover of mine, I'd have avoided it altogether if not for Peter and Kristin. The stopover provided them the opportunity to visit the movie sets, and Wallilabou falls farther inland. We dropped anchor by midafternoon, allowing ample time for their visit ashore before evening set in.

Rodney served as guide for the hike through the countryside, introducing them to the pleasures of sugarcane, mangoes, and other indigenous fruit found in abundance along the way. I used the time alone to commence piecing together the puzzle.

Later, Peter and Kristin back on board, the sun sinking toward the horizon, rum and cokes flowing freely, we watched the western sky glow crimson and mauve as the last vestige of daylight disappeared. The sky faded to black. Stars twinkled on. A handful at first, followed by more; countless more, until the pinpoints of light filled the black canopy above.

"Where did Rodney go?" Kristin asked in her soft accented voice. Both spoke English, slightly accented. When they lapsed into their native language I still understood their conversation, but didn't let on I spoke German.

"To arrange dinner ashore," I said. "You guys like local cooking?"

" I love the local foods," Kristin gushed. Peter merely smiled.

An odd pairing. I liked them both. But on the surface I didn't understand their attraction. Kristin friendly, extroverted, eager to try new things, a bit of a tease. Peter the opposite, introverted, given to quiet brooding.

Instead of the hotel at the anchorage, we ate at a local kitchen slash café off the main road in Wallilabou. I knew the family who owned it. Relatives of Winston. I preferred spending my money there. The tourist revenue from Wallilabou's newfound popularity not reaching many beyond the bay. Dinner entailed hot fish soup and flour dumplings, Jerk Chicken served with rice and peas, boiled greens bananas and plantains. Delicious and filling.

Later, well into the night, I sat propped by pillows on the bed in the master cabin. My laptop open beside me. A package of CDs labeled in Jolene's small handwriting and two flash drives beside it. Peter and Kristin remained on deck. Rodney asleep in the forecastle. Wherever secured for the night by a stern line run ashore to a stout coconut tree.

I picked through the CDs, contemplating where to begin. I eyed the flash drive containing the Daniels case file. I'd browsed through it before. Nothing there to shed any new light. I needed a lead. A single reference point to build on. The corner piece of the puzzle.

I needed to sift the raw intel myself. Develop my own feel for the ground. The players. The unseen variables. Uncertain of what I might be searching for. Hoping I'd recognize it when I saw it. Something out of place. A piece that didn't fit. Didn't belong. An anomaly. Maybe an obscure pattern underlying everything that had occurred. Experience assured me the picture would eventually emerge. A piece here, another piece over there, a seemingly unrelated piece corroborating a piece from somewhere else.

I knew how, when, and where Mike had been shot. I still didn't know the who, or the why. I'd seen nothing in the files linking Mike and the missing Sarah Holmes. But we had a confirmed link between her and at least one shooter. I put that piece aside for the moment.

I opened one of several CD jewel cases labeled 'Holmes Pictures'. I popped a disc into the laptop's drive. Opened a photo slide show application. Scrolled through the images on the disc. I'd been through the images before. I scanned them again for anything I may have missed the first time around.

After 40 minutes, a few more CDs, hundreds of images, and a nettlesome gnat-like buzzing around my brain, the pesky elusive thought swam into focus. All of Sarah's photos appeared ordinary, snapshots taken by an ordinary tourist. But observed another way, the photos had the flavor of a recon. Exactly the types of photos I'd want to study if I were scouting locations and the geography of the Grenadines. Which raised the question of what had Sarah Holmes been doing in the Grenadines.

I heard Peter and Kristin heading forward to the guest cabin as I inserted the Sarah Holmes case file flash drive into the USB port. I spent the next hour getting better acquainted with Sarah Holmes. At least the data compiled in the file. I scrutinized it with a skeptical eye.

Age thirty-five. Born and raised in Madison Wisconsin. After graduating High School she moved east to attend

Columbia University in New York City. She also attended Grad school there, obtaining a Master's Degree in Business. At the time of her disappearance she worked as a senior manager with Global Investments LLC, a boutique Wall Street investment bank. Considered a rising star in the field. Old, stale information. Nothing I hadn't known before.

Single. Dated periodically. No reports of a steady significant other. She traveled widely as a senior accounts executive for the firm. Ostensibly on a vacation cruise, she'd boarded the Nordic Star in Miami. Disappeared without a trace from Bequia. She had a connection to the dead shooter in Industry. He had her picture on his cell phone. Maybe in order to identify her. He was dead. Odds are so was she.

A significant piece of the puzzle remained obscure, the name whispered in the Florida Everglades. Eduardo Alonzo Ramirez. Nefarious head of a Columbian Drug Cartel. Wanted by the Columbian, Mexican, and U.S governments. The U.S had a standing bounty of five million dollars for his capture, or death. Mendez had emailed me a file. Preliminary. The file since augmented by new data when Mike had also tapped his sources after being read in. A burgeoning dossier compiled by DEA, FBI, DoD and Interpol sources. I'd have access to it soon.

I'd googled the name upon returning from Miami. Had been surprised by the large number of links to newspaper articles and other sources, even a Wikipedia page. I'd cut and pasted from these open sources and put it together with the material Mendez had emailed me to compile a tentative profile. Mendez hadn't exaggerated. Ramirez a nasty piece of work. My kind of guy. But exactly how his piece fitted in the puzzle remained elusive.

Morning. Another bright, hot day. I weighed anchor after landing Rodney ashore to make his way back to Bequia. After disembarking my guests on St. Lucia I had a rendezvous I needed to keep alone. My supposed charter a cover for the rendezvous.

The passage north to St. Lucia promised to be slow, long, and tedious. Except for the crossing between St. Vincent and St. Lucia, we'd be motoring most of the trip. No wind in the lee of St. Vincent's mountainous topography. Any breeze reaching us at all would be light, variable, and ineffective. It'd make sailing a futile exercise; a fond unfulfilled wish.

Wherever's Ford Lehman diesel hummed contentedly. She didn't like it. Didn't like being pushed by a mechanical beast and a bronze screw beneath her. She plod ahead uncomplaining at a sedate six knots, biding her time.

Playing tour guide, I pointed out sights of interest ashore to Peter and bikini clad Kristin. The landmarks ashore served a more important purpose, indicating our progress along the coast. That in turn indicated the tidal current, now running against us. We might be moving at six knots through the water, but only three or four over the bottom.

Wherever had instruments to provide such information in precise, technological, digital detail. I preferred sailing 'au natural', using instruments only when in instrument conditions. I didn't need instruments to confirm a long, tedious slog ahead.

The day wore on, accompanied by the diesel's muffled drone. The midday sun cast its scorching heat upon the land, the sea, the air, the searing deck; reaching its zenith as we neared the passage separating the two islands.

The long, slow crawl along the coast had allowed Peter and Kristin to practice at the helm. Kristin loved it. She took long delightful turns steering while Peter sat in the cockpit, disinterested. I coached her. Answered her enthusiastic questions. Got her to a decent point of competence. I'd need that competence when I went forward to make sail in the passage. The point of the entire exercise.

Approaching the passage I handed Kristin the wheel. I hoisted the mainsail. Made my way forward to the foremast, hauled up the foresail. By the time I had the jib up, small, aching twinges inched up my lower back. Barely noticeable. But enough to remind me of the passage of years.

I relieved Kristin at the helm as Wherever crept past the last bit of St. Vincent. Entering the channel the northeast wind caught and filled Wherever's flogging sails. She leapt ahead like a stallion catching the scent of a mare in heat. She put her port side down. Deck angled twenty degrees. Her sharp bow sliced the oncoming swells, throwing spray to either side. Tiny rainbows formed and disappeared as sea spray cascaded across her foredeck. Heeled onto her side she surged ahead for St. Lucia.

I trimmed her sails, easing her motion. She settled into a steady pace through the windswept sea. I kept the engine running, throttling it back, allowing me to point her a few degrees higher into the wind, countering the strong wind and current pushing us westward. I didn't want to be too far offshore when I made landfall on St. Lucia's southwestern coast.

Wherever galloped north, shouldering aside rolling mounds of water. The wheel alive in my hands. I ruminated on one Eduardo Alonzo Ramirez, aka el cuchillo - the knife. Fifty years old. In the drug trade most of his adult life, beginning as an enforcer and assassin for another big time drug trafficker. Acquired his alias due to a sadistic preference for bladed weapons. He liked to slice and dice his victims.

He'd risen to power in a cartel operating out of Northern Columbia. The Columbian Government, working with U.S agencies, had decimated the senior ranks of the older cartels through arrests, extraditions, and a few strategic clandestine assassinations. A long running, vicious war between cartel factions did the rest. Columbia and the U.S had targeted Ramirez as the new head of the Norte del Valle faction.

The Norte del Valle group itself grew out of the breakup of the Cali and Medellin cartels. Those cartels had wreaked havoc during the seventies and eighties. Surviving lieutenants, realizing large organizations were vulnerable to attack by the authorities, formed smaller more controllable groups having compartmentalized responsibilities. One group controlled production. Another transportation of the coca base from the fields. Another production in jungle labs. Another smuggled the drugs. And yet another controlled distribution.

At the top of the heap, Ramirez, who'd ordered a hit on my friend. A mistake which meant the end of his world. He just didn't know it yet. But I still didn't see the connection to Mike. Most of the Columbian and Argentinean cocaine headed for the States and Europe moved through the Caribbean. What did that have to do with Mike? A targeted hit meant they needed Mike out of the way. Or else Mike had been in the wrong place at the wrong time. In any case all the suspects so far connected back to drug trafficking. Where did Sarah Holmes fit into that picture?

Almost through the passage. The twin peaks of St. Lucia's Pitons loomed in the distance. The first signs of luffing shook the sails. Wherever's motion eased. Her head fell off as the southern coast of St. Lucia blanketed the wind and sea to starboard.

The sails slack and flogging, I asked Kristen to take the wheel while I lowered, furled and tied them down. St. Lucia's shoreline a stone toss to starboard. White beaches and waving coconut branches bathed by the afternoon sun. Lush, green, rolling hills ascended from the shore, rising three thousand feet to end in two pyramid shaped peaks, Gros Piton and its twin Petit Piton. Iconic landmarks welcoming visitors to St. Lucia, whether by sea or by air.

Three hours later I eased Wherever alongside Doolittle's dock in Marigot Bay. I hopped ashore and secured her lines to the dock, a line at the bow, one at the stern, and a forward spring.

I left Peter and Kristin below packing while I headed ashore to the immigration office. A uniformed immigration officer sat at a small wooden desk in the tiny immigration and customs shack at the end of the dock. I recognized him when he raised his head to see who had entered. His dark face turned from an annoyed scowl to a broad smile when he recognized me.

"Gage, mahn, yuh back agane." He put aside the outdated, excessively thumbed People Magazine he'd been reading, . "How long yuh stayin dis time?"

"Just dropping off a chartah. Leaving dis evening."

One of two officers who regularly manned the Marigot Bay office, Joseph, twenty-five or twenty-six, had the tall, thin build of a long-distance runner. Quick to smile and laugh, the tedium of his job sometimes buried his exuberant vivacious nature. Like many of his contemporaries he possessed a single-minded desire to immigrate to the United States, immersing himself in U.S culture. An immersion extending only as far as music, television shows, movies, tee shirts and jeans.

"Wheh yuh passenjahs?"

"On board packing. Dey staying at Doolittle's. Flying out tomorrow.

"Yu jus in time. I was gwoin close." He plucked a bag with a shoulder strap from a wall peg behind the desk. Slung the bag over his shoulder. He accompanied me along the dock to Wherever.

Peter and Kristin waited in the cockpit, backpacks at their feet. Joseph swung over the rail. Stepping down into the cockpit he greeted them.

"Sah, miss. Welcome to St. Lucia," he said, touching the brim of his peaked uniform cap.

Joseph set his bag on the cockpit table and asked, "Dese is all yur luggage?"

When they replied in the affirmative, Joseph asked, "Please to jus open dat one and dat one," pointing to the backpacks in the cockpit. "I'll jus tek a quick look." He performed a cursory examination without disturbing their belongings.

While they zippered the backpacks I handed Joseph the three passports, my passengers, and my own, bearing the Nicholas Gage identity. He gave the passports a similarly cursory examination, pulled a stamp and inkpad from the shoulder bag, stamped all three and handed them back to me.

I handed Peter and Kristin their passports and we said our goodbyes on the dock. A long tight hug from Kristin.

Joseph headed through the hatch down to the main salon, ostensibly to complete his customs check of the vessel. I followed him down, headed for the galley. I opened a cold red stripe, handed it to him. He walked forward, glancing into the guest and forecastle cabins. He returned to the salon. Made himself comfortable at the dinette, foregoing an inspection of the aft master cabin. Wherever and I a known quantity, frequently transiting in and out of St. Lucia.

I emerged from the aft cabin, handed him an unopened bottle of Wray and Nephew dark rum, a New York Giants tee shirt, and the latest Jay Z CD, brand new and unopened.

"Till nex time," I said.

His face lit up like a light bulb. His smile stretched from ear to ear, unveiling two perfect rows of pearl white teeth. He finished his beer, packed away the items I'd brought him. We shook hands at the companionway and he took his leave.

I crawled onto the aft berth and went directly to sleep.

A strong breeze, bearing the scent of rain, blew across Marigot Bay when I climbed on deck. Nighttime. A handful of stars visible in a dark sky blanketed by large swathes of dense black clouds. Perfect conditions for my rendezvous.

I donned black foul weather gear over black jeans, black long sleeved tee shirt, and black ski cap. I fired up Wherever's diesel. I untied her lines and eased her away from the well-lit dock. Clear of Marigot Bay I turned south. The sky's floodgates opened. The deluge reduced visibility to an arm's length. The first squall passed quickly. More to come.

I continued south through the black night. Wherever's running lights cast an eerie glow in the dark. The squalls came and went, moving east to west. Rain fell by the bucketful. Marble sized drops pelted Wherever's woodwork, providing a welcomed freshwater wash. After two more hours I doused her lights. Made the turn toward Vieux Fort harbor.

Invisible   in the black night I headed for my rendezvous.

CHAPTER 14

Wherever buried her bowsprit in an oncoming swell. Moments later her bow reared skyward from beneath the dark sea, flinging gallons of seawater onto her foredeck. She rose and dove with a steady, measured, living rhythm, caught in the lumpy, disorderly convergence of Atlantic and Caribbean waters in the bottleneck between St. Lucia to the north, and the soaring cliffs of St. Vincent to the south.

At the eastern end of the passage Wherever entered the Atlantic Ocean. The sea regained some normalcy. But unlike the gentle waves and calm breezes on the leeward side of St. Vincent, gale force winds lashed the windward side. Atlantic waves pounded its steep rocky coast.

St. Vincent lay in shadow to starboard. A wicked lee shore. Wherever clawed her way from it, like prey making a desperate dash from a stalking predator. The ocean held the schooner in its grasp, inexorably pushing her toward St. Vincent's jagged coast. Wherever beat eastward, gaining sea room, putting distance between her and the killer shore. Her bow plunged and split the dark water, rising to throw it aside, white and foaming. Salt spray flew back from her bow, sometimes reaching the cockpit. I had the deck to myself. The main hatch secured against sea and rain, no cabin light spilled into the cockpit. My vision had adjusted to the dark world around us.

Mike, Max and Mendez were below stowing their gear, settling in. Jolene in the galley whipping up something to eat. My emotions upon encountering Mike, gaunt, but on his feet, moving under his own steam, almost fully recovered, had surprised me. Emotions dormant for so long I'd considered them nonexistent. A distant memory. Their stirring like something new. An experience I didn't recognize.

The rendezvous and transfer had proceeded according to plan. Only a tight circle of eight people aware of Mike's return, including the Prime Ministers of St. Vincent and the Grenadines, and St. Lucia, who were cousins. They'd arranged Mike's transit through St. Lucia, forgoing the usual immigration and customs formalities. Jolene had flown up earlier to coordinate the arrangements. The private jet I'd arranged had landed after dark at Hewanorra, the international airport on St. Lucia 's southeastern end. The airport already closed for the night. Jolene had met Mike, Max and Mendez on the tarmac. She'd driven them the short distance to Vieux Fort, where Wherever had lain waiting.

I'd considered flying Mike's Piper Seneca the short distance between Bequia and St. Lucia. Mike had suggested sailing. He'd said he wanted to brief us all as a group before arriving on Bequia. But I figured he craved the openness of a sea voyage after being confined for so many weeks. And the sea air would do him good. Also there were security advantages to arriving by sea.

I savored the solitude on deck. Absorbed the transcendent magic of wind, sea, and sails. I gazed up at the sails, at Wherever's taut rigging. I peered under the boom at

St. Vincent's ever-present lee shore. Over my shoulder a green phosphorescent trail illuminated Wherever's serpentine wake. On my left, to port, white lines visible in the inky dark marked the tops of breaking swells hurtling towards us.

The main hatch opened. Max's wide shoulders and large torso filled the opening, blocking the light from below. He angled his shoulders diagonally as he emerged. Accustomed to tight spaces aboard ship, especially submarines. A competent hand in almost any kind of vessel.

"How's it going?" he said, his voice soft, mellifluous. He sidled into the cockpit next to me. A scraggy growth shadowed the lower half of his face. Like the latest masculine fashion trend. Though on Max not a fashion statement, representing instead days in the field. Shaving an afterthought. A similar stubble covered the lower half of my face. Shaving a chore I performed irregularly, most times waiting until my facial hair threatened to turn into a full on beard.

"Great," I said. "How's it going below?"

"Settled in okay. Great ride you've got here boss," his admiring gaze sweeping the deck and up at Wherever's sails. "Your lady friend's a keeper too," his smile complimentary. "She's got hot chow waiting, and the commish is ready to brief you. I got this."

"Okay. She's trimmed and running true. She'll let you know if anything's off. Hold this course for now." I opened a watertight compartment on the pedestal below the instruments. "Intercom," I pointed. "Third button is the salon. Call if you need anything." I closed the compartment and stepped to the high side of the cockpit. Max relieved me at the helm, taking the wheel in practiced hands. I smiled at his parting word as I stepped to the hatch. "Sweet."

At the bottom of the companionway steps I peeled off the foul weather gear. I hung the jacket and pants in a wet locket behind the companionway. Mike, Jo and Max sat on the settee in the starboard lounge. Manila files folders rested on the gimbaled coffee table before them.

"Hot soup on the stove," Jolene called.

The aroma of fish soup permeated the cabin and galley, emanating from a large pot securely clamped to the gimbaled stove, its lid locked in place. I braced myself in the moving galley, my right hip against the counter next to the stove, my left leg extended across the narrow space to the opposite counter. My position perpendicular to the canted deck. I ladled a bowlful of the delicious smelling concoction, ensuring I'd taken a hearty helping of fish, dumplings and bananas with the broth.

I sat on the high side of the U-shaped settee, facing the others. My back cushioned against a pile of throw pillows. My feet braced against the heavy bamboo legs of the mahogany coffee table bolted to the deck. The table's raised edges kept the files from sliding off as it gimbaled back and forth.

Sounds of Wherever under sail filled the cabin. Water sluiced along her side inches from where we sat. Her taut rigging twanged like bowstrings. Her keel stepped masts creaked under the strain. Rolling hills of water smacked against her bow, sounding like the inside of a bass drum. She reared and bucked and plunged like a wild stallion.

"So here's what we've got right now," Mike said, plucking a folder from the table. "Your guys already know all this," he said, indicating Mendez and glancing at me. He pulled an eight-by ten glossy photo from the file. Handed it to Jolene.

"Frank Tesca. The guy killed in Industry. I don't remember seeing him before I got shot. And the weapon found on him wasn't a match for the slugs they took from me. But the slugs pulled from him were a match. So we still have a person out there responsible for both shootings."

Jolene passed the photo to me.

"We found nothing at the house in Industry" she said. "But he had another rental in Villa on St. Vincent. We found personal effects including airline tickets and an American passport in the room. He arrived a week before Mike's shooting. American Airlines out of Miami, connecting with LIAT in Barbados. We have him on camera passing through customs and immigration at Arnos Vale. The place in Villa and the one in Industry were both booked in advance through a company named...." she fished through a file for a sheet of paper. "Futures Capital, based in Las Vegas Nevada."

"We ran that down," Mike said. "It's a small investment company. No information yet on their financials, investment portfolios, or clients. But I have someone working on that for me. Tesca is listed as a security officer with the corporation."

"Guy's a shooter," Mendez stated. "He's on the DEA's radar for a couple of bodies in New York, and a car bombing in Miami. They believe he's affiliated with Ramirez and the Norte del Valle Cartel.

"So this Vegas company isn't kosher," I said. "It's a cover. And he wasn't here on vacation. So what was he doing on St. Vincent and Bequia?"

"Don't know," Mike answered. "JJ had CID put together a timeline of his movements. But there're too many holes in it to tell us anything significant. I don't remember seeing him before or during the shooting. The guy I spotted seemed like he was waiting for someone. But I only caught a glimpse before he disappeared. Like he made me at the same time I made him. When I approached the spot, suddenly he was in front of me with the weapon already in his hand"

His voice changed audibly, hesitant, acquiring a distant tone. His gaze unfocussed, turned inward, probing his still fuzzy memory as he recounted the experience out loud.

"I'm pretty sure it had a silencer," he finished in a soft, distant voice.

"You okay Mike?" Jolene asked, the first to voice our concern. Her hand rested lightly on Mike's arm.

"Yeah... yeah. Okay," he said, shaking off the emotion. But his eyes remained haunted. "I didn't see the gun because of the angle. He just brought it up and fired. Next thing I remember is waking up in a hospital in Miami. The face is just a blur. Either I was focusing too much on the weapon, or I'm just blocking it out. Sometimes I just start to bring it into focus, then like smoke it's gone."

Jolene's eyes, wide, expressing her care and concern, never wavered from his face.

"Explains why no one heard the shots," I said.

"You don't remember making it to the road. Using your cell. Calling the station?" the concern in Jolene's eyes also in her voice.

"No." he said softly.

"Still you reacted quickly enough to save your life Mike," I said, a mixture of sympathy and admiration in my voice. "All three shots seemed targeted at center mass. You took them off center. Means you were moving. Turning away. Reducing the target profile. A ricochet caused the most damage."

Wherever shuddered under the impact of a wave on her bow. The deep bass sound resonated through the cabin. She staggered. I sensed her head falling off. My eyes involuntarily lifted toward the deck above me. She lunged forward, heeled far over on her side, almost sending everything on the table flying. She rose on a swell, her bow swinging back on course. I returned to my bowl of soup. Not a drop spilled.

"So this guy's here in advance," Mendez said. "Waiting for someone or something. Maybe part of a team. Maybe the opposition. The shooter who killed him may be cleaning up after what went down. Chief here walked into their business and all. Didn't know it was the Commissioner of Police until after."

"But why stick around?" Jolene asked. "Why didn't Tesca and this other person just take off?"

"Because shooting Mike created a couple of problems," I said, picking up on Mendez's theory. "The shooter hadn't completed his primary objective. He had to make sure the shooting didn't expose that objective. It'd explain the run at Mike in Miami, and me here."

"And when that doesn't work, a cleaner comes in," Mendez added.

"Maybe," I said. "But I'm not sure it tracks. Why kill him here? That only draws more attention. The smart move would've been to extract him then make him disappear."

"And we still don't know what his primary objective was," Mendez said.

"The only lead we have is that photo of Sarah Holmes on his cell phone," Mike said. "Maybe she was the primary objective. The photo so he could identify her."

"That's going to be your number one problem when you get back Mike," Jolene said. "Most of the news horde packed up and left. But the stragglers are still looking for answers we don't have. At least nothing we can go public with."

"We'll let the articles pave that road for us,' Mike said. "What's her name again? The reporter? Met with me in Miami too."

"Nora, Nora Austin," Jolene said.

"Yeah, Nora. Exactly what we needed. That was good work JJ. Let the articles speak for us until we're ready to say more."

"This Tesca guy have any connection to Calderon, or Ramirez?" I asked, finishing the last spoonful of soup.

"Who're Calderon and Ramirez?" Jolene asked.

"Philippe Calderon was the Miami drug guy who tried to have me killed in Miami," Mike answered. "Ramirez heads a Columbian drug cartel that supplies Calderon. According to Calderon, Ramirez asked him to do the hit."

"Gage never told me the names," she said, her gaze resting on me.

"Probably the best thing," Mike said. "And we still need to keep those names under wraps for now."

"Where does all this leave us?" she asked.

"Well, all the characters popping up in this thing indicate drugs, and where there's drugs there's money. In my experience when you have drugs and money, you follow either, or both. Between my contacts in Florida, and Mendez's contacts in the DEA, we can follow the drugs. I called in some favors that'll help us follow the money. Should have some results soon."

"I also have contacts following both," I said, without elaborating. "But two questions we need to get off the table first. Actually an observation and a question."

"How does Sarah Holmes fit into all this?" Jolene prompted.

"That's still an open question," I said. "But not the one I had in mind. The observation is Mike's right. Drugs and money go together. All the players are connected to drugs. Sarah's connected to money. Tesca is connected to both drugs and money. Doesn't prove anything, but maybe it paints a picture. What do we know about her beyond what's in the file?"

"Nothing much," Mike said. "I got a copy of the FBI file. They've done most of the background stuff on her stateside. She's smart, savvy, a go-getter, competitive, ambitious. I guess she had to be to make it in that world."

"I'm not sure the FBI file will provide any answers," I said. "Our best bet is to follow the money. Can you get your contacts to dig deeper into her firm, Global Investments. See if there's a connection to Futures Capital."

"What about while she was in the Grenadines?" Mike asked. "Anything there?"

"I retraced her steps in the Grenadines." I said. "If there was a pattern I didn't see it. But I must have triggered something because it was after that trip Tesca got interested in me. Or he may've just been covering the bases."

"Covering the bases?" Jolene said.

"Yeah. Mike had to be taken care of first. Then me. Then you next," I said turning to her. "And maybe even Nora."

"Merde," she said, absorbing the implication.

"Yeah," I said.

She fell silent, thoughts churning behind animated eyes. Returning to the present she said, "On our end, except for the photo we haven't been able to connect Sarah Holmes or anyone she came in contact with to Tesca."

"I went through her photos again," I said. "Something interesting there, maybe."

"Like what?" she said.

"They could be recon photos."

Jolene almost sprang out of the settee. "What?"

Mike's eyes weren't focused on anything in the immediate vicinity. I pictured wheels turning in his head.

Mendez wore his 'nothing surprises me' expression.

When Mike returned from his silent ruminations, he turned to me. "You said you also had a question."

"Huh?"

"You said you had an observation and a question."

"Right. Something we need to rule out. Are you, or were you, working on anything with Caricom, OAS, the Feds or Interpol, that would've made you a target?"

"No. I've thought about that. There're no specific cases. We're constantly passing intelligence back and forth, mostly forth and not a lot of back. Just routine reports. But since you mention it, I can tell you there's growing concern in the U.S about an increase in trafficking through the Eastern Caribbean.

"How so?" I prompted.

Mike sighed, pushing his frame, less bulky since the shooting, deeper into the soft settee cushions. Wherever bucked wildly beneath us, absorbing the onslaught of another huge swell. Mike raised his large hands to his face and rubbed his eyes. Jolene's concern reappeared. But Mike had merely been gathering his thoughts.

"Where to begin?" he said to no one in particular. He lowered his hands from his face, leaned forward, just as Wherever took another blow on her shoulder.

"Okay, from the beginning. During the late seventies and eighties, the Medellin and Cali drug cartels established networks of smuggling routes throughout the Caribbean, culminating in Haiti, the Dominican Republic, the Bahamas, Puerto Rico and finally the South Florida coast. They used a variety of techniques to smuggle their product to the States. You're probably a lot more familiar with that than I am," Mike said, his gaze directed at Mendez.

He continued, not expecting an answer from Mendez.

"The smaller islands in the Eastern Caribbean were used as stepping-stones for drop off points farther north. Thousands of tons of cocaine moved through the Caribbean to the States. Then the activity fell off when the Cartels were dismantled in the early nineties. Mexican cartels took over the trade and the shipping routes shifted, moving through Mexico and across the US southern border."

"But the Columbians weren't completely out of the game. The survivors reorganized into smaller, specialized groups, compartmentalizing and consolidating their operations. One of these groups began operating in the northern valley area of Columbia."

"The Norte del Valle Cartel," I said.

"You know them?" Mike asked, curious but not surprised.

"Not really. I've been doing some homework."

"I do," Mendez said in a dead pan voice. He didn't elaborate.

"Anyway," Mike continued, his gaze resting on Mendez, "The Mexicans charged fifty percent of each shipment to transport Columbian product through Mexico to the U.S. So the Columbians decided to return to their traditional smuggling routes in the Caribbean. More shipments started moving through the Caribbean again."

"St. Vincent, as JJ knows, but you guys may not," indicating Mendez and me, "along with other Eastern Caribbean islands is a signatory to the Inter-American Drug Action Task Force, the OAS Money Laundering Expert Group, and the Eastern Caribbean Regional Security System," Mike explained. "We participate in exercises with U.S. Southern Command, and joint counter-narcotics operations with the U.S. Coast Guard. And we all share information through Joint Information Coordinating Centers, directly linked to the DEA's operational and analysis center in Texas. It's called the El Paso Intelligence Center. The picture emerging after collating all the information is frightening."

Mike inhaled a deep breath, mentally organizing the continuation of his briefing.

"Couple years ago two St. Kitts police officers were shot on routine patrol. One officer was killed, the other injured. Two subjects were arrested, tried and convicted. They're currently in prison. They were tied to a narcotics smuggling gang, but there wasn't enough evidence to arrest any of the other gang members. But St. Kitts continues to report an increase in guns coming into the island by fishing boats. Their reports also show an increase in gun related crimes, and an increase in narcotics seizures."

"Last year, Grenada had an unusual number of murders, at least two of them directly linked to gangs trafficking drugs between Grenada's Petite Martinique and St. Vincent. Other shooting incidents have also been connected to narcotics trafficking."

"Over the last year St. Lucia's had a number of violent incidents connected to narcotics activity and weapons smuggling. Six murders have been connected to gangs involved in narcotics trafficking."

"Last year we seized over five hundred kilograms of cocaine right here in the Grenadines. That's double the year before. We also eradicated approximately 90 acres of marijuana plants. St. Vincent is now the largest producer of marijuana in the Eastern Caribbean, and the source for much of the marijuana used in the region. Even so, we aren't considered a major drug-producer since total production and shipment doesn't significantly affect the United States. But that designation is probably going to change. It now looks like the Columbians are moving the marijuana for our local boys, and funneling money back to them. Boats off-load cocaine and weapons in the Grenadines and return to their point of origin carrying marijuana. The amount of money coming into the island has already infiltrated the economy, and more rural farmers are becoming dependent on marijuana production and trafficking. The implications for official corruption is real, and threatening to become more entrenched."

"I hear that," Mendez said. "Seen it before. A year's pay in one envelope makes it easy for cops, customs, immigration, politicians to look the other way."

Mike nodded. "Anyway, taken separately, all this just seemed like disconnected incidents on different islands. But when the DEA put it all together in the analysis center, along with intelligence from other sources, a more ominous pattern emerged. We're seeing a definite increase in drugs transiting the region. Specifically through Antigua and Barbuda, Barbados, Dominica, Grenada, St. Kitts and Nevis, St. Lucia, and St. Vincent and the Grenadines. These are the new transshipment points for narcotics bound for the States and Europe. St. Vincent and the Grenadines in particular, is believed to be a storage and transshipment point for cocaine coming through Trinidad and Tobago on go-fast boats and interisland cargo vessels. Most of the drugs appear to be shipped from Nicaragua and Venezuela, but the source is Columbia."

Mike again inhaled a deep, labored breath. I wondered if all the talking might be taking a toll.

Mendez relieved him, picking up the cartel portion of the briefing.

"The DEA identified four major organizations based on the northern coast of Colombia. They believe these guys have established command and control cells in the Caribbean. With managers deployed to Puerto Rico, the Dominican Republic, and these other islands the chief here mentioned. And they're seeing more signs of money laundering."

"Like what?" I asked.

Mendez turned to Mike. I noted the silent exchange. A bond formed in their short time together.

"For one thing," Mike said, taking his cue from Mendez, "The US is pressuring OAS and CARICOM to make it a priority. They're pushing us pretty hard. They estimate at least half the drug revenue generated in the US is laundered through countries in the Caribbean. A couple of things are contributing to this. New banking entities are popping up all over the region, mostly because the islands as trying to diversify their economies, expanding into offshore banking services to clients in the US, Europe and far east. The US is convinced traffickers are exploiting this for money laundering."

"The other is the huge amounts of money pouring into the region in the past few years. Most of it focused on development and tourism. A lot of it legitimate foreign aid from Canada, the US, increasingly Asia, China and the Gulf States. That aid can be tracked. But a large part of it is private investment going into resort properties, rental properties, hotels, travel agencies, shops, finance companies, casinos, and other tourism related businesses. That's a lot harder to track. The feds are convinced traffickers are exploiting this. The funds are funneled through local banks from offshore accounts, and with so many transfers it's almost impossible to tell where the funds originate. And, because most of these tourist businesses are foreign owned, a lot of that revenue goes back offshore."

I noticed Mendez had zoned out. And I recognized the expression on his brown, bearded face.

"What're you thinking Mole?" I asked, interrupting Mike.

"I think you guys got caught in the middle of a war G."

"What does that mean?" Jolene asked.

Mendez gazed at her. Shifted his gaze to Mike. Without moving his head his eyes shifted to glance in my direction. An imperceptible nod my only response. Not so imperceptible. It hadn't escaped Jolene's notice. She studied us, her stare curious, her brow furrowed in thought.

"You guys do that a lot, you know?" her sudden nonsequitor surprising everyone.

"What?" I said.

"Sorry." She offered. "I just noticed you two have this whole communication thing going without having to say a word."

"JJ," Mike began. But she was on a roll, The first time she'd met anyone from my past. Her long submerged, unrequited curiosity surfacing.

"And why do you call him G? Short for Gage?"

"Short for ghostwalker," Mendez said, a passing glance in my direction, again without shifting his head. I hadn't given him the no signal. He continued, his gaze riveted on Jolene.

"The Norte del Valle Cartel the Chief mentioned before, it's the most powerful one in Colombia right now. Next to a smaller North Coast Cartel, and a bunch of guerrilla groups protecting cocoa fields and labs. The last intel I've seen shows there's a war going on. But with these guys there's always a war going on. The Columbians, Mexicans, Nicaraguans, Panamanians, They're all fighting for control of smuggling and distribution routes."

"The Mexicans are pissed at the Columbians and Jamaicans for trying to cut them out, and fighting among themselves for control of the U.S southern border. The Haitians and Jamaicans are fighting for control of the east coast, Miami, the Carolinas, New York. The Columbians are pissed at the Jamaicans for holding up their shipments, and the Jamaicans are pissed at the Columbians for trying to cut them out. The Panamanians are pissed at the Nicaraguans just because they're Nicaraguans. In Panama and Nicaragua there're factions that side with the Mexicans and others that side with the Columbians."

"Been there," I murmured.

"Yeah," Mendez said, introspection in the downcast eyes. "Typical in that kind of chaos. No idea who's who or what's what. Why you went off the reservation a few times." His gaze rose to meet mine.

Mike and Jolene both pinned me with their stare.

"Yeah," I said.

Mendez's gaze searched mine for his cue. I allowed him to continue.

"If you hadn't everyone in that village would've been slaughtered," he said.

"And you ended up on the shit list with me."

"Worth it boss. The brass didn't know their asses from their brains. Playing geopolitical games with people's lives. You did the right thing. That's why we had your back."

"Anyway," Mendez said, his attention returning to the present. "There's a real shooting war going on. Kept low-key on the mainland, but a high body count south of the border. The South Florida theatre was quiet until your recent visit boss," Mike and Jolene again fixed their gaze on me. "The local DEA and FBI guys are having a field day up there. Put this together with what the Chief told us, and I'd say your little paradise got caught in somebody's field of fire."

"I agree," I said.

Mike nodded, not voicing his thoughts, mental wheels churning behind his eyes instead.

"Mon Dieu Sacrament," Jolene said.

"If we can connect all the players we know, we might be able to figure what's what. Whose war this is, and the objective," Mendez said.

"You danced with these El Norte guys before Mole?" I asked, more a statement than a question.

"Couple of times. Once to pick up and transport a package, another time to find and return a missing package."

The cryptic response mightn't mean much to Jolene. Maybe more to Mike. Though their imaginations undoubtedly hard at work filling in the gaps. To me it meant Mendez had renditioned a narco trafficker on one occasion, probably delivering him to the DEA. The other a search and rescue op for someone held by the traffickers, probably a DEA agent or informant. And I knew from personal experience each of those ops entailed more, much more, than relayed in Mendez's understated response.

"Well our task boils down to identifying and finding one, maybe two shooters," Mike said. "And deciphering how Sarah Holmes fits into all this, and what happened to her."

Mendez and I exchanged a microsecond glance. Again it hadn't escaped Jolene.

"What?" she asked.

"She's probably dead," I said.

Mendez nodded his concurrence. In the silence no one dissented. Apparently all had been thinking the same thing.

"And even if we identify the shooters," Mike continued, breaking the silence, "Will we have the evidence to make any arrests? Right now all we have is a not so cohesive theory."

"This isn't about arrests anymore," I said.

Jolene and Mike stared at me, not comprehending. Mendez nodded.

"How do you see this playing out." Mike asked, searching my eyes.

I returned his stare. Held his attention.

"Ramirez isn't your concern. You can't touch him. But I can." The simple statement hung in the air surrounding the group. Mike and Jolene fixed me with laser-like stares.

"For you guys," I said, indicating both Jolene and Mike, "This is about intelligence now. You need to know why this war erupted here. Why now, why here. And if the government and police force have been penetrated or compromised. Then you'll have something in your jurisdiction you can act on. You'll never be able to prosecute the shooters or the people behind them."

I turned to Mendez. Didn't have to ask. "I'm in Boss. So is Max."

A minute nod. An acknowledgement perceptible only to Mendez. And maybe Jolene, who'd been tracking our silent signals like an eagle tracking its prey.

"There's a player we haven't mentioned yet," I said. "And can't rule out."

"Who's that?" Jolene asked. Mendez nodded, the thought already occurring to him. We both knew about waging war in the shadows. In the wilderness of smoke and mirrors. Where the distinction between friend and foe was often blurred, never a certainty.

"The States," I said. "CIA, DEA, DoD. Any, all, or a combination."

"You can't be serious?" Jolene protested. "You can't really believe they'd be complicit in something like this?"

Mike not convinced either. But he remained silent. Instead his eyes remained locked on mine, his stare inquiring.

I hadn't told anyone yet about my invisible watcher. But ever since I'd felt his presence I'd had a nagging, unshakable foreboding.

"It may not be sanctioned. It may be off book, very deep, very black. And no way to tell exactly who we may be dealing with. There're departments within agencies, shops within departments, units within shops. Each compartmentalized. Each with their own agenda. We can't rule it out. And with those folks, nothing is ever what it seems."

Mike and Jolene exchanged glances, a heavy silence between them.

"So what now?" Mendez asked, breaking the tension.

"The immediate objective, get Mike home safe," I said. "Arrowhead formation going in, sweep the perimeter. You take the house, I'll have the front, Max the rear."

"What the hell are you two talking about?" Jolene said, confusion in her stare.

"Better not to ask," Mike said, resignation in his voice.

"The terrain?" I asked Mendez, ignoring Jolene's question.

"Google earth images, updated by details from the Chief," he said.

"And the house?"

"Infrared scan before entry, then clear the interior."

"Would one of you please tell me what you're going on about? Jolene said, an exasperated insistence in her voice, accompanied by a determined demanding stare leveled alternately at me and Mendez.

"Just making sure it's safe for Mike to go ashore." I said.

"You believe that's still necessary?" Severity replaced by concern.

"Better safe than sorry," I said.

CHAPTER 15

Past midnight. The night as black as tar. A sprinkling of stars visible in a cloud laden sky. Wherever plowed on, diving in and out of rolling swells, flinging back spray tinted red and green by her running lights.

To leeward a dark looming landmass. Barely perceptible. Tiny specks of light sprinkled in the dark, villages along the coast. I eyed them periodically, ensuring they kept their distance. In two hours we'd lay the southern tip of St. Vincent and enter the passage, bound for Bequia Head. But a bunch more easting to do before then.

Mike and I had the deck to ourselves. The others had turned in. Max and Mendez occupied bunks in the starboard guest cabin. Jolene at home in the aft master cabin. Mike sat on the low side, his face turned to windward, breathing slow and deep. Savoring the briny night air.

"Interesting pair you sicced on me," he said following a lengthy silence.

"You wouldn't want either of them sicced on you," I said, smiling down at him.

"I gather. How long you guys known each other?"

"A short time which turned into a lifetime. Before Miami I hadn't seen them in about twelve years. But I've kept tabs on them."

"Twelve years!" he whistled softly. "Wow, that's loyalty."

"How'd you mean?"

"These guys haven't seen or heard from you for twelve years and they drop everything to help a complete stranger when you show up."

"They know I'd do the same for them. Besides, to them you're not a stranger."

"How so?"

"Being with me makes you family."

He stared at me, long and hard, an unspoken appreciation in his eyes, before shifting his gaze across the water.

"I get the same feeling talking to them I get talking to you. They don't say a lot. I swear, I'm not even sure I know their real names."

"Old habits," I said.

"Come to think of it, I'm not even sure I know your real name?"

"Nicholas Gage is as real as it gets. The name I was born with. Ironic too, in the peculiar way the universe has of making sense out of chaos."

"What does that mean?"

"I'll tell you about it sometime."

"God, I feel old," he sighed.

"Just the medication talking."

"No. And it's not just my aching joints either. It just never seems to end does it?" his voice plaintive, somber, lacking its usual authoritative tenor. I wondered if the shooting had produced his morose mood.

We'd had many long talks at sea, in the air, sitting around a bar. We'd discussed, debated, sometimes argued a variety of topics. Politics and religion among them. Two subjects I tended to steer clear of. We'd discovered a mutual appreciation for the other's perspective, sometimes shared, sometimes not. It'd formed the basis of our friendship.

In all that time we'd never explicitly explored the other's history. I knew he'd had a long law enforcement career. Had spent time in the Florida National Guard. I'd sometimes wondered if he'd ever taken a life, or been shot before in the line of duty. The portions of his body visible in swim trunks bore no such scars. He'd observed the numerous ones on mine. Commented on them at times. But the topic mostly avoided. He'd never pressed the issue. But he was no neophyte. Rather an astute student of human behavior, perceptive, a keen judge of character. Traits acquired through many years as a cop.

"When you were out there," his thrusting chin indicating an amorphous 'out there'. "did you think you were making a difference?"

"Never thought much about it until recently," I said, uncertain where the conversation might be headed, attributing his despondent mood to the shooting. He'd come within a hairsbreadth of dying. A trauma not easily overcome. And no psych counseling available on St. Vincent.

"What'd you come up with?" he pressed.

"When I started thinking about it, was when I also knew I was finished. Couldn't do it any longer."

We lapsed into another silence. A cloud of gloom hung over him. Something on his mind, gnawing at him. Not sure if I'd said the right thing.

"Why are you asking Mike? What's going on?"

He didn't respond right away. Then, "Like you, not sure I can do this anymore."

"Why? Because of the shooting?"

"How'd you manage to stay so....." he hesitated, searching for the right words, "so balanced?"

"What're you talking about?"

"Look. We've danced around it since we met. Never talked about it. What you did before settling here. But I'm no fool. I've spent most of my life dealing with life's ugly underbelly. With scum and garbage. Can only imagine the things you've had to deal with. What you've seen, had to do. It's a war, and it changes a person. Then something like this happens. You wonder why you're still in it. I've put in my time. Fought the necessary fight. Should be relaxing on the damn beach for christsake. Not continuing to risk my life."

I gazed over at him. Both of us held by the other's stare. A plaintiveness in his melancholy eyes, searching mine for some sort of answer; a need to understand; something solid to grab onto.

"How'd you come back from it?" He asked.

"I almost didn't," I said, my tone matching his somber mood. Not a period in my life I wanted to dredge up. But increasingly unavoidable of late. I pushed the memories of that dark desolate time aside.

"She saved me," I said.

"She? Who? Jolene?"

"Her too in her own way. But before her, Wherever. And someone else I know."

My response surprised him. Familiar contemplative lines creased his brow, dimly lit in the glow of Wherever's cockpit instruments.

"I've wondered about that," he said. "The way you refer to her. I mean, it's tradition and all, referring to a ship in the feminine. But I've noticed it's different with you. It's more. Like she's a real friend or something. One of the things makes me think sometimes you're as batty as hell."

"It's true though," I said, grinning as I faced him. "She is a friend. More than a friend. She saved my life."

"I take back everything I said about your mental stability. Now I know you're batty as hell," he said, the words accompanied by an affectionate smile.

We lapsed into another silence. I had an uncharacteristic urge to tell him more. An unburdening which might prompt him to reciprocate. I understood his mood. The dark despondency. The sense of being adrift, without purpose or meaning to provide an anchor.

"When I first saw her," I said, peering at him across the darkened cockpit, "I was a wreck. Like she was. In worse shape that she was probably. I was used up, burnt-out, disillusioned, depressed; angry at the world. I'd lost all sense of purpose and perspective. My inner demons baying at the door. Didn't know what to do about it. Didn't know if there was anything I could do about it. I was at the end of my rope Mike. Didn't much care if it ended once and for all."

His stare held mine. The expression in his eyes resembling recognition, empathy maybe. Or the resolution to something he'd been pondering a long time and finally understood.

"Anyway, I found her, or she found me," I said. "And everything changed. After her refit we took long cruises together, mostly alone. And eventually I figured a way out while putting some wrongs right. That part was worth it."

He nodded.

"How well do you know your Christopher Columbus?" I asked.

I'd meant it rhetorically, but he nodded, summoning the quote: "'And the sea will grant each man new hope, as sleep brings dreams'."

I smiled. He understood. "There you go," I said.

The silence returned. Except for the sounds of Wherever rushing through the black night on an equally black sea, cleaving oncoming swells. Water sluiced in swishing sighs along her sides. Wind whistled in shrill notes through her rigging.

"So back to my original question," he said, breaking his contemplative silence. "Do you feel you made a difference?"

"I think maybe toward the end, during the time it took to break free and before I left for good. Like I said making some wrongs right. Maybe hoping for a small measure of redemption. Reclaiming what little remained of my soul."

"Is that what Mendez meant by you going off the reservation?"

"Something like that. But that was before Wherever and I met. Before I got out. When I began questioning my role."

"What in the world made you chose that line of work?"

"Probably the same reason you chose to be a cop?"

He chuckled, amused by the absurd notion our choices had anything in common. "I just sorta fell into it." He said. "It wasn't what I wanted to be growing up."

"Exactly," I said. "Same here. You don't choose my line of work. It chooses you."

He thought about that for a moment. "Any regrets?"

"More curiosity than regret. The road not taken type of thing. What would my life be if I'd made a different decision here; a different choice there; taken a different road?"

"Some say 'all roads lead to the same place'."

I smiled, recognizing the reference. Another vice we shared. Odd, come to think of it. "'And many cross along the way'," I finished the quote.

He laughed out loud. A welcome sound, reflecting a lift in his spirits. Or so I hoped.

Another silence. Mike stared out at the white-tipped ocean. "How're things going with you and JJ?" he asked after a while, changing the subject.

"Couldn't be better. You getting shot sorta helped break down some barriers."

He laughed again. "Let me know when you need help again. I'll arrange to get shot for you." A healthier sign. Able to joke about the experience.

And then more seriously, "For a long time I wasn't sure about you two. As a couple I mean."

"You've said."

"Yeah, but we've never talked about it, have we?"

"Why didn't you."

"Wasn't my place. She's a grown woman. But It worried me. Still does."

"Like how?"

"Those barriers you mentioned. I know they exist. Between you and me. Between you and her. It's different for her. I know she struggled with it. Still does to a degree. Seems to have come to terms with it though."

"I know," I said.

"I have to admit you've been good for her," he continued. "When I first met her something was eating her up inside. A hungry passion she couldn't seem to find an outlet for. Then you came along. She started having fun."

"We both came along," I said. "You gave her direction, and purpose. Found an outlet for that passion."

"I think she's been good for you too. it works, I guess. But I still worry. Last thing I want is to see her hurt Gage. Especially by you. Don't know if I could forgive that. I'm sure you've thought about it too."

"All the time. It's a new concept for me Mike. And I know I'm starting late. For most of my life I've measured the future in minutes, hours; the next phase of the op. Truthfully, I never thought I'd make it this far."

He stared up at me, his eyes steady on mine. I waited. Wondered if he'd finally arrived at the point of unburdening himself.

Still not ready. Instead, "I appreciate what you and your guys did for me Gage. And them riding shotgun for the trip home. But I'm not sure two guys hanging around me is going to work. Miami was one thing. On St. Vincent they'll be more conspicuous. "

"They won't be. And they know what to look for. Your people don't."

"We'll see."

"I don't know if you're still a target Mike," the edge in my voice holding his attention. "There's still a shooter out there. And this whole thing has an unfinished feel about it. I have to assume there's more incoming headed our way." I still hadn't told him about the watcher. Not sure why I didn't.

Wherever had made enough easting to clear Bequia Head. Enough to thread the needle between Bequia's Diablo and Brute Points to starboard, and the small rock islands Battawia and Baliceaux to port, both invisible in the dark.

I turned to Mike. "Take her," I said. "Get ready to jibe. I'll handle the sails."

We'd sailed the route many times together. Mostly in daylight. Mike as familiar as I with the passage around Bequia Head. I scampered forward on bare feet. Careful of my footing, using handholds around the heaving deck.

I uncleated the foresail sheet. Hauled the boom in. Mike already easing Wherever's head to starboard, spilling a bit of wind from her sails. I returned to the cockpit, grabbed hold of the mainsheet. Mike took control of the jibsheet.

We waited.

When I'd drawn the long main boom all the way in, near parallel to the deck, Mike gently spun the wheel. Wherever's head came around, spilling the rest of her wind. A deafening pandemonium transformed her deck; banging blocks, slapping lines, flogging sails. A god-awful noise in the dark quiet night as she jibed. Her stern swung through the wind, until the wind blew from her starboard side. The sails on their booms made a cracking sound as they swung to her opposite side.

Wherever settled on a southwesterly course. The wind and swell on her starboard quarter. I trimmed the mainsail, the foresail, finally the jib. They filled and drew, propelling her along Bequia's eastern coast.

The noise on deck must've awakened Jolene. As I settled in the cockpit the hatch opened. She emerged from below, wearing jeans, and a wool turtleneck sweater against the cool night. She stepped to the helm and planted a kiss on Mike's cheek.

"How're you feeling?"

"This is the best medicine," he answered, sucking down a deep breath of sea air.

Jolene settled on the cushion next to me, snuggled close.

"Your friends are sound sleepers," she said innocently. I had an idea where that opening remark might be headed.

"Don't let that fool you. They're aware of everything happening around them. An acquired trait." I said.

"Well I'm glad I finally got to meet friends of yours. I like them. And I'm sorry about before. It's just they're the first, make that the only, friends of yours I've ever met. How long you known them?"

"A little over twelve years. We worked together a couple of times." She snuggled closer still. Lapsed into silence. Lost for the moment in her private thoughts.

Mike had the helm. He stared away to starboard at Bequia's dark eastern coast. To port, Battawia and Baliceaux islands barely visible in the dark. He focused inward, deep in silent contemplation. The reason for his depression still not vocalized.

Wherever slid through the still night. Mike's practiced hands made slight adjustments on her wheel, keeping her sails filled and her course on track.

"I thought I was done with this," he said to no one in particular, breaking the silence. The same wistfulness in his voice I'd detected earlier. "I always thought my second, and final, retirement would end on a high note. And I'd see the light at the end of the tunnel approaching as I got closer."

"You having doubts about that?" I asked

He nodded.

"Because of this situation." A statement more than a question.

"I'd got used to the idea this job was almost done. That I'd finally got the force turned around and heading in a positive direction. God knows it was like having daily root canals. And now I'm not sure it wasn't all for nothing. I'm not sure they're ready to handle what's coming."

"Don't sell yourself short Mike. I don't know anyone could've accomplished what you have," Jolene said, an assured sincerity in her voice. "You singlehandedly transformed the force. If it hadn't been for you it'd still be a cliquey old boy's club. Authority going to their heads, abusing the privilege that comes with the uniform. Totally unresponsive to the community they're supposed to be serving," the last spoken with an uncharacteristic vehemence. I silently questioned again why she'd joined the force.

"Not singlehandedly JJ. Couldn't have done it without you, and others," Mike said, a curious, searching gaze directed at her.

Glimpsing the uncertainty driving his mood I said, "You've made a difference Mike. And you did it in a way that'll outlast you. Quite a legacy I'd say."

"I'm not so sure," he said, the gloomy tone still present in his voice. "This threat could undo everything we've accomplished. We talking real money. Probably more than the entire national budget. Enough to undermine the economy, the government. Eventually the whole society. And we're running out of time."

"What does that mean?" Jolene said, turning to face him.

"It means this government has only another year and a half before elections. Defretas is into his third term. Even if he runs for a fourth the tide is against him. He's got a strong opposition, not to mention challenges in his own party for leadership. There's no guarantee he or the party will get another term. And I'll be out of a job. Frankly I wasn't planning on remaining in the job past the next election anyway."

Not much of a surprise to me. But I wondered about Jolene, observing her reaction. Her loyalty irrevocably tied to Mike, not the job, or the force. Yet she'd had her reasons for joining. Personal, unspoken reasons.

Silence returned as we lapsed into the privacy of our own thoughts, each contemplating an uncertain future. When Mike spoke again a transformation had taken place. Like a switch had been thrown. A loose connection repaired. A vital link reestablished. His voice possessed the strength of conviction and purpose missing only moments before. His doubts sloughed off like molted skin. His manner recharged, reenergized.

"I'll have to split my focus over the next few months," He said into the night, verbalizing his thoughts to no one in particular. "I'll have to reprioritize. But the top two priorities can be complementary. Work both tracks at the same time."

Long familiar with her boss's process Jolene didn't interrupt, until Mike fell silent again. "What do you need me to do?" her unquestioned willingness to follow his lead evident in her voice.

"First thing Monday morning I want you to initiate a review of all personnel. Start with the narcotics unit. Take your time. And don't make it obvious. Make it seem routine. Promotion evaluation or some such."

"What am I looking for?" She sat up, her attention focused on him.

"For now just background. An informal vetting. See if anything jumps out at you. But make a note of whoever you consider trustworthy. I'll do the same with the Coast Guard. Then we'll move on to the CID, the other special units, eventually the rest of the force."

He stared off into the distant dark, leaving us enveloped in another silence. Jolene and I aware of more to come, but maintaining the silence, allowing him time with his thoughts. We Waited.

"Once we've finished the review," he said, "We'll start placing handpicked people in the most sensitive positions," his voice growing in confidence. No longer uncertain. The old take charge confident Commissioner of Police emerged from the despondent depths. "I'm also going to accelerate our drug interdiction training and foreign liaison programs." About to say something further, he paused.

Jo and I focused on him. Waited for him to continue. His furrowed brow shadowed in the dim illumination of the cockpit instruments. His concentration focused and intense. His train of thought completed, a silent decision reached, he turned to me, a satisfied grin on his face.

"Gage, Mendez said he was DEA, or used to be?"

"He's done work for them from time to time," I said.

"Does he have DEA credentials?"

"He can have whatever credentials you need."

"Yeah. That figures. But this one stone could kill a whole bunch of birds."

"What're you getting at Mike?" Jolene said.

"The DEA is perfect cover for what we need. We'll go public with the narcotics angle in the investigations. And I'll announce a new round of drug interdiction training and exercises, with assistance from our DEA partners."

Before I had a chance to voice an objection his raised hand interrupted me.

"Not to worry Gage. I know the game. I'll take precautions not to expose your guys. The announcements are mostly for our local audience anyway. We say given the narcotics angle we've requested DEA assistance. Max and Mendez will represent that assistance. No one outside our little circle will know who they are. Or their real purpose, including the DEA."

"You'd make a helluva handler," I said.

"I've danced this dance before," he said.

I smiled in response, silently communicating my approval. "I've been rethinking this situation anyway." I said. "I want one of them on Jo too."

Jolene swung around to face me. "You can't be serious."

"Like a heart attack," I said.

Mike cut her off before she had a chance to protest further.

"Works for me. And for you too Superintendent," he said, ending the matter. "The other track is to entrench the gains we'd made. Make them politically toxic to reverse, regardless of who's in power, or who's the next Commissioner of Police. And I'll need to find the right people to put in our regional security organizations, especially the DEA training programs. That'll provide solid anti-trafficking indoctrination. And they'll develop useful relationships. Keep an eye out for those candidates too JJ."

"I can think of a few prospects already," she said.

"A few popped into my head too. Probably the same as yours. Let's compare lists and go to work on those first."

"And a couple of women too," she said. "They've done good work on the Drug Council, the CFATF, and the OAS group on money laundering."

More silence. Mike's revitalized energy had set our thoughts churning. A few minutes later I unwrapped myself from Jolene. Moved to the helm next to Mike. I scanned the instruments. A soft red glow emanated from the compass. To the right and just below the compass, the depth sounder, GPS, and radar displayed our progress along the coast, their backlit screens dimmed to the lowest setting.

Friendship Bay lay to starboard. The southern end of the entrance marked by white water bursting high against Saint Hilaire Point and tiny Semples Cay. The incoming tide had already entered the horseshoe shaped bay. But even at slack water, the passage through the entrance might prove treacherous. The landmarks ashore, the visible ones, deceptive at night.

Approaching the entrance I fired up Wherever's diesel. It rumbled to life. Settled into a dull hum, the throttle at idle and transmission in neutral.

Mike remained at the helm. I moved to the port side of the cockpit, readied the jibsheet. Jolene took charge of the main. Mike turned the wheel to starboard, lining up north of dead center to the entrance. I hauled in on the jibsheet. Jo hauled on the mainsheet. The sails flattened, held a firm curve. Wherever heeled, forging ahead, steady on her new course.

GPS and radar confirmed a good track. I flipped two toggle switches on the panel, dousing Wherever's running lights. In turn I extinguished every light on deck and below. A blacked out Wherever glided silently into Friendship Bay.

Mike eased the helm, steering a new course just west of north. Jolene and I retrimmed the sails. Before departing the cockpit for the bow I threw a quick glance at the depth sounder. Habit. I knew Mike included it in his instrument scan.

On my way forward I freed the foresail halyard. The sail slid down its mast. I bundled it onto the boom, a quick couple of ties around boom and sail. I secured the halyard. I'd tidy everything later. I continued forward to the staysail, repeated the procedure. Wherever slowed to a walking pace.

Abeam his house ashore, Mike spun the wheel to starboard. Wherever's head turned in a gentle arc, directly into the wind. Jolene let loose the jibsheet. I uncleated and let go the halyard. The triangular sail at the bow slid down its forestay to the deck. Jolene hopped to the mainsheet. She let it run. I continued forward to the anchor.

Wherever slid ahead, her forward momentum slowing, dissipating altogether. I released the anchor. The silence shattered by chain ratcheting through the sprockets. Lasting only moments as rope replaced chain. The wind carried the sound away from shore.

The shoreline remained dark. I'd planned the trip for an arrival two or so hours short of daybreak. And the weather helped. The night remained inky black. The three hotels spaced around the bay dark except for a single light burning at their entrances. Their few guests tucked in and asleep. Rental villas scattered on Friendship's rising terrain, providing open views of the bay, mostly empty this time of year. One or two occupied by their foreign owners during the off-season.

I tidied the deck, dressing lines, tying down sails, securing Wherever for the night. Jolene helped me unlash Wherever's dinghy from its aft davits and lower it into the water. She secured its painter to a stern cleat.

She turned from the aft rail, expelling a sharp "Holy Shit." Not loud. Enough to get my attention. Max and Mendez stood before her, dressed all in black, including gloves and balaclava masks.

"Sacrament. You scared the shit outta me." She said.

"Sorry." Max said. Accustomed to moving silently, they hadn't meant to startle her.

"I was just about to go below, see if you were up yet."

"We're up."

"I thought you might be hungry. Need some coffee, or anything?"

"We're good to go," Max said in his soft soothing voice.

Max and Mendez both wore backpacks, also black. In them the gear needed to clear Mike's house, and set up surveillance. A third backpack sat on the deck between them, mine. The weapons I'm sure both men carried, concealed.

Mendez had the dinghy pulled up to the transom as I approached. He climbed over the rail and landed lightly against its rigid fiberglass floor. He held it against the hull as Max handed down the third backpack and climbed in.

From the rail Jo stared into the dark toward the beach. Max did the same from the dinghy. Except he wore what appeared to be diving goggles. In reality state of the art optics, with night vision and infrared capabilities designed specifically for United States Special Operations Command.

"You think Mike's still in danger?" Jolene said when I drew next to her. Concern heavy in her voice. And not just for Mike. Her gaze lingered on the black clothing I'd worn since our rendezvous in Vieux Fort.

"I don't know. And since I don't know, I'm not going to assume anything, or take any chances."

I kissed her on the mouth. Her lips soft and responsive. I climbed over the rail into the dinghy.

The dark shoreline waited.

CHAPTER 16

Max and Mendez knelt on opposite sides of the dinghy, paddling silently. Wherever receded in the dark. I knelt in the bow, pulling gear from the backpack.

I hoped Mike might get some sleep. A vain hope knowing him. And Jolene would surely pump him for information regarding Max and Mendez. An oblique way of obtaining information about me. She'd do a fair amount of worrying too.

I donned the tactical ballistic vest and retrieved a com set from the backpack. I stuck the earpiece my right ear, its needle thin mike resting against me cheek. I double-checked the frequency. Enabled vox. We performed a quick radio check.

Weapons next. Max or Mendez, not sure who, had packed the backpack. It contained a modified Heckler & Koch 23, a Knight's Armament suppressor and six spare magazines. I thumbed a round from one of the magazines. Forty-five caliber ACP, full jacket hollow-points. I reinserted the round, stowed the magazines in the easy to reach compartments of the vest. I slid the magazine from the pistol's grip. Checked it, reinserted it. My fingers performed the actions in the dark; checking the ammo, the slide, attaching the suppressor, pressing the magazine release, dropping the hammer using the decocking lever, without having to think about it. Or see it. Pure muscle memory. My hand conformed comfortably to the grip.

I pulled two final items from the pack. Two tanto combat knives. One went into the vest sheath on the left side of my chest. The other in a waistband sheath at my back.

The night continued to cooperate. Darkness enveloped and concealed us. I signaled with a raised fist. Max and Mendez ceased paddling. I lowered the night optic goggles over my eyes. Adjusted the magnification. Scanned the beach. Back and forth. Paid particular attention to the beachfront on either side of our landing spot. I searched the line of coconut trees set back from the beach.

I didn't expect anything. But situations had a habit of turning to shit when you least expected it. Our approach might be overkill, but Mike had been shot. Almost killed. That wasn't supposed to happen on Bequia either. And the threat came from foreigners.

A small hotel located to the right of our intended landing might pose a problem. An insomniac guest. Or an amorous couple taking advantage of a deserted tropical beach at night. I switched to infrared. Repeated the scan. Clear.

Friendship Bay shallowed fifty meters from the beach. The oars contacted grassy bottom. Max and Mendez leapt from the dinghy, one on either side. Using the sidelines they pulled the dinghy forward. Water no higher than their knees. I went over the bow. My pistol up, pointing the way. We waded toward the beach in formation.

I raced ahead across the sand to the tree line. Dropped to one knee. Continued my scan. Max and Mendez dragged the dinghy onto the beach behind me. They too disappeared into the coconut trees. A sharp click in my ear. And another. Both in position. I tapped the mike twice, the signal to move. In my mind I pictured Max and Mendez moving across the dark landscape.

"At the house" I heard in my ear.

Followed by, "Sweeping the rear."

"Copy that." I acknowledged. For most of my career I'd worked alone. Preferred it that way. Max and Mendez, and two others, the only team I'd worked with. A team required different tactics than working solo. Hearing the calls in my ear, familiar, natural, automatic, stirred old memories; transporting me back in time, wiping away the intervening years.

"Perimeter clear," Mendez called. "Checking the entrance." A few minutes later, "Entry clear. Going in."

The nerve-wracking part. The part requiring, despite adrenaline surging through the bloodstream, slow shallow breaths, a slowed heart rate, steady painstaking movements, heightened senses; nerves of steel.

I pictured Mendez at the front door, completing the infrared scan of the interior. Gingerly probing for triggers and tripwires before opening the door. Cracking it mere inches. Clearing the opening. Peering into the dark, ominous interior.

I waited.

I scanned the front and sides of Mike's house for any movement. Unconsciously braced for the blinding flash. The concussive boom. Thinking it won't happen. That's when it usually does.

The earpiece remained silent. The waiting eternal. Mendez inside, moving cautiously around the room, an inch at a time. Technology only went so far. The rest up to Mendez; his training; his instincts. Taking one excruciating step after the other. Pausing. Peering into dark corners. Listening. Moving on.

"Clear," his voice said in my ear.

"Copy that"

"Clear in back," from Max.

"Copy that. Bring it in. Meet you in front."

"Copy."

Max appeared like a shadow from the side of the house. I approached from the front.

"Coming through the front," I radioed to Mendez as Max and I approached the front door. I retrieved Mendez's backpack from the verandah where he'd left it. Max and I entered the main living room. The night vision gear rendered Mendez a ghostlike specter at the far end of the room.

"Okay," I said when we'd gathered inside. "Mole, set up in here. Max, you place the cameras. I'll finish clearing the house."

They went to work in silence, pulling assorted gear out of their packs. Mendez pulled a briefcase sized aluminum case from his. He opened it, handed equipment to Max. Max exited the house. Mendez continued sweeping the house for electronic bugs.

I moved carefully through the kitchen, the hallway, the bathroom. Finally the bedrooms. Mendez completed his sweep. Didn't mean our shooter hadn't left a surprise package hidden somewhere else in the house. A timer unlikely. No one knew when Mike might return. Trip wires also unlikely, since other people, caretakers and the like, even animals, might trip them. That left remote detonation, or a booby-trapped personal item only the owner might touch.

As Mike's friend I took the job of going through his personal belongings. It preserved a modicum of privacy. And having spent time in the house with Mike I knew most of his things which might lend themselves to tampering. I methodically searched the living room and kitchen, using my eyes, fingers, and a hand held 'sniffer' to detect explosive materials. Not as reliable or accurate as a dog. But we didn't have one of those.

I headed along the narrow hallway to the bathroom. I checked the door jams and windows. The shelves, closets, and toiletries. The bedrooms next. I paid particular attention to the master bedroom, Mike's room. I examined the bed, the frame. Underneath the bed. Lifted the mattress after checking for pressure sensitive triggers. I went through the dressers, side tables, closets; everywhere an explosive device might be concealed. After an hour I'd found nothing inside the house designed to go boom.

I found it outside, next to the kitchen. In a small woodshed attached to the outside wall of the kitchen. The shed divided into two compartments by a brick wall. One compartment held a portable Honda generator, and three red gasoline filled five-gallon carboys. The other compartment held three twenty pound propane tanks. One connected to a regulator feeding gas to the kitchen stove. The valve closed. The small but powerful charge, pierced by a remotely triggered pencil detonator, taped to the side of a propane tank.

A rudimentary device. No booby-traps or tamper proof circuitry. No circuitry at all. The putty-like explosive inert. Until triggered by the detonator. The explosion amplified by the propane tanks. Enough to destroy the entire house. And if detonated with the target close to the tanks, checking or changing them, bits and pieces of body parts would be scattered far and wide.

It'd take a trained forensic arson investigator, which the local police didn't have, to know the explosion hadn't been a tragic accident. I pulled the device from the tank. I removed the detonator, rendering the explosive harmless.

If you found one. There might be more. A backup in case the primary failed.

"Mole. Max", I called on the radio.

"Here boss", from Mendez.

"Go," from Max.

"Meet me northwest corner of the house, outside the kitchen."

"Copy," from each of them. A moment later they materialized next to me. I showed them my find.

"Where there's one..." Mendez said.

"Exactly," I said.

No words necessary. They split off in opposite directions to work their way around the perimeter of the house. Like almost every house on Bequia this one had an underground water storage tank. Gutters collected rainwater from the roof and directed it into the tank. A second, smaller tank stood on a platform above roof height, providing gravity fed water to the house. Mike had installed a demand pump on the main tank to provide decent water pressure for the house. A 'Y' valve allowed the same pump to fill the overhead tank. An old style hand pump provided a manual backup when power went out, a not uncommon occurrence on Bequia. Or when the electric pump malfunctioned. I searched the spaces around the tanks and pumps, a logical hiding place for a second device. Found nothing.

The eastern sky had turned pink by the time we completed our search, including a small attached carport, another little shed filled with yard tools, and an unoccupied chicken coop in the backyard. Certain no other explosives lurked in or around the house, we gathered again in Mike's living room. Discarded the night optics. First light soon filtered into the room. Against one wall Mendez sat at a table Mike often used as a desk. Mendez had set up a laptop next to the aluminum briefcase. He tapped purposefully on the keys.

Max held the block of plastic explosive I'd pulled from the propane tank. "Doesn't make sense there was only one,"

"I know. Could be the guy's a novice. At least with explosives. More likely he didn't expect anyone to find it. Didn't expect the place to be swept before Mike arrived."

Despite what I'd said the anomaly bothered me. Something felt off. Too many mistakes. Too many loose ends. Too sloppy. Like killing Tesca. Too overt and conspicuous, attracting unnecessary attention.

"To use this he'd need eyes on the house," Max said, recapturing my wandering attention. "Didn't find any bugs. He'd have to see the Chief was in the house, alone, and ideally outside by the gas shed. No more than quarter mile radius on this," he said, picking up the dismantled detonator.

"We're up," Mendez said.

Max and I joined him at the table. Images from five miniature battery powered, motion sensitive video cameras appeared on a monitor. Max had positioned the cameras in the trees outside the house. One camera pointed east, capturing the beach approach to the house. Another pointed west, the approach from La Pompe. Another covered the front porch and entrance. One had a wide-angle view behind the house.

The final camera displayed a wide-angle view of Mike's living room from the kitchen, covering the front door. Mendez tweaked the images using the keyboard, until satisfied with the feed. Turning his attention to the briefcase, Mendez activated its built in electronics.

"So the chief's still in the kill zone," Max observed, turning his attention from the monitor to me.

"Yeah. And maybe Jolene too," I said. "We're gonna be stretched thin on this. Max you're gonna be on Mike. Mole you're on Jolene. Your cover is DEA. Mike's gonna set it up. He'll brief you."

"And you?" Max asked.

"I've got over watch. I'll switch off with you Mole when I'm with Jolene. And we also need to sweep Mike's other place in Kingstown, and his office. Max, you'll have to get those. The domestic staff is civilian. Police constables provide security."

"Aaand," I said, dragging out the word, "I have a watcher to smoke out."

Both heads swiveled toward me. Two pairs of eyes focused on mine.

"I've picked up a watcher. Don't know who. The why probably connected to all this. The watcher isn't following me. Just picks me up now and then, mostly in the harbor."

"What's your next move?" Mendez asked.

"Try to smoke him out. You get the items I asked for."

"In the pack," he gestured.

I flashed him an appreciative smile. He smiled back. He plugged a transformer into a wall socket, connected a final cable to the briefcase, stood up from the table.

"So what we've got here boss, is a digital video receiver, recorder, and server, all in one neat little package. Connect the laptop here," he said, pointing to a cable between the laptop and the briefcase, "and you can watch the camera feed on the monitor."

"The video server is connected to a sat receiver," he continued, pointing to another built in module. "Dial in from your cell, or connect to the server's URL from any computer. Log in with the user name and password, and remotely view the feed. We have three to five days' battery life in the cameras before we have to swap them out. Depends on how many times they get activated."

I patted his shoulder. Checked my watch. "The cat's gonna be out of the bag soon," I said.

"What happens when our bad guy triggers his detonator and there's no boom?" Max asked.

"He may not trigger it." I said. "May just be insurance. And if he does maybe we can use that. He'd have to break cover to check why it didn't go off."

A thought occurred as I said that. I turned back to Mendez. "How many more cameras you have?"

"Seven. I brought a dozen total and we used five for this package. Why boss?"

"Set up another one to cover the propane shed." I said.

Daylight greeted me on the front verandah. A new day. From habit my gaze lifted to the sky. A high grey overcast. Closer to the surface dark, moisture laden clouds marched in formation. I heard the sea's rhythmic rumble on the beach.

The air sweetened by the mingled scents of grapefruit, oranges and mango. Coconut branches rustled overhead in a breeze smelling of rain.

I studied the high overcast and scudding nimbocumulus. A warm front approaching from the east. Moving toward us. Had been for at least sixteen hours. I checked the wind direction. It'd already swung southward.

Exiting the coconut trees lining the beach I shifted my gaze to the sea. The tide running out. Thick, wet, brown-green seaweed deposited by the surf littered the beach. In the shallow water stalks of sea grass stood exposed to the air. Shallow enough to wade more than halfway out to Wherever, bobbing at anchor in deeper, indigo blue water.

I dragged the dinghy until I reached water deep enough for rowing. Arriving at Wherever I secured it to a stern cleat. Hoisted myself onto the deserted deck. Hoped Mike and Jolene had managed to get some sleep.

I opened the hatch. observed I'd been wrong. Mike sat at the dinette. Jolene stood to starboard of the companionway, half in half out of the galley. Both held nine millimeter service Glocks pointed at the open hatch.

"Permission to come aboard." I said, noticing the beginnings of a smile on Mike's face.

"Mon ostie de crisse," Jolene's reaction. "Gage Wah de bumbo." Checked herself from launching into a full stream of foul Bequian. Her expression alternately livid, worried, relieved and livid again. "Yu tryin fe get shot fe Christ's sake."

"Sorry," I greeted them both, displaying an appropriate amount of contrition, especially to Jolene. "Although I'm glad to see you guys listened, and were alert and prepared. Ready to go home Mike?"

I slid down the companionway. Put my arms around Jolene. Felt the subsiding tremors. She flung her arms around my torso, holding tight, her scented hair just below my chin, the Glock hanging limp in her fist.

Mike's wide smile answered my question. "How'd it go?"

"Good." I said. "No trouble. The house is clear, and we got perimeter security up and running." I glanced back at Jolene before continuing. "But we did find an unwelcome package."

"I don't like the sound of that at all" He said, the smile replaced by an intense inquiring stare. I told them about the explosive.

"I also come bearing gifts," I said. They glanced at each other before staring at me expectantly. I slipped the backpack from my shoulders. Set it on the dinette.

"New cell phones" I said, pulling two cell phones from the pack. I handed one to each of them. "You can still use your other phone if you want. But you might as well replace them with these. They'll work on the same local service network as the ones you use now. But these are encrypted. And satellite capable. All communications from me or the guys will be through these phones. Jo I'll show you how to use it. Mike, the guys will show you how to use yours. And one final thing. I'm giving both of you access to a secure server for emails, correspondence, and messages. Only five other people in the world have access. Jo, I'll install the encryption on your laptop. The guys will do the same on yours Mike."

Mike, anxious to return home after a month in hospital and eager to begin work on his plan, brief Max and Mendez, set up their covers, departed shortly after my return, rowing himself ashore. Max waited for him on the beach. I'd swim ashore to retrieve the dinghy later.

Knowing Mike, he'd be antsy for the next couple of days. Unable to plunge into work until Monday. His plans for the police force had lit a fire in him. A fire which had consumed his glum despondency.

I'd been awake for a full day and night. The second time in less than two weeks. And wanted nothing more than a few hours of blissful unconsciousness.

Jolene snuggled close, my arm wrapped around her shoulder. Her head of soft curls rested on my chest. Her fingers roamed my bare shoulders and torso. Combed through the patch of hair on my chest. Lingered on the mottled and stretched skin of my scars. She'd discovered each of them by sight and feel in the time we'd been together. Sometimes she'd ask me about them. Sometimes she just touched them. Sometimes she kissed them with a soft brush of her lips. She knew them intimately now, her practiced fingers unerringly finding them in the dark as though guided by a mental map. Each had a story. Each stirred a memory. Cambodia on the left lower torso, one of the earliest. Bolivia on the upper chest, almost ending it all. Congo on the right thigh; Sudan; Kosovo; others, like travel stickers. The touch of her fingers on my skin, I drifted into unconsciousness.

The face harsh and loathsome. A red scar along the right cheek, parting the stubble covering his jaw. Blue eyes beneath an unkempt patch of dirty blond hair registered surprise and disbelief. I'd spent weeks maneuvering him into position. To get this close. His mouth opened to speak as the first round penetrated his chest and perforated his heart. I wanted him to be aware of the end. His blue eyes registered shock, disbelief; the dawning realization of everything about to end, forever. Then rage. This couldn't be happening to him. Not him. Not now. Finally fear, a plaintive plea to stave off impending death. I put the second round through his forehead.

I awoke with a start. Consciousness fought its way up through the dim afterimage of the dream. Multiple dreams. But the dreams hadn't awoken me. Wherever had. She pointed in a different direction, her motion livelier.

I recalled the face. Remembered the ravaged countryside. The terrified villagers. The screams. The incessant automatic weapons fire. And the overpowering odor of bloated bodies littering the roadside mixed with cordite and wood smoke thick in the air. He'd been the last of the 'special squad'. Had gone into hiding as the others fell. One by one. Until they were no more.

I'd also had a recurring dream, one I hadn't had for a long time. Lying asleep in bed, in a house. Intruders in the house. My senses aware of their presence. Could hear them rummaging through the house. Approaching the bedroom. But unable to wake up. Like being trapped in conscious sleep. Unable to see them, or escape them. Then I'd awaken. But unable to move. Unable to get out of the bed. Couldn't hide. Couldn't defend myself. Lying helpless, listening to them moving about, getting closer.

Why those dreams now? I wondered.

Jolene sound asleep against me. I raised my left wrist to check the time. The watch no longer there. Earlier I'd consigned it to the chart table drawer, where it usually lived when I didn't need to keep track of time. Meaning most of the time.

I unwrapped myself from her and slid out of the queen sized master berth. She moaned in her sleep, pulled her arm up under the pillow but didn't awaken. I ached all over. Moving to the foot of the bed I pulled on sweatpants and a tee shirt. I set coffee brewing in the galley. Climbed the companionway to the deck.

A slate grey overcast hid the sun. Without it, late afternoon the closest estimate I could make of the time. Friendship Bay, despite its name, not a friendly anchorage. Winds from the north and east constantly swept the bay, lashing the La Pompe promontory and kicking up choppy water in the bay.

Wherever had swung her bow into the gusty wind. She strained on her anchor, and tossed her head as wind driven chop slapped against her bow.

I went forward to check her anchor. Set firmly, the line straight, stretched taut as a fishing line with a big catch. Foul weather on the way. I read it in the dark moisture laden clouds. In the shifting gusty wind. In the gathering white caps of the seascape. Smelt it in the moist salty air. But confident of Wherever's anchor holding. Not so certain about the handful of other vessels in the bay. If they dragged, Wherever lay between them and the beach.

The storm might reach us during the night. By morning at the latest. The weather system moving fast. What had begun as a low-pressure dust storm on the western coast of Africa had traveled west across the Atlantic Ocean, gathering strength. It had morphed into a tropical wave, then a tropical depression of squalls and thunderstorms. Feeding on the warm Atlantic water, its winds set up a cyclonic rotation, faster and faster as it gained energy. When those winds reached speeds of seventy-five miles per hours the system would officially be a hurricane.

Below deck the scent of Jamaican mountain roast permeated the cabin. Jolene sat at the dinette sipping from a large brown ceramic mug. Steam rose from it. An open laptop on the dinette occupied her attention. She wore a diaphanous black silk robe draped loosely on her shoulders. Open at the front. Nothing else.

Aboard Wherever she'd grown accustomed to wearing little, or nothing. And as accustomed as I'd become to it, the sight of her still left me breathless. The smooth, sun-burnished mocha skin; the exotic face framed by dark curled tresses; the toned arms and legs; the fascinating curve of waist and hips; the delicate line of jaw, throat, and neck; the proportioned pear shaped breasts, upturned nipples pushing against the robe's thin fabric. My crotch stirred.

Her gaze rose to meet mine. A smile parted her lips.

"What's it doing out there?"

"We may be in for a blow. A low moving to our north." I entered the galley, poured myself a mug of the aromatic brew. Fixed it to my liking with cream and sugar. I headed to the nav station.

"Probably just get grazed by it," I continued, punching instructions into the weather facsimile. "Could be a rocky night aboard though." While I waited for the fax to spit out its printed graphic I set an anchor watch on the GPS.

"Should we move Wherever?" a touch of anxiety betrayed in her inflection. Her gaze fixed on me across the cabin.

"Not an option right now. Not yet anyway. She should be fine. I'm more worried about those boats up by the hotel. If they start dragging we may be spending the night fending them off. And it's going to be nasty out there."

The weather fax ceased its clickity-clack printing. I ripped the page from the roll. The printed image also displayed on a flush mounted screen above the chart table. They confirmed my eyeball analysis.

Not a hurricane, not yet. But the system had grown to a tropical storm, diffused over a wide stretch of the Atlantic northwest of Barbados. Moving along 'hurricane alley', well north of St. Vincent and the Grenadines. But tracking straight for Dominica, an island smack in the middle of 'hurricane alley' which received so much rainfall it'd developed a tropical rain forest ecosystem.

I dropped the weather printout on the chart table. Joined Jolene at the dinette. Though her eyes remained glued to the laptop monitor, she sensed my gaze on her. Acknowledged by an amused curl at the corner of her mouth.

"What you got there?" I asked, with no real interest. My gaze roamed over her body, soaking it in, provoking an intense in my groin.

"Nora's latest article," she said, without lifting her eyes from the monitor.

I pondered the woman next to me. Her faint lavender scent like pheromones, beckoning. Pondered our bewildering relationship. A relationship I hadn't sought or desired. But had been inexorably drawn to. Pondered the ineffable quality surrounding her, infusing her, capable of unleashing my long repressed emotions, allowing me to believe in the possibility of a future. Of an us.

The women who'd populated my past had been either assets or pleasurable diversions providing a necessary biological release. A respite from an ugly world. A downtime entertainment. Professional lovers some of them, schooled in ways of pleasuring men. Others a means to an end. They'd provided a momentary tenderness; a softness; sometimes a sweetness. But without expectations or attachment. Until Jolene, who'd managed to stir a sweet, terrifying, tender, confusing longing deep inside me.

Her soft voice penetrated my thoughts. I met her eyes. Mine a blank stare.

"Where were you?"

"Huh?"

"You zoned out for a moment there."

"Sorry. Thinking about you," I said evasively, though not untruthfully.

Her worried expression transformed into a smile. She closed the laptop. Reached between my legs. Stroked me to a hard erection.

The rocking cabin, the gathering storm, thoughts from another lifetime, all dissolved in a tremendous wave of our own making. We rode the powerful surge as it intensified and grew, building higher, stronger, as we grasped and sucked and thrust against each other; propelling us to a dizzying height before cresting in an explosive roar, flinging us over the top to surf down other side locked in a blissful embrace; our naked bodies glistening from the wild wet ride.

CHAPTER 17

It rained for five straight days. Pausing intermittently. The passing storm halted in its tracks by two high-pressure systems blocking its path like offensive linebackers.

The steady monsoon-like downpour commenced before daybreak on Sunday. By Monday, normal life on Bequia ground to a halt. School, work, commerce; everything at a standstill. Foot traffic along the main roads disappeared. Dirt roads and footpaths turned into impassible mud streams. Vehicular traffic sparse, sporadic, eventually disappearing, like the pedestrians. A few shops opened. Usually those having a bar. Other establishments remained shuttered. Not a widespread storm, or even a full-fledged hurricane. But stationary, it packed the concentrated punch of a heavyweight boxer.

The rain fell in a fine drizzle at times. At other times in wind driven sheets, stinging exposed skin like tiny needles. More often it fell in a deluge, the marble sized raindrops denting roofs; the sustained winds stripping branches and fruit from trees.

At first Bequians welcomed the rain. Welcomed it as a respite from the daily routine; an unexpected holiday. Welcomed it for refreshing the dull, droopy landscape scorched by the dry-season sun. The parched ground soaked up the rain like a thirsty sponge until water bubbled up from the saturated soil. And they welcomed it for replenishing the nearly empty water tanks.

Mike chomped at the bit by day two. I welcomed the security advantages of his imposed seclusion. By day three he summoned a Coast Guard cutter to ferry him over to police headquarters in Kingstown.

Bequians' patience also worn thin by day three. By the fourth cooped up day, attitudes changed from water starved welcome to waterlogged cabin fever. The depressing absence of the sun took its toll. While street gutters continued to overflow, and yards turned into muddy ponds.

On the fourth day Jolene received a callout for a missing six-year-old child. The little girl, the second to youngest of six siblings, had disappeared from her yard at the top of a hill in Paget Farm. There'd been extensive flooding in the area. And dangerous mudslides.

Jolene had returned that evening heartbroken. They'd found the girl's lifeless body wedged in a culvert at Bottom Road in Paget Farm. Somehow she'd gotten caught in a mudslide. Had been swept down the hill to the culvert, where she'd been trapped, and drowned. What she'd been doing out in the yard, in that kind of weather, no one knew. A preventable tragedy. Senseless. Since the discovery Jolene had been occupied by the investigation in preparation for a coroner's inquest.

On the sixth day, Friday, the sky cleared. The truant sun reappeared. People moved about again. Some in a daze. Some possessing an enervating purposefulness. News of the little girl spread along the island's amorphous grapevine. The island mourned.

The mother of the little girl inconsolable for days. She and her family lived in a small two-room house, constructed of unpainted wood. Little more than a shack. The simple dwelling and dirt yard common on Bequia. More numerous than the landscaped lawns and comfortable hotels tourists encountered. A reality not shown on the brochures.

The yard, the land, whether large or small, rich or poor, held a central place in Bequian psyche and tradition. A part of their heritage. Passed down through generations. For many the only possession of any economic value. The yard fed the family. A small section planted with yams, sweet potatoes, or cassava. Another small patch covered in corn, as ubiquitous on Bequia as chickens and goats. The tall yellow-green stalks present in almost every yard. Yellow Ears and kernels spread out on rooftops drying in the sun. A staple, prepared and used in myriad ways from corn soup to chicken feed.

The storm left large rolling swells in its wake. And chaos ashore. But a sky unbelievably pure and clear. The air scrubbed so clean it smelled like fresh cut roses. Shops reopened. Bequians resurfaced to clean up after the storm. Mudslides covered roads. Fallen tree branches filled yards. Debris washed down by flooding had to be hauled away. Bequians took it in stride. Accustomed to storms, hurricanes, and the occasional eruption of Mount Soufrière, the volcano at the northern end of St. Vincent.

I joined the cleanup at the Green Boley. Alongside five generations of Winston and Rona's family, grandparents, parents, children, grandchildren, and great grandchildren; sweeping, raking, dragging, cutting, patching and repairing.

The structures escaped undamaged. The yard filled with torn branches and rotting fruit on the ground.

Jolene coordinated official cleanup efforts from the police station in Port Elizabeth, dispatching heavy equipment, vehicles, tools, hands, to where they were needed. Her constables and detectives busy cataloguing and reporting damaged property.

Mike remained on St. Vincent. He planned to return home for the weekend, following a press conference he'd scheduled for that afternoon. The first opportunity to do so. I watched the coverage on the Green Boley's television behind the bar.

Electricity had been restored around Port Elizabeth, Hamilton, and Belmont. Still out in areas farther from the harbor. Mostly due to downed lines and blown transformers. Electric power on the island more reliable in recent years. Failure of the single generator no longer a chronic problem. A check mark in development's plus column. Still, those who could afford to kept a portable generator handy. And many Bequians still lived in simple dwellings without electricity or indoor plumbing.

A handful of foreign reporters attended the press conference, hangers on after the Sarah Holmes story had gone cold, mostly magazine and print journalists. Newly promoted Assistant Superintendent Vincent Taylor, of the newly created Public Information Office, spoke from the podium. Light complexioned, charismatic, photogenic, a natural on television.

He announced Commissioner Daniel's return to duty. Tepid applause among the assembled press. The CID, Taylor said, had developed information indicating the shooting of

Commissioner Daniels, and the man found shot to death in Industry, were both connected to drug trafficking. He didn't elaborate. As a consequence, and the increasing dangers drugs and drug trafficking posed to the people of St. Vincent and the Grenadines, he announced that the government, and the Royal St. Vincent and the Grenadines Police Force, would be increasing anti-trafficking activities throughout the Grenadines, with the assistance of regional security partners. He didn't elaborate on that either. No mention of Sarah Holmes.

Taylor took a few questions, but his responses provided no more information than contained in the statement. A tour de force compared to Coffe's performances.

The foreign press interested only in Sarah Holmes. The shootings and drug connection insignificant side bars to their primary concern. No progress in the case, and not a single lead regarding the whereabouts of Sarah Holmes or her body. The small local press contingent on the other hand focused on the shootings and the drug angle. And about storm damage, and the cost to government for cleanup and repairs. The stories which would play locally. Exactly as Mike intended.

I returned to Winston's yard. The kids and I had dragged away the last bundle of fallen branches when Mike called using his new encrypted cell phone. Local cell service not yet restored. My phone's screen displayed a satellite identifier.

"Well played," I said when I answered.

"I guess. We'll see." He seemed preoccupied. "Listen. Let's get together at my place when I get back this evening. We've got some new information I need your take on."

"Sure. What time?"

"Say about eight"

"What time you think you'll be getting back."

"Can't tell yet. But I'm hoping before dark."

"See you then." I disconnected. The phone immediately chimed again. This time Mendez.

"Hey boss. When's the last time you checked the cameras at the Chief's house?"

"Not since this morning," I answered. "They're still down. I've been helping with cleanup. Haven't had a chance to check them recently."

"I'm still showing them down too," he said. "Want me to check it out?"

"No. You stay with Jolene. I'll take care of it. Mike's gonna be back this evening so I have to do it before then."

"Okay. The main battery's probably drained. Or the batteries in the cameras. Or the sat signal isn't getting out for some reason. It's IT stuff boss. Sure you don't want me to check it out?"

"No need. I'll make a full sweep of the house again anyway. Mike wants a meet this evening. Has some new information."

"Copy that. Catch you later then." He disconnected.

I had a few errands to run before heading back to Wherever. I also wanted to check in at De reef. Lend a hand there if needed. I surveyed our handiwork. Winston's yard had been cleared and cleaned. The restaurant/bar's concrete floor swept clean of sand and mopped. The kitchen in working order. The bar ready to open. I didn't expect it'd be busy anyway.

Pools of stagnant seawater still lay in the front yard. Nothing to be done about that. The normally sheltered harbor a roiling cauldron of swells driven by southeast winds. The tidal surge submerged the beach, reaching halfway up the stone seawall protecting beachfront properties. Rolling waves smashed against the seawall, sending spray and seawater over the top into the yards..

Winston thanked me unnecessarily for my help before I set off for Port Elizabeth. I needed a few items for Wherever. The beach, the normal route to the harbor, submerged underwater. From Port Elizabeth all the way to the Plantation House Hotel. I jumped the stone wall separating the Green Boley from the Gingerbread Hotel. My route to the harbor a circuitous path behind the Whale Boner and Frangipani, navigating piles of fallen coconuts and downed branches.

In the harbor seawater had surged inland as far as the main road, depositing stagnant saltwater pools, seaweed, and other debris. Floodwaters from Union Vale's high ground had delivered its own freshwater pools and debris. Muddy floodwaters mixed with seawater stained the shoreline a dirty rusty brown.

I collected the items I needed. Boarded a Suzuki pickup parked at the road's edge with its engine running. Five passengers sat on wood benches in back waiting for it to depart. The driver waited for more passengers. We were it for that trip. He put the pickup in gear, turned up the volume on Bob Marley's 'One love', and headed out of the harbor dodging water filled potholes, standing pools of water and debris.

Heading out of Port Elizabeth it occurred to me I hadn't sensed my watcher. I tapped the roof when we reached Lower Bay road. The pickup stopped barely long enough for me to hop off and pay the fare. Headed to Lower Bay I paused at my usual spot. Admiralty Bay a turmoil of marching swells and white water as the swells broke on the shallow sandbank off Belmont. Yachts anchored in the bay pitched and rolled with the passage of each swell, their bows pointed west. Some skippers had put out a second anchor.

I checked in at De Reef. The restaurant, set farther back from the surf line, had survived in good shape. The surf hadn't reached that far inland, though the surge covered half the beach. Coconut branches partially buried by deposited sand littered the exposed stretches of beach, their long green leaves sprouting like weeds from the sand.

Not needed at De Reef, I retraced my steps up Lower Bay Road. At the main road I turned right towards Friendship. A short walk to the turnoff leading down to Friendship Bay. Wherever serene on her anchor in the distance in the distance. I hiked along the concrete pavement, avoiding the litter of fallen branches and mangled fruit. At the beach I swung right in the direction of Mike's House. I'd left the dinghy tethered to a coconut tree. I dragged it into the water. Rowed out to Wherever.

Later, a little after six pm, I headed back to the beach. I'd completed chores aboard *Wherever* and changed into a clean pair of jeans and a clean tee shirt After sweeping Mike's house I'd hang there to wait for him, Jolene and the guys. Maybe try to rectify the camera problem.

I pulled the dinghy to the tree line. Tethered it as before. Headed through the dense line of coconut trees towards the house. The tree line ended at an open yard, citrus trees on either side. Oranges and tangerines on the right. Grapefruit on the left. Split coconut branches and fallen fruit littered the yard.

The house, brick and mortar, painted pale yellow, topped by a red galvanized A-frame roof, stood on a stone foundation on rising terrain overlooking Friendship Bay. A wide stone verandah at the front and along one side enclosed by a cedar porch railing, its cap and posts painted blue, the spindled balusters in white. Stained hardwood doors and blue window shutters all tightly shut.

As I moved into the yard my step slowed, an autonomous reaction to the prickling on my neck like a cold breath. I approached the house cautiously. No other indicators to set off my mental alarms.

I climbed the stone steps to the verandah. Approached the double doors. They remained locked. The master bedroom opened onto the verandah by another set of doors to my left. Nothing appeared unusual or out of place. I used the spare key Mike had given me. Unlocked the heavy front door. Pushed the left door open. Stepped over the threshold into the dark room.

An itch on the back of my neck. I sensed him behind me. The instinct honed over many years. Unexplainable. Perhaps the barely perceptible movement of neck hairs as his motions disturbed molecules in the surrounding air. Maybe the hint of cologne that shouldn't be there.

I reacted instantly. Automatically. Without conscious thought. I spun to my right in a slight stoop. My right arm raised. It connected with an unseen outstretched arm. The soft spit of a suppressed weapon. The supersonic buzz of a lead projectile past my right ear. The thud as it embedded itself in the opposite wall. Time slowed to a crawl.

Instead of spinning away the intruder attempted to swing his gun arm in my direction. My raised arm blocked it.

A handgun is a poor weapon in close quarters; its advantage is distance. A lesson my unknown assailant learned the hard way. Continuing my turn my outstretched right arm curled around his gun arm, pinning it against my chest. Two more spits from the weapon. Didn't see where the rounds went. Heard the sound of breaking glass.

Still continuing through the turn, weight balanced on my right leg, a nanosecond decision to forego the obvious choke hold. Too much time and effort involved. An opportunity for him to counter. Instead I drove my left foot into the back of his right knee. First strike. The leg buckled beneath him. He went down. On his way down I twisted the gun arm, still captured in mine. Heard sinews in his shoulder pop, accompanied by an agonized howl. His grimaced face turned in the direction of the pain, exposing the right side of his face. My closed left fist smashed down into the exposed side, just below his ear, where carotid, jugular, and vagus nerves all ran close together. Second strike. He went limp. I eased him the rest of the way to the floor.

I removed the weapon from his fist, a Browning nine millimeter. Felt for a carotid pulse. I'd measured the blow. More than needed to stun, less than needed to kill. I wanted him alive.

Bent over him the first stirring of unease caressed my heightened senses. Something wrong. My initial thought, he hadn't been alone in the house. I dismissed that. It didn't track. And what I sensed came from the front entrance. From outside.

I hefted my attacker's weapon. Decided against it. Pushed it into the waistband at my back. Felt its heat against my skin. I moved toward the open door. Slid next to the wall. Poised in a crouch, close to the floor. I waited.

The second assailant slipped through the open front door without making a sound, halting just inside the threshold, surveying the room. He noticed the unconscious shooter on the floor. His gaze didn't linger. His eyes quartered the room. He advanced farther inside. I waited. His movements precise and economical. A fish of a different sort, I concluded. Not at all like the shooter on the floor. Still I waited.

His back toward me, the moment to strike arrived. I moved off the wall, a knuckle punch aimed at the base of his skull.

He sensed it coming. Quicker than he looked. Much quicker. He twisted into the blow at the last second, blunting my strike. It jarred him. He used the force of the punch to turn, an elbow swinging behind aimed at my throat.

I raised my left arm. Blocked the elbow strike. His right elbow already swinging from the other side. Aimed at the same spot. He'd also backed up, closing the distance, still with his back to me. But I had no time to counterattack. Too busy fending off blows swinging nonstop from his left and right. Any one of them incapacitating, perhaps lethal. He turned full circle, a raised knee aimed full force at my midsection. I turned slightly to my right. Raised my own left knee. Took the impact on my thigh. It stung like hell.

This wasn't going well. Fights tended to follow a predictable pattern. A pattern I established and controlled. Typically lasting mere seconds, after no more than three blows, the other guy on the ground incapacitated, unconscious, or dead. This guy had me fighting for my life.

I recognized his tactics. Could almost anticipate his moves. Slowly he backed me toward the wall. Once I lost maneuvering room it'd be just about over. I needed space, and distance. I backed away from him, hit the wall, momentarily out of striking range. He moved to reclose the distance. Not before I planted a short, straight kick to his side. Not enough room to leverage much force into it. Not enough to cause damage. Enough to propel him a few feet across the room. I instantly moved to my left, away from the wall, farther into the room, searching for an opening, the weak spot; a way to end this quickly, on my terms.

He spun to face me. A 92F model Beretta, short stubby suppressor attached, aimed at my chest. I coiled myself to spring in the same instant I saw it. I'd certainly be shot. But moving quickly, and with luck, I'd take the bullet in a nonlethal spot. His arm abruptly fell to his side. The weapon pointed at the floor.

He stood across from me in a familiar stance. Apparently normal, casual even, arms hanging loosely at his sides, the weapon held nonchalantly, unthreateningly, by his right thigh. I knew better. Noted his solidly planted stance, the weight on the balls of his feet, his center of gravity squarely over his hips. More of his side than his front turned in my direction. Using minute movements I'd done the same.

We studied each other across the small intervening distance. Both frozen in place. Tall, languid. Pale blue eyes, cold, stared out from a lined, dark tanned angular face. Blond hair along the sides of his head. Absent from the top. He wore tan slacks, and a light blue shirt matching his eyes, open at the chest. He wore tan loafers and no socks.

No doubt in my mind I stood face-to-face with my invisible watcher.

I waited. Acutely conscious of the bulky weight in the waistband at my back. Its heat from being recently fired. To have any chance with the gun I'd have to move out of his line of fire. My eyes never left his face as my mind recalled the surrounding environment. The open door five paces to my right. Coffee table diagonally across on my left. Armchair next to it, a headlong dive away. No chance of cover anywhere.

He searched my eyes. Mine firmly focused on his. He smiled. An odd curling at the corners of his mouth. Thin lips stretching. A smile devoid of mirth. Practiced. Designed to inveigle. A reptilian kind of smile.

"Still have the chops." His voice deep, gravelly, a hint of amusement in his tone. "We need a meet," he said. "Without trying to kill each other." He sidled sideways toward the open door. Cold stare fixed on mine. Gone a moment later.

I didn't follow him. He obviously hadn't been there to kill me. But not a certainty. He might be standing in the yard waiting, the weapon pointed at the front door. Right where I'd be expected to exit. Pursuing him served no immediate purpose. Except to get into another fight. For some reason he'd wanted to test me. He'd chosen a dangerous way to do it. But his moves were practiced, second nature. Like mine. And familiar.

In any event I didn't relish another bout of hand-to-hand. Given the choice, I'd avoid a fight whenever possible. Unlike television or the movies, any combat, whether firefight or hand-to-hand, entailed real blood, real pain, real death. Whether doing the hitting or getting hit, flesh tends to bruise; to crack and break. Like teeth, ribs, wrists, and knuckles. It's fast. It's unpredictable. It can be deadly. A split second, a slight slip, a lucky strike, changing your life forever. Maybe ending it.

I'd learned to choose my fights. To strike when least expected. To put the opposition down hard and fast. No more than two, three blows at the most. Swift and lethal. That ability and skill slower on the backside of middle age. Emotionally I denied it. Intellectually I understood it. Physically I felt it. Maybe just a fraction of a second. Enough for someone younger, quicker. Like whoever had just walked out the door.

I'd discover his identity soon enough. But I knew with certainty I'd found my watcher. More ominously, he'd found me. Not good.

My arms and thigh ached. Definitely too old for this shit.

CHAPTER 18

The adrenaline surge subsided. No after action jitters or tremors. No racing heart rate thumping against my rib cage. Like the early days. I'd long since been desensitized. I calmly dialed Jolene's encrypted cell phone.

"What's up?" Her manner all business. The storm had left her a full plate of problems to cope with.

"You and Mendez need to get over to Mike's place right away. No one else. Just the two of you."

She fell silent. I pictured her straightening up from whatever she'd been working on. Her focus shifting. Her brow creased in concentration, a determined, inquiring look on her face and in her eyes.

"Not another.....?" She didn't finish the question.

"Not quite. You need to leave now."

She didn't argue. She'd learned to recognize that particular tone.

"On our way. Should I add 'boss'?"

I smiled as I disconnected.

While I waited I retrieved a pair of Mike's handcuffs from his desk and manacled the unconscious figure on the floor. I searched his clothing. Found nothing on him. No other weapons. No ID. Not even a scrap of paper.

His pulse remained steady. I left him face down on the floor, his hands cuffed behind his back. I pulled the handgun jammed against my back, examined it. Same caliber as the one used on Mike, and Tesca. I wiped it clean using a rag from the kitchen before pressing it into his hands again. Now only his prints were on the weapon. With any luck he'd also left prints on the magazine. Maybe on the rounds if he'd loaded it himself.

Something bothered me. Something not quite right. Something wrong with the entire picture. Why didn't the pieces seem to quite fit? Which pieces of the puzzle were still missing? What had I been sensing?

I heard Jolene and Mendez approaching from the rear. At least I thought it might be them. Hoped it might be them. I'd had enough excitement for one evening. They approached cautiously. Probably at Mendez's direction.

"Coming in." Mendez called.

"Clear." I called back.

Mendez entered first, a Beretta storm held down by his thigh. Jolene followed behind him. Her police issued Glock held in a two-handed grip in front of her. Her eyes glued to the unconscious figure at my feet.

Mendez moved to my side. "Who's he?"

"No idea. And he's got nothing on him. But that's not important right now."

"Not important?" Jolene said. Her gaze shifted back and forth between me and the man at our feet.

"Right now we need a story that doesn't involve me. I can't be here. I was never here."

"I got this boss. I'll give Super here the story."

"You have a problem with that." I held Jolene's gaze, searching her eyes.

"No. But won't he know you were here?"

"Maybe. Maybe not. He tried to take me from behind. It was dark. And fast. He may not have seen my face. At least not good enough to be sure."

"Get the story straight with Mendez and call it in." I said to her. But don't wait too long to call."

I handed her the weapon wrapped in the kitchen rag. "His prints will be on this but check the magazine and rounds too."

I walked them through it. The shots. Where the slugs might be embedded. The casings on the floor. Mendez had the scenario already worked out. He checked the video equipment. Either the cameras were down, or maybe the portable DVR. In any case he needn't worry about erasing any video.

"I'll let Mike and Max know." I said, heading for the door.

Deep in thought I returned to Wherever. Not so deep as to be unaware of my surroundings. Acutely aware. Senses on high alert. I wouldn't be surprised a second time. Yet the entire encounter still didn't sit right. Too cliché. Like a two-bit hit in a two-bit novel.

When I climbed aboard Wherever the sun hung low in the sky, casting shadows on the bottoms of low drifting clouds. The western horizon bathed in crimson and gold.

I sat at the chart table. Called Mike. "We've had another incident," I said when he answered.

"Tell me," he said.

"A shooter waiting inside your house when I went to check the cameras." I heard the low drone of heavy diesels in the background.

"Will we be able to question him?" disguising his real question.

"Yeah. Jo made the arrest after Mendez subdued the intruder."

"I see." He said, quickly accessing and understanding the situation. "Alright. Should be there in about thirty minutes."

"Check in with Jo. She may already be on her way to Port Elizabeth."

"Will do," he said

"What about later?" I asked. We still meeting?"

"I think it's even more imperative now."

"Okay." We disconnected.

My watcher had spoken American English. No trace of a regional accent. Meaning it'd been acquired. Practiced. Though not a foregone conclusion. His tradecraft smelled of spook. Didn't mean he belonged to any particular shop. He may be independent. His hand-to-hand 'tell' familiarly Russian. Didn't narrow who he might be working for given the number of ex-eastern bloc, ex-Soviet, and ex-Russian operatives on the international market.

I had few options. I needed more information on him. His connection to this situation. He wanted a meet. I'd play out that game with him. See where it led. The first priority remained Mike and Jolene. The continuing threat against them. It needed to be tied off. Neutralized forever.

Closer to nine o'clock, three hours later, when Mike called back. The CID had finished in the house. We'd still meet there. He and Jolene had processed the prisoner. Had attempted to interrogate him after Mendez revived him. Still groggy, the prisoner claimed not to recall much. Including what he'd been doing inside the home of the Commissioner of Police. The charges of unlawful entry, possession of a weapon and ammunition, intent to cause injury, and attempted murder, sufficient to keep him in Her Majesty's prison for the rest of his life. If ballistics tests connected his weapon to Mike's shooting and the murder of Frank Tesca, he might face the hangman. Mike finally had someone to arrest and prosecute.

Jolene and Mendez, in his DEA cover, provided statements detailing how they'd walked in on the intruder, who discharged a silenced handgun at Superintendent Johanssen and Special Agent Brown in an attempt to escape. Special agent Brown of the DEA, on assignment with the RSVGPF, had subdued the intruder, who'd been subsequently arrested by Superintendent Johanssen. His weapon had been recovered, along with the bullets fired in the home and the shell casings.

Mendez remained at the house after the CID investigators had departed. I met him there to wait for the others. The shutters and windows had been opened. A cool evening breeze wafted through, ruffling light blue linen drapes.

"How'd it go?" I asked.

"Solid." Mendez had been cleaning up. He picked up three drinking glasses from the coffee table. Deposited them in the kitchen sink. He picked up glass shards from a shattered jar on the kitchen counter, a bullet hole in the wall behind it.

"With the chief and Superintendent corroborating the story, it'll hold up,." he said

"How're they holding up?"

"Chief's a pro. Super's getting there too. She learns fast."

"Any idea why surveillance went down?" I asked, walking over to the electronics filled briefcase.

"Haven't had time to check it out yet."

"What about the rest of the house? And outside?"

"Clear. I guess after the last time he decided on the direct approach."

"Maybe."

He'd heard that tone before. Recognized the worrisome expression on my face.

"What you thinking boss?" His gaze leveled at me.

"What I'm thinking is something's wrong with this picture. And I haven't been able to figure out what it is." Pausing, I gave him the rest. "This is for you and Max only. My watcher was here?"

A puzzled frown on his rugged brown face. "Wasn't the shooter?"

"No. Spoke American. My take is somebody's spook. Probably an independent contractor."

Mendez's frown turned apprehensive. Aware of everything those words implied.

"He make you?"

"Don't know. But that's the assumption I have to go with."

"You make him?"

"Never laid eyes on him before. Says he wants a meet."

"You meet with him, maybe you find out who he is and why he's interested in you."

"That's what I'm thinking." Only part of my mind paid attention to the conversation. Another part focused on various scenarios involving my watcher, playing them out to various conclusions, some logical, some unconventional. Like a chess match without knowing your opponent's method of play.

Mendez crossed to the arched opening into the hallway. Disappeared into the guest bedroom. He returned with the backpack he'd carried on the first night at Mike's house.

"Think I'll just replace all the batteries. The one in the case too. Reboot the whole system. If it's not working after that I'll have to troubleshoot the system."

He headed out the door. I had the room to myself. It'd been close. Too close. My forearms still sore from blocking solidly delivered blows. They'd get sorer, with some ugly black and blues to match.

My watcher's involvement troubled me. Ironically the best-case scenario involved a connection to Mike and this situation in some way. The more ominous alternative, a connection from my past. If so, what were my options?

I wasn't prepared to abandon everything I had here. I enjoyed my solitude. Embraced it. Savored it like a cherished companion. But I hadn't opted for a solitary existence. Otherwise I'd have chosen a remote patch of mountain, or jungle, or an uninhabited island. Or just remained at sea, making port only when necessary. Bequia had been the middle ground. Not an isolated hideaway. Not a constant reminder of my past life either. And the island possessed a mythical quality. A way of capturing the spirit, of mesmerizing the heart and soul. A hard place to forget. Even harder to leave. And whenever the presence of other living souls encroached on my own, as during tourist season, I had Wherever and the sea.

They were my life now, attachments I'd formed here. Attachments I'd forsaken for so long. Attachments I hadn't the capacity to form before.

Shit. I thought.

No. The emotion ran deeper. A stronger, more dangerous sentiment lurking deep within me. A cold, deadly anger, buried, dormant, but not exorcised. The demon reawakened by whoever had threatened the people I cared about. Threatened my revitalized capacity to care, to hope, to live. Threatened to plunge me back into the darkness.

Mendez slid soundlessly into the house, closing the door behind him. He went to the briefcase on the side table. Tapped on the keyboard. Turned to me.

"Back online," he said.

A vehicle pulled up behind the house. Twin headlight beams illuminated the yard outside. The headlights went out. The sound of the engine died. Followed by three pairs of footsteps moving along the stone veranda. The door opened. Max entered first, followed by Mike. Jolene brought up the rear.

"What a fucking day?" Mike said, dropping his briefcase next to the wicker armchair. "You okay?" He moved next to me, patted my arm. Didn't wait for an answer. He'd seen it in my eyes. He continued on into the kitchen. Paused at the sight of the bullet hole in the wall. He returned carrying glasses. Set them on the coffee table.

"You guys know where everything is," he said, indicating an unfinished cedar cabinet against the far wall, below the big windows. The cabinet's raw wood chalk colored.

"Should be cold beers in the Cooler. Make one for me. Be back in a moment." He exited the room.

Jolene raised the lid of the refrigerated cooler in the kitchen.

"Guys," she called in the direction of Max and Mendez. "Heineken, Red Stripe or Hairoun?"

"Doesn't matter. Anything." Max said, making it sound like a melody.

"Same here," from Mendez, still hunched over the briefcase.

From Mike's liquor cabinet I pulled a half filled bottle of 'Jack Daniels', Mike's drink of choice. Myers rum neat for me. Jolene handed Max and Mendez an opened Heineken and placed a bowl of chipped ice on the table.

Mike returned. He'd changed into navy blue shorts and a light blue Hawaiian shirt with a white palm tree motif. He clipped-clopped across the tiled floor in rubber-soled flip-flops.

Jolene still wore the clothing she'd begun the day in. A tan shirt, long sleeves rolled above her elbows held by a buttoned strap. Dark slacks, the cuffs pushed into tan military boots. The boots stained and caked in dried brown mud.

Mike sat in one of two wicker armchairs around the coffee table. Picked up his half glass of JD on ice. He took a long swallow of the rust colored liquid. Over the rim of his glass his eyes held mine in an interrogative stare.

"We won't have an ID on the guy until morning." Mike said, his eyes difficult to read, reflecting different and conflicting emotions. "We shipped him over to Kingstown."

Not certain that'd been the best idea. Who else might have access to him? But I wasn't about to second-guess Mike. He knew his own backyard better that I did.

"He'll appear before a magistrate Monday morning. It'll be interesting to see if he has any local connections," he said.

Mike unfolded his crossed legs, placed his glass on the coffee table. Reached for the briefcase he'd dropped next to the chair. Propping it in his lap he opened it, withdrew a stack of files.

"Time to connect some dots." He took another sip from the glass. Placed it back on the coffee table.

"On the surface, both the firms Frank Tesca and Sarah Holmes worked for appear clean. But come to find out, they're both on the Fed's radar. The Vegas firm because of Tesca, and other unsavory types they like for a half dozen open homicides. Sarah's firm because it's owned by Banco Internacional, a bank which popped a couple of financial red flags over the past two years. Banco Internacional, by the way, also owns Future's Capital, Tesca's employer. And it's also the majority shareholder in Antigua Commonwealth Bank. All these entities own or control assets all over the Caribbean."

"And the money flows to El Norte," I finished.

"Bingo," Mike said. "At least that's what the Feds think."

"They can't make the connections?" I asked.

"Not all of it. The trail goes through a lot of blinds and dummy companies. Not to mention, when some of these islands decided to diversify their economies with offshore financial services, they set up some particularly restrictive secrecy laws."

"Sarah's firm has been opening new accounts in banks all around the Eastern Caribbean over the past two years. But we can't get any information on the account holders or their transactions."

Mike paused to swallow another sip of whiskey. I'd been nursing my rum during his briefing.

"I have people looking into it but so far we have no indication Sarah Holmes visited any of those banks," Mike continued. "But I don't believe it's a coincidence her firm has accounts on every island that cruise ship happened to make port."

"What about the guy Gage caught here?" Jolene said. She'd been silent until then. A combination of distracted, absorbed and broody. Several times she'd cast furtive glances in my direction.

"He's probably the guy who shot Mike and murdered Frank Tesca. But you won't find a connection to Ramirez," I said.

"Assuming the ballistics match, we can close both cases," Mike said. "But I agree. I doubt we'll be able to prove a connection to Ramirez."

"And somehow Sarah Holmes is mixed up in all this," Jolene continued. "But we don't know how. And if she's dead as we all suspect, we'll probably never find out. So what do we do, or say, about her part in all this?"

"There's no evidence to show, much less prove, she was involved in whatever went down here." Mike said. "And her only connection is a photo on a cell phone, and dubious ties by the firm she works for. Could be the guy just wanted to take her picture. Could be she knows nothing about illegal activities at the firm. We all know that's probably horse manure but the point is it isn't evidence of anything. And no evidence connecting any of this back to Ramirez. All we can do is pass this info on and let it be someone else's headache."

"Unless her body turns up here," Max said. His soft voice a melodic counterpoint to Mike's exasperated analysis. Like Jolene, neither Max nor Mendez had spoken much. They weren't sleuths. Their specialty intelligence. Trained to watch, listen, intercept. Sometimes they procured the intelligence. Sometimes they acted on the intelligence.

"How much do the Feds know?" I asked Mike.

"Not much." An unspoken question in the eyes scrutinizing mine. "They're probably aware of our inquiries. Frank Tesca is in their database. So might this other guy we're trying to ID. It's sure to pop red flags somewhere. But they wouldn't know why we're looking into him. I haven't sent any reports up the information chain yet."

So far only Mendez knew about the added player. He'd pass it on to Max soon. Still not certain why I kept it from Mike and Jolene. Habit maybe. Or some instinct telling me to keep it under wraps. For now.

"Good," I said. "How're the covers holding?"

A tight smile crossed Mike's face, the question in his eyes finding an answer. He'd correctly surmised my underlying concern.

"Solid for now," he said. "Could get complicated once this information goes stateside and federal types start asking questions."

I acknowledged by a small smile of my own. Both of us on the same page. "What about local questions?" I asked.

"No one's asking," Mike said. "I'm not sure if that's a good thing or not. Just shows how easy it'd be to penetrate us.

But these two," indicating Max and Mendez, a nod at each of them, "they're like finding buried treasure. Right now, the investigations are still open, and I still need their input, and the cover they provide for my other plan. But at some point I'm gonna have to send this up the chain.

"We're here until it's over." Max intoned.

"And you don't think it's over yet, do you?" Mike asked, turning to face him.

"The threat is the person running these guys." Max said. "The guy giving the orders. That threat has to be neutralized before this will be over. And evidence can't touch whoever is pulling the strings. You know that."

I observed their interaction. The dynamic formed in their short time together. A bond of trust and mutual respect between commander and advisor.

"Anyway," Mike said, his attention returning to the group, "My stateside contacts are running down the activities of these banks and corporations. Any others they can flag. And we got some more on Ramirez and his organization."

He shoved a file across the table to me. It contained a dozen or so pages. A five by seven photograph clipped to each page. And another thicker paper clipped sheaf with more photographs.

"Photographs of Ramirez, known associates, and lieutenants in the cartel," Mike said.

I scanned the pages and photographs. Paid particular attention to his presumed number two, and his chief enforcer. But most of my attention on the man himself. The photos old, mostly black and white, grainy, taken from a distance. And most from his younger years. He'd managed to remain out of camera sight following his rise to the top. The information portrayed him as paranoid, with good reason, indicating he seldom stayed in one place more than twenty-four hours.

We worked the information for another hour. Worried it this way and that. We'd gathered a great deal of data. The picture emerging, becoming clearer. But still nothing actionable. And Ramirez a hard target to get at. I asked Mike if I might hang on to the Ramirez file for a while.

Later, aboard Wherever, ensconced in the large aft berth, the cabin dark and silent except for water lapping against her hull, Jolene held tightly to me. I lay on my back, one arm wrapped around her. She lay on her side, her head on my chest, her hair draped across my neck and shoulder, its honeyed scent floating just below my nose. Her fingers traced their familiar path across the landmarks of my past.

I felt the wetness drip onto my skin and run across my chest. Teardrops shed without a sound. She remained still next to me.

"You okay?" I whispered.

"I love you," she whispered back in the dark. Words she gave voice to only occasionally, and without expectation of a reply. "I'm glad you're safe."

She loosened her tight embrace, still holding me close, with a tender fierceness. Like she never intended to ever let go.

I rocked her gently. My last thought before we both lapsed into unconsciousness the warm glow she unleashed within me. And the cold, frigid glacier lying beneath.

CHAPTER 19

Two days later. Early Sunday morning. Jolene and I awoke to the full-throated cocka-doodle-doos of a nearby roster. Maybe heralding a new day. Maybe crowing just to crow. They seemed to crow as it pleased them, especially at first light. Their crowing as natural to Bequia mornings as the clicks and chirps of inserts at night.

Almost every household on Bequia had at least one chicken, some more. A source of eggs and the occasional Sunday dinner. On Bequia they were as ubiquitous as the goats. They roamed at will, invading unfenced vegetable gardens, crossing busy roads in their slow, meandering, neck thrusting strut. Scattering helter-skelter in a ruckus of clucking and flapping of flightless wings as vehicles sped past them.

Jolene owned no chickens. Didn't matter. This particular rooster had laid claim to a piece of ground outside her bedroom window.

Sundays are special on Bequia. A day of rest and feasting. A day when families, aunts, uncles, cousins, siblings, grannies and pappies, visit each other and gather for church, meals, and the weekly 'sea bath'. The morning reserved for churchgoing. The churchgoers decked out in their best finery.

The afternoon for the beach. Huge Sunday meals an integral part of the day. The eating, drinking, games, and music continuing throughout the afternoon. The night for dancing and 'winenin' before the start of the new work week.

Jolene attended church irregularly, mostly when called upon in her official capacity. She'd risen to the rooster's crowing, showered, dressed, and departed early to attend a special service for the little girl from Paget Farm. The island's only fatality during the storm. Following the service the girl's body would be interred in a small hillside cemetery overlooking Paget Farm.

Unable to get back to sleep I decided to head down to Wherever. Jolene and I had sailed her around from Friendship Bay the day before. I bid good morning to late stragglers hurrying to church. The women in flamboyant hats, decorous dresses, and white gloves. Boys in dark pants, pressed white shirts and ties. Girls in colorful pinafores, shiny patent leather shoes, and bright bows tied to tightly braided pigtails.

The day smelled fresh and salty. The sun peeked above the headland, bathing the sloping green landscape and blue bay in increasing light and heat. I left the dinghy where I'd tethered it the night before, deciding to swim out instead. The surf rolling onto the sparkling white sand held a bracing chill as I dove in. A refreshing rush of bubbles raced along my skin through the denim shorts and cotton tee shirt.

I surfaced beyond the breakers. My tee shirt ballooned by pockets of air, flattening against my skin as I stroked farther from shore. I drew alongside Wherever. Pulled off the tee shirt, tossed it aboard. Turning, I plunged like a playful porpoise. Kicked in the direction of the open harbor. The water in the bay tranquil again.

By noon I was ready to return ashore following the invigorating morning swim, a leisured shower thanks to full water tanks, and a hearty brunch of scrambled eggs, bacon, toast smothered in homemade guava jelly, and mountain roast coffee.

Dressed again in shorts and tee shirt, this time army green, I dove from Wherever's rail. I waded ashore, tee shirt and shorts dripping wet, clinging to my skin. They'd dry soon enough in the midday heat. I dodged playful screaming kids running to and fro across the beach, jumping and diving into the surf. I opened a watertight fanny pack I'd worn around my waist. Donned my special sunglasses. Removed my phone and a few other items before securing the fanny pack out of sight in the dinghy.

Sunday afternoon at De Reef in full swing. Reggae music pounded from the restaurant's speakers. Churchgoing clothes replaced by beach attire. The beach given over to frolicking kids. Adolescent girls sat in the sand, hair being braided by moms, aunties, grannies or older female siblings.

At the front of the restaurant games of table tennis, cards, dominos, punctuated by excitable shouts of triumph and good-natured teasing. Other tables occupied by families eating lunch. The hunger inducing smell of food everywhere. A mixture of fish, chicken, conch, lobster, French fries, beef, and rice and peas.

The bar lined two deep. Drinkers in merry conversation between gulps of bottled beer. Among them a smattering of off-season tourists, sipping mixed drinks in highball glasses through straws.

I headed toward the back of De Reef. Exchanged greetings with knots of people along the way. Expats. A varied mixture. Americans, Canadians, British, Germans. A few other nationalities. They tended to socialize within their own nationalities. Some on Bequia for many years. They'd married locals, raised families, ran local businesses, owned hotels or rental villas. Some were cruising sailors whose Bequia stopover turned semi-permanent. The Island had that effect.

I cast a hello to G, a lithe leggy blond. A head turner in a bikini. A single mom, rumored to have been a Vegas dancer in her former life. A greeting nod to her friend and business partner Elaine, also blond, married to a Bequian. Elaine's two daughters, four and seven years old, both adorable. A gorgeous blend of mixed genes.

Others I knew by acquaintance. Helen, an American widow living aboard a thirty-four foot Joshua ketch moored in Port Elizabeth. She raised her rum punch glass in greeting. The young couple who'd come to Bequia as Peace Corp volunteers and never left. The teacher who'd founded a local school for children with disabilities. All of them having a story. All building lives far from their native homes.

Behind De Reef's bustling kitchen I entered an outdoor area used for cleaning and preparing food. A group of dwarf coconut trees stood next to the prep area. I grabbed a long pole which had a steel hook attached to one end. Hooked a green coconut. Yanked it from the tree. I picked three more. Traded the pole for a machete on a low-lying shelf. I sliced the top off one coconut in a single practiced stroke. The slice made at an angle, deep enough to expose the soft core containing the sweet, milky liquid.

"Meking yuh special?" the smiling black face peering out from the kitchen belonged to Dennis, one of De Reef's owners. Also Captain of a small interisland freighter anchored in Port Elizabeth. Also part owner of the supermarket in Hamilton.

I returned the smile. He turned away into the kitchen. I found the ice chest containing a block of ice. On Bequia ice is frozen in blocks. The blocks chipped into glass size chunks with an ice pick. Or shaved to make snow cones. Or smashed with a mallet or anything heavy close at hand to make crushed ice.

I crushed a small chunk of ice, poured it into the coconut. Dennis reappeared carrying an opened bottle of Mount Gay rum and a straw, saving me the trip to the bar. He handed over the bottle and straw. I poured a shot glass worth of rum into the coconut. As the day wore on the amount of rum in the mix usually increased. Grinning with good natured amusement Dennis took the bottle and returned to the bar.

With my coconut rum in hand I headed off to my right. Toward a quieter area of the beach. Where the view of the beach from the road was hidden by a high hedgerow of trees and shrubs. And a copse of manchioneel trees behind the hedgerow. I sat on an outcropping of rock rising above the sand, sipping my drink through a straw. I gazed idly across the beach in both directions.

A few yards in front of me another rock outcropping rose above the sand, probably part of the same formation providing my seat. It stretched parallel to the beach for maybe fifty yards, enclosing a shallow pool formed by seawater washing over its green moss-covered top. Squealing toddlers, all toddler cute and toddler adorable, romped in the clear tidal pool under watchful adult eyes. They crawled, sat, tottered on wobbly legs in the pool, splashing and shrieking in delight, making early swimming motions.

I smiled at their joyful play and exploration. Every so often one of them took a face first tumble into the water, instantly plucked out by a hovering adult. Sputtering, coughing, screaming in bewilderment. Followed by a dawning awareness of being okay, and a squirming escape from the adult's clutch. Right back into the water. No fear.

Farther down the beach, a full-throated pickup game of cricket underway, using sticks pushed into the sand for stumps, a cut piece of coconut branch for a bat, and a bald tennis ball.

He approached from the direction of Princess Margaret Beach. Didn't surprise me. It's what I'd have done.to remain clear of crowded areas. Ensuring sightlines to see, and more importantly, be seen. Assuming a non-hostile meet.

He appeared shorter than I'd first thought. Outdoors, in the full light of day, the creases in his face more discernible. Especially the deep furrows across his hairless brow. And the carved corners around his mouth. In daylight he also appeared older than I'd originally estimated.

Or maybe his skin had worn poorly, the deep lines obscuring his true age. The once white complexion darkened to a mahogany brown from long tropical exposure. But most remarkable, his eyes. Not for their color, a clear crisp blue like the petals of morning glory in the midday sun, but their lack of expression. As cold as the Nordic climes of his probable heritage. Windows not into a soul, but a dark empty abyss.

His eyes quartered the surrounding area before settling on me. He wore a loose fitting, short sleeved, faded Hawaiian shirt. Unbuttoned halfway down his chest. The tail hung over white cargo slacks. No obvious signs of a weapon. But he'd be armed, as I was. Probably a compact handgun tucked into the waistband at the small of his back. And an assortment of innocuous but deadly items on his person. Our previous encounter had taught me not to underestimate him.

"Mr. Gage I presume." He halted six feet off to my right. Deliberately beyond my personal space. Not to mention my reach.

"I don't know you," I said, gazing up at him through the sunglasses. I sipped my coconut rum.

"True. But it'd be to your advantage to get to know me."

"You don't say. And why is that?"

"I have information about something you want. I can help you get it." Deep lines punctuated the corners of his mouth like parentheses. His smile set, as expressionless as his eyes.

"And why would you want to do that? Like I said. I don't know you."

"I believe you know who I am. At least what I represent. Just as I know the same about you. As to what I want, we can get to that later. But believe me when I say I can help you."

Like hell you can, I thought. But we were playing his game. He'd get around to the point in his own good time. I'd danced this dance before. Usually the one leading. And he'd been correct. I did have a good idea what, if not who, he represented. Certainly a different caliber from the thuggish shooters I'd encountered so far. The 'tell' in his fighting style even providing an idea of his origins. The shops he might've trained and spent time in.

"At least hear what I'm offering," his deep voice smooth, nonthreatening, seductive. Just the right timber and tone. As before no discernable regional accent.

"I don't think so." I said.

The damn smile never left his face while his eyes evaluated me. A smile never reaching the glacial blue eyes. He bent at the knees, squatted. Sat cross-legged in the soft sand. Uninvited. His empty hands always deliberately displayed. I hadn't discouraged his presence. Or made a move to depart myself. He was a player in all this, whatever this was. He'd been watching me long enough to plan his approach, to be confident of initiating contact. I needed to know to what end.

"I can see why you like it here," he said, his gaze drifting along the beach. Kids at play. Families enjoying Sunday at the beach. His wandering gaze rested on Wherever. "I could see myself settling down here. Maybe get myself a boat and live on it. It's a special place. Something I'd want to protect and keep safe." The threat subtle, yet not so well hidden I didn't get it. The stick accompanying the still unoffered carrot.

The words fired my anger. My blood chilled and ran cold, freezing my emotions. My anger never ran hot. Instead it coalesced into an icy calm, emanating from the center of my being, freezing emotions in place, shattering whatever it touched. An anger recently reawakened.

Still not ready to unveil the carrot. He'd present it in his own time in this bizarre ritual.

No longer in the mood to play I said, "We both know how this dance goes so why don't you just tell me what you're selling, and the price."

He heard the honed steel in my voice. His gaze met mine. My eyes as cold as his. The set of his smile slipped for a fraction of a second. He decided he had to make his move or lose his opening.

"I can give you Eduardo Ramirez," he said.

My turn to smile. As mirthless as his. "And the price?"

"No price. Just a catch. You'll have to go get him. But that's what you want anyway isn't it?"

"Why come to me?"

"Because I can't take him alone. Because you've still got what it takes. And because it's what you want. You knew I've been watching you from the start didn't you?" Rhetorical. He didn't wait for an answer. "I saw the way you moved when you first felt eyes on you. You're in the game. Or were. Figured it'd be a waste of time to follow you. You'd have made me right off."

"How'd you make me?"

"Wasn't sure at first. But you have the look. And there was something familiar about you. Couldn't put my finger on it for the longest time. Then I remembered. We've crossed paths once. Never came face-to-face. But I remembered you. During the Panama operation right before the Noriega snatch. Back then the name was Alverez I believe. Heard the name a few times before that too. Other places neither of us would care to mention I imagine. Lots of people think you're dead. But here you are. And our little encounter in the commissioner's house clinched it."

Shit. My worst fear confirmed. A new situation now. A slender thread I couldn't have him or anyone pulling on. Unraveling it led to identities and events which needed to remain buried. Like Alverez. The implications of Alverez being found alive too ominous to contemplate.

Around us families played innocently along the beach. At the surf line two small boys, shirtless, wearing torn khaki shorts, raced makeshift boats constructed from dried coconut husks. Tree leaves threaded on a piece of stick served as sails.

"Bottom line is I just got lucky," he continued. "Followed a couple of Ramirez's crew here trying to figure an angle to get close to him. Was about to leave to set up on him when I spotted you. Learned you had a vested interest, the Commissioner of Police being your friend and all. And Ramirez won't stop at him. He'll go after her too."

The ice within me spreading, like a pond freezing in winter.

"And?" I said.

"And what?"

"What's in this for you? Why're you after Ramirez?"

"Part personal. Part there's a package I need your help to retrieve."

"What's the package?"

"A little early yet for that," he said. "Not until I know you're in. Then I'll tell you everything you need to know."

"I'll have to think about it."

"Fair enough. But there's a time constraint. A small window when he'll be vulnerable. So don't take too long thinking."

I rose from my seat on the rock. Left him sitting in the sand. I headed off in the direction of De Reef with my empty coconut. Time to cut open another.

The sun arced across the sky. The blinding silver orb transformed into a fiery orange ball as it slid closer to the horizon, disappearing in a splash of crimson, amber and gold. Evening swept in from the east. The sky a shade darker as the minutes following the sunset ticked away. Pinpoints of light twinkled on in the dark canopy overhead. Accompanied by lights ashore, muted and diffuse, winking through the trees. Shania Twain replaced Bob Marley through De Reef's speakers. The Sunday crowd long since thinned to a few dancing couples.

Jolene entered through the door closest to the road. Mendez close behind her. She hadn't seen me yet. Her eyes unobtrusively quartered the room. I hadn't paid much attention to it before. But I'd noticed her practicing it more and more, becoming adept. No one had taught her the technique. She'd absorbed it somehow, like osmosis, by observing Mike and me. Mostly me. And with Mendez constantly at her side, she'd soaked up even more tradecraft. A natural. Without the killing instinct. Though I wouldn't bet on it. On rare occasions her entrancing hazel eyes held a cold deadly edge, as though forged by a malevolent memory.

She spotted me against the wall. Veered in my direction, her scan continuing as she crossed the room.

God, I thought, observing her negotiate the dancing couples. How'd I ever deserve this? Deserve her? An exquisite, ineffable quality surrounded her, radiated from her. An understated sensuality and excitement. The simple orange sundress she wore draped and accentuated her enticing curves as she moved. The collar of the white tee shirt-like vest visible beneath the dress's high neckline. A pink frangipani tucked behind her right ear.

I met her in the middle of the room. Placed my hands on her hips. Pulled her into me. My arms circled her waist, moving her slowly against me in time to the sultry rhythm, feeling her response. I noticed Mendez moving toward an empty table. Caught his silent signal.

We remained locked in the swaying embrace through two more bluesy vocals of love found, love betrayed, love redeemed. Jolene soft and fragrant against me. Our hips, thighs, pelvises pressing and moving to the rhythmic mix of steel and acoustic guitars.

Max waited at the table for us. I sat opposite him. Jolene headed to the bar.

"What you got?" I asked.

"Nothing much. None of our contacts could ID the photos streamed from the sunglasses camera.

"Nothing then." I said.

"We're still digging. I want to ask the Chief to pull his entry card."

"What're you gonna tell him?"

"Person of interest we want to check out."

"He won't buy it. Tell him about the contact here at De Reef. Leave out the part about his house, and this guy watching me."

Mendez periodically glanced over my shoulder, keeping tabs on Jolene. And anyone taking an undue interest in her.

"He's trying to recruit me," I said. "Doing a good job too. Can't pin down who might've trained him. Probably the same place he got his hand-to-hand training. Russian style. Says he can deliver Ramirez. Also needs to retrieve a package Ramirez has. Wants me to help him get it. Don't give that part to Mike either. I'm still not sure where this is headed."

Jolene appeared at my side carrying a rum and coke on ice for me, a cold Heineken for Mendez. A large wine goblet containing a light golden liquid and the scent of Chablis for herself. She glanced at Mendez, at me, accurately read the scene. Sat down without voicing any questions.

She didn't ask until much later. Curled up against me under the mosquito net. A warm tropical breeze billowed the curtains at the open windows. On the cusp of sleep.

"What was that all about with Mendez?" she murmured, half asleep.

"There's a new player on the field." I said, deciding to tell her. If we were telling Mike, she needed to know too.

"What does that mean, a new player?"

"Someone else here on Bequia besides the guy in Mike's house. Someone involved in all this. Not sure how yet. He approached me on the beach earlier this afternoon."

"What does he want?" Her voice continuing to fade away.

"Being cagey about that at the moment," I lied.

"What do you intend to do about this new player?" almost a whisper.

"Not sure yet."

"Hmmm" she murmured, her fingers lightly tracing their usual path across my skin. Seconds later she sank easily into sleep.

I followed her moments later. My last waking thought her question. What to do about this guy?

CHAPTER 20

Midweek, Wednesday, before he approached me again. This time at the Frangipani bar where I'd stopped for a cold beer in between errands.

"You must have checked me out by now," he greeted, the smile set in place. The thought occurred it might be a facial feature. Not a smile at all. Just the unnatural contour of his mouth.

"For all the good it did me. Not much there to find," I lied. "You claim you can deliver Eduardo Ramirez."

"Yes"

"El cuchillo?"

"Yes"

"And you know why that would interest me?"

"Yes again."

"Okay. Let's dispense with the formalities. Here's what I propose. I don't decide if I'm in or out until I hear everything you have. And of course you won't give me everything until you know if I'm in. So let's do this in stages. We keep going to the next level unless I say stop and I'm out."

"I can live with that." A nice touch. Appearing not to be too eager. Aware he had me nipping at the line.

"Where do you want to meet?"

"How about your boat."

"Fine. When?"

"After dark, say about eight."

"See you then," I said, slipping off the stool, heading off toward the dinghy dock. I didn't ask how he intended to get out to Wherever. I didn't offer to pick him up.

I went about my day. I skimmed across the bay to the Hamilton Marina. Picked up six quarts of engine oil for the outboard. In need of a few items for Wherever's dwindling pantry I headed to the supermarket behind the marina. Just off the main road. A railed slipway separated the marina and the back of the supermarket. The slipway yard contained storage sheds constructed of chicken wire and corrugated tin roofs. Tall coconut trees populated the yard.

I stared at the area where Mike's life had almost ended. The spot bleak and dreary, the sun perpetually shaded by a canopy of palm branches high above. The ground littered with fallen palm branches and dried coconut husks. I stood on the spot where Mike had probably stood, absorbing the scene. I turned in the direction of the road. The blood trail long since soaked into the sandy soil. Washed clean by the storm. A miracle he'd made it to the road, and still possessed sufficient strength to call on his cell. A decade earlier, before cell phone service and reliable electricity, he'd have bled out before being found.

I imagined the thoughts which had probably raced through his brain as it slowly shut down. The darkness closing in. I'd been there. But I had no one to leave behind. Mike had a family. He'd have thought about his kids. He'd have thought how stupid he'd been to get himself shot. He'd have thought about dying. In this dreary place. Alone.

I knew then I'd continue down the slippery slope I'd embarked on. I'd questioned it. Had fought against it. Afraid of unleashing demons I'd buried and sought to forget. But I'd already travelled too far along it to back off now. I'd have to risk the demons; the barbarous beast. They'd already been awakened anyway. And I hoped, at the end of all this, I'd be able to put them back to rest. The new player provided the opportunity to end this once and for all.

A familiar contentment settled over me, like donning a favorite old tee shirt. A burdensome weight lifted. My brain already running scenarios, pondering exigencies, defining logistics, while I walked the aisles of the supermarket. I'd missed the mental exercise. Not so much the actions following it.

The aisles of the supermarket, Bequia's version of a supermarket, lit by natural sunlight streaming thought openings high up in the brick walls, close to the roof. No bright fluorescents illuminating everything. No clean tile floors mopped daily. Crude wood shelves partitioned the concrete floor. The shelves stacked with products bearing brand names unfamiliar in the States. Except for Kellogg's Cornflakes. And Coca Cola. Found everywhere on the planet.

I spent the remainder of the day doting on Wherever. She liked being kept in sailing shape. Ready to make passage at a moment's notice. In return she performed as I needed her to, flawlessly, her manners admirable in any wind or sea. Her mechanical and electrical systems allowed me the comforts of home. Her rigging and wardrobe allowed her to be what she'd been designed to be. She preferred close reaching the best. Liked to be stretched out like a thoroughbred given its head. With the wind directly behind her she had a tendency to steer wild and wander. She couldn't help it. She'd been born a schooner.

Her bottom had been recently cleaned of marine growth. Her booms lay idle like folded wings. She required a few minor adjustments to her standing rigging. Some minor repairs to her running rigging. I lubed her winches and slides. Replaced her worn tackle.

Come evening I lounged in the blacked out cockpit. A night vision scope on the cushion next to me. My visitor had to come out by water. I'd spot his approach early. He might come from the direction of Port Elizabeth, crossing Tony Gibbons Bay. Or he might take the land route to Lower Bay. Embark from there. I bet on Port Elizabeth, where he'd more likely find a water taxi.

Meeting on Wherever his suggestion. He hadn't done that mistakenly. Had to know it'd put him at a disadvantage, the schooner my home turf. He'd assume I'd prepare the home ground. Traps and weapons stashed within easy reach. His way of telling me he didn't mind. Building trust.

My take, the schooner somehow figured into his plan, whatever that plan might be.

I heard the water taxi before I saw it. The distinctive familiar drone of a Yamaha 9.9 horsepower outboard. A popular model among Bequia's fishermen and water taxi operators. The ghostly shape caught in the night scope. White water curled from an invisible bow as the water taxi sliced its way across the dark stretch of Tony Gibbons Bay.

I didn't switch on the cockpit lamp hanging under the awning until the small open decked launch came alongside. The mystery man grasped the rail, effortlessly hoisting himself on deck. I included a new item on the list of things I knew about him. He was comfortable on a boat. Probably knew his way around one too.

He ducked under the awning, entering the cockpit. I indicated a seat.

"Get you something to drink?" I offered.

"Whatever you're drinking," motioning to the glass on the cockpit table.

"Rum and Coke," I said, fetching another glass from the rack built onto the edge of the folding table. I dumped in ice from a cooler next to the binnacle. While I mixed the cocktail his gaze roamed Wherever's cockpit and deck. Not much to see in the darkness beyond the cockpit. But I'd bet he'd already memorized her details. Probably her interior layout too. I handed him the drink.

"So what do I call you?" According to Mendez he'd entered through immigration using the name Robert Carlson.

He stuck with the local ID. "Carlson. Robert Carlson." A pause while he set the smile in place. "Bob." He didn't extend his hand and neither did I. "And what do I call you?" He asked in return.

"Gage is fine," I said.

I studied his face as he sipped his drink. Over the rim of the highball glass his blue eyes stared right back into mine.

"Confirm for me, a couple of assumptions." I said.

"Go ahead."

"Assumption number one. You're coming to me because this is your operation and you want it kept that way. Anonymous. Off the books. Whoever you work for doesn't know about it.

"A plausible assumption." Neither confirmed nor denied. I needed to know if he was working alone. Or reporting my recruitment to anyone else. I let it go for the time being.

"Assumption number two. You want to leverage the package, whatever it is."

"Also a plausible assumption." Again, not sure if he wanted the package personally, or on behalf of someone he worked for.

"To what purpose?"

"Let's say it's my ticket out. Walking away on my terms, as you did. And maybe finding a little piece of this." He waved his arms in an all-inclusive gesture.

Reasonable. Made perfect sense. In our line of work you didn't just quit, retire and walk away. Getting out required a bargaining chip. Something to leverage. And an insurance policy to assure being left alone. But there were other ways to leverage a package, depending on its value. Retirement might not be Carlson's agenda at all. I didn't take anything he said at face value. Still not sure he wasn't working on behalf of someone else.

"And what, or who, is the package?" I didn't believe he'd reveal it this early, but worth a try.

"Not yet." He smiled. If a shark could smile it'd look like his.

I smiled right back.

"Tell me about Ramirez." I said, changing the subject.

"Ruthless. Paranoid. Has a five million dollar standing bounty on his head. But no one can touch him because he's too well protected. Never stays in one place more than twenty four hours. Never sleeps in the same place twice in a row."

"Tell me something I don't know," I said.

"He's going to be in Antigua next week, for the end of race week."

He knew he'd scored. The highball glass in my hand paused for the tiniest fraction of a second on the way to my mouth.

"You have confirmation?" I asked, swallowing a sip from the glass.

"One hundred percent guaranteed," he said.

Smug son of a bitch, I thought.

"And you've come by this information, how?"

"Let's just say I have sources outside the acknowledged channels."

In other words he had his own informant. Probably someone close to Ramirez.

"He'll be using decoys, as usual. Two or three yachts that he'll move between. A couple of villas ashore maybe. Maybe also an aircraft on standby. And he won't be there for more than twenty-four hours. But I know he'll be there for a face-to-face meet. And I also know who he's meeting."

"The person either delivering or receiving the package."

"Not too shabby," Mr. Gage.

I glanced at my watch. Close to nine. I had a date to meet Jolene.

"Okay," I said, standing. "I'll give you a ride ashore."

"Was it something I said?" The corners of his mouth curled in a mocking grin. "Or something I didn't say."

I flashed him an equally insincere smile. "Not that your company isn't captivating, but I have someplace else to be."

I headed to the stern, untied the dinghy painter, dragged the dinghy around the side.

He studied me as I handled the dinghy. Waiting for me to say something maybe. I remained silent, indicating the boarding ladder, the dinghy alongside.

"So what now?" He asked.

"We move to the next stage," I said.

We said little to each other during the fast ride across the Bay to Port Elizabeth. Both of us taking the other's measure. I dropped him off at the Frangipani dinghy dock.

There were good reasons to reject Carlson's proposal and this op out of hand. First and foremost I didn't trust him. His timing too convenient to be coincidence. I knew going in he'd been manipulating me. And would continue to do so. The trick, knowing when to break away. The timing essential. Too early, risk losing the objective. Too late, risk not escaping at all.

And the elephant in the room, my age. I'd long since deleted break-your-fool-neck risks from my repertoire. Mostly I'd gotten wiser. Now I'd gotten older. But even that might be turned to an advantage. As long as I kept in mind I no longer possessed the physical abilities of a twenty five year old.

Most important reason of all, I'd left the world Carlson inhabited behind for good. Buried that part of me. It'd been an addiction, like alcohol or crack cocaine. An adrenaline high producing a primal euphoric rush. And it had almost destroyed me. But I'd already made my decision. Already experienced the stirring of the beast. Even buried it'd always be a part of me. Like an arm or a leg.

And there were persuasive reasons to see it through. This place. Two people I cared about. Also part of me now. They'd awakened the part of me my beast had kept submerged. Had given it life and succor, allowing it to flourish. That existence, those people, my life now, were being threatened.

And maybe the one true reason for doing it? Because I could. Because the beast, as much a part of me as everything else, gave me the ability to not only kill, but also to protect.

I cranked the throttle down approaching the beach. The dinghy lost forward momentum, settling low in the water. As I shut down and tilted the outboard the swell created by the dinghy's wake caught up. It surged beneath the transom, lifting the inflatable clear of the surf line to deposit it high and dry on the beach. I hopped out, pulled the dinghy farther up the beach. Tethered and locked it around the trunk of a coconut tree.

Jolene sat at her dining table absorbed in a sea of paper. I walked over, put my arms around her shoulders, bent to kiss her cheek. Soft, jasmine scented curls brushed my cheek and nostrils.

"What you up to?"

"Finishing up some overdue reports. Not that they're much interest to anyone but me, it seems." She turned to face me. Clear hazel eyes, amber-green in lamplight, met mine. "And how was your evening?"

The lie on the tip of my tongue. Instinctive. And in this instance protective. I wanted to protect this extraordinary, wonderful person who'd found her way into my life. But a stronger, less familiar instinct took hold. A recognition of the unfairness of lying to her. She might not need to know. But she had a right to know. She wasn't an asset, or a package, or a mark, or any of the other euphemisms. But someone who loved me. Trusted me. And I felt the same about her. New concepts for me.

I told her the truth. "I met that guy again. He may be the key to ending this whole thing. But I still can't be sure yet. Just feeling my way for now."

She hadn't mentioned him since I'd told her about our meeting at De Reef. Her eyes searched mine, conveying something I didn't recognize.

"Thanks," She said, touching soft lips to mine.

She arranged, stacked and filed the papers scattered across the table. Max entered from the direction of the guestroom.

"Hey boss." His eyes met mine in silent inquiry. Instinctively cautious within earshot of Jolene.

"Working on it." I said.

"Copy that. See you in the morning." He headed out the door.

Jolene stuffed the files into a briefcase, set it on a chair and headed toward her bedroom. I headed for the fridge. For someone who ate like a bird the refrigerator contained an abundance of food. Maybe to accommodate her houseguest. I stared at the contents absentmindedly. Not really hungry. Deciding, I pulled a pitcher of white, creamy liquid from the fridge, poured myself a tall glass of soursop.

Jolene returned wearing an oversized, red, well-worn U Penn tee shirt. And nothing else. She moved about the room turning off lights, shutting windows and doors, buttoning up for the night. She took my hand, led me to the bedroom where homemade aromatic candles, placed strategically around the room, burned with the subtle fragrances of honeysuckle, jasmine, and rose.

She led me over to the bed, pushed me on to it. Leaning down she pressed her lips against mine, opening my mouth.

Her tongue flicked against mine as deft fingers worked at removing my clothes.

CHAPTER 21

"Ramirez has interests all over the Eastern Caribbean," Carlson said at our next meeting. Again we met aboard Wherever. After dark. We drank rum and cokes. Carlson closer to his objective. I'd taken the bait. He had me on the line. Ready to reel me in. The hook irremovably set.

"Real estate and banking mostly," he continued. "The type of entities you can wash a lot of cash through. I don't know all the specific holdings, or where." He swallowed a mouthful of his drink before continuing, as though talking made him thirsty.

"He has a controlling interest in the Antigua Commonwealth Bank. Practically owns the damn thing. I also believe it's one of his secret server sites."

It caught my interest. As Carlson knew it would. A server. Access to a large chunk of Ramirez's operation in one place. It'd be huge. Mega huge. I detected a scent of the as yet unspecified package.

Carlson studied me. Time for the net to land his catch? Hard to tell. His facial expressions expertly masked. His icy piercing stare unceasingly searching, striving to read me. As I aimed to read him.

"Okay," I said following a pause. Portraying the impression of pondering a decision. A decision I'd reached from our first encounter on the beach.

"The next stage comes with a set of ground rules." I said. "But before we get to that, one more question."

"Let's hear it." His tone agreeable, cooperative, self – confident. Aware he already had me.

"Why'd you wait to make contact? And why the Commissioner's house, that particular night, that particular time?" I had my own take. Knew what I'd say in his shoes. But interested in hearing his version.

"That's three questions," he said, his sarcasm witlessly thick and sappy. Accompanied by the damn smile; more a smirk since convincing himself of his control over me. His response also a classic delay tactic while he formulated his answer. He feigned a sigh and continued.

"I'd been following a couple of Ramirez's soldiers, like I said, when I spotted you. At the time I didn't know what you were doing here. Your role in all this. Until I made the connection to the Commissioner. Your friendship with him. Figured if you had a stake in this we might be able to work together. So I decided to also watch your back. I'd been surveiling the guy you took down. Followed him to the Commissioner's house. Saw you arrive. Figured you'd take him. But I had to be sure. Lend a hand if necessary. Also the timetable for bagging Ramirez was getting shorter. If I was going to get you on board I had to make contact sooner than later."

Consistent with everything he'd told me earlier. The veneer of truth masking bullshit.

"Why was this guy after the Commissioner?"

"Don't know. For some reason Ramirez wants the commissioner dead."

"Why?"

"No idea. My only concern was watching his people. Figuring a way to get close to him. Like I said they were dead ends. I was about to leave and set up in Antigua."

Plausible again. Though I assumed everything he'd told me since our first meeting to be bullshit, laced with a kernel of truth. But I hadn't been able to discern his agenda yet.

"And the guy killed in Industry? You said you were watching a couple of Ramirez's crew. He the other guy?"

"Could be. Not sure. I hadn't seen the second guy for a while. Figured he'd left. Or was set up somewhere on the mainland waiting for the Commissioner."

"But why would one partner kill the other?" I asked.

"Who said anything about partners? For all I know one got orders to clean the other when things started going south. It's how Ramirez operates."

"Must engender such loyalty," I said.

"Not loyalty. Fear," he said.

I paused long enough to convey another impression of cogitating. Of reaching a decision.

"Here's how we do this." I said. "The op is mine. Mine alone. I plan it. I execute it. You provide intel, support, logistics. You only have to get in my way once, and it's over. I abort and we're done." I held his gaze. His blue eyes steady on mine. The speech designed to assert my independence and my control. He'd have been suspicious otherwise. And of course he'd agree to it. After reasonable consideration. Allowing me the illusion of control, while he pulled the strings.

"Agreed," he said, not too quickly, begrudgingly. Our dance, like a tango, had a logical sequence and tempo.

"How're your sailing skills?" I asked.

"Fair. It's been a while. But probably like riding a bicycle, right. Why?"

"When's Ramirez going to be in Antigua?"

A pause. A crucial nexus reached. But Carlson confident of his control over me.

"Next Thursday," he said. "End of the month. For the end of race week. Slipping out with the rest of the regatta crowd departing over the weekend. If he leaves by sea at all. He may use a different exit."

"Okay. We'll sail up to Antigua. You as my charter. We spec out the op as best we can on the way. We leave day after tomorrow, Saturday. Be prepared to come aboard at first light Saturday morning. I'll pick you up at the Frangipani."

He made no objection. Didn't suggest an alternate plan. A split infiltration. I'd had a hunch Wherever figured into his plan somehow. He'd made infiltrating Antigua by boat seem like my idea. It'd be a risk having him aboard. But it also provided the opportunity to keep him close.

The next morning, Friday, I prepped and provisioned Wherever for a three-day sail north. I called Mike and Jolene to schedule a meet later at Mike's house.

Under a full moon Jolene and I hiked the steep hill from Lower Bay. The shining white sphere rose in a clear sky. Its muted light bright enough to illuminate the landscape and bathe the bay in a soft satiny silver glow.

We gathered in Mike's living room. When I'd finished my briefing on Carlson, our trip to Antigua, and the plan to take down Ramirez, a silence hung thick and heavy in the room. Thick enough to swat with an open hand. Each wrestled with their private reservations, questions, concerns.

Mike the first to voice his. As the senior law enforcement authority he deemed himself de facto leader of our little nonofficial task force.

"Who is this guy? What do we know about him? And what makes you believe he can deliver Ramirez?" The last directed at me. "And even if we can get him, we've got no evidence to hold or prosecute him with."

"We don't. But the Fed's can put him away forever." Mendez said. He threw me a covert glance containing the message "later."

"What I mean is," Mike said, "Why still go after Ramirez. Ballistics proved the gun taken off this guy Ortega fired the shots that killed Tesca and almost killed me. We have our man. If he isn't hanged he'll spend the rest of his life in Her Majesty's prison. We can close both cases."

"You're not interested in the whys?" I asked. "All the other questions we don't have answers to. Including Sarah Holmes. And this Ortega guy being the shooter doesn't track."

"What makes you say that?" Mike asked.

"Instinct. Something hasn't sat right about this from the outset. What do you have on this Ortega anyway?"

"That's the name he used to enter the country. But the hit on his prints came back with a dozen aliases. The authorities in Columbia, Mexico, Panama, the DEA, all had files on him, under different names. Apparently he's worked for a lot of different groups. Some believe he's a freelancer for hire. Others believe someone's pulling his strings. No one knows for sure. And he's not talking. Shut up tighter than a steel drum."

"Chief you know even if he's the shooter Ramirez can just send someone else. Ramirez is the threat we need to be neutralize," Max said.

"I know that Max. And I do care about the whys," turning a disapproving glare at me. "I don't like loose ends any more than you do. Don't much care for this harebrained scheme either."

"As far as I'm concerned, this is strictly an intelligence gathering operation," I said truthfully. At least concerning the initial phase. What might occur afterwards depended a great deal on the initial recon. "If there's a chance to take Ramirez down, I'll give you the word Mike." His perceptive eyes pinned mine, searching between the lines for things I'd left unsaid.

"In the meantime," I continued, returning his stare. "You need to contact Antigua. They need to be prepped to move at a moment's notice."

I leaned forward in the cozy wicker armchair for emphasis. "Mike," I said, holding his attention, "you have to be one hundred percent sure about your contact. Word of this leaks and the entire operation goes sideways, know what I mean?" hoping I'd conveyed the full import of my words. "If there isn't someone you can trust, maybe Max and Mendez can figure a way to alert the Feds."

"There's a guy," Mike said, a firm assurance in his voice.

I didn't press him, or the issue. Mike knew the drill. Aware of the stakes.

Although satisfied by the law enforcement approach of our strategy, Mike's discerning eyes still conveyed skepticism concerning my part in the plan.

"What's your take JJ?" he asked, turning to face her. Jolene had remained silent throughout, absently sipping a beer, and casting sidelong glances at me during my briefing and the ensuing discussion.

Eyes as skeptical as Mike's fixed on mine. "I'm not exactly sure what you hope to accomplish with this Carlson character. And you haven't answered Mike's question about who, or what, this guy is." Straight to the heart of the matter. A matter neither I, Max or Mendez wanted to discuss openly at the moment. Her stare conveyed a suspicion I hadn't told her and Mike everything.

Mike aware of it too. But neither pressed the issue. Mike switched the subject instead.

"So how does this go?"

Jolene's stare still fixed on me. She'd wait for her opportunity. Later. When we'd be alone.

"Carlson and I sail for Antigua tomorrow," I said. "I'll be in constant contact through Max and Mendez. They know the protocol and have the equipment," I added hastily, forestalling the frown forming on Mike's brow.

"If Ramirez shows as Carlson claims, we may get the opportunity to take him down," I finished.

"What does 'may' mean exactly?" Mike demanded.

"Depends on what I find on the ground," I said. "That's what gathering intelligence is about."

"Of course," Mike said, his tone sarcastic, his probing stare still skeptical. "You guys okay with this?" glancing in turn at Max and Mendez.

"No worries about the boss chief, Max said. "They picked the wrong place to come. The wrong guy to piss off." His soft mellifluous voice dropped an octave, producing a hard-edged quality not meant to appease or reassure. Instead it conveyed a rock hard deadly menace.

"He's not thirty anymore Max," Mike said skeptically.

"Wouldn't want to go up against him if he was seventy," Max said.

Jolene fixed him with a curious stare. Switched her gaze to Mendez. He merely nodded.

"It's the hand we have." I said. "We have to play it."

"Doesn't mean I have to like it," Mike said. He reached for an unopened file he'd dropped on the coffee table earlier. Searched inside for a specific page, pulled it out.

"We might be able to corroborate at least one thing Carlson told you. I asked my stateside contacts to flag any local or regional transactions involving the Ramirez companies we already know about. They got a hit on a couple of them. Two rental villas on Antigua leased by two different companies linked to Ramirez. Both leased for the entire month."

He handed me the page. My eyes held his. A smile curled the corners of my mouth. A silent acknowledgment of how deftly he'd played his hand. He'd been sitting on the information throughout our discussion of Carlson.

"They may be decoys," I said, scanning the page. "He may not use either of them."

"I know," he said, his eyes still fixed on mine, conveying a silent communication between us. Thoughts he didn't wish to voice aloud. His concern for Jolene primary among them. 'Don't want to see her hurt Gage', the words spoken in the Bequia passage repeated in his stare, echoing in my brain. Not for the world, my eyes answered his..

"I'll ask my contacts to flag any yachts, aircraft, vehicles, anything he might use around the island, or to get on and off the island. Probably won't have anything for you until you're in transit, or already on Antigua."

"Thanks. That'll help. According to Carlson we should arrive a couple of days before Ramirez shows."

We talked into the night, hashing out scenarios, refining the plan to capture Ramirez. The prevailing consensus being the attempted murder of a small island Police Commissioner wouldn't figure significantly in U.S considerations. They had bigger fish to fry. And no evidence connecting Ramirez to Mike's shooting anyway. Except the word of a Miami drug lord who'd disappeared. And a shooter who wasn't talking. Neutralizing Ramirez and getting answers the most we could hope for.

The scenario I privately envisioned remained unspoken. Known only to myself, Max, and Mendez. And possibly Mike, whose perceptive glances discerned much of what I'd left unsaid.

Mendez accompanied me and Jolene on the walk to Lower Bay. He'd sleep aboard Wherever. Not so much to sleep as to keep watch.

At the house Mendez met me on the front verandah carrying his 'go' bag. I followed him out into the yard. Jolene watched us leave but made no comment. Or any attempt to join us. Directly overhead the moon, bone white and bright, cast shadows beneath the trees. A gorgeous tropical night. The air fresh, breezy, lightly scented, jasmine and frangipani. We halted at the top of the path.

"Okay. What do we know about Carlson?"

"Can't get a definite bead on him. Guy doesn't exist. A ghost G, like you. But he fits the profile of a guy who operated in Central and South America for close to two decades. Lots of rumors, nothing solid."

"How close a fit?"

"Damn close. Showed up as an independent contractor during the Columbia drug eradication program. My source says this guy was 'spooky', his word. Shooter type. Had unusual latitude. And wasn't confined to just the Columbian theatre. Know what I'm saying? Probably on the Company's payroll."

"What about the rumors, specifically?"

"His specialty was infiltration. He'd worm his way inside, then he'd poison the well. Pitting one faction against the other. He spread whispers of one faction muscling in on another. Or so-and-so making a play for the top. Or someone sleeping around with someone else's woman. After the fireworks he'd move on. Sometimes taking remnants with him. One rumor was he'd put together his own paramilitary for a while. Another that he ran a Medellin faction back in the day. Always left a trail of bodies and destruction. The cartels never caught on. This guy was way out on the hairy edge boss. Know what I mean? No one will say whether any of it was sanctioned. Lots of off-book operations going down during that time. Lots of deniability."

"Any intel on how he operated? He have a team?"

"Except for the time he supposedly ran a paramilitary, or a cartel faction, he seemed to mostly operate on his own. But he disappeared after the cartels got broken up. His brand of operating stopped. Rumor is whoever was running him cut him loose. One version says he was killed. My guy said every now and again there'd be a rumor of a sighting. But no one could pin anything definite down. And no one seemed particularly interested. He was supposed to be dead. If this is the same guy he had access to heavy-duty resources. Money, arms, intelligence, muscle. And he's never resurfaced until now."

"What about the Panama reference?"

"After Noriega's removal they rolled up his network. Word was one of his lieutenants salvaged the remnants, took over the trade. Rival groups couldn't touch them. Couldn't make a move without getting hit. Everything from Production to personnel to their banks. Taken out one by one. While the new operation seemed immune to the takedowns. Like they enjoyed the blessing of a beneficent uncle. Know what I'm saying? Has the earmarks of our guy but none of his fingerprints."

"You dig up any names?"

"He operated under a couple of aliases. But if you're right about his origins it might be Dieter. Franz Dieter. East German, ex Stasi. Trained by the soviets. Operated mostly in South America, hunting defectors. So he was familiar with the terrain. Went independent after the wall came down. Gun for hire. Did work for Uncle Sam in Cuba and Latin America. May be the same guy."

"It's him. I recognized the style. Came across it a few times before. Anything else?"

"That's about it. And none of it solid. Except if this is the same guy then he's one dangerous son-of-a-bitch. Could be your profile. Only worse. Without the heart. Guy's a sociopath. Sure you want to play this game with him?"

"Unfortunately, he's the only game available. And there's more to this than just Ramirez."

"You been thinking that a while now." It wasn't a question. I turned to him and smiled.

"So how you want to play this. Max and me can set up over watch."

"No. I need both of you to stick with Mike and Jolene until this is over. Besides, involving anyone else might spook Carlson."

I'd left unsaid I wanted to do this alone. Having a team might've been the smart play. Especially at my age. But working with a team called for different tactics. Different methods. A different approach from working alone. Ramirez skittish by nature. Carlson an unresolved variable. And I still had an unsettling itch I hadn't been able to scratch. I didn't want anyone else involved.

"You need someone watching your six on this one boss," Mendez argued.

"I've been watching my own six a long time." I said. "You guys take care of Mike and Jo. They're my only blind spot."

"Copy that boss. Just make sure you take care of you okay. Usual coms?"

"Yeah."

We shook hands. A grasp of bent, interlocked fingers ending the handshake. I watched him walk down the moonlit path toward the road.

Jolene lay in the mosquito net draped bed waiting for me. She'd allowed me and Mendez our privacy. Had been quiet and reticent at Mike's. In the dim candlelight the inquiring intensity in her eyes could no longer be denied.

"What was that about?"

"Last minute details. Information on Carlson," I said honestly. "I intend to tell you everything," I said, hoping she read the sincerity in my eyes. "Just not right now."

"There's a lot you didn't tell Mike, or me, at the meeting." A statement. She'd been reading the silences as Mike probably had. Discerned the thoughts unsaid..

"You know most of it. What I can't tell you may have nothing to do with Mike's shooting. We think Carlson's a contract operative. Disappeared a long time ago and now suddenly he's here. I need to find out what his real agenda is."

"Spy versus spy."

I smiled at the reference. "Something like that."

"And dangerous. You're more concerned about him than Ramirez." An almost imperceptible tremor in her voice as she voiced her real concern.

"It might be," I said. "I'm not expecting it to be."

Her fingers traced a path across my scars. "How many times have you said that before?" She brushed lightly over the mottled patches of skin. Doleful eyes peered deep into mine. A tiny furrough of concern on her normally smooth forehead.

"Have you been compromised?" she asked, revealing her true concern, and a deeper awareness than I'd imagined. But should have expected. A smart, perceptive woman. An astute detective. And as adept as I at revealing only what she wished of her inner self. Still mysterious. Still able to surprise me.

"One of the things I need to find out," I said.

"And what if you've been?"

"Don't know. There're a number of options. Depends on the extent of the exposure."

"One of those options leaving?" I heard the small catch in her voice. The held inhalation. Downcast eyes snapped upward to hold mine in a beseeching stare. Her real fear revealed. And mine. Fear of the day when leaving everyone and everything behind remained the only safe option.

"That's not going to happen," I said, staring back into woeful amber-grey pools. "I already made that choice a while ago." The breath she'd been holding escaped slowly through parted lips.

"Listening to Max and Mendez you're extraordinarily good at what you do. Or did. Aren't you." A statement, not requiring a response. "You have to know I don't want you to do this. Not just for myself. But for you. For what this might do to you. Dredging up a part of yourself I know you want to forget." The depth of her perception astounded me. "But I won't ask you not to. Wouldn't even know how. All I know is I don't want to lose you. So do whatever you have to and get back home, safe." Her eyes held mine. A grim determination in hers. The rarely displayed, hardened edge. Rapier sharp. "Whatever you have to."

I remained silent. At a complete loss for an appropriate response. I stared in wonder into those mesmerizing pools; hard and determined, yet warm and understanding.

She didn't require words to fill the silence. No platitudes. No reassurances. No response necessary. She rolled over. Straddled me. Pressed her lips against mine. Gently at first, growing in urgency, tongues dancing in each other's mouth. My arousal intensified by the taste of her, the smell of her, the touch of her smooth skin, the brush of her erect nipples across my chest. Her hand reached for the stiffening flesh between my legs. Grasped it. Encircled it, hard and throbbing in her fist. Guided it into her warm, moist enclosure. Slid down its length, burying it deep within her. A throaty groan in response. A slow writhing. A pelvic bumping dance. Growing in ferocity, frantic, faster, harder. A wild abandoned frenzied fervor. Grunted breaths exploded on my face. Her voice hoarse, rose in volume, calling out my name as each quivering spasm swept through her. A crescendo of simultaneous eruptions consumed us both.

CHAPTER 22

V.C. Bird International Airport, Antigua. I waiting for the man flying in to meet Ramirez. Scheduled to arrive at midday. An air shimmering, tarmac melting hot day. The occasional breezes wafting across the dry landscape neither cooling nor refreshing. More like standing under a hot hair dryer. The man expected to arrive by private jet from Miami according to Carlson. Who'd also provided a description. The detailed intel he'd provided on the sail up from Bequia all but confirming he had a source close to Ramirez.

I hadn't been to Antigua in almost four years. The island not on my preferred itinerary of ports. Motoring into English Harbour two days before reminded me why I rarely visited. Too large - nearly twelve times the size of Bequia. Too crowded – a population also about twelve times larger than Bequia's. Too touristy. Too club medified.

We'd arrived at the end of race week. The sailing competitions over. The celebratory parties in full swing. English Harbour a dense forest of masts. Sailing vessels of every type and size from all across the globe. The annual regatta had grown from a few traditional classic sailing yachts racing for fun, to an international event featuring sponsors and multimillion dollar racing hulls. Anchored in the harbor as thick as weeds, and filling every slip along the stone quay.

Another dry, hot eddy drifted across the parking lot in front of the airport terminal, rustling palm trees lining a triangular shaped field behind the parking lot. The dry season left Antigua parched, and prickly dry. The hot breezes bore a fine powdery dust.

I'd set up on the far side of the field, across from the terminal access road. On high ground behind a strand of whitewood trees, 'Black Gregory' as Antiguans called them.

The sun reached its zenith. The airport shimmered in the distance. A Gulfstream Four approached over the placid blue Caribbean Sea. It turned final, its silver fuselage glinted in the sunlight. It grew larger as it descended from a bright, pale blue, cloud spattered sky. The jet screeched to earth on the single black ribbon running southwest to northeast, its engines a high-pitched whine in reverse thrust.

Another aircraft, a Britten-Norman Islander, without commercial markings, painted a drab green, also descended from the bright azure sky. It too lined up on final, touching down as the Gulfstream taxied to the terminal. I watched the new arrival slow, exit the runway, and taxi to park next to the Gulfstream.

I carried a digital camera equipped with a powerful telephoto lens. I trained it on the passenger pick up areas under the terminal's sun canopy. Private aircraft used the same tarmac and terminal as the commercial airlines. All arriving passengers had to clear Immigration and Customs in the same terminal. Unless they had juice with the local authorities. In which case the officers met the private aircraft, clearing its passengers on board prior to disembarking.

I panned my long lens along the length of the pink stucco terminal, waiting for the Gulfstream's passenger to emerge. A black Range Rover, its windows tinted, parked at one end of the terminal, caught my attention. It stood out. And it'd been sitting there a while.

When the passenger finally appeared he too stood out. Tall, six foot two maybe. Trim for a man I estimated to be in his mid-sixties. Wispy grey hair, thin on top, neatly trimmed on the sides. Attired like someone who paid attention to his wardrobe. Someone able to afford the best. The suit jacket fit his frame like a glove, well-cut, charcoal grey pinstripe, at least tailored if not made-to-order. A gold kerchief folded in the breast pocket. He wore a pale blue dress shirt opened at the collar. No tie, probably his sole concession to the tropical heat. Expensive dark burgundy loafers on his feet complemented the rest of his ensemble.

A black briefcase the only item he carried. No overnight stay I reasoned. He waited under the awning. Glanced back and forth along the pickup area. He pulled back French cuffs to glance at a wristwatch.

I'd been snapping photographs while observing him through the long distance lens. His having to wait in the open provided an unobstructed sight line, pure luck. Sparse vehicular and pedestrian traffic moved in front of the terminal. Only two arrivals in the past hour. Both private, noncommercial aircraft. The grandfatherly face, and the eyes behind round wire-rimmed glasses, expressed impatience. Not used to waiting.

I focused on the briefcase. It probably contained the package. According to Carlson, a dongle, a piece of computer hardware possessing an unhackable encryption. The software designed to take over any computer it was connected to, and run its own operating system. It made Ramirez's computer network, his emails, text, and other communications secure. Accessible only by other computers programmed with the dongle software. The software updated every six months. Hence the meeting on Antigua.

I shifted my focus to the Range Rover at the far end of the terminal building. A man dressed in khaki slacks and a white Guayabera shirt emerged from the passenger side. The bright white shirt a startling contrast to his dark brown complexion and straight black hair. The Range rover departed its parking spot and pulled up next to the waiting man in the immaculate suit. The driver exited, greeted the man, opened the rear door. The man got in. He didn't relinquish the briefcase. The driver returned to his seat. The vehicle pulled away from the terminal.

The man who'd left the Range Rover earlier leaned against the building. He scanned the meager activity around him. Midday. And scorching hot. Antiguans already at a leisurely lunch which would stretch into midafternoon.

I snapped a few face shots. His gaze followed the Range Rover leaving the terminal, heading away from the airport.

Mr. Suit had a shadow. A sweeper on his tail. There to make sure no one followed him. Probably for protection too. Assured no one had followed the Range Rover, the sweeper headed toward a blue SUV, some kind of Suzuki. It pulled away from the terminal as soon as he'd settled into the passenger seat.

A two-man detail in the chase car. A driver in the Range Rover and maybe, another riding shotgun. It'd been impossible to tell through the tinted windows. I'd seen only the driver, who'd gotten out, and Mr. Suit, who'd gotten in.

I abandoned my spot among the trees. Piled into a rented Jeep Wrangler parked off the road. Carlson had rented it. I called him on the prepaid cell phones he'd also provided.

"Heading your way," I said when he answered. "Black Range Rover, tinted windows, and a chase vehicle, blue Suzuki SUV."

Not many routes from the Airport into St. John's, Antigua's capital. Assuming that's where they were headed. Carlson and I planned to follow by leap frogging each other. We also had two other switch vehicles stashed. I'd follow them from the airport. Carlson to pick them up if they took an evasive route meant to spot a tail. Or in the congested confines of St. John's. One switch vehicle had been parked at a safe house on the outskirts of St. John's. Having a chase vehicle might mean they weren't planning an evasive route.

Carlson provided support and logistics. The role I'd delegated to him. In the two days we'd been on Antigua he'd procured vehicles, phones, and other essential equipment. We'd decided not to risk carrying handguns, a serious offense on Antigua. He'd also rented two safe houses. One in St. John's overlooking the harbor. Another on the southeastern side of the island high above English Harbour. Close to Wherever.

I'd swept any equipment he'd provided, including the vehicles, for tracking or listening devises. Everything came up clean. He'd probably assumed I would, deciding not to risk jeopardizing the relationship. Still, I'd arranged my own support and logistics. Whether my distrust of him, or force of habit, I wanted access to resources of my own. Resources known to no one else. Old habit.

On the sail up from Bequia we'd concocted a simple, straightforward plan. Phase one: find Ramirez by tailing the person he'd come to meet. Phase two: Take Ramirez down and retrieve the package. The plan for phase two depended on location of the meet and Ramirez's security. Phase three: exfiltration separately. Carlson left no doubt regarding the objective. Killing Ramirez. Probably how the operation might eventually end up. But not because Carlson wanted it. I had my own agenda. Still uncertain regarding his.

He'd been playing it straight thus far. We'd kept a low profile. Preserved operational security. He'd used local cutouts for all his transactions. As determined as I to leave no trace of our presence on Antigua. I maintained an acute alertness. Certain of the endgame approaching. The most dangerous part of any operation.

I allowed the chase to get some distance ahead. I watched for a tail the sweeper may have missed. Any such tail a complicating factor. Whose security had failed? Theirs? Ours? Or Carlson making his move.

No other tail. I started the Jeep. Pulled away from the spot off the road as the chase car passed the cricket ground. The Range Rover turned left onto the main access road winding past the airport, parallel to the runway.

Departing the airport environs, buildings gave way to cultivated fields on the right. Groves of fruit trees on the left. Rising terrain on both sides of the road. Traffic on the road sparse, permitting me to follow from a distance. The Range Rover drove at a steady, unhurried pace. Unlike the few Antiguan drivers on the road, who swung in and out of oncoming traffic to pass slower moving vehicles. Three garishly decorated minibuses passed me in this manner. Horns blared as they swept past. They closed and passed the chase car ahead. Repeated the maneuver upon reaching the Range Rover. We transited an area of industrial buildings and offices. I pulled the prepaid phone from my shirt pocket. Speed dialed Carlson.

"Coming up on the first intersection," I said when he answered.

"Got em in sight," he replied. He'd been waiting in the parking lot of a service station on the northwest corner of the intersection. The Range Rover came to a brief stop. Turned right onto the main road, heading away from the coast and airport. The chase car followed.

"I still got them," I told Carlson. "Close up and be ready to take over if I have to break off."

The route they'd taken led to the Capital. If they'd noticed my vehicle behind them, my taking the same turn wouldn't raise suspicions. Just another vehicle headed to St. John's. But the route presented other problems. More turnoffs. More chances to make evasive maneuvers. Take random turns. Attempt to spot a tail. Or lose one.

They did neither. The two vehicles kept to a leisurely pace along Old Parham Road. I considered they might be leading me into a trap of their own. I allowed a few cars to get in between us. Observed their maneuvers. Nothing out of the ordinary.

St. John's presented the real challenge. A compact, dense city. Crowded. Its narrow streets congested by pedestrian and vehicular traffic. I'd need to close up. My concern not losing them, the Range Rover hard to miss. But any alert observer in the Range Rover or chase car might recognize the same jeep from the airport close behind them.

We approached Antigua's largest car dealership on our right. The lot contained an assortment of Nissans, Suzukis and Daihatsus gleaming under the midday sun. We continued past. Neither the Range Rover nor the chase car made any attempt to spot or elude a tail.

Fifteen minutes after departing V.C. Bird International we entered the outskirts of Antigua's Capital. Close to the St. John's safe house, I decided to switch vehicles. I speed dialed Carlson.

"Pick them up at Government House. I'm going to switch vehicles."

"On it," he said and disconnected.

I watched him moving up in my rearview mirror. Directly behind me. We approached the traffic circle in front of the manicured lawn, trees, and flower beds of Government House, the official residence of Antigua's Governor General. The Range Rover and SUV turned left. I turned right.

The cell phone rang. "Got em," Carlson confirmed. "Let me know when you're on the way back. I'll give you a location."

"Roger that." I snapped the phone shut.

I drove the short distance to the safe house on Friar Hill Road. Switched from the Jeep to a lime-green Nissan. Something called a Tilda. A small four door. Ideal for the narrow streets of St. John's.

I headed down the hill into St. John's. Made a right onto Newgate Street, a steep sloping thoroughfare leading down to the harbor. A colonial era stone edifice, St. John's Cathedral, dominated the top of Newgate street. The

Cathedral's twin white baroque towers rose above the surrounding buildings, dominating St. John's skyline. A bombardment of bright yellows, reds, pinks, purples and violets filled its carefully maintained gardens.

I called Carlson. "I'm on Newgate Street heading toward the harbor."

"I'm across from the Antigua Commonwealth Bank on Market Street. Our man went in. He's still in there."

"I'm coming around. I'll take your spot if he doesn't come out before then."

Again we disconnected without further small talk or conversation. Partly operational security. Mostly we didn't have much to say to each other beyond the exigencies of the operation.

I turned left, maneuvering the little Nissan through busy chaotic traffic. The area around the cruise ship piers a congested choke point. Passing High Street I spotted the bank's white columned facade in the middle of the block. The building surrounded by palm trees and beds of dry, limp, thirsty flowers. I searched along the street for Carlson's parked vehicle. It pulled out in front of me as I reached it. I pulled into the spot he'd vacated. He'd drive to the intersection connecting the two main roads leading out of St. John's. A bus depot on one corner, the botanical gardens on the other. A logical place to intercept Mr. Suit departing St. John's.

I existed the car. Walked over to one of the multitude of street vendors lining the sidewalk. Some of them food vendors. Others sold everything from tee shirts to pirated CDs and DVDs. The sign on the vendor's cart I approached read 'Roti n Tings'. The other 'tings' listed in different colored chalk. I ordered a chicken roti and orange Ju-C. Found a bench next to a vendor's stall providing an unobstructed view of the bank. I sat. Waited. Ate as I staked out the front of the bank.

The Range Rover sat parked under the bank's front portico. Its engine running. Probably to keep the air-conditioning going. The chase car off to the side in a parking space. The engine off. The windows rolled down. No air-conditioning. Two pairs of languid eyes scanned the front of the bank. Not paying much attention to the street beyond.

The street itself overrun by swarming people. People on foot. People on bicycles. People on lunch break, eating, shopping. People hawking wares. People going about their business. Tall and short people, fat and thin people, black and brown and white and every shade in between people. Fine looking women people. And cruise ship people, pale, cherry faced, wandering about in a travel-fatigue daze. The decibel level raucous and discordant. Voices, music, horns, bicycle bells. Mixed odors hung in the hot stagnant air, cooked food, fresh produce, fruit, grime, sweat, and the stale saltiness of the waterfront.

I alternated between watching the bank and watching the street. The buildings lining both sides a patchwork of vivid reds, pinks, greens and yellows.

Mr. Suit emerged from the bank. As fresh and immaculate as when he'd stepped off the private jet. He'd been inside almost an hour. On the move again. The chase car again hung back to check for a tail. Not skillful at it. Both vehicles passed me, continuing south on market Street. Headed out of town. I pulled out, a few vehicles between us.

I speed dialed Carlson again. He answered on the first ring. A hint of anxiety in his voice.

"Been awhile. What's up?"

"He just left the bank. They're on the move. Heading south. You can move parallel on Independence."

"Roger that," and hung up.

The vehicles continued to the end of Market Street. Bore left onto All Saints Road, one of the main roads in and out of St. Johns. We traversed a dense residential area on the outskirts of the capital. Small brick houses packed against each other. I called Carlson to provide an update. The direction of travel parallel to his location. Driving south from his current location he'd intercept the road we were on.

We continued southeast, climbing through Antigua's interior toward the southern coast. Maybe English or Falmouth Harbours. Made sense. Despite Carlson's inside person, we still had no idea when Ramirez might arrive, his mode of transportation, or where he'd be staying. I didn't believe Carlson might be holding out. He appeared as eager as I to pinpoint Ramirez's location. For all we knew Ramirez might already be on the island. Our best bet remained Mr. Suit leading us to him. The Harbors might indicate a yacht. One amongst the hundreds gathered during race week and preparing to depart over the next couple of days. A perfect way to remain invisible.

In fact, I knew a great deal more regarding Ramirez than Carlson realized. I'd been receiving periodic updates from Bequia. Information gathered from Mike's, Max's and Mendez's sources revealed a labyrinthine trail of interlocking enterprises, companies, accounts, and holdings connected to Ramirez. His tentacles reached everywhere. As many paper companies as there were legitimate businesses. The former used to launder and move money. The latter for liquid capital.

I knew for example the Gulfstream hadn't been chartered or leased. But owned by a transportation company, a subsidiary of a shell company, itself owned by a holding company. All controlled by Ramirez. I knew of two mega yachts owned by Ramirez controlled companies. One anchored in Jolly Harbour, the other in Falmouth Harbour.

I'd already reconned the villas from Mike's list. The first thing I'd done upon arrival, while Carlson had been procuring equipment, the vehicles, and safe houses. One villa overlooked English Harbour on the south coast. The other overlooked Half Moon Bay on the eastern coast.

Farther from the capital, the road narrowed and wound through open fields, farmland, and rolling hills covered in foliage. The road outside the capital less well maintained, uneven, bumpy and potholed. It swung south and east, then south again. Cars rolled up behind, horns sounding, flashing past on the narrow, snaking road. I kept a few of them between me, the Range Rover, and the chase car ahead. Tall, thick trees bordering the twisting road also helped to conceal the tail.

We passed through dense dusty communities of small, wood houses packed against each other. The type of areas tour busses and taxis raced past. Areas tourists experienced from behind air-conditioned glass. Real life Antigua.

At the town of All Saints we intersected a road running in a north–south direction. The vehicles turned left, heading north. Away from Falmouth or English Harbour. I contemplated calling Carlson to switch tails. But neither vehicle half a mile ahead made any moves to spot or avoid a tail. And I had an idea now where they were headed.

They turned right onto Pears Village main road, heading east towards the coast. The road steeper, narrower, climbing into densely forested terrain. Tree branches on both sides hung over the road, forming shaded tunnels. Sunlight pierced the green canopy in slanting shafts. I downshifted, accelerating up the twisting, rutted road. The Nissan's four cylinder engine surged, its power surprising. I spotted the chase vehicle ahead.

I drove like a local. Pulled up behind the chase car. Waited for a short stretch of straight road. Passed the chase car while leaning on the horn. I closed on the Range Rover. The chase car kept close behind me, watching for any indication I posed a threat to the vehicle in front. At the first opportunity I pulled around the Range Rover, passing it too. I accelerated ahead, taking the turns as I tap-tapped the horn like a local would.

I phoned Carlson. Instructed him to lay back and stand down. I had their destination. Ready to commence the recon phase. I'd call him if necessary. He agreed. He'd wait at the English Harbour safe house. Still, I'd be watching my back.

By the time the Range Rover and chase car reached the long dirt tracks leading to the secluded villa, I'd already moved into the trees on foot. The wall of tall, thick, tightly packed trees hid the villa from the road. I moved through the underbrush, climbing the sloping hillside.

The villa sat in a manicured clearing at the top of the rise. Surrounded on three sides by hardwood forest. The pungent scent of white cedar thick in the air. The villa's front faced a well-kept, sloping lawn ending at a cliff face, providing a spectacular view of rocky Half Moon Bay below and the sapphire blue Atlantic.

I found a vantage spot providing a clear view of the villa. Pulled compact Leupold Katmai binoculars from the cargo pocket of my pants. I scanned the perimeter and front of the villa. No cover between the villa and tree line. The rear of the villa extended closer to the trees. Thick, sturdy branches hung over a narrow strip of intervening yard, and an attached structure at the back of the villa. The only way to get inside unseen.

Four guards patrolled the perimeter. They strolled casually about the yard. Telltale bulges beneath their shirttails and pants cuffs. If I needed a weapon besides the tactical knife I carried, I knew where to get it. I still had no idea how this might go down. And I didn't like what I'd observed so far.

A terraced pool on the far side of the villa from me. I didn't have a clear angle on it. Two individuals on poolside chaises. One a woman in a blue bikini, her face hidden by a broad brimmed hat and large sunglasses. I had a better angle on the man. Fully dressed, white silk shirt over white linen slacks, white socks, white loafers and a white hat. Obviously not there to swim.

The level of recon concerned me. I'd clocked the guards. Memorized the perimeter and outside of the villa. Automatically measured distances and judged angles. Still needed to get eyes on the target. Maybe get inside. Formulate the next move.

A guard approached the pool from a side entrance. Trailed by Mr. suit. The man in white rose from the chaise as the guard approached. The guard stepped aside as the man in white removed his hat and reached to shake Mr. Suit's hand.

Ramirez.

The guard retraced his steps, leaving the two men conversing at poolside. The woman hadn't moved from the chaise when Mr. Suit arrived. The two men ignored her. She ignored them. The newcomer wasn't introduced. After the greeting the men moved toward the villa.

I left my position. Moved silently through the trees toward the rear of the villa. I'd figured a way in. Didn't know how many more men might be inside. Or the interior layout. Though I had a general idea from studying the exterior. The structure resembled the letter 'H'. Two wings connected by a middle section containing large picture windows. Bedrooms on the second floor of the wings. The master bedroom faced the cliff, providing a view of the Bay and Atlantic Ocean. Sliding French doors led from the bedroom onto a stone terrace. They'd been left open, allowing me a partial view of the bedroom. Sheer lace curtains floated through the opening on each passing breeze.

The bedroom terrace sat directly above a porticoed stone porch facing the same direction, providing the same magnificent view. Plush wicker sofas, armchairs and glass topped wicker tables furnished the porch. Waist high urns containing colorful flower arrangements were spaced around the stone walls. I'd noticed a bowl of cut fruit, a platter of finger sandwiches, and a pitcher of an iced drink on a center table. I figured the business might take place there.

I entered through the back of the villa, moving silently through a spacious kitchen divided by a marble topped center island. A partially stocked pantry at the back. I encountered no one as I moved toward the front of the villa.

The secret to invisibility is the ability to hide in plain sight. Sometimes it's about blending into a background nobody pays visual attention to, a black waiter in an exclusive country club; a fireman at a four-alarm blaze; a nondescript office worker in an office full of cubicles. Other times it's about stealth, moving without sound; avoiding quick movements which register on the eyes' periphery. Most times its about using shadows.

I entered a hallway. Heard voices. Commands in Spanish. I heard a heavy door open and close. The guards ordered to station themselves outside the main entrance. The hallway ended in a large, high ceilinged reception area. A central floral display in the middle, potted trees against curved walls. The stone floor shone like polished marble. Maybe it was marble.

Wide stone stairs cantilevered from an adjacent curving wall rose to the second floor. No banister or handrail. At the top, an ornately carved balustrade enclosed the second floor landing, and the curved hallway leading to the bedroom suites.

The voices moved toward the outdoor porch. I caught a glimpse of Ramirez as he turned to sit. Square, grandfatherly face, though no older than forty-four. Drooping jowls, a bushy salt and pepper moustache, and thick, wavy black hair.

I ran the steps to the second floor. I hugged the wall along the hallway as I moved silently in the direction of the master suite above the porch. Passed into the bedroom, registering the neatly made four-poster bed and mosquito net canopy. The sides of the net rolled and tied. From habit my mind catalogued the furniture and memorized their placement. An antique dresser and vanity against the near wall. A tall armoire of dark red cherry and gold leaf filigree inlay next to the French doors. I sidled onto the terrace, hugging the shadowed side. Knelt in a crouch directly above the two men.

Their voices carried clearly. The men spoke in English. Ramirez's deep and accented. The suit's cultured, ivy league.

"The other updates went as expected?" Ramirez asked.

"No problems," the suit said. "I have just yours and the Puerto Rico office, and we're done for this upgrade."

"Bueno. Here."

I heard the briefcase latches snap open. Unable to see either man, or what they were doing. Certain of Carlson's 'package' directly below me.

After a silent interval, "Bueno," uttered again by Ramirez. "Now my friend, you have a plane to catch."

Apparently no hanging about. No chitchat. No socializing. Strictly a business meeting. Successfully concluded. The window for a take down at the villa closing fast. But not the last chance for the package. The suit had one more stop to make. Another contingency might come into play.

I moved back into the bedroom. Still in a crouch. Mostly due to an aching lower back and stiffened joints. The handle to the bedroom door turned. I sidestepped through the French doors. Squeezed against the side of the armoire, the side away from the door. The woman from the pool entered. She stepped to the center of the room. Tossed the hat and sunglasses onto the canopied bed.

Sarah Holmes.

Her blond hair now black. Cut shoulder length. Draped at the sides, bangs concealing her face. But no mistaking her at this distance.

Everything fell into place. The pivotal piece needed to complete the puzzle. The nebulous nagging in my subconscious coalesced into solid form. The damn itch finally scratched.

Ramirez on the move, she didn't linger. Didn't take in the view. Disconnected from it. From the room. From the house. Nothing more than a transient space. Not her own. A place to change. To spend a few hours before moving on to the next anonymous place. I knew the feeling. I empathized.

She undid the bikini top. Tossed it onto the bed. Then pulled down the bottom. It fall to her ankles. She stepped out of it, one leg at a time. Tossed that on the bed too. She strode across the room, retrieved a garment bag hanging from a hook on the closet door. She laid it on the bed. Headed toward the bathroom she paused briefly to inspect her naked figure in a full-length mirror mounted on the door.

The shower ran. I gave it a few moments before stepping away from the armoire. I strode across the room to the bed. Quickly searched the garment bag. It held an assortment of three dresses. All evening casuals. And changes of bras and underwear. Sufficient for a day and possibly evening. At the bottom of the bag a small silver clutch. I searched it too. No wallet or identification. Only a hairbrush, and a small kit containing eyebrow brush, eyelash comb, lip gloss and a small slim glass atomizer of perfume.

I put everything back exactly as I'd found it and added a extra little item of my own, concealed in the lining. I crossed to the door. Exited the room.

Voices and a lot of movement in the reception area below. Ramirez and his men preparing to move. I hadn't figured on exiting the same way I'd entered anyway. I moved in the few moments the sightlines from below cleared of men. Slipped along the hallway to the rear suite in that wing of the villa. The door unlocked. I stepped inside. Closed the door behind me. My back to it. A quartering gaze cleared the room. Rear bedroom suite. Same layout as the master suite, but smaller. A queen sized bed instead of a king. Less ornate furniture. I moved to the back of the room, to a window left of the bed. Peered out without exposing myself in the window.

Below the window a green corrugated roof. Top of the structure I seen from outside. Possibly a garage. Or storage room. Maybe a water storage tank. A short jump from the window. From the roof another short jump to the yard itself. Or to overhanging branches close by.

Once in the safety of the trees I pulled the cell phone from my pocket. My encrypted phone. Not the burner provided by Carlson, which I'd turned off and removed the battery. I sent a cryptic, one word text message.

From inside the tree line I watched the vehicles depart. Ramirez and Sarah Holmes in a Range Rover similar to the one used for Mr. Suit. No one remained behind. I hiked through the woods the way I'd come. Retrieved the little Nissan from where I'd hidden it off the road. Drove back the way we'd come earlier. I reassembled the burn phone, powered it up, speed dialed Carlson.

"How'd it go?" he answered.

"Better than expected. Some good intel for completing the op without leaving a lot of bodies lying around. And I know where the package will be. I'll spec it out with you when we meet up. In the meantime I'm going to need some gear."

"Like what?"

I gave him a list of items.

"What'd you gonna need this stuff for anyway?"

"Not your concern. You'll understand when we spec out the op."

"And where am I supposed to get all this stuff on short notice?"

"That's your concern. Use your imagination. Most of that stuff you can get at a marina. I believe there's a bunch of them around. I'll meet you back at the English Harbour safe house."

"Where're you gonna to be in the meantime?"

"I'm gonna see our passenger off. I'll tail him back to the airport. See if he makes any other contacts we need to know about. After that I'll head back to English Harbour."

I did return to the airport. Not tailing the passenger. He'd left the villa long before I did. And I knew he had a schedule to keep. I returned to the observation spot I'd used earlier, across from the airport. Observed the activity on the ramp. The Gulfstream ready for departure. Its engines spooled up, its nav lights on, its belly strobe rotating.

The Britten-Norman Islander, as common around the Leeward Islands as yellow cabs on a Manhattan street, still parked beside the Gulfstream. It too preparing to depart.

As I watched my personal cell phone beeped. I pulled it from my packet, read the text displayed on the screen. I smiled.

The Gulfstream lurched from its parking spot, accelerating forward until it built up sufficient momentum to roll at a smooth steady pace across the tarmac. Headed for a taxiway parallel to the runway. Given no other arriving or departing traffic the Gulfstream went from taxiway to runway without a stop. Lined up. Commenced its takeoff roll. Its engines a high-pitched scream as it flashed past the terminal, lifted its nose, and rose with a roar and a trail of shimmering exhaust into the azuline afternoon sky. The Islander departed a few minutes behind it. I watched it turn and climb away in the opposite direction.

I sent another cryptic message to Mendez before departing the airport.

A dark moonless night. Thick branches overhead obscured the stars. In the sun's absence the temperature abated. A cool sea breeze offered merciful relief from the day's searing heat.

Black as pitch among the trees. And Loud. A chaotic mélange of nocturnal sounds. Crickets, tree frogs, lizards, bats, something sounding like an owl. No owls on Antigua. And the incessant buzz of mosquitoes.

I'd been waiting a little over an hour. Covered head to toe in black to match the night. Black jeans, black tee shirt, black canvas topped rubber soled sneakers. Black cotton gloves and a black balaclava mask. My back pressed against a giant white cedar. I'd become part of the tree. I smelled like the tree. And like the stagnant decaying undergrowth I'd rolled around in not an hour before.

My prey headed toward me. I hoped. A hope built on calculation. I'd always operated by manipulating my prey to come to me. To pounce at a time and place of my choosing. To do so without warning. Operating solo, without a team, the tactic had always served me well. It'd work again here. I expected my target to appear at this time, at this place.

My eyes peered into the night, adjusted to the deep impenetrable black. I sensed his approach rather than saw it. No more than a shimmer of black against black. A mental extrapolation, like a planet observed only by the wobble it produced in its nearby star. But now I knew where to look. I squinted hard into the darkness. Squeezed my eyes to generate a bit more depth perception. I discerned a shape, black against black.

And I heard him. Just barely. The nighttime creatures maintained a constant background din I had to filter out. The dry underbrush betrayed his position as he moved. But he was good. Careful. He moved in small, cautious steps, treading lightly, pausing. The sounds of his approach as those of a small animal foraging in the bush.

I didn't move a muscle. Nor make a sound. Shallowed my breathing. He'd pass within a few meters of me, as I'd expected. Close enough now for me to smell him. And make out distinct shapes. A head. Arms and legs. Clad like me, in black. A thin line at the neck not completely covered. My target.

When he moved within reach my left arm whipped out and encircled his neck. A syringe in my right hand plunged into the exposed strip of flesh. His reaction instantaneous. Also futile. I had him pinned. The drug did the rest. And the more he struggled the faster it took effect. His struggle over in moments. His body limp against me. Deadweight. I'd have to carry him.

Shit. Too old for this crap.

CHAPTER 23

He revived in the villa. Hands and feet taped to an armchair in the rear bedroom. Pale blue eyes, cold as the icy glacier they resembled, stared up at mine. A moment to focus. Awareness set in. He smiled. The familiar mirthless smile.

"What's this about?" Carlson said, jerking his wrists against the restraints.

I didn't respond. I sat on the edge of the bed facing him. Pondered what I knew. Didn't know. Suspected. How to get him to confirm those suspicions.

Soulless blue eyes searched mine. "Whatever game you're playing here, I got you what you wanted didn't I?"

Still no response. I allowed him to stew in the silence.

"You did take him down?" He asked after a few moments, uncertainty creeping into his tone. A speculative leer in his eyes. His tone growing belligerent in my continuing silence.

"Tell me you took him down. You didn't let that asshole get away,"

"He's no longer a factor," I said, breaking my silence. Cold steel in my voice.

He nodded. The smile returned. He relaxed. The body language of someone in control. Being bound in a chair a mere inconvenience. He hadn't asked me outright. He assumed I'd killed Ramirez. His objective. Now he'd play whatever game I wanted. Make me feel better for being used. Didn't matter. He'd still be in control.

"So what's this about? He repeated. "I assume you got Ramirez earlier. And everything else, the equipment you asked for, the op we planned back at the safe house to take Ramirez here at the villa, all staged to get me here. You knew I couldn't just hang back without verifying the hit myself."

"I knew you'd need to clean up afterward," I said, observing his reactions closely. Reactions masked by the ever present predaceous smile. His expressionless eyes gave nothing away. and he maintained an unconcerned calm.

"What about the package?"

"In safe hands," I said.

"So you never had any intention of handing it over?"

"None."

"So who was playing who?"

"Touché," I said. "Anyway, I'm more interested in something else."

"And we can't discuss it without these?" again jerking at the restraints.

"I'm afraid not. I'm getting a little old for the physical stuff."

"Coulda fooled me. You took me easily enough."

I smiled at him in acknowledgement, not amusement. My own icy dispassionate smile a reflection of the freezing fury within me.

"So what is it you want?"

"You already know that too."

"Why don't you enlighten me?"

I leaned in closer to him. Out of reach of his head or teeth. My eyes drilled into his, held his attention.

"As you already know a very close friend of mine was shot. Came this close to being killed," I said, the words spoken in a slow, deliberate manner, my index finger and thumb held a millimeter apart. "Because of you," I said

"What the hell're you talking about?" A tactical stall. Now aware of the real reason behind his capture. The reason for the interrogation. Not a gambit to keep him out of my life. Discover what he might know regarding my past. Or an attempt to scare him off. But something much different. Deadlier.

He needed time to recalibrate his responses. He hadn't prepped for this contingency. At this point in his op I should be dead.

"Right out of your playbook Dieter," I said, deliberately pronouncing the name. And scored. Observed the infinitesimal dilation of the pupils; the microscopic adjustment of the masking smile.

"Infiltrate and provoke. Manipulate someone else into doing the dirty work. None of your fingerprints left behind. You were behind this from the beginning. Running an asset, Sarah Holmes, who I happened to meet in this very villa earlier this afternoon. How long ago did you put her next to Ramirez? And how in the hell did you manage to recruit her in the first place?"

Not a muscle in his face moved. But now I knew what to look for. Knew I'd scored again. More confirmation. Hearing his East German name had rocked him. Made this an entirely new situation for him. He'd lost control. Needed desperately to regain it.

"No matter," I said, waving away the questions, not expecting any answers.

I pressed my advantage. "This was a long-term op," I continued. "Your op. And when you made me on Bequia you saw an opportunity for another cut-out. To use your playbook. You pointed me at Ramirez. I was supposed to eliminate him for you. Maybe the woman too. You knew she'd be with Ramirez. Knew I'd see her sooner or later. But it didn't matter. Even if I'd left her alive you'd have killed her too. And killed me here tonight. No loose ends. And you nowhere near any of it."

His stare drilled into mine. A deadly expression in the icy blue eyes. I'd used the phrase 'happened to meet' referring to Sarah Holmes deliberately. Time to play a wild card.

"We talked." I lied, leaning closer. My eyes drilled into his. "I know you shot my friend," the whispered words laced with a menacing chill.

He glared at me. Cold blooded malevolence in his eyes. As if his stare alone could strike me dead. His expression a dispassionate desire to reach down my throat and rip my heart out whole.

But no fear. On a different level, a different caliber from Calderon. But I didn't need to extract information from him. Only confirmation. I didn't need him to utter a word. Merely to listen.

He studied the chair, the furniture, the room, as though contemplating redecorating. But I knew his thoughts. Could almost hear them. I'd been on that side of the chair too. Searching for a way out. The chink in the captor's armor. A hook to get inside the interrogator's head. An angle. The single thing needed to change the game.

"You and me are alike," he said, his tone neutral, nonthreatening, seductive. "We're the same." He didn't push it. Waited for my response. For me to provide the hook he needed. Something he could use to reach me. To get inside.

I didn't respond. Didn't provide the thing he needed. But recognized the kernel of truth in his words. Years of duplicity and lies. Constant paranoia. The callous devaluation of human life. Day after day, month after month, year after year. An entire adult lifetime of it, until nothing remained of your soul. I'd stared into that abyss. Pondered often my inexplicable salvation.

The difference between us, I'd recognized the cost, albeit late in the game. Had clung to the last vestige of my humanity before it disappeared altogether. Had sought a measure of redemption, unrequited, as I clawed my way back clutching the tiny remaining piece of my soul. 'There but for the grace of whatever...'

"Look. The Commissioner was just part of what we do. You know it. You've done it. Just like me."

"Be that as it may, this time you went after a friend of mine. And you kept going after him, in Miami and here. But it didn't make sense until today. The randomness, the sloppiness. You're way better than that. But killing him wasn't the point. And may even have been counterproductive. You just needed me to keep chasing the shooters. Until I'd be so hungry for Ramirez I wouldn't question it when you served him up in a neat little package. You manipulated everything. Revising and improvising as you went along, moving the players around the board. Me, Mike, Sarah Holmes, the shooters on Bequia, all the pieces. The Bequia shooters were yours but you were playing them too. Like you played Sarah

Holmes. Like you tried to play me. You killed Tesca in Industry. Did you know I was there? Doesn't matter. You'd have let me be in any case. You needed me alive. But Tesca had become a loose end. And you set up Ortega in Mike's house. Supplied him the weapon. The one you used to shoot Mike, and Tesca. Your plan almost went off the rails there."

"He wasn't supposed to kill you," Carlson said. For whatever reason confirming the story. Perhaps still hoping to make a connection. Put us on the same side.

"Coulda fooled me," I said. "Came real close to putting a bullet in my head. And I guess you figured I'd kill him. Tie up another loose end for you. Must've surprised the hell outta you when he was arrested instead. At any rate you were running out of time. The shooter at Mike's place the final piece to get me on board. That's why you were there. Ready to make contact."

His blank stare still fixed on me while the mind behind it whirred and calculated.

"I'm curious why you want Ramirez out of the way. Is it you, or someone paying you? But that doesn't matter either. My only concern in all this was finding the person who shot my friend. And I've found him."

I'd obtained my confirmation. Didn't need to prolong what had to happen next. Not something I took any pleasure in. Not back then, when it'd been just a job and I didn't really care. Certainly not now. Then, as now, it boiled down to necessity. Survival. Eradication of a deadly predator. Alive he remained a threat. He'd make me pay. Someday. And he'd come at me sideways, through people I cared about.

He continued to study me, still searching for an angle. His eyes uncaring. Devoid of emotion. I rose from the bed where I'd sat facing him. Beneath my thigh, hidden from his view during our little chat, a Colt SSP modified to accept a suppressor. His eyes widened involuntarily. Still dispassionate, displaying no emotion.

"Killing me won't end this," his voice still unnervingly calm. "You have no idea what this is about. And without me you never will. You want to protect your friends? The only way to do that is if I'm alive."

I remained silent. My expression unchanged.

"Ramirez is nothing," he said. "The person who wants him put out of business more powerful than you can imagine. With ambitions and resources Ramirez couldn't even dream of. And he's got his sights set on your precious islands. Kill me and you'll have no idea what's coming your way. Without me you'll never see it coming, or be able to stop it."

May or may not be true. It might confirm my suspicion Carlson hadn't targeted Ramirez for his own purposes. But had either been contracted or was in the employ of someone who needed Ramirez removed. Didn't matter. I wasn't going down that rabbit hole. And if true, it wouldn't save him. On the contrary it'd sealed his fate. I couldn't allow Carlson to reveal my existence to whoever had hired him. That person a worry for another day.

"It doesn't matter. Your time's up," I said. I leaned forward again. Held his stare. "Back on Bequia you called me Alverez. Said you'd heard the name a few times before Panama. That person also went by another name. I leaned in closer, from the side. Whispered in his ear.

His eyes opened wide. A flicker of fear finally. A sudden, futile struggle in the chair. Only momentary. Ceasing as abruptly as it began. His gaze rose to meet mine. Defiant.

"You're....."

Before he uttered another word I fired. Twice. Both rounds in the heart. His body jerked back in the sturdy armchair. The chair remained upright. The force of the rounds pushing him backward not enough to topple it. The loads and projectiles designed to shred tissue at close range. To produce instant shock and shut down the brain. No death throes. No parting emotions. He died instantly. Perhaps not feeling a thing. A mercy he perhaps didn't deserve.

CHAPTER 24

English Harbour, a slice of Antigua's colonial history. Declared a national park by the Antiguan government in order to preserve it. The harbor's historic setting attracted both land bound tourists and cruising yachtsmen.

It'd been originally developed in the eighteenth century as a base for the Royal Navy. The headquarters of the Leeward Islands fleet under Admiral Nelson. It'd been ideal. A natural 'hurricane hole' gouged into Antigua's southwest coast. In its secure, protected anchorage, the fleet sheltered from storms, effected repairs and resupplied.

I sat on the upper deck of what used to be the officers' quarters. The old stone building one of many original eighteenth century structures around the harbor. Converted into shops, inns, restaurants, and marina offices. The open sides of the restaurant overlooked a stone quay, its line of ancient cannons as though protecting the anchorage beyond.

Race week had ended. Most of the visiting yachts had already departed for all points of the compass. When uncrowded, English Harbour possessed a quaint beckoning charm, allowing its visitors to lose themselves in a bygone era. Its restored Georgian buildings and nautical artifacts imbued by two hundred years of British naval history. Capstans for careening ships; cauldrons to boil tar; cannons to maul enemy ships and their crews. Buildings to house naval officers, seamen, slave laborers. And as storage for cooper, wood, tar, shot, gunpowder, ropes and sailcloth. All the accoutrements of eighteenth century naval warfare.

I gazed across the water. Focused on Wherever riding at anchor. A new bright red boot stripe sparkled against the blue water. She'd been 'splashed' the day before, following a short-haul at Nelson's Dockyard. I'd completed a thorough inspection of her interior and rigging, just in case Carlson had left any nasty surprises. And I'd dry-docked her, ostensibly to clean and repaint her bottom. But more importantly to inspect every inch of her hull, inside and out. No Carlson surprises there either.

I scanned a half-folded copy of the International Herald Tribune. Also on the table in front of me the latest editions of the Antigua Sun and the Antigua Observer. And the remains of a conch salad sandwich I hadn't finished. It'd been four days since I'd texted Mendez the 'go' code following Ramirez's departure from the villa, accompanied by Sarah Holmes and the RFID tag I'd planted in her handbag.

A task force of Antigua Cops had captured Ramirez attempting to flee the Island. He, or at least his men, had put up a fight. The operation had been closely compartmentalized and controlled by Mike and his contact in the Antiguan National Drug and Money Laundering Control Department. Ramirez undoubtedly had tentacles inside the Antiguan police and national defense forces. Except for Mike's contact, no one on the task force had been given prior knowledge of the raid's real objective or target.

During our briefing on Bequia we'd discussed the possibility of arresting Ramirez. A contingency dependent on intelligence on the ground. I hadn't considered putting the contingency into play. Hadn't envisioned Ramirez being alive to arrest. Until the appearance of Sarah Holmes changed everything.

Ramirez's arrest triggered an international news sensation, placing Antigua in the international spotlight. The Tribune headline in bold black letters read: 'COLUMBIAN CARTEL LEADER ARRESTED.' A photograph of a bullet scarred yacht tied against a dock accompanied the article.

Falmouth Harbour, Antigua (Reuters).

Antiguan authorities arrested the Columbian drug cartel leader Edwardo Alonzo Ramirez, an international drug trafficker on the US most wanted list. The arrest occurred after a shootout in Falmouth Harbour involving members of the Antiguan T.A.S.T Drug Enforcement Unit. Mr. Ramirez is said by US authorities to be the head of a Columbian Cartel embroiled in a violent struggle for control of lucrative drug routes in the Eastern Caribbean.

Authorities received an anonymous tip regarding Mr. Ramirez's presence aboard a luxury yacht in Falmouth Harbour during the final days of Antigua's annual regatta. Police were met by gunfire when they approached and attempted to board the yacht. A two hour gun battle ensued during which the yacht attempted to flee. It was chased and eventually disabled by units of the Royal Antiguan Coast Guard. The gunmen on board surrendered to Police. There were several unconfirmed reports from the scene that as many as five policemen were wounded, and two killed. Four of the gunmen aboard the yacht were also believed killed according to initial unconfirmed reports.

The United States indicted Mr. Ramirez in 2003 on drug trafficking, money-laundering and murder charges and had offered a reward as high as $5 million for his capture.

When Mr. Ramirez was arrested he was found in the company of Sarah Holmes, an American who had been the subject of an extensive search after she was reported missing on the Caribbean Island of Bequia two months ago. No explanation for her presence on the yacht have been provided by either the US or Antiguan authorities'.

Another article, about the size of a quarter page classified ad, but also on the front page probably due to its connection to Antigua, carried the headline: 'MISSING JET FEARED CRASHED IN THE CARIBBEAN'

St. Johns, Antigua (Reuters)

A private Gulfstream IV jet that departed Antigua International Airport at approximately 4:15 PM last Thursday was reported overdue for a scheduled stop in Puerto Rico. After four days authorities have called off the search around the area where the pilots last made radio contact with the ground. Since there is no radar coverage over the Caribbean Sea, authorities are unable to determine if the aircraft was on the course or at the altitude given in its last position report to ground controllers. No signs of wreckage were found in the search area. The aircraft manifest listed two pilots, David Moore 34, and George Herman 32, both of Miami; a cabin attendant Sandra Jones 28, of Vero Beach; and a New York financier, George Anderson, a Senior Vice President of Equity

International Group, who was the sole passenger. Mr. Anderson had flown to Antigua for a business meeting.

A smile crossed my face. An op worthy of Monk's larcenous heart. One I'm certain he'd thoroughly enjoyed. Especially since it'd provided a new aircraft for his fleet. I had no doubt in his ability to 'procure' the necessary paperwork and history for his new acquisition.

No mention anywhere in the local media of a body found in a villa above Half Moon Bay. A situation continuing to haunt me. Guilt weighed on me like a four ton elephant on my back. Not for killing Carlson. Rather the manifestation of the dread I'd experienced on Bequia the night Mike had been shot. It'd been my attachment to him, and Jolene, that had put them in jeopardy. My perpetual curse. I doubted I'd ever escape it. So what then?

Carlson's words echoed in my head. 'You and me are the same....' And I finally understood a more profound truth surrounding those words. To deny a part of myself wasn't the answer. For too long I'd buried the emotional side. A survival mechanism. And it'd almost destroyed me. To bury the darker side, deny it, refuse to confront and face it in open honesty, also a mistake. I needed both to survive. To be whole. And to protect the ones I loved.

I worried too about whoever discovered Carlson's body. Preferably the police. Even so, encountering a days old decomposing body would shock and scare the bejesus out of anyone not hardened to such a sight. It'd leave a lasting psychological impression. I hoped it'd be the police who found the body, and not a caretaker or maid.

But I'd needed to stage it as I did. Ensuring everyone's attention remained focused on Ramirez. The bullets eventually retrieved from Carlson's body would match a weapon recovered from Ramirez's yacht. I'd already planted the Colt among the police haul from the yacht. There'd be no useable prints on the weapon. No one would care. Despite the denials of Ramirez and his men. They'd been at the villa. The murder weapon found among others seized from the yacht. They'd injured and killed Antiguan policemen in a shootout. They'd brought undeclared firearms illegally into the country. The Antiguan authorities would quickly and confidently add Carlson's death to the charges against Ramirez.

Carlson's true identity, beyond the cover aliases, might never be known to the Feds or Antiguan authorities. His true identity and origins scrubbed, as mine had been. He'd be deniable.

Three days following the arrests of Ramirez and Sarah Holmes the international news media descended on Antigua. International meaning mostly U.S cable news channels. Their focus unsurprisingly on Sarah Holmes. Most reporters unaware of Ramirez's existence prior to his arrest. The same chattering heads unashamedly uttered the same incoherent noises. Unapologetic for having been so incorrect and mistaken in their opinions and speculation regarding Sarah Holmes. None had foreseen this development. None knew what it meant. Though some commentators had the temerity to claim otherwise.

I sensed her presence before I saw her. Superintendent Jolene Johanssen strode through the entrance like a ray of sunshine, instantly brightening the room. Luxuriant, straw streaked hair hung loose about her radiant olive face, straight on the top, a mass of tight curls cascading onto her shoulders. She wore a pale blue pinstriped formfitting shirt, the sleeves rolled and buttoned above her elbows. The dark blue skirt fell just above her knees, accentuating the narrow waist, the sensual flair of her hips, the heart shaped slope of her buttocks. A small handbag hung at regulation length against her right hip, held by a thin black leather strap over her shoulder. She wore closed-toe, soft black leather shoes with sturdy kitten heels. Comfortable and functional.

As usual she wore no makeup. Fetchingly glamorous without it. Her only jewelry small pearl stud earrings, and a thin crescent shaped wristwatch with a silver bracelet-like band.

"Hi sailor," her face lit by a smile of genuine delight. She leaned forward, planted a quick kiss on my cheek.

"You hungry?" I asked.

"No," she said, taking a chair opposite me. "I want to get out of here, get out of these clothes, and rock the boat." Hypnotic hazel eyes, like peridots floating in sparkling champagne, projected pent up desire and relief as they gazed into mine. Accompanied by a coquettish grin. Her forthrightness invitingly charming. Irresistible. She signaled a passing waitress. Ordered a bitter lemon, tall, lots of ice.

She perused the papers spread on the table in front of me. "Looks like it went down just like you said it would," tapping the Herald Tribune article.

"Not exactly," I said.

A row of tiny creases furrowed her brow. "How so?"

"Sarah Holmes," I said.

She nodded.

Michael W Smart

"How'd it go on your end?" As the lead investigator on Mike's shooting and Sarah Holmes's disappearance, Jolene had been dispatched to Antigua to question Ramirez and Sarah Holmes.

"I think we've got most of it. The Americans have Ramirez under wraps. Wrangling over extradition. He isn't saying anything anyway. So I've been told. But Sarah Holmes told us everything she knew once she had a plea deal with the US attorney. They'll place her in witness protection in exchange for testimony against Ramirez. She told us about the evening Mike was shot."

She hesitated. Inhaled a deep breath. The passage of almost two months hadn't blunted the raw memories of that fateful night. Her gaze wandered around the room before she spoke again.

"She said she was waiting to meet a currier to deliver financial information for her client. She'd been meeting curriers at almost every port on the cruise. Routine. Until Bequia. The currier never showed. She was about to leave when she noticed the two men. Before she knew what was happening one of them shot the other. She didn't hear the shots, or get a good look at the two men. She just remembers the man who'd been shot reeling back... twisting around.... then falling to the ground." Her words halting as she verbalized them. Her gaze again wandered the room. The Adams apple in the sensual stretch and curve of her throat slid up and down as she swallowed hard.

The bitter lemon she'd ordered arrived. She drank a long gulping mouthful, lubricating her dry throat. Not dried from thirst. She placed the glass on the table and eyed my unfinished sandwich. Plucked a conch morsel from the plate. Popped it into her mouth.

"Anyway," she continued. "She fled the area. Not sure what to do. Stayed out of sight until she made contact with the man she worked for, who was also scheduled to meet her on Bequia. He instructed her to lay low and wait for him to come get her."

"She say who this man was?" I already knew the answer. Wanted to hear Sarah's confirmation.

"Man named Fowler. He didn't show up in anyone's investigation. Not ours. Not the FBI's. According to Sarah about two years ago her firm was acquired by another firm with a broader international reach. They'd been searching for a boutique firm like hers to handle select clients. After the merger she was assigned to one client. And one client only."

"Let me guess. Ramirez."

"Correct. According to her that's when she first met this Fowler. He was some sort of a managing director with the firm that acquired hers. She answered to him and only him. And received her instructions only from him. She said the single client kept her busy. Busier than she'd ever been. And she had to travel a lot. Scouting businesses and investment opportunities for the client. Evaluating and overseeing acquisitions. Occasionally meeting with the client. Always in exotic locations. The Caribbean. Argentina. Brazil. Never in Europe. Never in the States. Always with tight security. Often travelling with Fowler. They even had an on again off again affair."

She popped another sauce smothered piece of conch in her mouth.

"Why'd she take off? Disappear? Instead of just going back to the ship and carrying on as normal."

"According to her this Fowler had always been tight assed about security. To the point of paranoia. The shooting freaked her out. When Fowler got to her he told her the currier had been killed. Their security had been breached. Someone was after her and the information she'd been gathering. She had to secure the information. Get it to the client as soon as possible. And without being spotted. Said Fowler told her he didn't know who they could trust. Except for the client. She'd be safe once she got to him. He told her she'd have to disappear for a while until they figured out what was going on. Who was after her and the client. And why. She said Fowler kept in regular contact with her and the client. Said he'd let her know when it was safe for her to resurface. Said it looked like he'd have it all wrapped up while they were here on Antigua."

"Did she know the uproar her disappearance created? All the people searching for her?"

"No. Said she was kept pretty much in seclusion. Under tight security. According to her it wasn't until then she began to suspect what kind of business her client was in."

"The Feds buying that?"

"They believe she's lying about that part. She's too intelligent to have not figured it out before this. They believe she became a willing part of it a while ago. Seduced by the money and the lifestyle. They think that's why she ran and disappeared, aside from anything else. But Ramirez is the one they want. They're willing to cut her a deal. And they're interested in this Fowler guy too. She gave them a description.

They're searching for him. One of a couple of loose ends still remaining in this whole affair."

"Won't' matter," I said noncommittally.

She ceased chewing. Her eyes, more green than amber in the shaded sunlight, settled on me in an inquiring gaze.

"Did she say what else she might've been doing in the Grenadines?" I asked quickly.

"You mean the pictures? I asked her about that. She said it was Fowler's idea. Scouting opportunities for another of the Firm's clients. Nothing to do with Ramirez."

The other person Carlson mentioned? I wondered.

"You said there were a couple of loose ends. What else?"

"This thing about the missing aircraft," she said, her curious stare still focused on me. "According to Sarah the passenger on that aircraft was here to meet Ramirez. Upgrading some kinda computer software."

It made me wonder why no one had checked the villa yet. "Did she say where the meet took place?"

"She couldn't say for sure. Some villa on the other side of the island. Said she didn't pay much attention to directions or names."

Jolene popped another scrap from the plate into her mouth. Her eyes never left mine.

"Anyway the plane goes missing, but the flight crew shows up stateside safe and sound, saying how lucky they were to be taken off the flight. According to them at the last moment they got instructions to layover and take a commercial flight home the next day. Another crew came in to fly the rest of the trip. The Feds think Ramirez wanted his own people to take over the flight. That maybe he was heading to some destination he didn't want anyone else to know."

"Maybe," I said.

She leaned back in the chair. Certain now of an unspoken something she'd perceived while studying me.

"Why do I get the feeling there's a whole lot to this story you know that I don't?" After a moment, "Because of course you do," she said, answering her own question. "So?"

"For your and Mike's ears only." I waited. Her elegant curved eyebrows rose, opening her eyes wider. Their expression shifted from questioning to acutely attentive. She leaned forward again. Nodded.

"You don't have any loose ends," I said. "You can close your cases. The aircraft was repayment of a debt."

Chartreuse eyes continued to stare, uncomprehending.

"A wha...?" Unable to complete the sentence. her words replaced by soft laughter. It bubbled up out of her. A quiet chuckle at first, blossoming into a long rippling string, like melodious hiccoughs. She laid an open palm on her chest.

"I swear Gage. You do take my breath away. In more ways than one. Repayment of a debt?" Another ripple of laughter shook her. It subsided. Replaced by a more serious tone.

"I'm not sure I know or want to know what that means. And what about the passenger. This guy Anderson who met with Ramirez?"

"He's in the hands of people who will make good use of the information he has. And after that, I don't know. But he's out of the money laundering business for good."

Her eyes locked on mine again. Her mirth disappeared as abruptly as it'd been spawned. Attentive again. And something else in their hypnotic pools. A compassionate concern. As though perceiving the guilt swimming behind mine. The involuntary part I'd played in the near death of our friend.

"What else?" she said, her voice reflecting the concern in her eyes.

"Carlson was Fowler," I said quietly. "He was behind everything that happened. The endgame of an operation he'd been running for some time against Ramirez. Sarah was his asset. He placed her next to Ramirez. Played her from the beginning. Just like he played the rest of us. His real name was Dieter, Franz Dieter. And he shot Mike."

"Was...."

"He's dead." I said. Her eyes flickered wider. Held me in their steady gaze. I told her everything.

Jolene sat motionless across from me. Moments passed in silence. Woeful, moist eyes peered into mine, conveying a mixture of sympathy, understanding, love, and strength. She reached across the table. Her hand grasped mine.

"Let's get out of here," she said.

Aboard Wherever she held me in comforting arms. And gave herself unselfishly, unstintingly. A Long, lingering, loving cathartic release. Through the afternoon. Into the night. Until in the wee hours, long before the sun's expected rise, we hauled Wherever's anchor and slipped anonymously into the night.

An hour out from Antigua we encountered the syncopated rhythm of offshore swells. Wherever plowed through the long, undulating rollers, moving with an assured grace, her wings spread wide. A glowing green phosphorescent swath in her wake.

The night black. The sky a bewildering abundance of stars, like sprinkled diamonds. Bright and luminous.

The next three days ours together. Me, Jolene, Wherever. Alone. Embraced in the boundless solace of a vast indomitable sea.

About the author

A native New Yorker, Michael W. Smart spent eight years sailing around the Eastern Caribbean. Dead Reckoning is his debut novel, the first in a series of Bequia Mysteries, which draws on his intimate knowledge of the islands, its people, and his sailing adventures in the Caribbean. Following diverse careers as a charter and delivery captain, yacht broker, pilot, air traffic controller and marina manager, he now writes full time

Thank you for reading my book. If you enjoyed it please take a moment to leave a review where you purchased it and spread the word to your friends. Thank you. Fair winds and following seas.

Preview book 2 of the opening trilogy of the Bequia Mystery Series.

Eight months following the near fatal shooting of her boss, mentor and friend Commissioner of Police Mike Daniels, Police Superintendent Jolene Johanssen is dispatched to a fatal vehicular accident on Union Island. Her investigation in its initial stages Johanssen catches a second case, the apparent suicide of a prominent Vincentian and advisor to the Government. The two cases lead her and Nicholas Gage on a chase culminating in New York City, and a shocking discovery which threatens St. Vincent and the Grenadines.

CHAPTER 1

Confusion and chaos greeted me at the scene. Horns blared in the midmorning heat. Vans piled up one behind the other, their drivers lending voice to the loud animated shouting already present at the roadside. The disordered dissonance smothered the pleasant afterglow of my flight down from Bequia, the first time I'd flown Mike's Seneca on my own.

Pedestrians milled about, lining both sides of the narrow mountain road. Women with laden baskets on their heads; children in school uniform who should've already been in their classrooms; men apparently with no place they needed to be. Goats grazed at the roadside, their plaintive baaing joining the chorus of excitable voices.

A uniformed constable stood in the midst of the chaos. Unable or unwilling to control the mess. Just another loud voice in the chaotic cacophony.

Alighting from the battered police Toyota 4runner I noticed yellow police tape stretched across a section of the road. Each end of the tape tied to stakes made from cut tree branches and driven into the ground. Off to the side, away from the crowd, a full-figured, buxom woman in a simple pink batik sundress, and sensible grey flats, stood before a distraught older man. She said something to the man before heading in my direction.

Zelina McIntosh, late twenties, one of the few female CID detectives on the Royal St. Vincent and the Grenadines Police Force. And among the handful who investigated criminal complaints beyond the limited purview of sexual and family offenses; the reason she'd accepted the Union Island station assignment. As the only CID detective on the island, Zelina investigated all criminal complaints. While she didn't have as many cases as she might on St. Vincent, she'd make her bones quicker on Union Island than on the mainland. I considered myself fortunate to have her in my Division.

Reaching me she stood at attention and saluted. I returned the salute, before flashing a welcoming smile and shaking her hand.

"Suprintendent," she greeted in a lilting Vincentian contraction of Superintendent, releasing my hand.

"Cut the formality Zelina. Jus we gurls heah."

She smiled in turn, a pleasant, broad separation of full lips revealing straight, pearl white teeth. The smile lifted the chubby flesh covering her cheekbones. A thin patina of perspiration glistened on her ochre toned face.

"Before I forget, terrific job on the Delves case," I said, referring to a fatal stabbing on the island she'd successfully closed.

"So what we have heah?" I asked her.

She flipped pages on a spiral stenographer's notebook in her left hand.

"Passahsby discovahed de vehicle approximately seven o'clock dis mahnin," she began, consulting her notes. "Dey made a repoht at Clifton Police Station. Names are in de repoht at de station. Sargent Baptiste and Constable Quashie responded to de scene."

"Where is Baptiste by the way?" I asked, interrupting her.

"Said he had business back at de station since dis a CID case."

"I see," I said.

Her exasperated expression indicated she did too, Baptiste purposely avoiding me. Fine by me.

"Anyway," she continued, "De registration plate is listed in de ownership of...." she flipped more pages, "Samuel Gooding. Dats him ova dey," pointing to the man she'd been speaking to when I'd arrived.

"Accordin to Mr. Gooding he loaned de vehicle to an American frend."

"When? When de las time he see de vehicle?" I asked.

She flipped more pages. "Accordin to Gooding, last evening jus befoh dahk."

"And de name of dis friend?"

"John Smith," she said reading from her notes.

"John Smith?" I repeated.

Zelina noticed the inflection in my voice. "Yuh noh dis man?"

"I noh it's probably a false name," I said.

"How come?"

"Is an American ting. Smith and Jones are common aliases. Any description of dis so called friend?"

"White, American, early sixties about. Big. Dress in dahk pants an a light blue polo shirt wid dat horse ting on it."

"And he's supposedly staying on PSV?"

"Dat accordin to Mr. Gooding."

"What yuh tink?" I asked.

"I tink he hire out de vehicle fe money. It's a criminal offense, but no way to prove it widout de American or de money."

"And what being done to locate dis American?"

"Nuttin yet. Sergeant Baptiste stop doin anyting aftah yuh call me. And I didn't av a chance to staht inquirin into dat yet. Anyhow, if he been drivin he might be dung dey in de wreck."

"Dats de reason Commissioner Daniels give CID de case and why I'm here," I said, recalling the astonishing phone call earlier that morning from Mike ordering me to Union Island to personally take charge of the investigation. A vehicular accident not the sort of case usually assigned to the CID, unless it involved a fatality. And usually handled by an investigator well below my rank. An American staying on the resort island Petit St. Vincent might be involved Mike had explained, a situation requiring delicate handling. He'd also suggested, practically commanded, I save time by flying down in his personal aircraft, a twin engine Piper Seneca.

His call had set my heart racing. Mike had dispatched me into a lion's den. First, the situation had the potential to blow up in our faces given the combination of a wealthy American tourist, and a foreign owned island resort where the management vigorously protected their guest's privacy.

Secondly I'd have to contend with Union Island's Station Sergeant, Garrett Baptiste, a misogynistic, incompetent bully who used his position to conceal his own insecurity and ineptitude.

Primarily my heart had raced at the prospect of flying the Seneca, and also the chance to see Gage. He'd sailed down island from Bequia two days before.

I'd missed him even after just two days apart. Missed waking up beside him; watching him get dressed; smelling his scent; reaching for him at night and feeling his arms close around me.

But the scene before me dominated my attention and monopolized my thoughts.

"Corporal Radcliff," I shouted, turning to the constable who'd driven me out from the airport.

"Ma'am," he said, stiffening to attention.

"Move dis police vehicle off de road and you an de odder constable start moving dose people and vans. I want dis road clear in five minutes."

"Yes ma'am," he acknowledged.

"Constable Johns," I called next, searching for the gangly nineteen year old rookie who'd accompanied me from Bequia. I'd shanghaied him for this assignment. He wasn't complaining. It meant an exciting change from his usual boring routine. And the flight down had transformed him into a wide-eyed kid on a fantasy adventure; when he wasn't clutching his seat in white knuckled apprehension.

"Ma'am," he said, materializing like magic at my side.

"Mek sure dat man don't go anywhey," I instructed, pointing to Samuel Gooding.

"Yes ma'am," he acknowledged, running off.

Loud voices rose from the roadside. Corporal Radcliff's above everyone else. He and his partner gesticulated in wild abandon, shooing, prodding, cajoling at the top of his voice, moving the knot of people and vehicles along the roadside.

The road clear, I called out to Corporal Radcliff again. When he arrived I gave him further instructions.

"Okay. One of you at dat end of de road," I said, pointing in one direction, "the odder ovah dat end," pointing in the opposite direction. "Keep any traffic moving and dis road clear." I shouldn't have had to direct them, but neither had taken the initiative to control the scene.

I walked to the opposite side of the road, to the yellow tape. Far down in a steep ravine, maybe a hundred meters, the tail end of a yellow Volkswagen 181 'Thing' stuck out of the treetops. The dense packed trees had arrested the compact jeep's fall. It'd left a trail of smashed rocks, torn foliage, and vehicle debris in its tumble down the ravine. The soft, convertible canvas top had been shredded. A small portion of the front end visible from the road appeared crushed.

A thought struck me. I turned to Zelina surveying the scene alongside me.

"Why didn't Gooding drive de jeep himself? Why give it to de American?"

"I was jus gwoin ask im dat when yuh ahrived."

"What about photos of de scene?" I asked.

"I tek some wen we was putting up de tape," she said, fishing in the cloth handbag under her left armpit. She pulled out a small Nikon digital camera, powered it up, selected playback mode and handed it to me. The jeep had gone off a narrow winding road halfway up Mount Olympus, northwest of Ashton Township. It had tumbled over a cliff of rock and dry forest. Zelina had taken shots of the jeep's destructive path, including the mangled bits of yellow and red debris. She'd done everything correctly since receiving my call earlier that morning to take over the case.

An hour to go before noon. The sun a blinding silver orb high in a pale blue almost cloudless sky. Scattered cumulus balls hovered over Union island. The remainder of the sky clear and bright. Frequent rainy season showers had nourished the verdant landscape and brightened the vibrant reds, oranges, purples, yellows and blues of fruit trees and wildflowers populating the hillsides.

From our vantage point on the mountain Union's entire three square miles spread out before us. The green sloping landscape gave way to white sand and turquoise bays surrounded by a sapphire sea. Mayreau, Canuoan, Bequia and St. Vincent all visible to the east and north. Palm Island and Petit St. Vincent to the southeast. Petit Martinique and Carriacou belonging to Grenada lay to the south. And rising from the distant haze, the volcanic peak of Grenada itself.

I rummaged in my handbag, retrieved my cell phone, and dialed the Coast Guard dispatch desk in Calliaqua Bay on St. Vincent. I requested an ETA on the cutter Commissioner Daniels had dispatched. I'd flown over it on the trip down, a forty foot aluminum cutter throwing a white bow wave as it plowed south for Union. I waited while the dispatcher radioed the vessel. The background noise of multiple active radio frequencies heard through the phone. Twelve minutes the dispatcher informed me. I hung up and turned to Zelina.

"Let's go see Mr. Gooding."

"If I may suggest Suprintendent."

"What?"

"Follow my lead."

She stood directly in front of Samuel Gooding. Zelina shorter by a head, but her authoritative presence clearly intimidated him. He kept his eyes focused on the ground while she addressed him.

"Mister Gooding, yuh know we can bring a chahge gainst yuh fe unlawful hire of a vehicle. Dis is Suprintendent Johanssen of de CID." She emphasized my rank, as if by itself it increased the seriousness of the trouble he faced. In fact, absent evidence demonstrating he'd hired out the vehicle we couldn't charge him.

"Why yuh no drive de jeep yuhself?" She continued in the same aggressive tone.

"I dun tell yuh me nevah hire out de jeep. Me loan it to a fren," he insisted, his gaze still downcast.

"Okay. So yuh loan it," she said, going along. "How yuh know dis man can drive? Yuh see him drivah license? Him have permit to drive on St. Vincent and the Grenadines? Why yuh no drive him yuhself?" She repeated more forcefully.

"He say he meeting sombady in private."

"Who?" She pressed him.

"How me fe noh? Him no tell me an me no ask."

"Whey dis meetin supposed to be?"

"Me no noh."

"Yuh no noh? Yuh len him yuh jeep and yuh no noh whey he gwoin wid it? Yuh edah stupid or lyin. So now we goin ahress and chahge yuh."

Zelina's threat produced a mournful muttering. He hadn't done anything wrong. Just being neighborly and helpful to a visitor. Didn't know nuttin bout nuttin. Repeated 'Lord have mercies' liberally interspersed in his mutterings.

Zelina turned to me, a knowing expression on her face. I nodded. We wouldn't get much more from him. She informed him he was under arrest and left Constable Johns to guard him.

We walked back to the spot where the vehicle had left the road. A typical rural Vincentian road. Narrow, winding, poorly maintained and potholed, with dangerous drop-offs sometimes marked only by a low stone wall. Local drivers knew the dangerous stretches and deadly curves. A stranger had no chance, especially at night.

Evidently he'd been heading down toward Ashton. He'd misjudged the sharp curve, and half mounted, half plowed through the stone wall. It meant the jeep had been moving fast. But if the driver had been aware of impending disaster, the scene showed no evidence of it. No skid marks; no other indication the driver had tried to avoid hitting the wall. The jeep didn't appear to have hit side-on and rolled. Rather the destructive path indicated it had travelled straight over the low wall before tumbling end over end.

If one could believe anything Gooding said, I wondered who the driver planned to meet. Why it had to be kept private. It might mean a woman. I wondered if he'd been on the way to or from the rendezvous.

I walked over to Gooding again who remained under the watchful eyes of Constable Johns.

"Mister Gooding," I said approaching him, his gaze still firmly fixed on the ground.

"Look at me when I speak to you," I commanded.

His gaze slowly left the pavement and rose to meet mine. He had deep set eyes in a heavily lined coal black face. Dark irises, surrounded by dull chalky sclera; the corners streaked in red.

"Where yuh len dis man de jeep?" His gaze moved back and forth across my face, not focusing, avoiding my eyes.

"In Clifton, ma'am," he eventually answered, making momentary eye contact before quickly averting his gaze. His entire manner meek and submissive.

"What time?"

"Time? Time? I dohn noh time. Was jus gettin dahk."

"And how much he give yuh?"

"Him give me...." he began before catching himself and shutting his mouth. I glanced over at Zelina. She stifled a laugh.

"He nevah ge me nuttin, inspector... officer... suprintenden...." he continued in a nervous stutter.

"Riiight," I said. An when he supposed to return it?"

"Was fe leave it by Clifton Harbor wen he done wid it."

Satisfied, I returned to the still chuckling Zelina.

"So what now Suprintendent?" she asked.

"I need to get down to that jeep," I said in non-patois English, glancing at my watch. "An whey de hell de Coast Guard be?" lapsing right back into it as my exasperation grew. Again checking my watch. Checking it every few seconds wouldn't get the Coast Guard and SSU officers on site any sooner. On these islands things happened on Vincy time.

Mon ostie de saint-sacrament de câlice de crisse! My silent frustration switched from patois to French, one of three languages I'd grown up hearing in my household.

"Suprintendent, ow we gwoin bring up de jeep from down dey?" Zelina asked, channeling my own thoughts. I'd been contemplating the problem on and off since arriving on the scene. Anywhere else it'd be a no brainer. Call in a crane, a hoist, whatever. Haul it up. But in the Grenadines it presented a challenge requiring creative thinking. Another reason to get a move on. No telling what this operation might entail and how long it might take.

"Not sure yet," I said to Zelina. Won't know til I get down dey, see what we have. Yuh have yuh VHF?"

"Yeah Suprintendent."

"Call de Coast Guard fo me. Find out whey de hell dey be," my patience running on empty.

She fished in her handbag, pulled out her handheld VHF and tuned in the Coast Guard frequency. The cutter had to be in range of the portable radio by now. Standing next to her I heard both sides of the exchange.

"We jus leave de harbor, be dey just now," came the answer to her inquiry. 'Just now' a distinctly Vincentian concept. A subset of Vincy time, indicating an indefinite period which might be soon, maybe later, but in practice meant whenever.

We waited in the tropical heat. The scenery magnificent and unchanging. Distant specs of white sail appeared motionless in the blue expanse. Zelina and I discussed what we knew so far, formulating theories regarding the accident. I told her my idea the driver might've been meeting a woman, wanting to keep the meeting discreet.

He'd picked up the jeep in Clifton, and judging from the angle it went off the road, he might've been on the way back. Did he meet the person and drive up here together? Or did the meeting take place farther up the mountain? Not much up there. No villas or hotels. A few rudimentary island homes sparsely scattered in the dense forest. A few clearings offering spectacular views. Maybe they'd wanted the view and privacy; an impromptu lover's lane.

Who had the driver met? And was that person also in the vehicle when it went off the road and down the cliff? I wondered.

Merde! I needed to get down to the wreck.

A glossary of nautical and aviation terms used in the
Bequia Mysteries

Abeam - A relative bearing perpendicular to the sides of a vessel or off the wingtip of an aircraft.

Abeam the Runway – Indicates the runway is directly perpendicular to the right or left side of the aircraft.

Aboard - On or in a vessel or aircraft.

Adrift - Afloat and unattached in any way to the shore or seabed, but not under way. Also refers to any gear not fastened down or put away properly.

Aft - Towards the stern (rear) of a vessel or aircraft.

Aground - Resting on or touching the sea bottom (usually involuntarily).

Ahead - Forward of a vessel's bow or aircraft's nose.

Ahoy - A shout to draw attention. Term used to hail another vessel.

Air Data Computer (ADC) – An instrument which displays information on the surrounding atmosphere and the aircraft's flight through it, such as pressure altitude, outside air temperature, airspeed, and aircraft attitude.

Aileron – A control surface attached to the outer trailing edge of an aircraft's wings allowing the aircraft to bank.

Alee - To leeward. Referring to the lee side (away from the wind) of a vessel.

Aloft- In the rigging of a sailing ship. Above the ship's uppermost solid structure; overhead or high above. An aircraft at altitude. High altitude winds.

Alongside - By the side of a vessel or pier.

Amidships (or midships) – At the middle of a vessel.

Anchor – A metal hook or plough-like object designed to dig into the seabed and hold a vessel in place. Attached to the vessel by a line or chain. A sea anchor is used to prevent or slow a vessel's drift at sea.

Anchor/Mooring buoy- A small floating buoy secured by a line to an anchor or mooring to indicate position of the anchor or mooring.

Anchor Chain - Chain connecting the vessel to the anchor. (See Ground Tackle)

Anchor Light – A white light displayed by a vessel at anchor usually from the tallest masthead. Anchor Rode - The anchor line, rope or cable connecting the anchor chain to the vessel. (See Ground Tackle)

Anchor Watch – An electronic instrument (GPS) or crewmen assigned to monitor the ship while anchored or moored, to ensure the anchor is holding and the vessel is not drifting. Most marine GPS units have an Anchor Watch Alarm capability.

Anchorage - A suitable area for a vessel to anchor. A harbor or port.

Anchors Aweigh – An anchor pulled clear of the bottom.

Aport - To port. Referring to the port (left) side of the vessel.

Apparent Wind - The combination of the true wind and the headwind caused by a vessel's forward motion.

Approach Charts – An aviation chart displaying instrument approach information such as holding fixes and procedures, approach and missed approach procedures, in addition to the plan and profile views of various instrument procedures. Other information on approach charts include obstacle location and clearance height; navigational aid frequencies and identifiers; transition altitudes and levels; airfield elevation; approach, tower, ground and ATIS radio frequencies; the location of outer, middle and inner markers; approach fixes and missed approach points; minimum safe descent altitudes; final approach course; decision height/altitude, and other airport information.

Approach Control – Air traffic controllers assigned to the approach segment of a given airport who provide directional guidance (vectors) to the final approach course.

Approach Segments - The parts of an instrument approach to an airport: arrival, initial approach, intermediate approach, final approach and missed approach segments.

Area traffic Control Center – Air traffic controllers responsible for large areas of enroute airspace, as opposed to approach, departure, tower and ground controllers.

Ashore - On the beach, shore, or land, as opposed to being aboard or on board).

Astarboard – Referring to the starboard (right) side of the vessel.

Astern – Referring to the stern (rear) of a vessel.

ATIS (Automated Terminal Information Service) - A continuous broadcast of recorded airport information updated hourly including active runways, arrival and departure procedures in use, weather, radio frequencies and other safety information.

ATR - A twin-engine turboprop regional transport aircraft used by many regional airlines in the Eastern Caribbean.

Attitude - An aircraft's position in flight relative to the three axes: pitch, roll and yaw.

Auto-flight System (AFS) - The combination of autopilot, autothrottle /autothrust, flight director, and autoland systems used to control flight through an aircraft's Flight Management System (FMS)

Autoland - An autopilot function which enables a "hands-off" automatic landing.

Autopilot (AP) - An automated computerized system which enables an aircraft to pilot itself.

Autothrottle (ATHR) - A computerized engine power control system enabling an aircraft to automatically adjust its power settings in different flight configurations.

Backstays - Lines or cables from the stern of a vessel to the masthead to support the masts. Part of the vessel's standing rigging.

Backtrack – To taxi on a runway in the opposite direction used for landing or takeoff.

Bank - A large area of elevated sea floor. The angle at which an aircraft is inclined about its longitudinal axis, used mostly during a turn.

Bareboat Charter – To hire or charter a vessel without a crew or provisions.

Base Leg - Part of the standard airport circuit an aircraft completes when landing. The aircraft parallels the runway on a downwind leg and turns to a base leg perpendicular to the runway before turning to the final landing leg. Referred to as "turning base".

Beam - The width of a vessel at the widest point, or a point alongside the vessel at the midpoint of its length (abeam).

Beam Ends - The sides of a vessel. "On her beam ends" may mean the vessel is literally on its side and possibly about to capsize. More often the phrase means the vessel is listing 45 degrees or more.

Beam Reach – A point of sail with the wind directly over the vessel's beam.

Bear down or bear away - Turn away from the wind. Also fall off.

Beat or Beating - Sailing as close as possible in the direction from which the wind is blowing.

Becalmed – A sailing vessel unable to sail due to lack of wind.

Belay - To secure a line around a fitting, cleat or belaying pin. Belaying Pins - Short movable iron bars or hard wood to which running rigging may be secured.

Berth (navigation) – Safe distance to be kept by a vessel from another vessel or an obstruction, hence the phrase, "to give a wide berth."

Berth (sleeping) - A bed or sleeping accommodation on a vessel.

Berth (vessel) - A dock, slip, or mooring area provided for vessels to tie up or moor.

Bilge - The compartment at the bottom of a vessel's interior hull. The lowest area of a vessel's interior.

Bimini Top - Canvas top covering the cockpit of a vessel, usually supported by a metal frame.

Binnacle - The stand on which the vessel's compass is mounted.

Bitt or Bitts - A post or posts mounted on the vessel's bow for fastening ropes or cables.

Bitter End - The last part or loose end of a rope, cable or chain.

Block - A pulley or set of pulleys.

Boarding Ladder - A portable flight of steps down a vessel's side or over the stern.

Boat-hook - A pole with a hook on the end, used to reach into the water to catch buoys or other floating objects.

Bobstay – A cable or chain which supports the bowsprit from below, counteracting the upward pull of the forestay.

Bollard - A stout vertical pillar on a dock or pier around which dock lines are made fast.

Booby hatch - A sliding hatch or cover.

Boom – A spar to which the foot (bottom) of a sail is attached.

Boom vang - A line which applies downward tension on a boom, countering the upward tension of the sail. The boom vang anchors the boom and allows control of the sail shape.

Boomkin (Bumpkin) - A spar, similar to a bowsprit, but projecting from the stern to extend the backstay or mizzen sheets.

Boot Stripe (Boot Top) - A painted stripe along a vessel's hull at the design waterline.

Bow - The front of a vessel.

Bowline - A type of knot, producing a strong loop of a fixed size.

Bowsprit - A spar projecting from the bow used to extend the forestay forward allowing the headsail to be set further forward.

Brightwork - Exposed varnished wood or polished metal on a vessel.

Britten Norman Islander – A twin engine light utility aircraft manufactured by the Britten-Norman company in the UK in the 1960's and still used by some regional airlines in the Caribbean for its STOL characteristics.

Broach - When a sailing vessel is forced by wind, sea, or too much sail into a sudden sharp turn which may lead to a capsize. The sudden change in direction is called broaching-to.

Broad Reach – A point of sail with the wind between the beam and stern, or 'on the quarter'.

Broken (BKN): A meteorological terms indicating cloud cover between 50% and 90% of the sky.

Bugs (Speed, Heading, Altitude) - Small plastic markers on analog instruments, or dials for digital displays, which are set at critical airspeeds, altitudes or headings during takeoff, climb and descent. When autopilot is engaged it automatically pursues the bug setting.

Bulkhead - An upright, watertight, load-bearing wall within the hull of a vessel or separating compartments on an aircraft.

Bulwark - The extension of the vessel's side above deck level.

Buoy - A floating object of defined shape and color used as an aid to navigation. A floating object indicating the position of an anchor or mooring.

Burgee - A small flag, typically triangular, flown from the masthead to indicate yacht-club membership.

Cabin - An enclosed room inside a vessel or aircraft.

Cabin Altitude (Pressure) - the artificially maintained atmospheric pressure inside an aircraft during high altitude flight, approximately 6,000- 8,000 feet inside the cabin.

Cabin Sole - The cabin floor, also referred to as an interior or lower deck.

Cable - A thick rope or bundle of spun wire.

Calibrated Airspeed (CAS) - The indicated airspeed (IAS) of an aircraft corrected for airspeed instrument errors.

Call-out – Verbal readout of flight data by a co-pilot or automated synthetic voice.

Capsize - When a vessel lists too far and rolls over, exposing the keel, often resulting in sinking.

Cardinal Points- Refers to the four main points of the compass: north, south, east and west.

Careening - Tilting a ship on its side, usually when beached, to clean or repair the hull below the water line.

CAT III Conditions - When visibility is very poor and aircraft require ILS automation for take-off and landing.

CAT IIIC - The crew, aircraft and airport are qualified and equipped to land in CAT III Conditions of 0 feet longitudinal visibility and a Decision Height of 0 feet.

Catamaran - A vessel with two hulls.

CAVOK - Ceiling and Visibility OK, spoken by pilots as "CAV-O-KAY".

Chafing - Wear on a line or sail caused by constant rubbing against another surface.

Chafing Gear - Material applied to a line or spar to prevent or reduce chafing.

Chain Locker - A space in the forward part of the ship containing the anchor chain and rode, typically behind the bow in front of the foremost bulkhead.

Checklist - A series of checks which are performed and confirmed during specific phases of a flight.

Chine - The angle formed where the sides and bottom of a vessel join. Soft chine is when the two surfaces join at a shallow angle, and hard chine is when they join at a steep angle.

Chocks - Rubber or wooden blocks placed against an aircraft's tires to prevent the aircraft from rolling while parked.

Circuit Breaker - An electrical safety device on vessels and aircraft which opens a circuit in case of current overload. On vessels the CB panel is located with or in close proximity to the main electrical panel. In large jet aircraft circuit breakers are located on the cockpit overhead panel, and at the bottom of the instrument panel on smaller aircraft like Mike Daniel's Piper Seneca.

Clean Up- To retract an aircraft's flaps, gear, slats and other exterior devices which may affect aerodynamics and speed.

Clew - The forward corner of a sail attached to the deck or forward end of a boom.

Close Aboard - In close proximity to another vessel.

Close-hauled – A vessel sailing as close to the wind as possible, referred to as beating.

Close Reach – A point of sail with the wind between the bow and beam.

Clear (CLR) – A meteorological term indicating a clear sky with no clouds.

Clearance (Cleared) - Authorization from air traffic control to proceed as requested or instructed.

Coach- roof – A cabin roof higher than the main deck.

Coaming - The edge of a hatch, cockpit or skylight raised above the deck to keep out water.

Cockpit - The area on deck containing helm and other vessel controls. Compartment from which a pilot operates an aircraft.

Companionway - A ladder leading from an entrance hatch to cabins below deck.

Compass – Navigational instrument indicating the direction of the vessel in relation to the Earth's geographical or magnetic poles.

Control Tower - An air traffic control facility located at an airport.

Controlled Airspace - Airspace of defined dimensions within which air traffic control is exercised and mandatory for aircraft flying through it.

Crabbing - Flying with drift due to crosswind.

Crossfeed - A valve which allows an aircraft's engines to obtain fuel from any of the available fuel tanks. A crossfeed also allows transfer of fuel from one tank to another.

Crosswind - A wind blowing at an angle to an aircraft's flight path, not necessarily perpendicular, which is a direct crosswind.

Dash 8 - A twin engine turboprop regional transport aircraft manufactured by De Havilland Canada (now Bombardier).

Davit – A paired set of cranes used to hoist, lower and hold a dinghy in place, usually affixed to the stern of a sailing vessel.

Dead Ahead - Directly ahead in front of the vessel.

Dead In The Water - Not moving; used only when a vessel is afloat and neither tied up nor anchored.

Dead Reckoning – To navigate without the aid of precision instruments or celestial observation where current position is estimated based on time and distance travelled from a know fix.

Deadeye - A wood block with holes (but no pulleys) which is spliced to a shroud. Used to adjust the tension in the standing rigging of a sailing vessel by lacing a lanyard from the deck through the holes. Performs the same job as a turnbuckle.

Deadlight - A strong shutter fitted over a porthole or other opening and closed in bad weather.

Deadrise - The design angle between the keel and vertical rise of the hull as measured from the horizontal.

Deadwood – The structural reinforcement of the aft portion of a vessel's hull between the keel and sternpost.

Decision Altitude (DA) - The altitude at which a pilot must decide to land or go around.

Decision Height (DH) - The height above the ground as displayed on a radio altimeter at which a pilot must decide to land or go around.

Deck - The top surface of a vessel. An interior floor below the top deck (See Cabin sole).

Deck Hand - A person (crew) performing tasks which aid in sailing and maintenance of the vessel.

Decks Awash – When the deck of a vessel is partially or wholly submerged.

Dinghy - A small inflatable or rigid hull boat carried or towed as a transport tender for the vessel. May be rowed, powered by an outboard motor, and some types can be rigged for sailing.

Displacement – The volume (weight) of water displaced by a vessel's immersed hull. Exactly equivalent to the vessel's weight.

Displacement hull - A hull designed to travel through the water, rather than planning over it.

Distance Measuring Equipment (DME) - A radio transmitter located on the ground which provides distance information for aircraft. Though still used its been mostly replaced by GPS.

Dock – A pier or wharf which a vessel can tie up to. Also maneuvering a vessel against a pier or wharf to tie up.

Dockyard - A facility where ships or boats are built and repaired. Dockyard is usually associated with vessel maintenance and repairs, while shipyard is usually associated with vessel construction.

Dodger - A hood with a clear plastic section to prevent wind and spray from entering the cockpit. Functions like a windshield.

Double Ender – A boat with its stern shaped like the bow enabling it to move forward or backward equally well.

Downwind Leg – Part of the standard airport circuit an aircraft completes when landing. On the downwind leg the aircraft parallels the runway before turning onto the base leg perpendicular to the runway.

Draft -The depth of a vessel's keel below the waterline.

EGT (Exhaust Gas Temperature) - Indicated by a gauge in the cockpit. EGT is a principal engine performance parameter monitored during flight.

Elevator – A part of an aircraft's horizontal tail section which controls pitch.

Empennage - the tail section of an aircraft, consisting of the fin, tailplane or elevator, and the part of the fuselage to which they are attached.

Endurance - The time an aircraft can fly without refueling.

Engine Room – The space containing the vessel's engine, batteries and other machinery like a generator.

Engine Run-up - Operating an aircraft's engine on the ground over its full power range. Usually conducted following repair and prior to takeoff.

Ensign - The principal flag or banner flown at a vessel's stern to indicate its nationality.

ETOPS (Extended Twin Operations) - The term for long distance twin-engine operation over the ocean, desert or arctic regions where there is no suitable airport within 60 minutes of flight in case of an emergency. Referred to by pilots as "Engines Turning Or Passengers Swimming".

Fairlead - A ring, hook or other device used to keep a line or chain running in the correct direction or to prevent it chafing or fouling.

Fall- The part of the tackle or line a crewman hauls on.

Fall Off - To steer away from the direction of the wind. Also to bear away, bear off or put the head down. The opposite of pointing up or heading up.

Fast – Secure, as in tied or held securely.

Fathom – A unit of length equal to 6 feet (1.8 m). Particularly used to measure depth.

Feet Per Minute (FPM) - A unit of measurement indicating an aircraft's rate of climb or descent.

Fender - An air or foam filled bumper used to protect the sides of a vessel from rubbing against a dock or another vessel tied alongside. Used tires are most often used on locally owned boats in the Grenadines.

Fetch - The distance across water the wind or waves have traveled. Also to reach a navigational mark without having to tack.

Final Approach Fix (FAF) – A navigational reference point from which an aircraft begins its final approach to an airport. The beginning of the final approach segment.

Final Leg (On Final) – Part of the standard airport circuit an aircraft completes when landing. The aircraft turns onto the final leg inbound for landing from the base leg, referred to as "turning final" or "on final".

Fitting-out – The interior construction of a vessel after the hull has been completed and launched.

Fix - A radio transmitted beacon or GPS coordinates indicating an aircraft is in a specified position, either an enroute waypoint, or a point from which to begin an initial approach (IAF) or final approach (FAF).

Fixed Base Operator (FBO) - An airport operator serving General Aviation aircraft.

Flare – A nose-up pitch movement to slow an aircraft just prior to touchdown.

Flight Deck - Compartment from which the crew operates an aircraft. Also cockpit, flight compartment, or control cabin.

Flight Plan - Specified information relating to the whole or portion of an intended flight.

Flight Management System (FMS) – An onboard computerized system using preprogrammed route data and flight instrument data to interface with an aircraft's Automatic Flight Control System (AFCS) and Electronic Flight Instrument System (EFIS) allowing automated flight.

Fluke - The wedge-shaped part of an anchor's arms which dig into the sea bottom.

Following Sea – Waves or tide moving in the same direction as the vessel.

Foot – The lower edge of a sail. The bottom of a mast.

Fore/forward - Towards the bow (front) of the vessel.

Forecastle – The area (usually a cabin or locker) at the forward end of the vessel just aft of the bow.

Forefoot - The lower part of the stem (bow) of the vessel.

Foresail - The headsail on a sloop. The sail directly ahead of the mainsail on a schooner.

Forestays – Lines or cables from the bow or bowsprit of the vessel to the masthead to support the mast. Part of the vessel's 'standing' rigging.

Frame - A transverse structural member which provides the hull's shape and strength.

Freeboard - The height of a ship's hull measured from the waterline to the highest gunwale.

Furl - To roll or gather a sail against its mast or spar.

Fuselage - The main body of an aircraft excluding wings, tail, landing gear, etc.

G-IV – A twin engine jet aircraft designed and built by Gulfstream Aerospace for private and business use.

G-V – Larger and improved version of the G-IV with a longer range.

Gaff – On a Gaff rigged vessel the upper spars (a short boom) which hoists and stretches the upper edge of the four sided Gaff sail.

Gaff Rigged – A vessel rigged to use a four-sided fore-and-aft sail with the sail's upper edge supported by a spar or gaff which extends aft from the mast.

Galley - The kitchen on a vessel or aircraft.

Gear - The landing and ground operation apparatus on an aircraft, including the wheels, tires, struts and other mechanisms connected to them.

General Aviation Pilot - A pilot who flies for pleasure, business or hire.

General Aviation Terminal – Airport terminal serving private, business and leisure aircraft.

Genoa (Genny or Jib) - A large triangular sail flown at the front of the vessel from the forestay. Referred to as the pulling sail since it functions in the same manner as an airplane wing.

Gibe or Gybe - To change from one tack to the other by turning a sailing vessel's stern rather than its bow through the wind. Also known by the historical term 'wearing' or 'to wear'.

Glareshield – A cockpit panel above the main instrument panels and below the windshield in an aircraft to protect the instruments and prevent reflected glare.

Glide Path - The flight path of an aircraft during landing approach to a runway.

Glideslope - A cockpit instrument depicting an aircraft's glide path during an instrument landing.

Global Positioning System (GPS)- A satellite based navigation system providing continuous worldwide coverage of position and time on the ground, at sea, and in the air.

Global Navigation Satellite System (GNSS) - A GPS based instrument Landing System which combines satellite and local data to provide accurate navigational positioning for landing.

Go-around - Pulling up and flying to a hold position or reentering the airport traffic pattern after discontinuing an approach to landing.

Grounding - When a vessel while afloat touches the seabed or goes 'aground'. A vessel hard aground is stuck in the sea floor.

Ground effect - the increased lift an aircraft's wings generate close to the ground. When landing ground effect may cause the aircraft to 'float' and delay touchdown. On takeoff ground effect allows level flight just above the ground in order to accelerate to a safe climb airspeed. Especially useful when taking off from a short runway.

Ground Tackle - All the parts of the anchor system including the anchor, anchor chain, anchor rode and shackles.

Gunwale – The top edge of the hull or Bulwark.

Halyard - A line used to raise a sail. Also refers to any line used to raise any object aloft, like a flag, pennant or spar.

Hangar – Building for garaging aircraft on the ground.

Hank - A fastener attached to the luff of the headsail which then attaches the headsail to the forestay. The hanks slides along the forestay as the headsail is raised.

Hatch - An opening or entrance in a vessel's deck providing access to the vessel's interior. The cover or door to the opening is also called a hatch.

Hauling Wind - Pointing the vessel in the direction of the wind.

Hawsepipe, Hawsehole or Hawse – A shaft or hole in the side of a vessel's bow, bulwark or stern through which the anchor chain or dock lines pass.

Haze - Fine dust particles causing the sky to appear unclear and reducing visibility.

Head - The forwardmost or uppermost part of a vessel. The forwardmost or uppermost part of any individual part of the vessel, e.g., the masthead, beakhead, stemhead, etc. The top corner of a triangular sail. The toilet on a vessel.

Heading – The direction in which a vessel is sailing or an aircraft is flying as indicated on a magnetic or electronic compass, and distinct from the directional track of the vessel or aircraft.

Header - A change in wind direction which forces the helmsman to steer further away from the current course or requiring a tack. The opposite of a lift.

Headsail - Any sail flown in front of the most forward mast. Usually attached to the forestay.

Head Sea – A sea in which the waves are directly opposing the forward progress of the vessel.

Headwind - A wind blowing in a direction opposite to an aircraft's flight path and affecting the aircraft's speed over the ground (SOG). The opposite of a tailwind.

Heave - A vessel's up-and-down (pitching) motion in a seaway.

Heel/Heeling - The lean of a sailing vessel onto its side caused by the wind's force on the sails. Also measured by the angle the deck is tilted sideways from horizontal.

Helm – The Vessel's steering mechanism connecting the wheel in the cockpit to the rudder.

High Frequency (HF) – Radio frequencies in the 3 to 30 MHz range used for aeronautical and marine communication beyond VHF (Very High Frequency) range. HF is not affected by the line of sight limitations of VHF, but are susceptible to atmospheric conditions including ionization by solar flares.

High Intensity Runway Lighting (HIRL) - Airport runway lighting where the brightness can be adjusted by the Tower depending on atmospheric conditions and time of day.

Hitch - A knot used to tie a rope or line to a fixed object.

Hold - An interior space in a vessel used for storing cargo. A circular flight pattern around a specified fix flown by an aircraft waiting to descend and land (Holding Pattern).

Horizontal stabilizer – The horizontal tail section of an aircraft's empennage which articulates up and down to control the aircraft's pitch. Also referred to as the tailplane or elevator. It can be trimmed by a control in the cockpit to reduce the aerodynamic pressure on the tail which the pilot feels as resistance on the control yolk.

Hounds - Attachments on the masts for connecting stays and shrouds and to support topmasts.

Hull - The shell and framework of the flotation part of a vessel.

Hypoxia - An inadequate amount of oxygen reaching the brain which occurs in an unpressurized aircraft cabin above 10,000 feet, requiring the use of supplemental oxygen.

Indicated Airspeed (IAS) - The relative speed of an aircraft through the surrounding air as displayed on an airspeed indicator in the cockpit.

Inertial Navigation System (INS) - A self-contained computerized navigation system using laser gyroscopes and accelerometers to sense an aircraft's movement and velocity around all three axis and calculate its precise position without external references.

In Irons - When the bow of a sailboat is pointed directly into the wind and the vessel is unable to maneuver.

Initial Approach Fix (IAF) - The point from which the initial segment of an ILS approach begins.

Iron wind/Iron Jenny – Using a sailing vessel's engine.

Instrument Approach Procedure (IAP) - The procedure for a specified ILS approach at an airport.

Instrument Landing System (ILS) - A system using radio signals to guide an aircraft down to the runway in poor weather conditions. The system depicts a Localizer for horizontal guidance and a Glide Sloop for vertical guidance on cockpit instruments.

Instrument Meteorological Conditions (IMC) - Weather conditions (cloud, fog, rain etc.) making it impossible to fly by outside visual references (VMC). The pilot has to fly solely by reference to the aircraft's instruments (IFR).

Jenny (Genoa or Jib) - A triangular headsail flown at the front of the vessel.

Jeppesen Charts – Aviation charts manufactured by the Jeppesen Sanderson Company used by pilots worldwide.

Jib (Genoa) - A triangular headsail flown at the front of the vessel.

Keel - The central structural foundation of a vessel's hull. The vessel's 'backbone'.

Ketch - A two-masted sailboat with the aft mast (the mizzen) shorter than the main mast and stepped (mounted) closer to the stern.

Knot - A unit of speed: 1 nautical mile (1.8520 km; 1.1508 mi) per hour.

Landing Distance Available (LDA) - The actual length of runway which can be used for landing and roll-out.

Lanyard - A rope or line which ties something off or from which something is suspended.

Lay – The direction (relative bearing) of a designated mark in relation to a vessel's course.

Lazarette - A small stowage locker on deck, usually toward the aft end of a vessel. Also seat lockers in the cockpit.

Leading Edge - The forward edge of an aircraft's wing, engine blades, tail fin and stabilizers.

Lee - The side of a vessel or island away from the wind.

Lee Shore - A shore downwind (to the lee) of a vessel. A vessel which cannot sail well to windward risks being blown onto a lee shore and grounded or smashed against a rocky coast.

Leech - The aft or trailing edge of a sail. The leeward edge of a spinnaker.

Leeward - In the opposite direction from which the wind is blowing.

Leeway - The amount a vessel is blown sideways by the wind.

Length Overall (LOA) - The maximum length of a vessel's hull measured parallel to the waterline, including any overhanging ends which extend beyond the bow and stern. In sailing vessels this might include the bowsprit, boomkin, or stern swim platform.

Liferaft - An inflatable, covered raft, used in the event of a vessel being abandoned.

Lift – A change in wind direction enabling a close hauled sailboat to steer up from its current course to a more favorable one. The opposite of a header.

Line - The nautical term for the cordage or ropes used on a vessel. A line may have a specific name specifying its use, such as main or jib halyards, or main and jib sheets.

Luff - The forward edge of a sail.

Luffing - When a sailing vessel is steered too close to the wind causing insufficiently filled sails to flap. The luff of the sail begins to flap first.

Mach Number – Commonly used to express a jet aircraft's airspeed, measured as a ratio to the speed of sound.

Main Deck - The uppermost continuous deck extending from bow to stern.

Mainmast - The tallest mast on the vessel on which the mainsail is hoisted.

Mainsheet (See Sheets) – A tackle line attacked to the main boom used to controls the trim of the mainsail by controlling the angle of the boom. The downward tension on this line also affects the shape of the mainsail, sometimes aided by a boom vang.

Making Way - A vessel moving under its own power.

Marconi Rig – A fore-and-aft sail rig using triangular sails, as opposed to square rigged or gaff rigged. Also call the Bermuda Rig.

Marlinspike - A tool used in rope work such as unlaying rope for splicing, untying knots, or forming a makeshift handle.

Mast - A vertical pole on a sailing vessel which supports sails.

Maximum Landing Weight - The weight at which specific aircraft can land without risking structural damage.

Maximum Takeoff Weight - The weight at which specific aircraft can take off without risking takeoff and climb performance.

METAR - A weather report from an airport or other ground weather station used by pilots during flight planning, enroute, and approaching the destination.

Minimum Approach Speed - The minimum speed at which a specific aircraft can safely maintain flight in the approach to landing configuration (flaps, slats and gear extended).

Minimum Descent Altitude (MDA) - The altitude in the terminal area (around an airport) below which no aircraft must descend unless it is on its approach path. At some airports the MDA may be different in different directions depending on terrain.

Missed Approach - When a aircraft aborts its landing approach usually due to low visibility or a runway obstacle and performs a go around.

Nautical Mile - A unit of distance corresponding to one minute of arc of latitude. 1,852 meters; approximately 6,076 feet; 1.1508 mile.

Navigation Display (ND) - In an aircraft cockpit equipped with LCD panel screens navigational data is digitally displayed on a screen in front of the pilot next to the Primary Flight Display (PFD) screen.

Navigation Lights – Required on marine vessels and aircraft to avoid collision by indicating position, relative angle and direction of travel. The location and type of lighting is specified by international law to include lights visible on both sides of a vessel or aircraft - red on the port side or wingtip, green on the starboard side or wingtip; and a white light visible from the rear of the vessel or aircraft. Aircraft also use high intensity flashing or rotating strobe lights.

NOTAM (Notice to Airmen) - A printout providing information regarding changes to aeronautical facilities, services, procedures or hazards used during flight planning.

Outhaul - A line used to tension the foot of a sail along the boom.

Outer Marker – A radio beacon used for ILS approaches positioned 4 to 7 miles from the runway threshold and aligned with the runway centerline. The outermost of three beacons including a middle marker and inner marker.

Painter - A rope attached to the bow of a dinghy used for towing or tethering the dinghy.

Phosphorescence – A bright blue-green luminosity in a vessel's wake seen at night, caused by the bioluminescence of marine organisms disturbed by the vessel's passage.

Pilot Flying (PF) - The pilot actually doing the hands-on flying of the aircraft at a given moment.

Pilot In Command - The pilot in command of the aircraft, not necessarily the pilot flying.

Pilot Report (PIREP) – Updates of weather or other flight conditions provided by pilots when they encounter them enroute or during approach and landing.

Pitch - A vessel's motion in a seaway in which the bow and stern rise and fall repetitively (See heave). The nose up or down attitude of an aircraft in flight.

Plane - To skim over the water at high speed rather than push through it.

Point Up - To change the direction of a sailboat so it is heading more upwind. To steer toward windward. Also called heading up. The opposite of falling off.

Points Of Sail - The course sailed in relation to wind direction. Close hauled (sailing as close into the wind as possible); Close reach (wind between the bow and beam); Beam reach (wind on the beam and the vessel perpendicular to the wind); Broad reach (wind on the quarter between the beam and stern); Running, sailing downwind with the wind behind.

Port - The left side of a vessel or aircraft when facing forward.

Port Tack – Sailing with the wind blowing from the port side of the vessel. Must give way to vessels on starboard tack.

Porthole or port - An opening or window in a vessel's side for admitting light and air, fitted with thick glass, and often a hinged metal cover.

Precision Approach Path Indicator (PAPI) - A series of flashing lights leading to the runway threshold providing pilots with a visual approach reference.

Radio Management Panel (RMP) - A control panel located on the center pedestal between the two pilot seats where the pilots tune and manage the aircraft's communications radios including VHF, HF and satellite up and down links. On smaller general aviation aircraft like Mike Daniels' Piper Seneca the radios are usually located in the center of the instrument panel.

Reaching – Any point of sail from about 60° to about 160° off the wind including close reaching, beam reaching and broad reaching.

Reefing - Temporarily reducing sail area in strong or gusty wind conditions by reducing the amount of exposed sail. Mainsails usually have reef points constructed into them.

Regatta - A series of sailboat races.

Rigging - The system of masts and lines on ships and sailing vessels.

Rode - The anchor line, rope or cable connecting the anchor chain to the vessel. Also Anchor Rode.

Roll - A vessel's motion in a seaway in which it rolls from side to side about the fore-aft/longitudinal axis. An aircraft in a bank about its longitudinal axis.

Rollout - An aircraft's ground roll along the runway after landing. A return to level flight after banking.

Rudder - A steering device attached at or near the aft end of a vessel controlled by a tiller or wheel. On an aircraft the rudder is attached to the trailing edge of the vertical tailfin and controlled by foot pedals in the cockpit.

Run Up – An engine test at full power prior to takeoff.

Running Before The Wind or Running – Sailing with the wind behind the vessel. (See Points of sail).

Running rigging – The lines and tackles used to manipulate sails, spars, etc. in order to control the movement of as sailing vessel.

Runway - The paved surface of an airport designed for aircraft take-offs and landings. Runways are designated by the compass direction in which they are aligned.

Runway Edge Lighting - White lights, usually on stalks, on both sides of the runway.

Sail – A dacron or nylon fabric (formally canvas) designed and arranged so it causes the wind to drive a sailing vessel along. Sails are attached and manipulated by a combination of masts, spars (booms), and ropes (running rigging).

Sampson Post- A strong vertical post near the bow of a vessel used to support a vessel's anchor windlass and the heel (back end) of a vessel's bowsprit.

Scattered (SCT) - A meteorological terms indicating clouds distributed irregularly in the sky.

Schooner - A type of sailing vessel characterized by two or more masts with the mainmast being the tallest.

Scuppers - Openings in a vessel's bulwarks to allow seawater to drain from the deck.

Seacock - A valve fitted through the vessel's hull.

Sea Shanty – Song about sailors or the sea.

Shackle - A metal U-shaped device secured with a clevis pin or bolt across the opening used to connect rigging to an object or one piece of rigging to another.

Sheer - The curve of a vessel's sides.

Sheet - A rope attached to a boom or clew of a sail used to control the sail's trim.

Shoal - Shallow water.

Shrouds - Ropes or cables which hold and support a mast from the sides. Part of a sailing vessel's standing rigging.

Sloop – A sailing vessel with a single mast for a mainsail and headsail.

Solo – The first flight of a student pilot unaccompanied by an instructor, usually confined to the traffic pattern.

Speed Over Ground (SOG)- Speed of a vessel over the ground irrespective of its speed through the water. The speed of an aircraft over the ground irrespective of its airspeed. A vessel's speed over the ground is affected by tidal currents, while an aircraft's speed over the ground is affected by headwinds, crosswinds and tailwinds.

Speed Through The Water (STW) - Speed of a vessel through the water as measured by a speedometer log attached to the hull below the waterline. While STW indicates a vessel's performance, SOG is the relevant measure used for navigation.

Spar (Boom) – A wood or aluminum pole used to support rigging and sails.

Spinnaker – A large light fabric sail hoisted in front of the vessel when sailing downwind.

Spreader - A short spar positioned on both sides of a mast to deflect (spread) the shrouds allowing greater support of the mast.

Stall – A sailing vessel in irons. The position of an aircraft's wings relative to the surrounding air (angle of attack) at which lift is no longer generated.

Stanchion - Vertical posts spaced along a deck's edge to support a bulwark, rail or lifelines.

Standing Rigging – The combination of stays, shrouds, attachments and tensioners used to support masts and spars.

Starboard - The right side of a vessel or aircraft when facing forward.

Starboard tack - When sailing with the wind coming from the starboard side of the vessel. Has right of way over boats on port tack.

Stay – A line or cable running forward (forestay) and aft (backstay) from a mast to the hull to support the mast.

Staysail – A small triangular sail behind the jib or headsail attached to an inner forestay (between the head forestay and mast). On large vessels the foot of the staysail is usually attached to a staysail boom.

Steerage - The helm's effect on the vessel's steering.

Steerageway - The minimum speed at which a vessel will answer the helm, below which the vessel cannot be steered.

Stem (Stempost) – The upward extension of a vessel's keel at the forward end of the vessel, to which the bow is attached.

Stern (Sternpost) – The upward extension of a vessel's keel at the rear end of the vessel, to which the transom is attached.

Stick Shaker - An aircraft's stall warning system which when triggered by angle of attack sensors causes the stick or control column to vibrate. In small aircraft like Mike Daniels' Piper Seneca a stall warning horn sounds.

STOL – Short takeoff and landing.

Stow - To store or to put away personal effects, tackle, gear or cargo.

Straight-in - Approaching an airport's runway without executing any legs of the airport's traffic pattern. Also referred to as a long final.

Squawk - An identifier code which identifies transponder equipped aircraft on ATC radar screens.

Squawk Sheet - A list of maintenance items to be performed on an aircraft indicated in the aircraft's logbook.

Standard Pressure Setting - The 29.92 inch Hg altimeter setting universally used above the 29,000 feet transition level.

Superstructure - The parts of the vessel which project above the main deck not including masts.

Tacking – Turning the vessel's bow through the wind to bring the wind onto the opposite side of the vessel. Such a zig-zagging course is necessary to sail a vessel toward a mark in the direction from which the wind is blowing.

Tackle – The combination of rope passed through a pulley (block) or set of pulleys to provide mechanical leverage for hoisting, lowering or applying tension. (See also Ground Tackle).

Tailwind - Wind blowing in the same direction as the aircraft's direction of travel. The opposite of headwind.

Take-off Roll - The process of accelerating down the runway in order to take off.

Tarmac – Commonly used to refer to an airport's paved surfaces including runways, taxiways, terminal and other parking ramps. Short for tarmacadam, the name of the surfacing material.

Taxiway - Paved roadways for aircraft to move about an airport. Indicated by blue lights along the sides and named for letters of the alphabet pronounced phonetically.

Tell-tale (Tell-tail) - A light piece of string, yarn, or plastic attached to a stay or a shroud to indicate the apparent wind direction. Also sometimes attached to the body and/or leech of a sail to indicate air flow over the sail's surface.

Terminal Aerodrome Forecasts (TAFs) – Weather information similar to METARs but providing forecast information for an airport. Used by pilots during flight planning.

Terminal Control Area (TCA) – Controlled airspace around an airport used for departures and arrivals.

Threshold - The beginning of a runway usually marked by broad white stripes.

Thrust - The propulsive force generated by an aircraft engine; the other three forces which act on an aircraft are lift, weight and drag. The force generated by wind on a vessel's sails.

Thwart - A bench seat across the width of an open boat, like a dinghy.

Topping Lift – A line attached from the masthead to the aft end of a boom to control the boom angle and therefore the shape of the sail.

Topsides - The part of the hull between the waterline and the deck.

Touch and Go - A pilot training exercise in which pilots practice approaches and touch downs on a runway without rolling to a stop, instead taking off again for another circuit in the traffic pattern. This 'touch and go' or 'circuit and bump' is repeated several time in a single practice session.

Touchdown Speed - The airspeed at which the aircraft makes contact with the ground on landing.

Touchdown Target – A point on the runway a pilot aims for during the landing approach.

To Weather - The side of a vessel exposed to the wind. Turning toward the wind.

Track – The actual directional path (course) of a vessel or aircraft due to the effects of leeway, tidal currents or crosswinds.

Transom – The aft (rear) section at the stern of a vessel. May be vertical, or raked (sloped). Traffic Advisory – An air traffic control message advising a pilot of the presence of traffic in their vicinity. An advisory does not require pilot action but allows the pilot to visually locate and observe the traffic.

Traffic Pattern - A predefined flight circuit of the runway intended for landing consisting of downwind, base and final legs.

Trailing Edge - The rear edge of a wing, stabilizer or propeller blade on an aircraft. A sail's leech.

Transponder - A radio which transmits a coded response to identify aircraft on ATC radar. A mode C transponder also provides the aircraft's altitude.

Trim - Adjustments made to sails in relation to wind direction to maximize their efficiency. Adjustment of an aircraft's control surfaces to minimize control pressure on the yolk.

Turbo-Prop – an aircraft with propellers driven by turbine (jet) engines.

Underway - A vessel moving under control that is neither anchored, moored, tied up, aground nor adrift.

Vertical Speed Indicator (VSI) – A cockpit instrument which displays an aircraft's vertical speed, (rate of climb or descent) in feet per minute.

VHF- A marine and aviation radio using the very high frequency band.

Visual Approach Slope Indicator (VASI) – A system of 3 lights at the side of a runway which provide a visual descent/glide sloop when landing.

Visual Flight Rules (VFR) – Flight by visual references outside the aircraft in visual meteorological conditions (VMC). As opposed to Instrument Flight Rules (IFR) when flying by instruments in instrument meteorological conditions (IMC).

VOR – A ground based omnidirectional radio transmitter used for aircraft navigation. The intersection of two VOR radials provides the aircraft's position.

Wake – The trail behind a vessel caused by its passage through the water. The turbulent downdraft caused by the passage of a large aircraft through the air. Also referred to as wake turbulence or wake vortex.

Walkaround – An external inspection and check of an aircraft prior to flight.

Weatherly - A vessel which is easily sailed and maneuvered and makes little leeway when sailing to windward.

Weather helm – The tendency of a sailing vessel's bow to swing to windward.

Weigh Anchor – To pull up an anchor prior to sailing.

Weight and Balance – A document recording an aircraft manufacturer's approved weight distribution and center of gravity (CG) for that type aircraft. Required to be kept aboard the aircraft at all times. A pilot calculates weight and centre of gravity when loading the aircraft to ensure it meets the aircraft's weight and balance parameters. An overweight and out of CG aircraft may not get off the ground, and even if it does, it may be impossible to handle in the air.

Whaleboat (Bequia) – A narrow open boat pointed at both ends (double-ended) enabling it to move forwards or backwards equally well.

Whaler (Bequia) – A fisherman specializing in catching whales.

Wick Static Discharger - Located on the trailing edges of an aircraft's wings to discharge static electrical built up in the airframe during flight.

Winds Aloft – Forecasts of winds at altitudes above 3,000 feet. Upper level wind forecasts provide information on winds up to 39,000 feet for the polar jet streams and at higher altitudes for the subtropical jet streams.

Windward - In the direction the wind is blowing from.

Wing on Wing - A method of sailing downwind with the mainsail extended on one side and the Genoa extended on the opposite side.

Yaw – The tendency of a vessel's bow to swing off course in a seaway. The turn of an aircraft's nose left or right due to rudder input. The adverse tendency of an aircraft's nose to swing left or right, controlled by rudder input or a yaw damper.

Yoke – The control wheel and column in an aircraft cockpit.

Zulu – Used in marine and aviation radiotelephony for Universal Coordinated Time (UTC), also Greenwich Mean Time (GMT).

Printed in Great Britain
by Amazon